Dying with Angst

David J. Pedersen

Cover art by:
Alessandro Brunelli

Editing by:
Angela D. Pedersen
Danielle Fine

Dedication

When I started writing Angst, my goal wasn't to get rich or famous (good thing.) I had a story to tell. I wanted to share a part of me and only hoped that people who read my books would be entertained. In eight years I've written over a half-million words and have published six books. Because of these books I've had the great honor to meet people from all over the world, many who I now call friend. Readers have sent me emails, messages, and even a handwritten letter telling me that they enjoy my stories and relate to the characters. They've shared that my books make them laugh. I consider that a gift to me.

Thank you for reading my books. You have kept me writing, and thanks to you I completed my goal. That means a lot.

I have a team that has helped me get there. My lovely wife Angie is always there for support and encouragement. Whether critiquing early drafts or helping me peddle books at cons, I would be lost without my dear friends, Cristi, Becky, Matt, Mike, Marina, Mayra and Sarah. Thanks to Danielle Fine for editing my mess and making me a better writer. I'm also very grateful for my cover artist, Alessandro Brunelli. Every cover he makes is my new favorite. Also, a special thanks to my Advance Reader Team who helped provided a fine polish to this book.

I hope you have enjoyed my Angst, and I look forward to our next adventure!

Dedication

For Angie Pedersen

My wife, my love, my passionate friend.
Thank you for your undying support
and your incredible patience.

Books by David J. Pedersen

Angst Five Book Series:

Book 1: Angst
Book 2: Buried in Angst
Book 3: Drowning in Angst
Book 4: Burning with Angst
Book 5: Dying with Angst

Young Adult / Middle Grade Fiction:

Clod Makes A Friend

Map of Ehrde

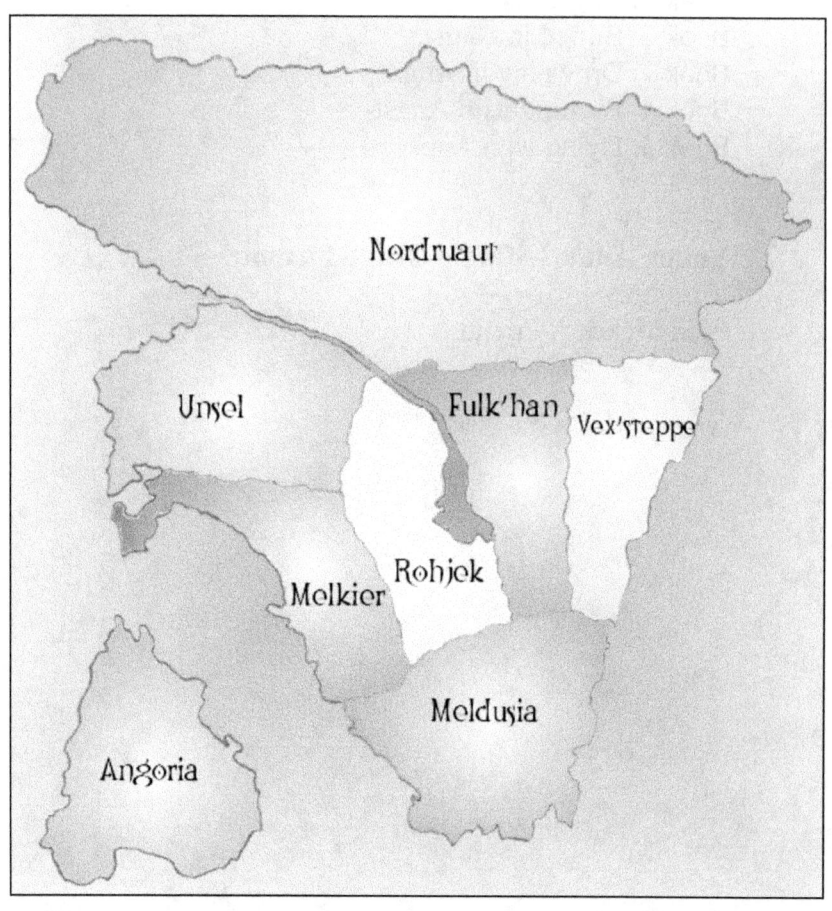

Prelude

18 Years Ago

Angst ran fingers through his thick, dark hair in a final attempt to tame it. He should've made time earlier in the week for a haircut. Not that it would've helped; his hair grew like weeds in spring and probably would've grown back overnight. He longed for thinner hair that would be easier to manage, but that was as likely as gaining weight.

"Are you done primping yet, pretty boy?" Hector asked in his gravelly voice. "Just remember, the only one you have to impress tonight is me. And so far, I'm not impressed."

"I'll be impressed if my pants stay on," Angst said, pulling them up for the hundredth time. "I thought your training would bulk me up. At this point, I'll never gain weight."

"The way you flirt," Dallow said with a cautious smile, "I'm surprised you bother wearing any."

"Heh," Hector replied, coolly.

Angst flashed Dallow a broad grin, even as his friend retreated from the conversation. While grateful that both men had agreed to accompany him, he was wary about the evening since they didn't exactly get along. They couldn't have been more different. Dallow was a tall, lanky bookworm, who practically lived for his job at the library. His long blond hair, tanned skin, and intelligent gaze caught the eye of many women, but he ignored them all as he was already married. Between his job and wife,

Dallow seemed happily stuck in his life like a bug in amber. Angst wouldn't have described him as boring, exactly. At least not to his face.

Hector was a soldier-for-hire, and widely recognized as one of the best. His efficiently cropped dark hair and piercing blue-gray eyes were practically wolf-like as they took in everything, always. A wincingly fresh scar stretched along his jaw from ear to chin. His friend was the definition of intense, and knew it.

"Still happy you came to the capital?" Hector asked.

"Best decision I've made yet," Angst said.

The largest city in Unsel was always alive, except for maybe a brisk nap between 3 am and 5. Twenty-two was the perfect age to live here, and his first two weeks had already been an adventure. The food was amazing, the booze even better, and there were so many beautiful women that it always felt like his birthday. Thanks to his friends, Angst had landed a job filing papers at the castle. It was entry level, but an opportunity for greater things. Yeah, Unsel was the best, and it could only get better. Starting tonight.

"Whatever you do, please don't embarrass me, Angst," Hector said. "The king and queen will be here, along with Commander Tyrell. You should save drinking for after the party…"

Hector continued talking about something, and Angst politely nodded after every pause as he took in the crowd. His ears were buzzing, but not from his mentor droning on about expectations. The king and queen had thrown this party in honor of the castle staff, and he was overwhelmed by the extravagance. So many important people had shown up, from dukes to knights to everyone in charge. Not only was this his chance to make an impression on royalty, but maybe even meet young Queen Isabelle. He grabbed another goblet of mead from a passing tray, earning a frown from both the servant and Hector.

"Good advice," Dallow said, interrupting his thoughts. "I'd like to keep my library job. I've only had it for a short while, and it's everything I've ever wanted. Have I told you how many books they have on—"

"No," Hector said, holding up a hand. "And I don't care."

"Did you ask Tyrell if he would duel me in a training match?" Angst asked, quickly taking a sip before Hector could snatch the drink away. "I hear he's the best."

"I'm the best," Hector corrected, his thick brows furrowed. "He said he'll consider it. Tyrell only trains with commissioned soldiers, but I asked, as a favor."

"Did you tell him I plan to be a knight?" Angst asked.

"I may have mentioned that," Hector said with a thin-lipped smile.

"A knighthood's unlikely," Dallow said. Pressing his hands together, he tapped two fingers to his chin. "It's been a long time since wielders have been knighted, and longer since we've been allowed to wield openly. I'm sorry, but the chance of that happening—"

"Is great," Angst said. "Once I pick up that beautiful sword."

Hector and Dallow's mocking laughter didn't dissuade his hope or his hunger.

"Angst," Hector said, resting a hand on his shoulder. "You realize it's a hazing ritual, right? That thing's a statue, not a real sword."

"I dunno," Angst said, approaching the monument. "It looks real to me."

The centerpiece of the courtyard featured a gigantic broadsword resting horizontally on a low marble stand. The blade of the sword was five feet long and two feet wide. It was thick in the center, featuring a riser instead of a fuller. The handle was so thin compared to the bulk of the thing, it looked like it could snap off.

It was rumored that whoever actually lifted the sword would be knighted. Wouldn't it be nice if something in life was that easy? He reached for the monument, his ears still buzzing with...something. Anticipation? Magic? Before his hand touched the sword, Dallow grasped his sleeve and drew it back.

"You can't pick up a statue," Dallow said, rolling his eyes.

"And even if you could, do you really think they would award you a knighthood for wielding a giant sword?"

"They'd better," Angst said, his tone serious. "You forget, I can move the earth when I try hard enough. If I focus, maybe I can use magic to pick that thing up."

"We can't wield magic here," Dallow whispered, looking about nervously.

"And you can't control it," Hector said, his words clipped. "Do you want to create another earthquake, here, with royalty present? The guards will line up to take turns gutting you."

"Hey, hey, hey," Angst said soothingly, holding out both hands until they calmed. "I've got this."

Their shoulders dropped, and his friends looked at each other in despair. A pretty waitress with dark skin and a beautiful smile swayed up with a tray of goblets.

"Hi, Angst," she said airily. "Sweet wine?"

"Right now, you're my favorite person," he said with a smile, placing his empty goblet on the tray and taking a fresh one. "Thanks, Nally."

"Just one more," Hector said, sternly.

He winked at the young woman before taking a deep draw, warmth and relaxation spreading through his body. "Another one more would be better."

Nally giggled.

"If it means you won't do anything," Hector waggled his fingers to indicate magic, "she can bring you five."

"That's a good start," Angst said.

"Let me know if you need anything else," Nally said, her voice sultry as she sauntered off.

"Oh, I will," Angst said under his breath.

Hector coughed, interrupting his leering gaze. "Here comes the royal party. Be sure to bow when they pass."

"I know what to do," Angst said. "You're worse than my dad."

King Riann, Queen Isabelle, and their new baby, Princess Victoria, passed by with all the flair and pomp you'd expect from royalty—expensive, shiny clothes, long, flowing robes, and an indifferent nonchalance that made Angst cringe to his bones. They walked slowly, making his bow last longer than his patience, so he glanced up. Queen Isabelle was hawked closely by Commander Tyrell, but Angst still caught her gaze. She blushed. Did he see the barest of smiles in her eyes? It was hard to tell with all that makeup, but she looked familiar. Tyrell gently pulled her along.

"Really?" Hector asked, his whisper practically a growl.

"It feels like we've met," Angst said, not quite able to place her.

"Probably," Hector said. "You've spoken to every woman in Unsel."

"I have not," Angst said, mocking offense. "At least, not yet."

"We should sit," Dallow said anxiously. "They'll be serving dinner soon."

"Hey, my buddy Wilfred's waving us over," Angst said, already moving through the crowd.

"That know-it-all?" Hector asked with a grunt. "He makes up half the crap he says."

"He's not that bad," Angst said dismissively. "I'd trust what he makes up over other people's truths any day."

They joined Wilfred at a nearby table. His chubby friend looked at the three analytically, sizing them up, even as he licked appetizers from his fingers. Wilfred was so intelligent he was someone to know, even when he knew it all.

Angst's meager lunch had consisted of a bacon sandwich that still tasted like burnt grease hours later. This dinner came in courses, each with generous helpings of delicious food he'd never experienced. Sweetmeats, boiled vegetables, and delicate cakes that were too small. Even better was the sweet wine, which Nally delivered with her own flirting. Her winks and smiles only made his warm buzz that much better.

Entertainers performed between courses; jugglers and singers and dancers and other distractions that made him wait too long. Angst worried that his opportunity to wield the giant sword, his giant sword, was going to be forgotten. Finally, finally, the king stood and raised a goblet. *"To the knight* fortunate enough to wield the great sword that has decorated our lawn for all history."

Until now, Angst thought as he stood, wobbling.

"Please," Hector whispered, gripping his sleeve. "No magic."

"I couldn't if I wanted to, probably," Angst said with a wink.

Hector didn't look comforted.

"Every new employee, and everyone wanting to try again, line up to give it your best," King Riann encouraged with a reserved grin.

Angst waved off Hector and Dallow's further concerns about wielding magic before weaving into the line of hopefuls and dreamers. He was slow enough to be last, which made him nervous. What if someone picked up the sword before he had his chance? What if someone else became a knight when he knew it should be him?

It took for-ev-er. The line felt like it was getting longer or moving backward. Men and women, both young and old, took time with their lottery attempt. Some were comical, playing to the crowd. One woman spat on her hands, squared her shoulders, and pulled until something popped loud enough to make everyone wince. A burly man took a running start in an attempt to topple it over. His landing looked painful. The result was always the same. Frustrated grunting followed by another round of laughter from the crowd. They'd given up, all of them, except Angst.

He stood alone, the rest of the contenders gone, and he was very aware of all the eyes on him. Princess Victoria let out a baby yelp that caught his attention. Isabelle coddled the child and, with some assistance from Tyrell, stood to leave. He took that moment to rub his hands together and focus his concentration.

Angst did his best impersonation of sober and waited for the sword to come back in focus. The weapon was obnoxiously large, but that wasn't the reason he hesitated. He'd wanted to be a knight, a hero, ever since he could remember. Angst had always wanted to help people, to make it better. Maybe, just maybe, this was his chance. This wasn't just for him; this was for everyone.

"Come on," a nearby soldier grumbled. "Get to it before the queen passes through."

"Right," Angst said. He took a deep breath and drew in the tiniest bit of magic before placing his hands on the hilt. It really wasn't that much.

There was an audible click as the sword seemed to wiggle in his hand. He gasped as his senses were bombarded. A flash of heat, a rush of wind, the coolness of water, and the cold strength of stone all coursed through him with an overwhelming sense of power. This wasn't what he'd expected at all. His hands were frozen to the hilt, and the only way to be free was to pick the sword up. His vision dimmed as though a storm had suddenly appeared over the courtyard. On the verge of lifting the sword, Angst heard a malevolent voice, "And so it begins."

Victoria's crying snapped him out of the moment. Queen Isabelle and Commander Tyrell were standing right beside him. They paused long enough for Isabelle to hold the baby against her shoulder. Victoria burped out a smile as she looked at Angst with beautiful green eyes—eyes that flashed white for the briefest moment.

Angst stepped back, releasing the sword in surprise. "Uh," he said, holding up a finger.

"Mind your own business," Tyrell whispered, gripping his hand firmly and forcing it down. "Do you understand, Angst?"

"Yes," he said, his mouth suddenly dry.

"Now go sit with your friends," he said coolly.

"But, the sword," Angst said, staring at his hands. They itched and tingled. His heart was pounding in his ears, and he felt dizzy. Whatever had happened was the most frightening experience of his life. Was it magic, or something else? If it *was* magic, picking the sword up wouldn't make him a knight, it would make him a prisoner, or a dead man. He didn't want anything to do with it, which meant he would have to become a knight the hard way. He took a deep breath and braved asking, "So, about that sparring match?"

"Fine," Tyrell said with a sigh.

"Thanks," Angst said, patting the commander roughly on the shoulder. He waved at the king, who nodded back.

"And we go another year without a new knight," the king said to cheers and laughter.

Angst bowed with a flourish before slowly making his way back to the table. Walking away from the monument felt worse than leaving a puppy behind at a pet store. Despite the temptation, that sword may be more trouble than it was worth. That rush of elements had felt like an oncoming storm…or maybe just too much booze. The moment had passed too quickly and was already like trying to remember a dream. He collapsed in his seat with a deep sigh.

"Are you all right?" Hector asked, placing a hand on his shoulder. "You've gone pale. I told you not to drink too much."

"You…you guys didn't feel it?" he asked. "The rush of heat, and cold water?"

"I felt uncomfortable at you eying the queen again," Hector said with a grunt.

"What about that voice?" Angst asked with a shiver. "Just as I was going to lift the sword, it said, 'And so it begins.'"

Dallow, Hector, and Wilfred all looked at each other before losing themselves to laughter.

"I love your jokes," Wilfred finally said, wiping his eyes.

"I've never seen someone try so hard," Dallow said, gasping for breath. "You were up there for ten minutes, maybe more. You should be grateful our king is so patient."

"Ten minutes?" Angst asked in disbelief.

"I'm sorry it didn't work out with the sword, Angst," Hector said, with a knowing smile. "But, like the bookworm said, it takes more than that to be a knight."

"I've always wondered why that sword is here," Dallow said, tapping his chin with steepled fingers. "It looks like it has a greater purpose than being a statue."

"Until someone picks it up," Hector said, "I guess we'll never know its potential."

"I wish it had worked for me. Knighthood, lands, gold, and admiration from everyone," Wilfred said with a sigh. "I wonder if anyone's ever lifted it?"

"No way," Hector said. "What kind of person would give up all that."

"An idiot," Angst said, sinking into his seat. "A complete and total idiot."

1

Unsel—now

Angst was distraught. He had the patience of a tea kettle already boiling over. After months of friends telling him to "move on" or that his idea was "not possible," he'd decided there was really no other choice.

The two soldiers guarding the dungeon entrance came to attention on his approach. They glanced at each other nervously.

"You…you shouldn't be in here," the first guard said as he shakily drew his sword. "Her Highness, Princess Victoria, said not to let anyone through."

"I'm not just anyone, though. Am I, Richard?" Angst asked, taking a step forward.

"It's Dick, Mr. Angst," the guard said, his eyes dancing between the two enormous swords hovering over Angst's back.

"Richard," Angst said, with a gentle smile. "Let's make this easy. Why don't you just let me in? I'll be brief, and nobody will know."

"You know who's down there," the other soldier said. "She's dangerous."

"So am I, when I have to be," Angst said, casually brushing a spot on his dusky vambrace. "Why don't you just run for help?"

"We swore on our lives to keep everyone away from her," Richard said.

"On your lives?" Angst asked. "Gentlemen, my life is already lost. I have no reason to stand down, and there's no force on Ehrde that will keep me out. Put down the swords before you get hurt."

Both guards slowly lowered their swords.

"Run," Angst said, drawing in enough power to make his eyes flash red.

They looked at each other, their faces pale, and they ran.

Angst sighed with relief. Scaring was so much better than killing, but their speedy departure meant a quick return with more guards. His optimistic goal was to get a few questions answered then leave without having to brawl his way out of the dungeon. Optimism had been poor company of late, and realism made his stomach churn.

Having never been in the Unsel dungeon, he hadn't known what to plan for and admonished himself for not borrowing keys from the fleeing guards. Tori wouldn't be happy when he broke her castle, again. Well, he'd just have to fix it and apologize later. After so many years of being married to Heather, he'd gotten pretty good at apologizing.

Angst's ability to wield had always been about controlling minerals. He'd originally thought it was limited to moving and forming rocks, convenient for creating underground bookshelves. Since bonding with his two foci, Chryslaenor and Dulgirgraut, he'd learned so much more. He could now do almost anything imaginable with minerals. Stone, steel, even bones were malleable and movable. But that wasn't all. Over the last year, the swords had also taught him something about controlling water, air, and even fire. He was reluctant to wield fire after what had happened to his family, after what had happened to Faeoris. Fortunately, this was about minerals.

With a gentle nudge of magic, the lock rusted away to sand, and he opened the steel door. Wide stairs led him down to a long, cave-like hallway with barred rooms on either side. The red and blue auras shining from his swords were overly bright. Criminals grasping onto bars backed away slowly at his approach.

At the end of the hallway was a wide, metal door with a small, barred window. The lock disintegrated as easily as the first, and he opened the door to the largest room in the prison.

Alloria stood from her plush chair and rested her steaming cuppa of soup on a short graymowl table. Even the heavy gray robes of her prison uniform couldn't completely hide her voluptuous curves. Honey brown hair curled down her olive cheeks and poured over her shoulders. A finely jeweled tiara was tucked neatly into her hair, standing so apart from the rest of her plain attire that he felt bad for the person who'd lost that argument. She looked at him nervously with her large green eyes and chewed on her pouty lip. It was the first time he'd seen her without makeup and fancy clothes. Those things didn't seem to matter; the young woman was still stunning.

Angst tore his eyes away to take in her room. This prison was nicer than anywhere he'd lived. The gentle smell of flowers completely masked the stench of sweat and urine behind him. Heavy draperies hung along the walls, hiding the cold stone enclosure. A plush round carpet covered the sandy floor. She had a wide, cozy chair, a table with an oil lamp, and a tall bed with plenty of covers. All of it in soft pastel colors accentuated by gentle candlelight that made it appear comfortable. It was the most gilded cage he'd ever seen.

Glancing past him, she crouched down as if preparing to escape.

"I'm not going to harm you," he said, reaching out with calming hands. "I need you—"

The young princess leaped forward, wrapping her arms around him and planting a kiss on his mouth. It took a minute to pull away from her lips. Maybe two; it was a nice kiss.

"Six months was a long wait, but I knew you'd come to save me," she said. "My champion."

Angst peeled her off and grasped her shoulders, gently holding her away. "I need you to tell me where Prendere is. Can you help me?"

"Of course I can," she said, rolling her eyes. Reaching out, she brushed his cheek with the back of her hand. "Anything for the man who fought death to save me."

"Right," Angst said. He hadn't really wanted to save her. She'd deserved to die after trying to kill Victoria. But Alloria was also the only one who could save her, so Angst had let her live. "You're right. I did save you."

She nodded quickly, her smile wide and eyes wider than they should've been. He glanced over his shoulder; the dungeon hallway was still empty.

"I'm in a hurry," he said. "Tell me."

"I can't tell you, silly," she said. "I have to show you."

"No chance," Angst said. "Not after what you did to those guards a few months ago."

"It was a misunderstanding," she said, crossing her arms and frowning. "They brought me the wrong dinner. It's not like they died."

"Right," he said with a grimace. Rose had healed their wounds, but not their nightmares. "I don't have time to argue. I need to leave."

"Whatever you want, baby," she said, looking at him hungrily.

"I want Prendere," Angst said. "If you can get me there, then...then I'll set you free."

She looked at him with hope, and love, and longing. They'd always flirted. She'd always flirted a lot, even kissing him once. That was fun; this gave him goosebumps. But really, what choice did he have?

"Together," she said firmly.

He nodded.

"But there are conditions," she said, holding out her fingers and preparing to count them out.

"Of course there are," he said with a knowing sigh as realism set in deeper. "What are your terms? Hurry, we don't have much time."

"Don't bring me back to this dungeon when it's over," she said.

"That's easy. I promise to bring you someplace safe," Angst said. "Go on."

"Be my champion," she said, raising her chin royally.

He hesitated. Victoria had never asked, but like an unspoken agreement, Angst had always assumed he would become the queen's champion. Victoria would be distraught and furious if he promised to be someone else's champion. Her feelings wouldn't be hurt if she didn't hear him lie. Reaching out with his mind, Angst sensed a mass of armor and bodies approaching fast—Victoria and his friends probably amongst them. They weren't here yet, and he was desperate for Alloria's help. With a sigh, he finally agreed. "Fine," he said. "I'll champion you. Is that it?"

"Tell me you love me," she said, looking at him like that crazy neighbor who owned way too many cats.

This one made him take a step back. That wasn't anything he'd ever lied about. Just how badly did he need her help? "I'll be your champion," he said through gritted teeth.

"Traitor," Victoria said from the top of the stairs.

Angst spun around. A dozen guards flanked her, but worse than that, Dallow stood to her left and Rose to her right. The look of hurt on Tori's face stabbed his heart, as if this was his last chance to make it right. And maybe it was. Everyone else looked at him like he was as crazy and dangerous as Alloria. They waited at the top of the steps.

"Quit looking at me like that. I'm no traitor," he snapped at his friends. "I let you see my future, Tori. You know what I'm planning. I'm going to fix all of it."

"Your choices at Prendere could also split Ehrde in half," Victoria said, her voice quivering with worry. "I've seen that future of death and chaos. The risk is too high. I can't let that happen."

"You've got to believe in me," he pleaded. "I can do this. I can set everything right."

"I believe in you," Alloria said. She leaned against him, placing a hand on his chest.

14

CHAPTER ONE

"Shut up," Angst and Victoria said.

"The war's over," Victoria said, raising her hands to hold off the soldiers gathering behind her. "I'm sorry. I'm so sorry that your family and friend are gone, but there's nothing you can do—"

"The war isn't over," he shouted. The anxiety that typically gnawed at his belly took a bite between his shoulders. The pinch made him wince, and his head jerked to one side.

Now they really were all looking at him like he'd gone mad. And maybe he had, but it was too late to stop. Tori held her arms out like she was holding back the tide. Rose pushed past and drew the twin blades of her foci, Jormbrinder.

"I think we could stop you," Dallow called out. "I may not be Al'eyrn—"

"I don't think I am either," Angst said. "Not anymore."

Rose and Dallow glanced at each other. Dallow's eyes went white, and he began muttering something in Acratic.

"Stand down," Victoria shouted.

"There's too much at risk if he escapes," Rose said, her face flushed and her voice strained.

"You said you would be my champion until he's ready," Victoria snapped. "That means you do as I say."

Rose crouched low, ready to leap at Angst and Alloria.

"Please, Angst. I'll offer you anything to stay," Tori said. "What do you want?"

"I want my family back," he said, choking down his grief. "I want Hector and Faeoris back."

"That's not possible," Dallow said.

"It is. We both know that's possible at Prendere," Angst said. "I'll set it all right, and I'll get them back. All of them."

"Please don't do this," Victoria said. "It's wrong."

"I've been doing it wrong this whole time. That's why everyone keeps dying," Angst tried to explain, unable to keep the desperation out of his voice. "This is the only way. I have to go back and fix it. I have no choice!"

"No," Dallow said. "Angst, you'll destroy Ehrde, or you'll

15

die, or both. We've talked about this."

"We've got to leave," Angst said under his breath to Alloria. "Will you help me?"

"Say it," Alloria said haughtily. "Say you love me."

His heart sank. It would be a betrayal to utter those words. He'd only said them to maybe a dozen people in his life, and she hadn't been one of them. He hated her for trying to kill Victoria. Out of desperation, she'd attempted to kill Rose and Dallow too. It was wrong, but there was no time to argue. Saying those words felt like another sacrifice, but what would one more cost him?

Angst turned to face her. He looked into Alloria's eyes and said, "I love you."

"No," Victoria said with a gasp.

"Take me wherever you want, honey," she said, planting a kiss on his cheek.

"Don't do this," Victoria cried.

"It's the only way," Angst said. He reached out with both hands, grasped at the air in the room, and pulled.

Victoria, the guards, and his friends all clutched their throats as he drew air from their lungs. He didn't want to kill them, just steal enough so they would pass out. The accusing look in Tori's eyes was heartbreaking, but shouldn't she have known better? She'd seen his future and known this could happen. She'd trusted him too much. Guilt washed over him as everyone collapsed to their knees—everyone but Rose.

"You forget, old man," she said with a determined glare. "I'm Al'eyrn now."

"I didn't forget," he said. "Old friend."

"We aren't friends," she shouted. "Not if you're doing this."

Rose blurred toward him. There was a loud crack as he anchored her foot to the stone floor. She screamed and slammed hard against the prison floor, the daggers flying from her hands.

"Gross," Alloria said at the bone jutting out near Rose's ankle.

"It's a bad break, but she'll only be down for a few minutes," he said, releasing Rose. "Deep breath like you're jumping in a lake. You won't like this. I don't."

"I hate you," Rose shouted, rocking back and forth, clutching her foot.

"So do I," he said before nodding at Alloria.

She took a deep breath and pinched her nose. Rose glared at him, and he tried his best to apologize with his eyes. Hers didn't forgive. With a gasp, he wrapped his arm around Alloria and, just as his gamlin had taught him, they dove into the ground like it was water.

2

Tarness waited in the ice cave, staring at the enormous burlap sack he had dragged for miles. He asked himself the same questions every day. How deep in was he? Could he still use this situation to help his friends? Was it even possible to escape this trap?

After six months with the Nordruaut, Tarness had come to only one conclusion: he hated the cold now more than ever. He despised the "summer" in northern Nordruaut even more than Unsel winters. The cold was as relentless and tiring as Angst's flirting. Maarja had assured him that southern Nordruaut was warm enough for farming. He'd playfully argued that they must be farming icicles. She hadn't found that funny, another reminder that he hadn't quite grasped Nordruaut humor. But it was so cold he felt bad for those crops they'd planted. If he'd been a seed in that field, he would've lived just to spread himself on a southern wind.

Despite the cold, he enjoyed being in the company of Nordruaut. They liked big meals with generous amounts of cold ale, and they were an efficient people who left nothing to waste—even their attitude toward sex was a little too practical, as if the cold had numbed most of their passion. At the same time, he couldn't complain about quantity over quality. Maarja was voracious, and now more than ever, he needed that link to his humanity.

CHAPTER TWO

There was still much about them he didn't understand. Their jokes, their drive, and their internal struggle to be hunters or warriors. They took all of it in a matter-of-fact stride that was slowly methodical and more evenly paced than he'd ever experienced. It always surprised him how inclusive they were. They seemed to trust him implicitly, which often left him with deep pangs of guilt.

Seven months ago, Tarness had died. He'd helped save his friends Hector, Dallow, and Rose by tossing them like ragdolls into a mage city just before the doorway shut. After telling Hector to thank Angst for the adventure, he was alone, in a blizzard, at night without Dallow's protective shield. Tarness had collapsed to the snowy ground and leaned against the barrier that separated him from his friends. The inevitable didn't take long. He remembered all of it too clearly.

* * * *

The fear of facing Death had rushed through him and was gone, leaving him ready for whatever came next. He'd done the right thing, something heroic. As the Nordruaut would say, it was a good death. But when time stopped, it wasn't Death who came to visit.

"Freezing is a terrible way to die," said a man in a high-pitched, nasally voice. "Almost as bad as drowning."

Tarness forced his eyes open to see the blurry image of a tall, awkward-looking man. He hovered over an unmoving blizzard. An aura of gray light surrounding him, purging color like gray-mowl trees.

It took a moment to realize that the painful battering of sleet had stopped. He could breathe, and the freezing air didn't burn his lungs. Not only had feeling returned to Tarness's fingers and toes, but all of his pains had been washed away. What would that cost him? No one had the power to stop a storm as if holding firm the hands of a clock. No human could do that and take away his pain at the same time, not even Angst.

19

"Magic," Tarness said with a grunt.

"Vivek," the ageless man corrected, his eyes peering. "Or Dark Vivek, if it frightens you more."

"Sure." Tarness shook his head.

"I'm surprised you recognized me," the man said. "You're smarter than your friends give you credit for."

"Sometimes, but not always," he said with a sigh. "What do you want? I'm trying to die here."

"You're doing a fine job," Magic said, brushing snow off his sleeves. "I'm here to keep that from happening."

"Like I said, what do you want?" he asked.

"I can keep you alive," the man said. "But I need your help."

"I won't betray Angst," Tarness said firmly.

For barely the tick of a clock, the onslaught of raw blizzard and the madness of dying returned. All that numbing pain closed in like a sheet of darkness, and then it was gone. His heart raced with fear and he took a stammering breath.

"Well?" Magic asked.

Tarness stood, dusted off what snow he could, and stepped forward until he was within head-butting distance. "Is that it?"

"What?" Magic asked, incredulous.

"I was already dying," he explained. "Continuing to die isn't exactly a threat."

Magic's eyes went wide, and he stomped several times in a tantrum. Tarness barked out a laugh. He wished his friends were here to enjoy the scene.

"Humans are so frustrating," Magic said.

"Feeling's mutual," Tarness said defiantly.

The Dark Vivek eyed him up and down before taking a deep breath and letting it out with a sigh. Dusky circles under Magic's eyes and shadows along his cheeks made the element seem tired.

"As I said," Tarness frowned and jabbed a finger at Magic's chest, "I won't betray Angst."

"Will you betray Unsel?" Magic asked, staring down at the threatening finger. "What about Ehrde?"

"What are you talking about?" he asked.

"Will you allow one man to destroy Ehrde?" Magic asked. "Even Angst?"

"Of course not," Tarness said.

"Angst is going to break Ehrde in half," Magic said, pushing Tarness's hand away. "You're his best friend. You may be the only one who can stop him."

Magic had to be lying. Angst would never harm Ehrde. All he'd ever wanted was to protect it. But Aerella had said Angst would go crazy, and now that his friend had bonded to two foci, who knew what he would do? His friend needed help now more than ever—something a dead Tarness would be unable to do.

"I don't believe you," Tarness said, staring at the morsel of hope. "But I won't let Angst, or anyone, destroy Ehrde."

"Then take this ring," Magic said, a ruby ring in his outstretched hand, "and you will live to protect those you love."

"Fine," Tarness said, swallowing back the bitter taste of bile and self-reproach. He grabbed the ring and placed it on his finger.

"Excellent," Magic said, placing it on his finger. "Because you will be Ehrde's last line of defense. You could save everyone."

* * * *

He didn't feel like the 'last line of defense' with a frozen bag of body parts at his feet. Anger, frustration, and guilt were his unfortunate sources of strength. That power was enough to forge his way through the cold and complete Magic's tasks. Unfortunately, it wasn't enough to escape this trap.

Alone, surrounded by glassy ice, he tugged at the ring for the hundredth time—literally the hundredth time; he had counted, desperately hoping there was some magic behind that number.

"That still won't work," Magic said. "I won't let anyone I save remove their ring again. Not after Alloria gave hers to Angst. You know this."

"Yeah," Tarness said in frustration. "But I'll still try."

"I thought you wanted a foci to yourself," Magic said. "So

you could be a hero, like Angst."

"What?" Tarness asked.

"Consider it a poor man's foci," Magic said. "Which is appropriate, since I gather you're poor."

"If it's a foci," Tarness said, "why can't I use it to kill you?"

"Maybe you aren't the man Angst is," Magic said, peering at him. "Ooh, did I hit a sore spot?"

"Maybe," Tarness said, doing his best to let the slight roll off. It hit a few bumps along the way. "But I like being Tarness, I like Angst being Angst, and you're not good at making foci. If you were, I'd have killed you with it already."

"No, I can't make foci like the Mendahir," Magic said with a grimace. "But I can imbue an item with enough power to keep you alive. Without it, you will complete your visit with Death."

"So you've told me," Tarness said. "But making foci isn't the only thing you're bad at, is it?"

"What do you mean?" Magic said. His browless frown was more than little creepy.

"All your plans fall through. All of them," Tarness said, calmly. "Even these rings don't work like they're supposed to, or Angst wouldn't have saved Alloria. You're a crappy element."

Magic's eyes flashed black, and dark clouds formed around his hands. Light from the cave vibrated as the element took a deep breath. Tarness's stomach churned as he closed his eyes and stuck out his chest.

"Kill me and end this," Tarness said. "Fuel Angst's anger, so when you do battle, he makes it hurt that much more. I'll rest easier in death."

There was a fizzle, and a pop, and a sigh that made Tarness open his eyes. Magic shook his head and lowered his hands.

"In the beginning, I always won," Magic said. He waved his hands and muttered something until the cave was gone.

They stood in an enormous grassy field surrounded by mountains. Animals unlike any Tarness had ever seen roamed freely in peace. Giant white butterflies danced in the sky, swooping down to touch unicorn horns with their antennae feelers before soaring up. Schools of flying, golden fish swarmed around silver dragons as if polishing them. There were rainbows without rain, blue trees that grew on floating islands, and pinpricks of light that made his eyelids heavy. It was all a beautiful madness.

"Every two thousand years, it was either Water or me," Magic said. "When I won, my Ehrde was a world of beauty, with creatures you couldn't imagine. Some so beautiful, you would go insane just to look at them for more than a glimpse."

"I don't see any humans," Tarness said.

"Exactly," Magic said, waving his arms until the scene was gone. "There were no humans in my Ehrde. No place for them. I didn't create them, nor have I ever dealt with them, until Angst."

"That's why you hate us," Tarness said.

"Hate you?" Magic asked in surprise. "I don't hate you. I just don't get you. No matter how hard I try to understand or fit in, humans don't make sense. My Ehrde is a sensual portrait that's a reflection of me. Your Ehrde is a wooden bucket of smelly children, muddy dogs, and fried chicken. They are nothing alike. I'm not a bad element. I'm a bad human."

Tarness struggled as his well-structured common sense was tossed aside by the dawn of creation and other stuff. "What do you want from us, from me?"

"The winning element receives one wish, for lack of a better term, at the end of every battle," Magic said. "And that prize is given to the winner at a place we refer to as Prendere. But it's more than just a wish—it's a cornerstone of creation. If a human...if Angst were to acquire that gift or accidentally let someone else acquire it, the consequences could be devastating. Angst could inadvertently destroy Ehrde, or split it asunder, or turn it into mead."

"Or save all humans from the element's agendas for the next two thousand years," Tarness retorted, even if he didn't quite feel it.

"It's possible," Magic said. "But despite his bravado, Angst isn't an element. Which is probably a good thing. From what

I've learned, his Ehrde would contain nothing but beautiful women."

"And they'd all have large breasts," Tarness said, laughing.

"I've tried something with you that I've tried with no other human, ever," Magic said.

Tarness looked at him quizzically.

"Reason," Magic said.

"Why?" Tarness asked.

"As I've said, I don't understand humans, and I don't necessarily like them," Magic said. "But I don't hate them. I don't even hate Angst. I'm just afraid of what he'll do."

"What do you want from me?" Tarness asked. "Why show me all of this?"

"Think on it," Magic said. "Angst trusts you. He loves you, whatever that is. You're his best friend and may be the only one who can stop him. You won't try if you believe he's right."

Of course Angst was right. Despite some of his friend's bad choices, things tended to work out. Angst wouldn't destroy Ehrde, at least not on purpose. While Magic's argument made some sense, his chaotic vision of Ehrde wasn't exactly a winning sales pitch. The element could keep Tarness alive to do menial tasks, but that wasn't enough leverage to make him turn on Angst.

"I've brought you what you wanted," Tarness said, nodding at the ice-coated bag. "These are the last parts."

"Yes," Magic said, with a hopeful smile. "It has to be here."

"Now give him to me," Tarness demanded. "That was the deal."

"Come back in a week," Magic said, dismissively. "I'll have what I promised. But you won't like it."

Tarness nodded, hoping the element wasn't lying. Magic rubbed his hands together and pulled an enormous toe out of the burlap sack. Tarness swallowed bile and left the cave.

A cold wind blew across the frozen desert, lifting enough fine snow that it appeared like mist. This creature who called himself Magic, this element, who'd been on Ehrde since the dawn of creation and could destroy Tarness in a blink, had just spoken to him in a way that made far too much sense. Angst had killed elements with one foci. Now that he was bonded to two, how could he manage so much power? His friend's intentions were always good and heroic but sometimes seemed self-serving. And the longer Angst remained bonded, the more erratic his decisions had become. Or was it just his way of managing the unmanageable? Could his best friend actually destroy Ehrde?

Tarness closed his eyes, took a deep breath, and held it. Because that was how deep in he was.

3

A tidal wave of pain washed over Rose. She did her best to breathe through it as her ankle knitted itself back together. The pain wasn't just physical; it went far deeper. Angst had betrayed her, had hurt her on purpose, and that gouged at her heart. She felt like she'd just lost a friend, as if he'd died. How could Angst do this to her? To Victoria? Dallow was Angst's oldest friend, and he lay still on the ground, like the others. She drew power from her foci, Jormbrinder, to heal faster and, with a grunt, forced her ankle back into place.

"Wh...what just happened?" Victoria asked, pushing herself up from the dungeon floor. She shook violently. "Did Angst...did he really just escape with Alloria?"

"They jumped into the ground, like gamlin," Rose said, sniffing deeply as tears streamed down her cheeks. "He betrayed you. betrayed all of us. He really has gone crazy."

Reeling as if slapped hard, Victoria gripped her chest and coughed. Everyone else in the room was still unconscious, and it took several long moments for the princess to gather herself. "See to the others," she finally whispered. "As soon as you can."

Rose nodded. She stood, stretching out her repaired ankle with a wince. It still stung, but that would pass soon enough. She made her way around the dungeon, kneeling beside fallen soldiers and healing them awake.

Healing used to be a chore. She would have to absorb the in-

26

jury, essentially becoming injured herself then wait for her own body to heal. That was no longer the case with Jormbrinder. Dallow had taught her healing spells, and her foci provided more than ample power to cast them.

Jaden ran down the dungeon stairs, his curly blond hair bouncing with every rushed step, showing off dark roots underneath. He slowed mere steps before Victoria. She looked at him, her lip trembling slightly. He reached for her hand, and she looked away. The rejection made his cheeks flush, and he peered at the princess with his sharp blue eyes. After a deep intake of breath, Jaden looked around the room, studying everything until his firm jaw set.

"It was Angst," Jaden said with a grimace. "Wasn't it?"

"Who else?" Dallow said, pushing himself up. "He escaped with Alloria."

"How?" Jaden asked. "They didn't run past me. I wouldn't have let them."

Dallow pointed at the ground. Jaden shook his head in disbelief.

"They're swimming to freedom right now," Rose said.

"I told you he's going to destroy Ehrde," Jaden snapped at Victoria as she stood. "You refused to listen to me. We need to hunt him down and kill him before he kills everyone."

Victoria slapped him hard across the mouth. He jerked back in surprise, covering his cheek with a hand.

"He may be right, Your Majesty," Rose said, taking a step back. "Please don't hit me."

"Well, whatever we decide to do, they couldn't have gotten far," Jaden said, rubbing his face. "Angst may know how to swim through earth, but he's not a gamlin. I doubt they can hold their breath for very long."

"Fine," Victoria said, glaring at them. "Where do you suggest we go? And then, how do we stop him?"

Rose looked at Jaden, and then the princess. Their shoulders dropped as the rush of urgency deflated.

"The next steps will be my decision," Victoria said, looking at Dallow. "Until then, we stick to the plan."

"The plan?" Jaden and Rose said together.

Dallow nodded at Victoria, who said nothing more, instead patting dust off her hot pink satin dress. Rose shook her head at the apparent secret and checked on the soldiers again. They stood jerkily, like broken reeds preparing for the next attack of wind.

"We should do something, at least to keep up appearances," Dallow said to the princess. "It would appear unusual not to search for them."

"Thoughtful advice, Mr. Dallow," Victoria said with a nod. She turned to a guard. "I want a troop of soldiers to sweep the city. Have them split up but tell them not to engage. Then inform Captain Mirim and her zyn'ight to search the castle grounds but nothing further. I want them to remain close."

"Yes, Your Highness," the soldier said with a wobbly bow.

"There will be consequences if anyone approaches Angst," she said. "Do you understand?"

He nodded briskly before she waved him away.

"So, we just wait?" Jaden asked.

"No," Victoria said, staring down her nose at him. "You and Dallow go search the damaged area of the castle near the sinkhole. Meet us in the war room in two hours."

"There's no way Angst went there," Jaden snapped. "You're just trying to keep us busy, and I don't understand why."

"I can't help that. You trust me or you don't," Victoria said. "Do as you're told or leave."

Rose whistled softly as Jaden went rigid. He nodded stiffly, and both men rushed out of the dungeon.

"I should go with them," Rose said, practically pleading. "I'm the only one who has a chance of stopping him."

"Exactly why I don't want you out there," Victoria said. "It isn't time."

"Not time?" Rose asked, a little too loudly. That made no sense. Were Victoria's feelings for Angst, whatever they were, clouding her judgment? "You've spent more time with Angst than anyone since his family was killed, and you didn't see any of this coming?"

"I did, Rose," she said, her face growing dark. "You forget, I see all futures, including the one where you try to knock me out so you can chase after Angst, the one where you leave with Dallow and never come back, and the one where we both collapse in a heap and sob it out."

Rose gasped. It was true. All those ideas had crossed her mind.

"Nobody has just one future," Victoria said with a sort of forced calm. "I see all the possible futures when someone's nearby. Well, everyone but Al'eyrn. I can't see any of Angst's futures if he doesn't let me, nor could I see yours if you kept your guard up. I can see mine, and Dallow's, which also give me glimpses of your futures and Angst's."

"So you knew this could happen?" Rose asked, shocked.

"Angst let me in for a brief glimpse of how he could save Ehrde," she said. "That told me a little, but visits with Alloria told me more."

"If you'd said something, we could've stopped him." Rose clenched her fists, struggling to hold back her anger.

"Could we?" Victoria asked. "It's going to take more than you and Dallow, or even Jaden and the zyn'ight. It requires timing, and I believe we only have one chance."

Rose struggled to believe this young woman, who was soon to be queen, could see past a mirror. Victoria spent far too much time worrying about being pretty. Her full lips and large, green eyes were perfect. Her tight, hot pink satin gown was perfect. And she made sure her perfect breasts were always on display. How many hours had Rose endured Victoria's court gossip and flirting while brushing out her long, perfect black hair—or curly blond locks if she was seeing Angst? It all made Rose want to gag. How could this ditsy child with serious daddy issues suddenly become a master tactician with plans to save all Ehrde? Not to mention, what queen would ever wear hot pink?

"I look nice in pink, and so would you," Victoria said with a broad smile.

"I hate pink, and it doesn't go with my hair," Rose muttered. "I thought you couldn't read minds."

"I know what people want to say. Sometimes that's enough. You rarely hold back what's on your mind, so it was an easy guess," Victoria explained, "At one point, Angst and I could communicate without speaking."

That made her head spin. Victoria was glimpsing into possible futures to decide on her favorite. Did she actually use her power for all decisions? How could she possibly choose the right one? The very concept that the princess saw only one of many options was frightening. If true, it seemed like a fragile thread to hang their hopes on. She shuddered.

"Enough conjecture," Victoria said, coolly. "You may not like it, but you're going to follow my orders, or we will part ways and you'll hate yourself for it. Are we clear?"

"Yes, Your Highness," Rose said, battling every urge to strangle Victoria. "What orders would you like me to follow?"

"Go see Flint and Teedle to get fitted for armor," she said.

"Armor?" she asked in surprise, but the princess's steely gaze told her it was an order to follow, not question. "I will. Is there anything else?"

"Gather General Mirot and Wilfred and have them meet us in the war room. Tell them we need to make final preparations for battle," Victoria said, swallowing hard. "We're going to war. With Angst."

4

Alloria lay still on the grass, covered in flecks of mud as if she'd crawled out of a grave. She didn't move. Or breathe. They'd swum a long way through the earth to get to the practice field. He hadn't figured out how to breathe while swimming through the ground like gamlin and had almost passed out getting here.

"Please don't be dead," he wheezed, shaking her gently. He needed her more than anyone; she was the key to setting everything right. "Too many have died because of me, and you're the only way I can get them back. Please."

She remained still.

"How do I revive her?" he asked over his shoulder. The swords remained frustratingly silent. "Tell me, or I'll leave you here and we'll all die."

Dulgirgraut reluctantly told him how to help her breathe. He leaned over the young woman, placing his lips on hers. Just as the mermaid Moyra had breathed air into him, Angst blew into Alloria's mouth. He did it again and again until her eyes opened and her tongue flicked playfully against his. Angst jerked away as Alloria laughed between coughs.

"My hero," she wheezed, wiping mud off her face.

He sat back on his rear and sighed deeply. What was he doing? Everything about his great plan felt wrong. He'd just freed the most notorious criminal in Unsel—the woman who'd usurped the throne by murdering his best friend's mother, Queen Isabelle. He'd said he would be Alloria's champion in front of Tori. Could there be a worse transgression? Oh, yeah, he'd also said something about love. Angst did his best to shake off these thoughts like a dog shaking off water. This wasn't the time to question his actions, however foolish, or wallow in guilt. It was time to follow his plan.

"We need to hurry," Angst said crisply, standing and taking a step back. "We didn't get far, and I don't want to fight our way out of here if they find us."

"Why are you moving away, Angst?" Alloria asked, brushing a lock of muddy hair from her face. She frowned as if he were speaking another language. "You feel...distant."

"Distant?" Angst snapped. He stood over her and leaned in, his fists shaking. "What do you expect? Of course I'm distant!"

"You can hit me, if that would help," she said. "That's what Dark Vivek did when I'd tell him to leave you alone."

Her words punctured his fury. He drew away, unclenching his fists and squeezing his eyes shut. The hate driven rage that made him lash out so quickly wasn't for her. Not really. After so many failures, and so much loss, he hated himself. All it would take was one strike to free that hatred and become something terrible and dark.

Alloria was ready to let him. She sat on her rear with her legs tucked neatly by her side. Her eyes were closed, and she faced away, as if making it easy for him to strike. She took shallow breaths, and a single tear trickled down her cheek. Resting on his knees beside her, he brushed the tear with the back of a finger, and she flinched before grasping the hand and holding it there. He had to remember that the war of elements had affected everyone, not just him.

"What did Magic do to you, Alloria?" he asked.

She continued holding on for dear life, but, after several deep breaths, finally let go. She opened her eyes, which were suddenly far too old for her seventeen years, and gave him a tight-lipped smile. "You first," she said. "Why was it so hard to say you love me?"

"I…" He swallowed his frustration as he thought about her exposed cheek and single tear. "Alloria, you killed Queen Isabelle and Captain Guard Tyrell, and tried to kill Victoria. I almost died fighting Fire to save her. You ask me to say I love you, but I can't even trust you."

"You fought Death to save me. I know it was to save her, but you released me from his hold," Alloria said. "You can trust me because I'd do anything for you. Anything."

"I released you?" Angst asked.

"Magic controlled almost everything I did," she said. "But he couldn't kill me because you wore my ring around your neck. At first, when I agreed to take that ring, I didn't realize the influence he would have over me. I could make some of my own decisions, but I had to do what he said…his will was too strong. He made Vars kill Queen Isabelle, and Tyrell, and Rook, and so many. But even worse, he made me try to kill my cousin." Alloria started to cry.

Instinctively, he placed a hand on the back of her head as she wept into his grungy red cloak. Her cry became uncontrollable, wracking sobs that would've challenged Heather's on her very worst day. Angst might never know everything Alloria had been through, might never completely trust her, but she might also be the only person more broken than himself. He could relate to her endless tears. Angst held her, rocking back and forth for a long time until she composed herself.

"I always hated Tori," she said bitterly into his shoulder. "So self-righteous, so perfect, so everything. I was in line for the throne, but she would never treat me as an equal. I tried not to care and drowned myself in fun with friends…until Cliffview."

There was a lot more crying, and he knew why. Water had destroyed Cliffview, killing hundreds of people as the element created a path of enormous sinkholes to Unsel. Alloria had lost her father and her friends to that attack.

"You were the only one who believed me," she finally said. "You were the only one who cared, and I fell in lo—" Alloria took a deep, wracking breath. "When I learned how much you loved Princess Victoria, I was more jealous than ever."

"So you tried to kill her," he said.

"No!" she said pulling away. She pushed him back roughly. "No! Angst, that's when I kissed you and gave you the ring that kept me alive. I gave you the ring because I loved you, and I thought a little part of you loved me, so you would keep me safe. I hoped it would give me back control."

"I…" he said, searching for words that weren't there.

She saved him by placing a hand on his mouth. "Magic made me try to kill Victoria," she said. "But I didn't want to, Angst. I hated her, I was jealous of you both, but she's family. I wish I'd never taken that ring."

"I understand," Angst said. "I wish I hadn't picked up Chryslaenor. I wish I'd never bonded with it. My selfish desire to become a knight is what killed my family."

"What?" Alloria asked.

He hadn't expected the look of pure horror on her face. She didn't know.

"They're dead," he said. "All of them, gone. My wife Heather. My son Thom and daughter Eila. Our dog Scar, and Kala. Faeoris…"

It was his turn to weep at the memory of Fire's attack on his family. Grief is a vicious, uncontrollable monster that rips out the heart when least expected, its brutality only challenged by its timing.

She shakily placed a hand on his shoulder. When he didn't jerk away, she pulled him in for a hug. Angst was grateful until she began kissing his cheek. He pulled back and wiped away his tears.

"I'm sorry," he said awkwardly, sniffing deeply. "I can't…"

"Was it me?" she asked in a small voice.

"Was what you?" he asked.

"Was it my fault your family died?" she asked, her lip trembling.

"No, Alloria," he said grimly, the anger returning. "No. It was

Fire."

"I'm sorry," she said, a quiver to her voice. "I shouldn't have asked. Please don't be upset at me."

"I'm upset at everything, Alloria," he said. "I'm angry at the elements and their war. I'm furious at what Fire did to my family." He took a controlling breath as a shudder passed through his body. "Even though I know I'm going to save them, hope isn't enough to make my anger or pain go away. Not completely."

"You don't have to talk about it," she said, refusing to make eye contact.

He took her chin between two fingers and gently lifted it until she looked at him with those big, beautiful eyes. "Actually, I do. You deserve to know what a screw-up your champion is. It's only fair that you understand what could happen to you if I fail again."

Her shoulders dropped, her face relaxed, and the young princess sat back and waited.

"When the elements go to war, they consider humans pawns and not opponents. They imbue human hosts with power, like Air did with Aereon," Angst said. "Those hosts lead nations into war alongside minions. This time Water's minions were gargoyles, Air had cavastil birds, Dragons fought for Fire, and the Gamlin belonged to Earth."

"What about Magic?"

"I guess Vex'kvette monsters, or the Fulk'han," Angst said, scratching caked dirt from his cheek. "My point is that they don't typically get involved. Not directly. They move their pieces around the Ehrde chessboard until one of them wins."

"But it didn't happen that way," Alloria said.

"I may have messed up their war," Angst explained. "Ivan, a knight of Unsel had been turned into a giant monster by Magic. Right after bonding with Chryslaenor I killed him, somehow releasing the element. Magic had changed into this beam of dark light that I chased across Ehrde. I eventually trapped it by removing the bond with my foci."

"The end," Alloria said with a clap.

"More like the beginning," Angst said with a sigh. "Earth explained that releasing Magic had changed the rules, and the elements were free to battle in the open. Since then, I've had to fight all of them. Giving up the bond to Chryslaenor made me ill. We found Dulgirgraut in Melkier just in time to fight a city-sized dragon. After Tori and I killed it, Fire threw a sun at us."

"A sun?" Alloria asked in disbelief.

"Or something like that," Angst said. "The sun destroyed half of the Melkier capital and killed Earth. We barely escaped, only to learn Magic was controlling Rose through Chryslaenor. He tried forcing her to bond with the sword, but I took it on just in time. Bonding with a second foci should have killed me, but I only exploded."

"You exploded?" She asked with wide eyes.

"That's what happens when I get angry now," he said.

"Really?" she asked, inching away.

"No," he said with a smile. "Just the once."

She playfully smacked his armor.

"The explosion destroyed Air," Angst said. "Faeoris, Victoria and I flew to Unsel and that's when I killed Water."

"That leaves Magic," she said, counting on her fingers, "and Fire."

"Yeah, him," Angst said, taking a deep breath. "Scar and I almost destroyed Fire in Nordruaut."

"Wait a second," she said, her brow furrowed in concentration. "Your dog fought an Element?"

"Scar isn't just any dog," Angst said, proudly. "He was a giant, Vex'kvette monster-dog when we found him. He almost died when we fought, so I healed him with Chryslaenor. Something about that changed the pup. In Nordruaut, I sort of bonded him to the swords with a spell. So, Scar was pretty much an Al'eyrn, like me."

"But he's just a dog," she said. "How could a dog handle that much power?"

"I told him to protect everyone *at all costs*," Angst said, almost hesitant to utter those words. "He grew even bigger and attacked the element. When Scar was done, I finished the job with a bolt of lightning the size of a castle. I thought Fire was dead."

"But he wasn't," she said.

"No, he wasn't. After Rose bonded with the foci and healed Victoria, the princess had a vision. She said Fire was going to kill my family." Angst leaned back awkwardly in his armor and wiggled until it was less pinchy. "Fire's hatred for me was a sort of madness. Maybe it was because I killed his giant dragon."

"It's because he was scared," Alloria said. "Fire and Magic both said they were scared of you, Magic more than any of them."

"He should be," Angst said darkly. "I'm not done yet."

"Go on, Angst," she encouraged. "What happened next?"

"Fire was waiting for me with an enormous fireball. When he threw it, the impact knocked me into my house and broke my back. It was so hot I could feel my armor melting into my skin. Somehow, the swords kept me alive, but it must've taken all of their magic because there wasn't enough left to fight. Before finishing me, the element attacked my family. Just as Fire threw another ball of flame at them, Kala and Scar arrived. They blocked the path of the fireball, trying to shield Heather and the kids, but it was too much. In a flash of light, they were gone. My family, Scar, Kala...all of them."

"Fire was gone too?" she asked.

"Not yet," he said. His cheeks were wet with tears again. He was so sick of tears. "At this point, Fire had used up most of his power and wasn't much taller than me. He was so upset that I'd lived, the element threw a tantrum, an actual tantrum like a toddler—stomping around and shaking his fists. When he finally came over to finish me, Faeoris arrived."

"Your pretty friend with the wings?" she asked.

Angst let out a bitter chuckle. "It's a blurry memory—I was in a lot of pain—but I remember her battle cry as she struck him with her sword over and over again. She fought Fire like she had a foci, moving around so fast he could barely keep up. *I* could barely keep up, it was everything I could do not to pass out. At the last moment, Fire wrapped his arms around her. She cried out and was gone in a flash of light. Fire was gone. Faeoris was gone. All that remained was a golden feather."

"I'm sorry," she whispered. "Faeoris meant a lot to you."

"I only knew her for a short time," Angst said, "but our friendship was right. She was exactly what I needed. She didn't deserve to die because of my failure. And after losing her, and Heather, and Thom, and Eila, Scar and poor Kala...all I wanted to do was die. That's when Rose and Dallow arrived."

"Rose healed you," she said.

"Eventually," he said. "She told me that I wanted to die so badly that her healing wouldn't work. I was fighting it, but my foci wouldn't let me die. Rose and Dallow brought me back to the castle, and after several months, she healed my body. It wasn't an easy time for Rose, or for me. It's driven a wedge between us."

"And then you came to save me?" she asked hopefully.

"Well, no," he said. "Months passed. At first, I wouldn't believe they were dead. That flash of light that enveloped Faeoris and my family was too bright to be just Fire. Dallow convinced me that in my condition I'd seen what I wanted to see. I still don't understand, but Dallow's smarter than I am. That's when I began to grieve."

It was so quiet, he could hear his racing heart. He longed for the music from his swords, Dulgirgraut and Chryslaenor, but they remained silent. Alloria waited, pursing her lips as if holding back words.

The break in conversation was timely. Holding a finger to his mouth, he turned away and reached out with his mind.

"What is it?" she whispered.

"Someone's close enough to spot us," he said. "I can sense them walking nearby."

Angst closed his eyes and focused. He could sense the armor of two soldiers inching closer. He willed the gauntleted hand of one soldier to strike the other in the head. They immediately turned and ran to the castle.

"Are they coming?" Alloria asked. "Do we need to go?"

"Not yet," Angst said, his shoulders relaxing. "Just a couple of guards who realized they shouldn't attack by themselves. It will take them fifteen minutes to get to the castle, another twenty to gather the zyn'ight... We've got time."

"Good," she said, looking relieved. "So, what am I supposed to be afraid of?"

"A lot of people have died since I picked up these swords," Angst said. "I'm not much of a champion. I've failed so much, I don't think I can ever forgive myself."

"Angst, you've destroyed elements. People have died, but I bet you've saved more," she said. "You're not just my champion, you're a hero."

He smiled at this, not knowing what to say.

"You're also not done yet. You said you've got a plan," she said, hopefully. "You don't think Scar could've saved them? Since he was Al'eyrn?"

"I did," he said with a sigh. "I told Scar to save them *at all costs*. I'd hoped that flash of light had brought them somewhere safe. But it wasn't anything like a portal, and that was six months ago. I'd know if they were alive by now. They would have sent a message or Tori would have seen their return. It took a long time for me to accept that they were gone."

Without any warning, Alloria launched forward, kissed him on the mouth, then pulled back, placing her head on his chest. She wrapped her arms around him, holding tight, and he didn't know what to do. Alloria had kissed him once before, but it was a peck. This was something more. Only Heather had kissed him, and meant it, in the last twenty years, and it was jarring. Despite Alloria's issues, and there were a lot of them, more than you could count on fingers and toes, she must've been trying to console him in her own way. It wasn't the worst therapy he'd received.

"Uh, thanks," he said, his cheeks and ears burning.

"It's okay to grieve," she said, resting a hand on his.

"There's no reason," he said, taking a deep breath. "Even though I watched them die, I refuse to give up. I had an idea, and after some research, I now have a plan."

"And that's when you saved me from that horrid dungeon!" she said excitedly.

"That's when I saved you," he replied with the barest of smiles. That hadn't been the plan, but when did his plans ever go smoothly? "Now, I need you to help me save them."

"How?" she asked, her pretty brows furrowing. "Angst, I'm sorry, but I can't bring the dead back to life."

"Prendere," he said. "It's an Acratic word for 'The Prize.'"

"I like prizes," she said, hopefully. "I won a kitten once. Are we going to win a kitten?"

"No," he said, gently. "This prize is a wish, Alloria. It's not a little wish, like wishing to be younger, or thinner, or that my hair would grow back, or…"

She cocked her head to one side.

"Never mind," he said, clearing his throat. "This is the wish elements get after winning the war. They use it to shape Ehrde into their own image for two thousand years. Water usually wins the war, which is why Ehrde is mostly covered with water…but not all of it. You can imagine how dangerous that wish would be in the wrong hands. If Fire or Magic were to win…"

Her eyes went wide, and she nodded slowly.

"I think my wish is possible."

"You're going to wish your family back to life?" she asked.

"It's not that easy," he said. "From what I've learned, I'm not supposed to wish anyone back to life."

"Then what are you going to wish? I still hope for kittens," she said innocently.

"I'm going to wish this had never happened," he said. "I'm going back in time to stop myself from ever picking up Chryslaenor."

5

Victoria *fwumped* into the center seat of the war room, feeling more like a child in an overstuffed chair than the soon-to-be-queen of Unsel. She squeezed her eyes shut and pinched the bridge of her nose, hoping to draw out some of the steady, constant headache that others referred to as leadership. After six months of ruling Unsel, she would've hoped for a little more confidence in her new job.

During her brief tenure in the big chair, the day-to-day running-the-kingdom chores had gone smoothly. Wilfred took on the brunt of the issues, with Tori stepping in if they would have long-term ramifications. That was where she excelled. Her gift of seeing someone's futures, all the possible things that could happen based on their choices, made those decisions easy. If she saw too many paths, it only took the briefest physical contact to clarify. Proximity was important, and when she touched someone, she could practically read their mind. Rumors and speculation of her abilities stopped everyone from questioning her decisions, or by proxy, Wilfred's.

Her power helped a lot when it came to stuff like land, and cows. It did little to help her manage a country facing world-threatening annihilation. Her inexperience had challenged her patience, her abilities, and her wardrobe.

Queen Isabelle had made it look so easy. Her mother had been decisive and confident, and looked good doing it. The young queen-to-be had tried to appear strong. Today, she wore a tight, navy ensemble with pale blue embellishments, the type her mother referred to as a "power dress." It was great for turning heads but terrible for stuff like breathing. Emulating her mom's wardrobe wasn't hard, but there wasn't a dress in the world that could imbue her with the skills required to see this through.

Sure, she'd seen the future of Angst breaking Alloria free and running off with her, but it was the worst future. Her ability to tell the future had set Angst on a path to bonding with the sword, and then everything had gotten fuzzy. When Angst bonded with Chryslaenor, her visions became misty. When he wielded a second foci, they were more like a thick fog on a stormy night. On occasion, he would let his guard down, allowing her glimpses into his many futures. She tended to hold onto the ones she liked best, which was why today had taken her by surprise.

Her best friend had always been there for her, and now he was gone. With Alloria. It made her want to cry. Not only had Angst left with her mortal enemy, he hadn't taken Victoria instead. Her mind was a storm. She rubbed her temples, and a cool hand touched her arm.

"Please don't," she said, opening her eyes.

Rose pulled her hand back slowly, as if hoping to heal as much of Tori's headache as possible. Her champion was like that. A good heart hidden by the resilient armor of bitch face. She cared, more than she'd ever admit, but always on her own terms.

Rose was pretty, with porcelain features and dark red hair. Her eyes were the deepest of dark pools, always attentive, and always judging. And she cursed like she'd been raised by a team of angry ranch hands.

Rose had agreed to temporarily take the position of champion while they both waited, and hoped, for Angst to come to his senses. Captain Guard Tyrell was her mother's champion. He'd protected the queen and advised her. They were close enough to generate more than a few rumors around the castle. But being a champion wasn't just for good advice or ignoring court gossip.

Tyrell had practically died protecting Queen Isabelle from Aereon, the avatar of Air. Champions do that too.

Rose was a good choice, most of the time. She took her job so seriously, she'd cut her hair into a military buzz cut more practical than flattering. As an adviser, she was a delicate balance of incredible common sense and judgmental hatred for anyone she didn't like—which, from what Victoria could tell, was almost everyone. Even worse, she hated authority and accepted orders like any toddler unwilling to nap. Getting to the truth of Rose was easy; getting the young woman to stop from cursing in the great hall was impossible. It had taken a while to learn how to filter Rose's venom. But, as a protector now bonded to the foci Jormbrinder, none could best her, as she'd already proven time and time again.

"If my headache were gone, I'd probably fall asleep," Victoria said with a smile. "If I were well rested, I'd start being nice to people, and Unsel wouldn't know what to do with a nice queen."

"As you say, Your Highness," Rose said with a disapproving sigh.

"Where are the others?" Victoria asked, sitting up and straightening the bunch of her satin dress with a tug.

"Jaden's doing another sweep," she said, her dark brows furrowing dangerously.

"For Angst?" Victoria snapped. "Why is he wasting time?"

"For assassins. I told him Jormbrinder would let me know, but the ass wouldn't believe me," Rose said. "I only missed sensing one Melkier assassin. It wasn't my fault Dallow and I were felking in the—"

"We know," Victoria said, holding up a hand. "You've told us. Several times."

"I just want it to be clear that when I'm not being distracted by Dallow," she said with a mischievous smile, "you're safe."

"You seem to get distracted a lot," Victoria said, looking at Rose with a mockingly stern face.

"I'm surprised you don't get distracted with Jaden," Rose

43

said. "Is he still jealous about you and—"

"Rose," Victoria said sharply enough to make her stand at attention. "I said not to discuss that. Ever."

"Yes, Your Majesty," Rose replied, crisp as a thin sheet of ice.

"Mr. Jaden is a powerful ally. He's also untrusting, and a liar," Victoria said. "I would never marry a liar."

Rose looked as though she'd eaten something sour but nodded once.

"Be wary of him, my champion," she said gently. "I don't trust someone whose future I can't see clearly, especially when they aren't Al'eyrn."

"I'm telling you," Jaden said, his voice echoing down the hallway, "Dallow and I should've been told where he was the minute the guards came back. We could've stopped him."

"I'm not convinced of that," Wilfred said, his voice pitched higher than normal. "But I am worried that Angst is out there alone. Too many nations want him dead."

"Every time he leaves the castle," Mirot said, "he makes a new enemy. Our army isn't large enough to fight off the entire planet."

Jaden, Dallow, Mirot, and Wilfred filed into the room, their arms directing the argument as if there were too many conductors in front of a band. When they finally arrived, their voices were seething with anger, and they almost forgot to bow. Rose reminded them by clearing her throat. The four men bowed with apologetic glances at Victoria. Her headache wasn't getting any better.

"The answer is no," she said, hoping to take them by surprise.

Angst had taught her that humor was a great way to diffuse an argument before digging into the real problem. Happy people tended to be more willing to share their thoughts and feelings than angry people. Angst was also better at it than she was, clearly, because the incredulous, distraught stares she got from the men weren't exactly filled with laughter.

"I wasn't reading your minds," she said, sighing at the lost joke. "But the next time you come storming in like moody teen-agers, you'll be doing laps around the castle until I'm tired. Understood?"

They muttered sorries and bowed, more appropriately this time. She hated being sharp with them, but if she didn't give them the occasional reminder of who was in charge, nothing would ever get done.

Captain Mirim rushed into the war room, sweat beading her dark cheeks. She looked around nervously before stopping to make a very formal bow.

"I'm sorry for being late, Your Majesty," Mirim said. "I spend my time in the practice field and not the castle. I got a little turned around."

"It's okay," Victoria said. "At least someone knows how to treat me respectfully."

Mirim nodded and found a seat. The attractive young captain was a head taller than Victoria, with attentive eyes even darker than her skin. She'd done a fantastic job readying the zyn'ight for battle. Not only a hard worker and an excellent tactician, she had a knack for pairing wielders with abilities that complement-ed each other.

"Where did your guards find them?" Victoria asked.

"At the practice field, Your Highness," Mirim said.

"That's to the east," Jaden said, his tone angry. "You sent us west. You knew—"

"I did. Now shut up," Victoria said before turning to Mirim. "For expediency, a little less formality in the war room."

"Yes, Your…" Mirim said, looking as if she were about to do something wrong. "Yes, ma'am."

"Wilfred," Victoria said calmly. "Tell us your concerns. Why are you worried for Angst?"

"Assassins," he said, gasping for breath, his cheeks ruddy from the walk. The man was in worse shape than Angst had ever been, and leaned over his formidable girth to rest. It was worth the wait for him to catch his breath; he was probably the smart-est man in the room. He finally stood upright and mopped his brow.

"Take your time," she said sincerely.

"We have no time," Jaden snapped.

"Liars will speak in my court when called on," the princess said sharply.

Jaden's jaw dropped, and Rose sucked in a breath. Dallow took a step back as if expecting fiery daggers to shoot from Victoria's eyes. They all found chairs, opposite Jaden.

"Every assassin Rose and Jaden have stopped, whether they were from Fulk'han, Vex'steppe, or Melkier, came to kill Angst," Wilfred said. "From what I've learned, those nations are just waiting for him to be out in the open. His death could leave Unsel in grave danger should other nations team up to attack."

"We are lacking in allies," General Mirot said.

"Have we heard back from our envoy to Angoria?" she asked. "If the Berfemmian would be willing to help us…"

"Our ambassador's been gone too long," Mirot said. "The Berfemmian could've flown him back by now. It's possible they're upset about Faeoris."

Jaden raised a finger to say something, and quickly lowered it at the sight of her glare.

"We all are," Victoria said with a nod. "Send a full team and make it all women, as Rose suggested. If what Angst told me is true, the Berfemmian could still be in their mating cycle, and the male envoy could be dead."

"Not the worst way to die," Dallow said with a smirk.

"Oh," Rose said dangerously. "Want to find out?"

"Please, flirt later," Victoria said, rolling her eyes.

"What are we even discussing?" Jaden said. "Are we going after him, or not?"

She wanted to scream at him, again. His constant impudence was grating, especially when he was right. She took a deep, calming breath and tried to remember not to throw him in the dungeon.

"We are going after him. We're leaving in two days," she said, raising a hand to stop the complaints. "That's not what we're here to discuss. When we catch up to him, and we will, do we offer to help, or do we...stop him."

Mirot raised a hand, and she nodded.

"I agree with Wilfred, Your Highness," he said. "Unsel is in danger without Angst. We should assist him."

All heads turned to the general. He was a known bigot toward wielders, who'd barely cracked the shell of acceptance.

"Everything he's done has been to save you, and Unsel," Mirot said. "A man who would sacrifice his family for his queen would not turn around and destroy Ehrde."

"Thank you, General," she said, her throat tight. Angst hadn't actually chosen Tori over Heather and his children, but everyone in Unsel believed this to be true. It was the worse type of court-gossip and was completely thoughtless of what Angst had gone through. She turned to Jaden and lashed out. "You were going to say something, liar?"

Jaden paled. He looked ready to scream, or cry, or both, and the hurt on his face melted a little of her ice. He composed himself slowly before speaking.

"Angst has two foci. That's too much power for one man to wield, and they are slowly driving him crazy. I'm from the future, and history says it's true. It's not his fault, but it is our problem," he said. "We've seen it over the last few months. He was a broken man who suddenly became giddy with hope. When he completely loses himself, it will happen. He'll break Ehrde."

"Jaden's concerns are founded," Dallow said. "Angst thinks he's found something that could bring his family back. Prendere is the prize that elements win at the end of their war. He doesn't know how to wield that sort of power. Nobody does. If he is going mad and acquires that prize, it could be the end of all things."

"That's why we need to stop him," Jaden said. "That's why I was sent back."

"Sent by who?" Rose asked.

"This is a lie made up by a jealous man," Victoria said, pointing at Jaden. "Another word and you're dismissed."

Jaden grimaced, his cheeks flushing red, but remained quiet.

"I can't believe that Angst intends to destroy Ehrde," Wilfred said, setting his hands behind his back. "His intentions sometimes cause more problems than they solve, but maybe if we're there to help, we will all survive this."

"But?" she prompted.

"I agree that his mood change was abrupt, but not without reason," Wilfred said. "Angst is planning something, to be sure, but that was a bit too much happiness and excitement. I worry that he's already slipping."

She really wanted to ask what she should do. Her magic wouldn't give her the answer, and she wanted Wilfred to provide it. But according to her mother, that would be a weakness. She was at a loss for words, and Wilfred was kind enough to offer her something.

"I've always thought you were a bright kid, Your Highness," he said, almost casually. "I've been here the whole time, watching you grow up. Even when I learned what you could do with magic, I knew there was more to you than wielding. Sure, you can see all those future possibilities, but you decide which one to take. It's your instinct, your gut that tells you what path to choose."

He was right. Even when she took up a sword, she had to choose what to do with it in the midst of battle. It was practically instinct to know which swing to parry, but it was a choice. "Go on."

"These last few weeks, since our friend's 'discovery,' he's been a little too Angst. It's hard to tell if it's crazy, or if he knows something the rest of us don't. It's hard for *me* to tell, but not for you, because you know him better than anyone."

"What's your point, Mr. Wilfred?" she said, uncomfortable at so much revelation.

"Magic is a gift, a force to be reckoned with, but it can be a crutch. My point is that your abilities only play a small part in your decisions, and I don't think you need to see his future to follow your gut feeling. You'll know what to do when it's time."

CHAPTER FIVE

"Thank you, Wilfred," Victoria said with a smile. "And you're right, we don't need to decide, yet."

"That's it?" Rose asked. "The decision is to not make a decision?"

"No," Victoria said. "For now, we follow him."

"Do we even know how to find him?" Rose asked. "Do we even know how he's going to destroy Ehrde?"

Victoria looked at Dallow, and everyone turned to him. The tall, thin man brushed blond bangs from his forehead before pressing his hands together.

"We do know where he is," Dallow said. "And exactly what he's planning to do."

6

"What he wants to do is simple, in concept," Dallow said. "He wants to go back in time and stop himself from wielding Chryslaenor."

"We can't let that happen," Victoria said. "I remember seeing a future where Angst didn't bond with the foci, and it was disastrous. That's exactly why I put all of this in motion."

"You what?" Rose asked.

"I first met Angst when he stumbled into the Maiden's Courtyard," Victoria said. "I hid because I was scared. He started imitating my mom, and he was so funny that I couldn't keep myself from laughing. Angst introduced himself, and he was so charming—"

"I'm going to vomit," Rose said, rolling her eyes.

"Shut up, champion," Victoria said, sternly.

"Yes, Your Highness," Rose said, her face stiffening.

"Please continue," Wilfred said, his tone gentle and cautious.

Victoria slowly drew her burning gaze away from Rose and closed her eyes. "He flirted like Angst does, and my fears washed away. It was the first time I really tried to wield. I was bombarded with all his potential futures, and all the things that could happen to Unsel. I was overwhelmed, but then he created a rose out of stone for me, and everything seemed okay. Of course, that was right before he lost control of his magic. There was an earthquake, and he saved me from a falling pillar."

She glanced at Rose, who swallowed hard, squinting as if forcing her eyes not to roll.

"It was our moment, and that rose gave me focus. I spent days with Angst in the maiden's courtyard and nights sorting through my memories of his futures." Victoria sighed so deeply Angst would've been proud. "Eventually, I found the path that would save Unsel, and make Angst a hero."

"You used him," Rose said, accusingly.

"Of course I did. That's between Angst and me, and not your concern," she snapped. Taking a calming breath, she continued, "So much has gone wrong. Angst's family, my mom…but that was the only safe path, and we barely got here."

"And now he wants to destroy it all by going back in time to undo it," Dallow said.

"Angst is an idiot. He can't do that," Rose said looking at Dallow with a steady gaze. "Can he?"

* * * *

"Of course I can," Angst said with the smile of a conman who'd just sold a bridge. "I can do anything."

"I believe you," Alloria said, her face glowing. "That's why I chose you to be *my* champion."

He struggled to maintain that smile. He truly needed her help to make this happen and would do his best to keep her alive. So, sure, champion was more or less accurate. Maybe less.

"But if you go back in time and stop yourself from picking up the giant sword," she began, "who will protect us from the elements?"

* * * *

"My head hurts," General Mirot said, rubbing his temples. "How does this time thing work?"

"Time is fragile," Dallow said. "Let's pretend I gave Rose a bouquet of flowers and asked her to marry me."

"It's going to take more than flowers," Rose grumbled.

"What if someone from the future comes back in time and steals those flowers?" Dallow continued.

"If I don't even get flowers," she said, "I'm definitely not marrying you."

"Really?" Dallow asked.

She kissed him on the cheek then shook her head.

"Note to self, remember the flowers," Dallow said under his breath. "But, exactly my point. If the flowers are gone, we don't get married. That future never happens. Angst wants to undo what he believes he started."

"Angst stopping this mess from happening doesn't sound so bad," Mirot said. "We've lost a lot of good people. Tyrell, the queen, Rook…it's a long list. Why wouldn't we just help him?"

"The elements will just go to war anyway," Victoria said. "They go to war every two thousand years, with or without Angst."

"Exactly," Dallow said. "Angst is so desperate to save his family, Kala, Hector, and Faeoris that he's forgetting the most important point. He's the hero who saved the rest of us. Without that foci, nobody will be able to."

"I told you he was an idiot," Rose said.

* * * *

"They think I'm an idiot," Angst said. "Or crazy."

"We can be crazy together," Alloria said, her eyes a little too wild again.

Angst took a cautious step back, and she moved close, following him like a puppy. He sighed. "If I go back a year to stop myself from wielding Chryslaenor, the elements will still go to war and nobody will be able to protect everyone. What they don't realize is that I'm going back eighteen years to stop myself from ever trying to pick up Chryslaenor."

"What?" she asked, dumbfounded.

"This is all my fault," he said, unable to hold back the guilt. "I think my first attempt to lift the sword triggered the element war."

"How?" Alloria asked, taking his hand.

"It happened right after I started working at the castle," Angst explained. "I was attending the annual party for staff. As a sort of hazing ritual, they would tempt every new employee with knighthood if they could pick up the sword. I was determined, really determined, so I summoned a little magic—just a trickle, I swear. When I grasped the hilt, there was a click, and it loosened."

"Wow," she said. "And nobody noticed?"

"Nope," he said. "But I felt the elements, each of them, wash over me as if I'd set them free. When it was done, I stood there alone, holding the hilt of the sword, and Magic whispered 'And so it begins.'"

"Why didn't you keep it?" she asked. "You would've become a knight."

"I've told myself it must not have been the right time," he said. "But really, I was scared. I thought I'd broken something. In a way, I did."

"So going back and stopping all that from happening will save everyone?" Alloria asked. "That sounds like a great idea!"

* * * *

"This sounds like a terrible idea," Wilfred said.

"It's worse," Dallow said. "Going back in time will kill Angst. Not only do we lose our champion, but we also lose our friend."

* * * *

"Of course, I'll probably die," he said. "But that's okay."

"Why will you die?" she asked, her voice filled with desperation. "Why is that okay?"

"A change like that will break time," he said. "When I go back, everything that happens from that point on will cease to exist. Young Angst should live, hopefully, but old Angst, me, will die."

* * * *

"It's a paradox," Dallow said. "While Angst may think he's going to die, he may end up killing us all. Breaking time that much—"

"Will break Ehrde," Victoria said, gripping her stomach. "I've seen it. The entire world could split in half."

"Will split in half," Jaden corrected. "I've been there. It's a dark and dangerous place, and Angst was the catalyst."

"And that's what Aerella meant when she said he's going to go crazy," Rose said.

* * * *

"That doesn't sound crazy to me," Alloria said. "But what about us?"

"Us?" Angst asked. "Uh, oh, right...us. Well, things will change."

"I don't like that," she said, frowning. "You're the only person I have left."

* * * *

"What do we do, Your Majesty?" Mirot asked.

"We either try to reason with him," Victoria said, "or we have to stop him."

* * * *

"No one can stop me. No matter what, I have to fix all of this," he said, waving his hand around. "You'll get your dad back, your friends, and maybe we can still be close too."

"I still don't get it," she said, with a confused frown. "But you seem happy, Angst. I'm happy too, now that I'm out of prison. I'll be even happier in a change of clothes and after we take a bath."

"We?" he asked, taken aback.

"Me," she said. "I meant me, of course. I'm just a little bit in shock after swimming through all those rocks."

"Right," he said, summoning his swifen.

"I really would like to see them again," Alloria said. "I still miss my dad. I even miss my step-mom what's-her-name. And all my friends…"

"I get it," he said with a nod. "That's why I want to do this, even if it kills me."

"Just tell me what you want," Alloria said, her tone sultry. "I'll do anything."

"Great," he said, the pinch between his shoulders abating. "I need you to help me find Magic."

"Noooo," she said, reeling. Her hands shook, and she held herself, practically folding into a fetal position. "Anything but him."

He took a surprised step back. What had the element done to her? He wanted to ask but worried she would lose herself in whatever hole she was hiding. "Alloria, I'll protect you."

"No, you won't," she said in a tiny voice, as if another person had suddenly taken her place.

He needed the element's help to find Prendere. Magic hadn't shown up to visit over the last six months, probably because Angst was planning to beat the information out of him. Alloria had ties to Magic. Angst had thought she was a partner, not a prisoner. It completely changed his approach.

"I'm your champion, aren't I?"

"Yes," she squeaked.

"I've destroyed other elements, and I've already beaten Magic once," he said. "You believe in me, don't you?"

"Sure," she said, sounding unconvinced.

After years of emotional parrying with his wife, his instinct was to placate and be gentle. He always gave Heather the time she needed to recover from being upset, and did everything in his power to help. But now, they didn't have time, and Angst wasn't convinced he could pull Alloria from her dark place with soothing words.

"You love me," he said firmly.

"Yes," she said, looking up.

"Then stand up," he said.

She stood straight, arching her back. Flecks of dirt and grass fell from her.

"You'll do this because you love me," he said. "And I'll protect you because I'm your champion."

Alloria looked at him with her big eyes, gazing into his as if he'd suddenly reappeared. Her smile returned, as did her uncomfortably longing gaze. "Okay."

It was as if the dark moment had never happened. *"Nothing to be nervous about here,"* screamed the sarcastic voice in his head continually giving him sort-of advice.

"But not like this," she said, looking down at her grungy prison garb.

"Agreed," he said, a little surprised she was making sense. "We'll find a town with an inn where we can take a quick bath—"

"Together?" she asked, grabbing his hand and leaning in, so his arm was lodged between her boobs.

"That's not what I meant," he said, his heart skipping several beats as he pulled away.

She laughed as he gathered himself. Alloria's flirting was way out of his league.

"As I said, we'll find a town," he said. "After *you* take a bath, dry off, are fully clothed and fast asleep, then, and only then, will I take a bath."

"Boo," she said with a mocking pout. Even caked in dirt, she was pretty. "Baths can be fun…"

"We need a place small enough where we can go unnoticed," he said, completely ignoring that last comment. "But big enough to have a shop for your new clothes. Maybe we could buy a horse, since my swifen stands out a little."

Alloria laughed.

"What?" he asked.

"Are you going to hide your giant swords, too?" she asked.

"Well, yeah," he said, scratching his head. "That's a good

point."

"Not just pretty," she said, tapping her temple with a finger. "I know where we can get lost in a crowd, even with your swords. We'll go to The Fette."

"The what?" he asked.

"It's a hidden town where people my age hang out," she said. "They have shops, baths, places to crash, and parties. Lots of parties."

It sounded like a distraction, a great distraction, but also a waste of time. Was Alloria dragging out their adventure so she wouldn't have to face Magic? Either way, if his plan was right, they had time to spare. Maybe she would be more prepared to face the element if she had that time. And, she really needed a bath. They both did.

"I've never heard of The Fette," Angst said with a frown.

"Exactly why it's safe to go there," she said. "The innkeeper at Potterton will know where it is, and then I'll introduce you to paradise."

7

The tent Tarness shared with Maarja was spacious by human standards—far larger than the single-room rental he squeezed into back in Unsel. It was easily eight feet tall, giving him enough height to stand. Large, down pillows rested along the far edge over a worn, fur-covered pallet. The floor and walls were all lined with skins from her hunts. Smoke billowed up through a hole in the top of the round tent. A stone fire pit in the center provided warmth and a place for cooking. That was his favorite part, the heat.

The first time they made love on warm fur before the fire, he'd thought it was romantic—until she told him to focus. The furs weren't for romance or decoration. They were effective insulation and blankets. After months passed, he'd wondered how there were enough animals in Nordruaut to furnish all the tents. And then he'd decided it was probably better to stay on task during sex before getting corrected again.

Maarja crawled through the tent entrance, and he beamed at her beautiful, tanned face. Beneath her light blue eyes were three vertical lines of paint like white tears that almost reached her cheekbones. Long, platinum blond braids swung back and forth before her white fur tunic. After entering, she escaped her fur coverings like a butterfly leaving its cocoon. Except this butterfly was almost naked, his other favorite thing about their tent. While short for a Nordruaut, she was a third taller than Tarness, and far too tall to stand in the tent, so she sat cross-legged in front of the fire.

"Your boots are off," she said with a nod. "We don't have time for sex, husband. Jintorich has already left for your training, and you don't want to keep him waiting...unless you do want to keep him waiting."

She gave him the barest of smiles, which he took as being coy. To say that the Nordruaut were reserved was like saying a blank piece of parchment is plain. That shy-yet-alluring smile meant she was ready to make their friend wait for hours. He crawled closer to kiss her full on the mouth. It was far better than their first romantic adventure, where her kiss covered half his face, and she tossed him around like a toy. Not his worst memory, but it had taken awhile to figure things out, after the bruises healed.

"I wouldn't want to be disrespectful of Jintorich," Tarness finally said, pulling away.

She nodded curtly, but there was a hint of disappointment in her eyes. "You are a good husband to work so hard."

"I try." Tarness inched to the edge of the tent and began pulling on his boots.

"I would like to attend this session," Maarja said.

"Not yet," he said, gently. Gentle apparently didn't mean much to her, because her gaze was cold. She'd asked every time, and he'd always given an excuse. It was much harder to tell her no after she offered sex, but he had no choice. Per Jintorich's advice, he tried thinking like a Nordruaut. His low voice became firm. "I will not have you see me fail."

"You do not fail when you try," she said. "I will be your inspiration to succeed."

"You always are, but I have to do this on my own," he said.

Her terse smile reminded him of the disapproving look Heather frequently gave Angst. He smiled until she gave in with a sigh. After crawling over to their bed, Maarja removed her leather top, providing him a glimpse of breast before covering herself with fur blankets. She looked delicious, and Jintorich would certainly understand why he was late, again.

"I will be here when you return," she said, huskily. "Wake me, or I will be upset."

"I won't be long," he said before reluctantly leaving the warmth and nakedness of their home.

The felking cold outside was felking cold. He wouldn't admit that this was the real reason he was late to meet Jintorich. The Al'eyrn knew spells to keep himself warm, but Tarness hadn't been able to cast a spell beyond summoning his swifen—an obsidian stallion that also wasn't warm. His secret wish was for the war between Eastern and Western Nordruaut to end so he could travel with Maarja. They could visit Unsel, or warmer Meldusia, or possibly a volcano or two.

A fifteen-minute trudge through the snow brought him to a secluded alcove that Jintorich had magically carved out of a freezing hill. High, snowy walls surrounded most of the nook, keeping them from prying eyes. A bonfire blazed in the center, and the walls kept out most of the wind. Tarness relaxed in the warmth and nodded at his small friend.

Jintorich was apparently the only Meldusian to survive the Vex'kvette, a river of orange sludge created by Magic that had killed every creature it couldn't change into a monster. He was 18-inches tall, if you included the hairy ears that were thin and pointed up most of the time. The little man was bulbous, from his pumpkin-shaped forehead to his ruddy nose. Dark hair pulled back in cornrows draped down to his shoulders. Jintorich's eyes were rich blue marbles that peered out from under long, animated eyebrows. Despite the cold, he wore nothing more than a white terrycloth robe, thick nails peeking out from beneath them.

"Sorry I'm late," Tarness said, rubbing his hands before reaching for the fire's heat.

"Did you tell her?" Jintorich asked, his squeaky voice filled with concern. "You said you might."

"I don't think I'd be here if I had," Tarness said with a sigh. "Are we alone?"

"Yes, my friend," Jintorich said, his eyebrows drooping in

disappointment. "I sense no one nearby."

"Maarja won't trust me if I tell her about the deal I made with Magic to stay alive. None of them will." He held up the hand with the ruby ring. "That's why we need to remove it."

"I understand," Jintorich squeaked softly. "But I fear she suspects something. Maarja is no fool, and if she were to find out, it would be far worse than if you told her."

"That's exactly why I want it off," Tarness grumbled. "If it's off, and I tell her, I know she'll understand. I know she'll forgive me."

"Will she?" Jintorich asked. "It's still a lie."

Tarness shrugged and sighed. He stared at the ring that kept him alive and gave it a tug, stretching the skin underneath. It seemed fused to his finger and wouldn't budge.

"Any new ideas?" Tarness asked.

"For the spells you're supposed to be learning?" Jintorich asked. "Or removing the ring?"

"The real reason we're here," Tarness said, not enjoying the Meldusian's judgement. "To remove the ring."

"You'll need to learn a spell one day," Jintorich said. "Just in case someone asks why we come here so often."

"We've tried. I can't even learn how to change the color of my hair," Tarness said, his shoulders dropping. "You said that was almost as easy as summoning my swifen."

"Yes, something is keeping you from learning another spell," Jintorich said, rubbing his chin thoughtfully. "Maybe it's the ring. Or it could be the guilt…"

"Let's call it the ring," Tarness said.

"Of course," Jintorich said. "I've been conferring with my foci, Maehtikyn, and there may be another way. We could remove your finger or your hand."

"What?" Tarness snapped. "No way am I losing any body part. That's worse than this thing keeping me alive, or being dead." He shuddered. "Anything but that."

"You're not making this easy," Jintorich said. "There is a fire spell I could use. It may burn, but you'll probably keep your hand and fingers."

"Burning is good," Tarness said. "Well, better than the other thing. What do I do?"

"Just hold your hand out where I can reach it," Jintorich said.

Tarness rested on his knees and held out his hand as if preparing for someone to kiss it. There was an audible *tink* as Jintorich placed his tiny staff on the ring. It quickly warmed to the point of discomfort, and Tarness took deep, calming breaths. As the heat grew past the point of unbearable, so did his temper. The pain was like a fan to his own flame of anger as the ring went from red to white.

"It's moving," Tarness said as the ruby listed to one side then the other.

A small, dark circle appeared over the fire. Shadowy tendrils grew, soaking up the color around it like an oblong whirlpool.

"Death," Tarness gasped. It was the same void that had almost killed Alloria. "You're doing it, keep—"

Crack! A sound like lightning followed by a flash of bright, white light made Tarness wince. The skin on his face and arms rolled back in waves from the explosion while he remained in place. It was practically impossible to move him when he was emotional, especially when he was upset.

It took several minutes of blinking away the spots in his vision to see the results of their experiment. The fire was out, the void was gone, and so was Jintorich.

"Jin?" Tarness called out. "Jin, where are you? Are you okay?"

A high-pitched mumble came from the nearby wall of snow. Tarness rushed over to see a Jintorich-shaped indentation. He reached deep into the snowbank until he felt robes, and gently pulled.

Tarness set him on the ground, and Jintorich gave him a wide-toothed smile. He was covered in so much white, he looked like a creepy snowman.

"That was exciting!" Jintorich said. With a squint of concentration, steam rose from his clothes until they were dry.

"That's the spell I need to learn," Tarness said.

"I could try teaching you again," Jintorich said. "If you don't want to make another attempt to remove the ring."

"It feels like a waste of time to keep trying," Tarness grumbled. "It's always the same. We get close, death shows up, and then that flash of white interrupts your spell. I still think it's Magic."

"Possibly," Jintorich said. "But whatever it is, it's definitely a counter-spell."

"Counter-spell?" Tarness asked, rubbing warmth into his hands.

"According to Maehtikyn, there are spells that conflict with each other," Jintorich said, his thick brows drooping sincerely. "They cause a reaction, sometimes creating a spark."

"That was a big spark," Tarness said in frustration.

"It certainly wasn't from the spell I cast," Jintorich said. "I would call it unnatural."

"I'm not sure what natural is anymore." Tarness barked out a laugh. "Thanks for trying again. I'm going to head back to camp."

"What about the drying spell?" Jintorich asked.

"Next time," Tarness said. "Maarja is waiting, and I'd hate to disappoint."

8

"I think I look ridiculous," Rose said, staring down in disbelief as if she wore her dad's hand-me-downs. She shook her head, hiding most of her new armor with a black cloak.

"We're wearing the same armor," Victoria said, raising an eyebrow. "Do you think I look ridiculous?"

"You look great. It suits you. This is not my, uh, style," Rose said, carefully. "Also, why is your breastplate so much more...breasty than mine?"

"I'm going to be queen," Victoria said sincerely. "I have to stand out and be impressive."

"They certainly stand out," Rose muttered.

Victoria ignored the slight. She loved her new armor. It was very similar to Angst's zyn'ight armor, except for several design modifications she'd requested. Angst's chest piece covered the top half of his torso and was shaped to be muscular. Rose's was similar with two small bumps for her breasts. Victoria had designed hers to be more like a steel corset that squeezed her breasts together and presented them like a Berfemmian top. Chainmail covered her midriff, dangling over steel bottoms that rested low on her waist. Plate armor covered the tops of her hands and front of her legs, only wrapping half-way around, leaving the back of her limbs unprotected, save for leather leggings. She proudly wore a long, red cloak that looked quite a bit like a cape.

"I just wish it wasn't so…gold," Rose said, looking at her arms.

"I love rose-gold," Victoria said, barely able to contain a twirl. "Are you going to be grumpy this entire trip?"

"Maybe," Rose said, flopping noisily onto a nearby bench.

They waited impatiently in an antechamber where soldiers readied themselves for the training grounds. It was an ideal place to slip out in the dewy hours of early morning. Victoria hid her gnawing anticipation behind excitement—not only for her new armor, but also the upcoming adventure. It was a thin veil she would have to peek behind soon to face tougher decisions, like what to do with Angst. Fortunately, now wasn't the time to ponder or dwell; it was time to leave the castle's confines.

"Sean, Simon," Victoria said, beaming at the brothers as they entered. "I'm so glad you're here."

They bowed respectfully. The two appeared more like brothers in spirit than actual kin. Simon was six feet tall with a dark-brown military haircut, pale skin, and sharp blue eyes. His brother was easily a head shorter and had a long, wispy mane of black hair. Both men were in their fit-twenties, but neither looked like a muscular knight or burly soldier. Sean seemed especially thin like a runner who never ate, and overly tan as if he ran everywhere naked.

"Thank you for having us, Your Majesty," Simon said, standing tall. "With Jaden's guidance, I'm now ready to heal anything, within reason."

"Why do we need another healer if I'm here?" Rose asked with a frown.

"In case Angst kills you," Victoria said in an overly sweet tone. "Or I do."

Rose peered at her but said nothing. Sean was also quiet but smiled briefly before looking away to the door.

"And are you ready, Sean?" she asked, gently.

"He's ready." Simon looked at Sean nervously. "My brother rarely speaks, Your Highness. Usually just to me. He thinks a little differently than us, but he's reliable."

"Maybe you can start by healing Sean," Rose said, mocking the man's gaze with an open-mouthed stare at the door.

Victoria shook her head and was about to say something when Captain Mirim entered.

Mirim was tall, muscular, and beautiful enough to be Berfemmian. Her skin was so dark she could've been a member of the Vex'steppe tribe, if there were women. She had a pretty, yet stern face with keen eyes that took in everything. Her broad shoulders and confident approach gave Victoria some relief. At least one of them knew what to do on the battlefield.

Bowing stiffly, Mirim nodded, her full lips tight as if holding back every reservation on her tongue. Tori could sense Mirim's concern that there weren't enough of them to face Angst. Despite having done an exceptional job training with the zyn'ight, she didn't know the full scope of Victoria's plan.

"Your Highness," she said. "I appreciate the opportunity to lead this team."

"In battle, Captain," Victoria said. "Otherwise, I'll be in charge."

"Of course," she said, crisply.

"I wish they'd shut up," Nikkola said, rushing in and closing the door behind her. She latched it and spun around, bracing the door with her back. "Can we just do this without the men, Tori...Victoria...Your Highness?"

Simon cleared his throat and Sean glanced at Nikkola with a disapproving pout.

"Oh," Nikkola said, noticing the brothers. "Maybe you can hold them off while we escape?"

The 39ish-year-old woman seemed harried and uncomfortable. Nikkola had the pasty skin and ruddy cheeks of someone who drank too much—not a surprise. She'd lost her daughter Kala to Fire, and her sister Janda was killed by Vars. Despite this, she'd begged to come with. Captain Mirim had warned caution, wary about Nikkola's motivations. No one could deny the woman's raw power.

"Are you sure you're up for this?" Victoria asked, calmly approaching Nikkola. She brushed a strand of long, black hair from the woman's pale face.

"I've lost too many, Your Highness, I won't let anyone else die," she said, fury in her eyes. "Except maybe them."

The pounding on the wooden door made everyone jump. Whatever they were arguing about was loud enough to fill the small room. Nikkola's advice to leave the men behind may be right.

She closed her eyes and reached out with her mind. It was rarely possible to read minds unless someone actually let her, but she could view people's futures, all of their futures. Their wants, wishes, and demands appeared in her mind like moving pictures. Most of the futures she filtered out because there could be so many. Some she fought to block because people could be disgusting or morose.

Fortunately, or unfortunately, their thoughts were as loud as their voices. General Mirot, Jaden, and Dallow were arguing about whether she should be allowed to leave. Allowed? It seemed, at least, that Dallow had her back.

"Let them in," she said stiffly.

The three men practically tripped over each other as the door opened. They became silent at the sight of Victoria's armor. Mirot's cheeks went so red, she worried that his quick bow might actually be a heart attack. Jaden opened his mouth wide enough to put his foot in but caught himself and swallowed hard. Dallow bowed smoothly, placed his hands behind his back, and strolled to stand behind Victoria.

"If even one of you suggests that I should stay at the castle ruling Unsel and making heirs," Victoria said, "your future will be constantly reliving your worst nightmares, and I know what they are."

"I was just going to say that you look," Jaden stuttered, glancing at Mirot, "you look, uh…"

"Incredible. And powerful," Mirim said, impatiently. "As does her champion."

"Thank you, Captain," Victoria said.

"Fierce," Dallow said with a respectful nod.

"Sexy," Jaden whispered in her ear.

"Those were the right answers," she said.

"You look like a target, Your Majesty," Mirot said, his eyes wide. "That rose-gold is not subtle."

"That's my fault," Dallow said, raising a finger. "Two thousand years ago, the creators of the zyn'ight armor were concerned that so much of the body was exposed. They created a spell to harden the armor, not only making it more durable, but also magically protecting the unprotected parts. That spell changes the armor from dusky black to silver."

"And yet, this is gold," Rose admonished.

"It's a complicated spell," Dallow said, reaching behind his neck and rubbing. "It worked, mostly, but I didn't get it quite right."

"Dallow," Victoria said. "I would pay for more mistakes like this."

"Good," Rose grumbled. "Because this mistake will cost him plenty."

Dallow looked at her, squinting. She nodded, as if silently expressing that there would be a punishment that Victoria didn't understand, and didn't want to.

"How will this protect us from Angst?" Rose asked. "He can just turn it to sand."

"It's to protect us from everything else," Victoria said. "I'm sure you're all familiar with the many assassination attempts on my life over the last six months. The truth is, they were trying to kill Angst."

"Is it because the Fulk'han hate him so much?" Simon asked.

"Maybe," Victoria said. "But there have been attempts made by almost every nation on Ehrde. We've stopped or killed Nordruaut, Tribesmen, several from Melkier, and even a cavastil bird."

"That one sucked," Rose said with a grimace.

"When Angst left, the assassins stopped coming," Victoria said. "We've been spying on several Fulk'han and Vex'steppe camps, and they've all moved off. They must be on the hunt for Angst, like us."

"How many?" Mirim asked with a frown.

"We have no way of knowing," General Mirot said. "But we believe quite a few. Nobody is going to face Angst alone."

"How do we get through them to find Angst?" Mirim asked.

"Carefully," Dallow said. "We have a plan to stop Angst, but it has to be at the right time. Until then, we're going to have to stay far enough away that he doesn't sense us, and close enough to follow whatever path he clears."

"You're expecting Angst to fight off hordes of enemies, so we don't have to?" Mirim asked.

"That's a lot of faith in someone who's going crazy," Nikkola said.

"I don't think he's going crazy," Victoria said, tugging at a strand of hair.

"Right," Rose said, rolling her eyes. "So, basically, we're going to our doom."

"Some champion," Jaden said with a sneer.

"Don't make me champion your ass, jerk," Rose said, peering at the young man.

"Stop," Victoria said, holding out a hand before Rose. "For now. I may need you to champion him later."

"How do you propose we find Angst?" Mirim asked. "Do we know how the other nations are tracking him?

"We aren't sure if, or how, the other nations know where he is," Victoria said, her eyes dancing to Dallow nervously. "I spent some time with my cousin. Alloria's future is as fractured as her mind, but she gave me some direction. As for Angst, I believe Rose, Dallow, and I know how he thinks."

"As do I," Jaden said, lifting his chin.

"Care to explain what that means?" Rose asked.

"I'm from the future," said Jaden, coolly. "History has taught me about the disaster he will bring when he goes insane."

They all looked at each other nervously.

"Right," Rose said in disbelief. "Maybe I'm from the future

too."

"No," he said. "You don't make it."

"Where to first?" Victoria abruptly turned to Dallow.

"I believe he's at Potterton," Dallow said.

"That harlot," Victoria said, balling her hands into fists.

Everyone stopped breathing to look at Victoria, who blushed furiously.

"Is she…is she taking him to The Fette?" Rose asked, putting a hand to her mouth. She burst out in laughter. "This is going to be easy. He'll never want to leave!"

"Why would she take Angst there?" Jaden asked.

"I know my cousin," Victoria said. "She won't want to travel in that prison outfit, and The Fette has clothes…more her style."

"I'm sure that's not all she wants," Rose said, laughing again. She quieted quickly under Victoria's steely gaze.

"I'm sorry," Dallow said. "What is The Fette?"

Sean and Simon looked down at the ground as if they'd stolen a cookie.

"It's a sort of party in the woods that moves every week or so. There's lots of music and dancing and drinking," Victoria said. "Under twenty-five only…usually."

"Oh," Dallow said, hopefully. "Parties are good."

"How do you know so much about it? Unless…" Rose's jaw dropped. "Did I see you there? I remember…strawberry blond hair."

"Hey, you can change your hair color," Dallow said, as if suddenly struck by realization. "It's always straight and black when you're at the castle, but curly and blond when you're out here with us. Wait, you told us that the trip to Melkier was your first time out of the castle."

"We should probably get going," Victoria said, her cheeks so warm she was practically sweating.

"A constant party filled with hedonistic youth," Mirot huffed. "It sounds like trouble."

"Yes," Victoria and Rose said at the same time, matching twinkles in their eyes. Both of them laughed.

"Rose is right. He won't want to leave," Dallow said. "It sounds like we should definitely go and investigate."

Rose slugged him with her tiny stick arm, which didn't make him wince. Much.

"He won't stay, but it will definitely slow him down," Victoria said. "It's a window for us to catch up if we leave now."

"So, there's no talking you out of this," Mirot said, already sounding defeated. "You're more stubborn than your mother."

"Yes," Victoria said. "I am. And, I don't see another option."

"But, Unsel needs you to be queen," Mirot pleaded.

"Didn't she mention a future of your nightmares?" Rose asked, placing a hand on one of the long dagger handles by her side.

"This isn't just about protecting Unsel anymore. Angst is putting all of Ehrde in danger, and I'm one of the few people who can get through to him." Victoria sighed. "Make Wilfred king if I don't survive."

"He doesn't wish to be king, Your Majesty," Mirot said.

"Another reason why he's the perfect man for the job," Victoria said.

"Are eight enough to hunt down Angst?" Mirot asked. "Please, let me send a garrison with to keep you safe. Or more zyn'ight."

Victoria looked over her crew with pride. Captain Mirim stood tall and resolute in her plate armor. Everyone else wore flat black zyn'ight armor, except for Dallow. The tall, skinny man had argued that steel would exhaust him. His arguments had exhausted her, and they'd settled on an armor of light black leather.

"We need to move fast," Victoria finally said. "And this party will be more than enough. Rose is Al'eyrn now and will keep me safe, just like Angst did the last time I snuck out."

"You'll even get to keep your clothes on," Rose muttered.

"What?" Victoria snapped.

"Nothing, Your Majesty," Rose said.

Victoria peered at her before continuing. "Not only does

71

Jaden claim to have some knowledge of the events that are coming, he's also gone toe-to-toe with Angst."

"For about five minutes before he kicked my ass," Jaden said under his breath.

"Those five minutes may just save us," Victoria said.

"I'm willing to go again," Jaden said, beaming.

"Dallow has more knowledge of magic than anyone else alive," Victoria said. "He's both powerful and Angst's oldest friend. Between the two of us, we may be able to reason with him."

"Thank you, Your Highness," Dallow said with a short bow. "I'll try."

"Nikkola is one of our most dangerous zyn'ight. Simon can heal when Rose is fighting. Sean, well, Sean communes with animals or something."

"He'll be there when we need him most, Your Highness," Simon said.

"I hate to say this, Your Majesty," Mirim said, "but I don't feel like I bring a lot to the table. I have no magic."

"Mirim," Victoria said, placing a hand on her shoulder. "You are possibly the most important person here. While I can fight better than any of them—"

"Hey," Rose said, defensively.

"It's true," Dallow said. "She beat Hector. She's amazing."

Mirot's eyebrows rose in surprise.

"I'm no tactician," Victoria continued. "You were chosen to lead the zyn'ight for that reason. You're comfortable around magic, know their strengths, and can see situations in a way I can't. We need that experience."

"You'll be our Hector now," Dallow said, softly.

There was a brief moment of silence.

"I can't replace him," Mirim said, standing tall. "But I will do my best to fill his boots."

"It sounds like you're in good hands," Mirot said reluctantly.

Without another word, Victoria opened the door and led them outside. She summoned her swifen. The feathery pink unicorn appeared and nuzzled her cheek. Rose rolled her eyes at the sight as she summoned her wood chip buck. The others did the same until there was a menagerie of large glass, steel, and wood animals.

"My pinto is in the stables," Captain Mirim said. "It will only take a minute to fetch her."

"Sorry, Mirim," Victoria said, "but you'll have to ride with one of us. Your horse will slow us down if there's a chase."

Jaden summoned a Nordruaut Bokeen made of soft grass and large enough for several people. "I promise, it smells better than the real thing," he said with a smile.

"General," Victoria said. "As discussed, take our entire army and the remaining zyn'ight. Skirt the borders of Rohjek and Melkier then wait for us at the appointed spot in Meldusia."

"Yes, Your Highness," he said, tugging nervously at his long mustache. "But is it wise to leave Unsel undefended?"

"If we don't succeed," Victoria said, "there won't be an Unsel left to defend."

9

Angst and Alloria rode the steel ram swifen along a path not much wider than a deer trail. The ram he'd summoned was as powerful and confident as ever, thudding noisily against the forest floor with every step. Alloria rode in front of him because she was afraid of falling off. She settled more comfortably into him than Tori ever had. At least, she seemed comfortable.

The path finally widened to reveal two barely clothed young men leaning against trees and casually chatting.

"We're here," Alloria said, wistfully.

"Welcome," a scruffy young man said with a bow. "I'm Kale, and this is Gahn."

"Dropping off your daughter, sir?" Gahn asked, eying the large foci over Angst's shoulders.

The twenteensomething had wiry muscles and a friendly face. Long dark hair fell to his tanned shoulders in a way that screamed, *"Do you notice how much I don't care?"* The little blue vest that covered his nipples looked like it belonged on a monkey, and his pants were baggy enough to carry potatoes. Angst hated him.

"He's with me," Alloria said.

"Oh?" Gahn asked in surprise.

Alloria stretched back, revealing her tummy as she wrapped her arms around the back of Angst's head and pulled him closer. Both men were mesmerized as her prison top crept up to reveal

74

the bottom of her breasts.

"Gold," she whispered into his ear before licking it.

He jerked back, making her laugh and sit upright. The men sighed in disappointment. Angst pulled out two gold coins that made Gahn roll his eyes. The eye rolling stopped eight coins later.

"Just passing through," Angst said, handing over the coins. "Won't be here long."

"Right," Gahn said, taking them greedily.

"We're weapon-free here at The Fette," said his dark-skinned, equally perfect counterpart. With an extra twenty pounds of muscle, he braved the pleasant weather by forgoing any sort of top. His navy pants were so tight that his 'weapon' made Angst uncomfortable. Angst hated him too.

Both young men looked at him with broad smiles and bravery. They positioned themselves in some sort of action-stance as if bracing against a strong wind. Angst wondered how much effort it would take to scare them into peeing themselves.

"Angst?" Alloria said. "It's safe here."

"Right," Angst said sharply. "My swords are what keep us safe."

The olive-skinned man lifted two fingers to his mouth and let out a loud whistle. Within seconds, three more men pranced toward them with bows notched, each making him feel old and fat. Oh, and short. Don't forget the thinning hair. There were a lot of people here to hate. Their eyes did a funny little dance, darting between the swords, the metallic ram, the gorgeous young woman between his legs, and each other. Angst wrapped an arm around Alloria's waist, making her 'ooh' as he released the swifen. He dropped to his feet as it disappeared and set her on the ground.

"Ehrde isn't safe anymore, so I don't like leaving my friends behind," Angst said to the crowd, jerking a thumb at the swords. "Would you like to take them from me?"

"Angst, it's okay," Alloria said, gently. "This is a happy place, a safe place."

"But—"

"I feel safe here," she said. "And we won't stay long, I promise."

Something about Alloria's words eased his tension. Her promise was as good as any salesman's selling hair-growth tonic, which Angst had no experience with at all, ever. But the fact that she felt safe meant something. He didn't, but would he ever?

"Fine," Angst grumbled. He removed the swords from his back and pressed his way through the young herd. He placed both foci upright on their tip to hover vertically over the ground. Chryslaenor stood on the left side of the entrance, and Dulgirgraut on the right. He whispered something fancy in the ancient Acratic language before saying aloud, "If they touch you, turn them into slugs."

A thin trail of red and blue lightning snapped back and forth between the swords, making everyone jump.

"Um," one of the new members of the perfect-boys club said.

"Yes? Is there something else?" Alloria asked, her voice like bells.

"How old is your dad?" he asked.

Angst expected her to laugh. If Rose had been here, he never would've heard the end of it. Alloria actually looked nervous, like she didn't know what to say.

"I'm forty-one," he said, stiffly.

"You can't be older than twenty-five to enter," one of the newcomers said.

Hadn't he paid the entrance fee already? He had enough gold and could always make more, but slapping these kids around sounded like a better idea.

"But he's my champion," Alloria pleaded.

"I'm sorry, but he'll have to wait here," he said.

"I'm done here," Angst said, waving her to follow him. "Let's go in."

The man-child whistled again, and again.

"He's calling for more. Please don't hurt them," she said, hurriedly. "We should leave."

"No need," Angst said. "I only sense fourteen in the vicinity. They'll be here for a while."

"I can't move my legs," Gahn said from behind them.

It was an old trick, one he'd learned long before bonding with the swords. Angst could anchor leg bones to the ground like a strong magnet. With the help of two foci, it took nothing to hold all fourteen in place.

"That's why I lov— Why you're my champion," Alloria said.

"I'm here to serve," Angst said with a bow of his head. "As promised."

Alloria beamed at him, her eyes so wide they seemed more crazy than compelling.

Angst leaned over to the nearest 'guard' tugging at his legs and whispered, "I'll cause no problems if you leave us alone. Got it?"

The young man nodded, his eyes wide.

"And it'd be best if you forget that we were here," Angst said.

"It's part of the deal." Alloria wrapped her arms around him awkwardly as they ambled down the path. "They won't tell anyone who was here. Like I said, we're safe."

The Fette was a large tent city that covered a vast field encircled by thick woods. It was so well hidden, Angst wasn't sure he could find his way out. Hundreds of simple brown, ivory, and navy canvas triangles were scattered like flower petals tossed by a child. The smell of sweaty youth, campfires, incense, and sex was overwhelming. At the distant end, a line of young men and women brought logs to a growing pile that stood before a raised platform. They were either planning to gather around an enormous bonfire later or burn down the forest. There was plenty of space between the pile of logs and tents for whatever orgy was going to happen.

This was either paradise or the place he was meant to die. Probably both. Everything was a distraction. Everyone was a distraction. Actually, every young woman was a distraction, and there were more than a few. They wore crop tops and low leather pants, or tiny dresses that barely covered his fantasies, and often less. Partially naked youth surrounded them in glorious nonchalance. If Alloria hadn't been leading him through the crowd by hand, he would've passed out from dehydration. Drooling can do that, right?

Oddly enough, Alloria wasn't the center of attention. He was. Many of the women they passed, who were every bit as young and beautiful as Alloria, watched him closely. At first, Angst thought it was the two giant swords hovering over his back until he remembered his foci were at the entrance. He paused briefly to make certain he wasn't naked when several dreams approached. A redhead in a crop top of red homeweave who'd spent her life doing sit-ups instead of eating came practically nose-to-nose with Angst. He held his breath as she reached up and brushed the gray hair from his eyes.

"Ooh," she said. "It's not dye. You're really older."

"Unfortunately," he said.

Her lips parted, and he wondered if he was finally going crazy. The best kind of crazy.

"Mine," Alloria snapped, turning on the redhead. She jerked Angst away to follow a new path. "This way."

"Dance with me later," the young woman called after them.

"Was she talking to me?" Angst asked.

"Probably both of us," Alloria said with a grunt, rushing him through the crowd. "As the guards mentioned, older men aren't supposed to be at The Fette, but some sneak in. They tend to be popular."

"Really?" Angst asked in disbelief. "Why would anyone want an old, ugly, short—"

She stopped abruptly and spun around. He struggled to slow so he wouldn't run into her. They were a breath away, and Alloria looked upset.

"Stop," she said. "You're not ugly. I don't care if you're short or tall or thin…it doesn't make a difference. You're Angst, and I love you because of who you are."

He swallowed hard. Not only was it unusual for beautiful young women to compliment him, but she was also close enough to lick.

"So, you're into ugly guys," he said. "It's cool."

Alloria rolled her eyes and let out a sigh. Before he could stop her, she pecked him on the lips, turned around, and pulled him through the crowd.

Angst followed numbly. He was torn. Part of him wanted to get lost in the youth of this place, and Alloria's attentions, but it was hard not to be held back by his own loss and what he hoped to regain. He was going to save his family, but, right now, they were dead and gone. And here he was, surrounded by beauty and so much raw energy. Shouldn't he revel in this, just to experience life? Wasn't that his due? There wasn't much time to dwell as she led him into one of the larger tents, and he sighed with a sudden sense of reality.

The tent smelled heavily of incense and was filled with too many racks of clothes. This wasn't a store, it was a trap. Angst hated bullies, and dragons, thoughtless people, and elements. But it was likely that he hated shopping more than anything.

"You first," she said.

"What?" he asked. "I'm fine. I've got my armor."

"And I love you in your armor," Alloria said, her voice soft. "But it doesn't fit in here."

"Because I'm not naked like those kids?" he asked. "Why do I need to fit in?"

"We're staying here tonight," she said.

"What?" Angst asked, loud enough to turn heads. He lowered his voice. "You were taking me to Magic."

"Magic isn't ready yet," she said, her voice husky. "I promise I'll bring you to him, but this first."

He couldn't argue with husky, and time really wasn't an issue. Whether he went back in time tomorrow or in a month didn't make a difference; it would kill him either way. And as much as he despised shopping, he really wanted to see what this place was about.

"Fine," he said, reluctantly. "Let's get this over with. It shouldn't take long."

"Yeah, only a few hours."

"Hours?" he asked, incredulously. "Aren't we just buying clothes?"

"Just?" she asked in shock. "No, Angst. We're buying the right clothes."

Before he could argue, she was handing him pants and leggings in fabrics and bright colors he didn't even recognize.

"Are you sure I need these?" he asked. "Nobody seemed to mind what I'm wearing."

"You can't wear armor all the time. It's stinky, and it chafes," she said.

"Chafes?" he asked. "I don't have any problems."

"Chafes me," she said firmly.

"Oh," he said, his cheeks warming.

"And you'll want something fun to wear for tonight," she said.

"What's tonight?" he asked.

"You'll see," she said mysteriously, pushing him through the drapes of a changing room. "Try these on."

"I've never tried on fancy clothes before," he said, shuffling forward.

"I've noticed," she said dryly.

He couldn't have felt more naked in the changing room surrounded by nothing but four thin sheets and tiny feet to the left and right of him. His neighbor's giggling didn't help.

After lots of his grumbling and a string of her nos, he ended up with a loose-fitting blue tunic that was cut low to his sternum. Charcoal leather strips trimmed the short sleeves and loose-fitting bottom, which did an admirable job of camouflaging his gut. The coordinating charcoal leather pants she chose were a bit tight, and tucked into soft black boots that made him as uncomfortable as her "mmmm," but he was too embarrassed to argue.

Alloria's turn at trying on outfits took so many exhausting hours that he felt like he'd walked to Nordruaut and back. While she took great pleasure in presenting clothes that were too tight, he did his best to carefully let her know when items weren't flattering. She quickly learned from his winces that he wasn't a fan of yellows and oranges but was most disappointed at his reaction to a tight, pink number that made her look like a tropical bird.

"How's this?" Alloria asked as she walked out from behind the curtain.

She looked like something out of a drunken fantasy—a really good fantasy that would require apologies afterward. Her light-gray, leather leggings were painted on and tucked into knee-high, shiny black boots that were practical for looking at and nothing else. She turned from side to side until he noticed her pants. They were tied from calf to hip with a red ribbon that showed plenty of skin. A gap of tight, tan stomach was almost enough to distract him from the gray half-corset she'd squeezed into. Two red racing stripes rose up the center in a V, just enough to cover nipples. Her breasts had always been fantastic, but they must've been held into the corset by willpower or magic because the red ribbon crisscrossing her sternum couldn't possibly have the strength to last that long. He may not last that long.

His cheeks were warm, his ears were warm, and Angst felt like he was coming down with a fever. The shop had gone quiet, and a quick glance around told him why. Patrons and clerks were all openly gawking at her with wide eyes or dropped jaws. For the first time since arriving, not a single person paid attention to his gray hair. She looked that good.

"From the expression on your face," she said with a stunning smile, "I'd say this is the right outfit."

"Subtle," he said, licking his lips. He felt like he'd swallowed a desert.

"Like your swords?" she asked.

"You can't wear this," he said, coughing. "It's not, uh, practical. Maybe something a little more…baggy."

"I can take it off," she threatened, tugging at a red ribbon.

"Nope," he said, mostly hoping she'd stop. "But—"

"You look wonderful, miss," a clerk interrupted.

"I do," she said, turning around slowly. "Don't I?"

"Of course," the snivelly man said. "I'm assuming that's for tonight's party. Can I package that for you?"

"I'll just wear it," she said. "You can burn what I left in the changing room."

"Of course," he said, taking it in stride. "That will be 200 gold."

"What?" Angst asked, his head whipping around like he'd been struck across the mouth. That was more than it cost a family to eat, for months.

"My poppa will take care of it," she said, giving him a peck on the cheek.

Heads turned to face him. Her *what*? He didn't know what poh-pah meant, but part of him wanted to vomit, the rest of him felt dizzy. What was she thinking? All eyes were now on him. The glares, and stares, and under-breath-mutterings were too much. He quickly handed over his 'emergency funds' pouch containing several gems as Alloria swayed out the door.

"Looks like you'll have a fun night at the party," the man said crisply. "Poppa."

Angst closed his eyes. "What's this party you're talking about?"

"You'll see," he said, as he emptied the pouch with a surprised smile.

10

Angst had always prided himself on being young at heart. Many in their forties were just bitter and cranky. They wallowed in their bad luck, poor choices, and creaky joints like there wasn't anything to look forward to and it was already time to die. Sure, most people he knew weren't doing what they wanted and acted as if their destiny had been just out of reach. Rather than doing something about it, though, they wore their bitterness like a badge with bold letters that screamed, "*I HATE Mondays.*"

It was the very reason he gravitated to a younger crowd. Rose was fifteen years younger, Victoria almost twenty, and he probably shouldn't even think about Alloria being a teenager. He definitely shouldn't think about that. Sure, being seen with them fed his ego, but, more than that, they were so fun and filled with hope. Oh, and pretty.

He'd worried that his thinning gray hair and desire to go to bed before midnight was a sign that the younger crowd would find him creepy instead of charming. Alloria had temporarily set that to rest when she kissed him in the hallway in Unsel, until he realized that her mind was like a basket of drunk cats. And now...now he sort of wished this younger crowd did find him creepy. Just until they were out of The Fette because when fantasies become real, they can be overwhelming.

Alloria had left him sitting on an old stump, grabbing his largest pouch of gold and promising to find a tent for the night.

"Two tents," he called out after her.

She blew him a kiss before running off into the crowd, making him sigh deeply. At first, Angst didn't mind his surroundings. He did his best to blend into the stump, and just people-watch. It was one of his favorite pastimes. He always enjoyed observing the patrons at Graloon's bar The Wizard's Revenge, but in comparison, that was whelming. Here, a frenetic energy buzzed about him in youthful, vibrant colors. The Fette attendees kissed and hugged and squeed in their barely clothed, incredibly fit bodies. It was as if they'd all been overtaken by a spell of inconsequence—like nothing they did would be judged. A tiny part of him wanted to join in.

"Hi," a young woman said. "I'm Ren."

"And I'm Dub," another woman said. "Do you mind if we have a seat?"

They were perfect. Dub had dark skin, abs that must've been carved from marble, and wide eyes filled with energy and hope. Ren's hair was long and pink. She had a tiny nose, and eyes far too sultry for her age. They were also naked. Mostly. Both women wore sheer yellow pants that flowed with any breeze, and his heavy breathing may have been enough to make them flow off. Matching yellow circles oh-so-barely covered their nipples, and that was it. The nipple covers must've been held on by the same magic that kept Alloria from bursting out of her top. He felt overdressed.

Practically convinced he was still in the infirmary at Unsel, dreaming away, Angst said, "Sure, have a seat."

And before he could stop them, the young women found a spot on his knees. He instinctively wrapped an arm around their waists, which brought on a few too many giggles. Their perky, nipple-covered breasts were at eye level, and so close he could feel their warmth. His cheeks and ears burned so much, he glanced up in the sky, anticipating a dragon attack.

"Uh, hi," he said. "I'm Angst."

"Are you here by yourself?" Ren asked.

"We've got a tent," Dub said. "You could share with us."

CHAPTER TEN

"You should buy us a drink, poppa," Ren said.

His head went back and forth like he was watching a jousting match as they continued with their requests. In the matter of five minutes, they'd decided he was going to buy them food, drinks, clothes, puppies, and a farm where they could throw more parties like this. He felt more like a pet than a love interest, and they kept saying poppa—which had gone from weird to uncomfortable. His legs were getting numb, and he was about ready to stand when Dub leaned over, twisted around, and planted a full kiss on his lips. She held the back of his head as her tongue darted in and out of his mouth.

She pulled away, leaving him speechless in his heart attack. They giggled. Giggled. As if it were a game. A game he would've loved to play twenty years ago.

"Angst!" another woman said from nearby.

"Thanks for saving our spot," came a lower voice. "Ladies."

Ren and Dub stood as abruptly as if he'd pinched them.

"We're sorry," Dub said sadly.

"Your poppa looked lonely," Ren said with a well-practiced pout.

In an odd sort of ritual, the four women all took turns kissing each other. When the ceremony was done, and without another word, his two lap buddies, their puppies, and future party farm walked away. He shook his head in disbelief, his eyes slowly coming back into focus to see the twins.

To his relief, they were both clothed, and he sighed to see somewhat familiar faces. The young women had shown up at Oakhaven when he was deep, deep into the kegs. They were every bit as beautiful as he barely remembered.

The twins were so jaw-droppingly perfect that Angst worried Alloria would immediately spew jealous dragonfire at the sight of them. They were both on the verge of being too thin, falling somewhere between impossibly toned and emaciated. Their skin was a moonlight-in-winter pale that captured every shadow, accentuating muscular abs and eye-lingering cleavage. Blocky-heeled boots made them taller than Angst, but he didn't care.

Despite being identical twins, Bella and Karina made some efforts to distinguish themselves from each other. Bella's hair was ripe-apple red, most of which was pulled back in a practical braid except for the right side of her head which was shaved low. She had unnaturally long lashes and dark eyes, either from makeup or exhaustion. Her low-cut silk ivory blouse was tied beneath her breasts, holding them up just for Angst. She wore black leather leggings and knee-high boots that were both eye-catching and practical, great for a seedy glare, riding horses, or kicking someone in the face.

Karina seemed ready for fun. Her long platinum hair was barely tamed by a wide leather wrap. She wore a too-short red leather skirt and shiny, black thigh-high boots. Her tiny, red leather vest sort of covered the bottom of her breasts while simultaneously putting them on display. Her tailor deserved more gold coin than Angst could make.

Karina's eyes were sultry, as though whispering, "Come hither or miss the opportunity of a lifetime." Bella's eyes dared you, immediately sizing you up for a challenge you would probably fail. On closer inspection, there was more to those eyes. A deeper concern, a constant awareness of all things. It was the occasional glance over the shoulder, or the quick look of wariness between the sisters as if expecting danger from every shadow. There seemed to be a lot of shadows.

"Jaw," Bella said crisply.

"Right," Angst said, straining to close his mouth.

His legs were still sprawled as the blood had just started flowing again when they both found a seat on his knees. He swallowed a grunt, refusing to be old, and placed his hands on their hips. Really, what was there to complain about? He probably wouldn't need to feel his toes for days.

"Move your hand, or I'll break it, Al'eyrn," Bella said.

"No," Karina corrected. "We need to fit in, and I don't mind."

"Of course you don't," her sister snapped.

Karina stuck out her tongue but didn't retort. Her cheeks glowed.

"These things haven't changed." Bella was taking in everything around them with a knowing smirk. "I really hope that fitting in doesn't mean we have to start calling him poppa."

The blond giggled.

"Why do the young women here call me poppa?" Angst asked. "I'd expect to be seen as some old, creepy guy. It's weird."

"And disgusting," Bella said. "Older men sneak in and throw around a lot of money. Some just want attention from younger women, most are looking for sex—"

"What?" Angst asked, standing up.

The twins sprang from his knees, landing lithely on their feet before crouching to a more defensive position. He had the sudden desire to take a long bath. The amazing view of half-naked young bodies didn't make up for his discomfort. Older men were coming here for their attention, and some young women would apparently do anything for the right man. It was inappropriate, and wrong, and maybe hit a little too close to home. He'd been friends with Victoria since she was a young teen, drawn in by her need and loving her attention. Their relationship made everyone else uncomfortable, but did they all judged him like he was judging other poppas? His relationship with Tori was different, right? And with Alloria? The veil between the two worlds was as thin as cheesecloth. He wouldn't give up his time with Victoria for anything, and who had the right to judge? Apparently his skin, which crawled.

Bella and Karina looked about nervously, both half-crouched with their shoulders relaxed and fists clenched. They reminded him of Hector, prepared to fight at the drop of a hat, any hat. Both stood incredibly still, like cats ready to pounce. They were too young to be so vigilant, especially when they should've been here to carouse and party. His concern thoroughly washed away his ogling.

"I hope he hasn't lost his mind already," Karina said, her voice quivering.

"Do you see what he's wearing?" Bella asked, eyeing his

tight-fitting pants. "He looks crazy to me."

"You're safe here," Angst said, holding his hands out.

"Never safe," Bella said, her gaze darting about.

"Always safe with Angst," Karina said, looking at her sister.

"I won't hurt you," Angst said. "And I won't let anyone else hurt you."

"They're starting to take notice," Karina said under her breath as a crowd gathered. "They are mostly harmless, but there are a lot."

"Sit, Angst. Please," Bella whispered, nodding slowly to the stump. "Help us play this off."

"There's no way we can fit six in one of those small tents, ladies," Angst said aloud with his cheekiest grin. "The three of us is more than enough."

Several onlookers barked out laughs before moving on. He sat cautiously, and they returned to their perch on his knees. They looked at each other with pensive stares that echoed his own concerns. Who were they? Where had they gone when they disappeared from the Inn at Oakhaven? Why were they here now?

Just as he was about to ask, they spoke in a language he didn't understand—if it was a language. They made chittering noises that he couldn't make out, and his eyes widened in wonder. He had heard of 'twins' language,' but twins were so rare he had never experienced it. He sat there for long moments, looking back and forth as they discussed, and argued, and then went quiet.

"Hey, poppa's still here," he said with a grin, hoping a little humor would break through their walls.

"Gross," Bella said, rolling her eyes.

Karina giggled. "You don't change, do you?"

Bella shot her a look, but Karina just shrugged.

"Nope, always Angst," he said. "So, are you going to tell me what that means? How is it you know me, but I've only met you once? I'm not smart like Dallow, but this reminds me of Aerella and how she never stayed anchored to any one time for long.

When are you from?"

"That's what we were arguing about," Karina said. "How much we can tell you."

"I need a drink," he said, waving over a nearby server.

"Why?" Bella asked.

"One sec," Angst said. He purchased three drinks and winced through his first sip of cheap mead. It tasted like the alcohol a physician would use to clean wounds. "Ugh, I'm too old to drink crap booze."

"That's all I have on me," the woman said apologetically. "But we've got a few jugs of expensive port."

"Please," Angst said, handing her more gold than necessary. "And hurry. This may kill me."

She laughed and scurried off. He drank the rest of the poison and dropped the cup.

"Why booze?" he asked Bella. "Because you're from the future, and anything to do with time gives me a headache."

They both looked at each other in shock.

"I didn't tell him," Karina said. "I promise."

"You didn't have to," Angst said. "From your comfort with me, or discomfort, I can tell you both know me pretty well. You aren't from the past, I'd remember. That means you're from the future. Why are you from the future when I'm trying to go back into the past?"

"Why do you want to go to the past?" Karina asked.

"I was twenty-two when I first tried picking up Chryslaenor. It triggered the war between the elements. I didn't realize it at the time, but it was my fault. I'm going to go back in time to stop myself. Dallow says it will kill me, but I believe it will save everyone else, and that's all that matters."

"Oh, Angst," Bella said, leaning over to give him a side hug. "This is why I love you. When you stop being a dumb flirt long enough to be heroic."

"Flirting's not dumb," Angst said with a frown.

"I like your flirting," Karina said.

"Angst," Bella said, her brows furrowing. "You're right. You may have triggered the war when you picked up Chryslaenor. But it would've happened anyway. We've seen war too. It's inevitable. You weren't their reason. You were their excuse."

"My family died because of me. Going back in time could save them," he said quietly. His hands were shaking, and he let go of their waists. "It has to."

"You'll save them, Angst," Karina said. "That's what you do."

Angst struggled to pull himself away from that dark place. His family, his friends, were all going to be fine. They were going to make it. He had to believe that to keep going or it was all over. He shook his head like a dog shaking off water and forced a smile.

"Aerella once said that she couldn't tell me my future because it could cause problems. That's why this gives me a headache, and the port is here just in time."

He took a brown jug and handed the woman more coins, enough to make her eyes wide.

"This is too much, sir," she said with a worried look. "I can't offer you, uh, anything else. I'm sorry, but my boyfriend—"

"Miss," Angst said, sternly. "You're hanging around the wrong people if you think I'm buying anything more than this port. There should be enough extra to get away from this place, and you should."

"Thank you," she said, looking at the coins in disbelief. "I think I will."

Dropping her apron, she marched away.

"Hero," Bella said, fondly. "You never did need the swords, did you?"

"Stop," Angst said with a wink. "Or I'll start flirting again." He removed the cork and took more than several gulps of thick, sweet wine. It was delicious, and he handed it to Karina, who'd already finished her mead. "Please, tell me what you can."

"What you're trying to do will break Ehrde," Bella said. "It won't happen the way you expect, and our world will literally split in half. Hundreds of thousands will die, and you won't save anyone."

Karina was mid-drink, and Angst pulled the jug away from her to take another long draw. He handed it back and wiped his lips with the back of his sleeve.

"Go on," he said stiffly.

"We want to help you save everyone," she said. "But you need to save us too."

Angst hadn't had enough port for that. This was the second time they'd met, and he already needed to save them, too. Sure, why not? "How do I know that Magic didn't send you?"

Both women held up their hands.

"No rings," Karina said.

He nodded slowly.

"Jaden was supposed to stop you, but something went wrong when we brought him back," Karina said.

"Wait," Angst said, looking back and forth between them. "You brought him back?"

"Karina," Bella snapped.

Karina stuck her tongue out at her twin. "Is he...is he okay?"

"Sure, the jerk is just fine," Angst said.

"Jerk," Karina said in surprise. "You two are like brothers."

"Ha," Angst said. "He showed up out of nowhere, not remembering why he was here but knowing all sorts of magic. I had to kick his ass to get him to shut up, and... Wait. Brothers?"

"We can't say anymore," Bella said. "We promised, Karina."

"Fine," Karina said, suddenly distracted by a mostly naked young man who winked at her.

Bella rolled her eyes. Angst crossed his arms and stared after the man. It took a minute to shake off his jealousy, and another to question where it had come from. How could he feel anything? They'd just met. What *was* their connection?

"Look, I'm not sure I believe you, or would even understand if you explained it all to me," Angst said. "If I can save you, I will. I'll do everything I can to help, but not if it keeps me from saving my family. That means I'm going back in time to set everything right, so none of this ever happens. If you're here to stop me, then you should probably get off my lap…which would really suck."

Karina laughed, the sound of tinkling bells, even while Bella's face became sad.

"We'll help you, Angst," Bella said with a sigh. "Have you found it yet? The foci?"

"I've found two, and both swords are acting like a couple of babies," Angst grumbled. Dulgirgraut and Chryslaenor threw a fit in his mind that made him wince. It passed quickly, and they returned to quiet as if pretending to ignore him.

"But no horn?" Bella asked.

"Horn?" Angst asked with a frown. His tongue felt thick, and despite it all, he was happy. How strong was that drink? "No, no horn."

Bella frowned, tapping a finger against her cheek.

"Wow," Karina said. "Is that Victoria? She's delicious."

"No," Angst said, surprised she knew about Tori. "That's Alloria."

"Oh," they both said at the same time, looking at each other in concern.

"Isn't she, a little bit, uh," Karina said. "Not sane?"

"She's been through a lot," Angst said. "Magic tortured her and…" Despite their comfort with him, he remembered that he really didn't know them at all. "She's been through a lot."

"Angst," Karina said. "Don't have sex with her."

"What?" he said, defensively. "No, I wouldn't."

"Of course you would," Bella whispered in his ear. "She is sex. Even I want her. But please, Angst. Don't do it. You'll hate yourself."

"I already do," he muttered, a bit shaken. They began to move but he held them tighter. "Don't leave yet, please."

"We'll stay as long as we can," Karina said, kissing him on the cheek. "Won't we?"

"Yeah," Bella said, her tone wary. "For you, we'll try."

When Alloria saw the twins, her sexy gait evolved into a raging storm. She stomped toward them, and Angst was surprised the ground didn't shake. Her eyes were too wide, too dangerous, and she reached for a dagger in her boot.

"We kept your seat warm," Bella said. Her tone had changed from sincere to silly as if all intelligence had seeped out. "We thought your poppa was alone, but he said he was taken."

"Oh," Alloria said, suddenly happy again. She let go of the hilt and smiled broadly as if slicing the twins into pieces had never crossed her mind.

She leaned over, which was great, and planted a kiss on his mouth, which was even more awkward now that he was being watched by the twins. Alloria's eyes were closed, and he looked to them for help. Karina seemed perturbed, but Bella nodded encouragingly. Why? They must know something that he didn't, so he finished the mouth-sucking rather than pulling back.

"Thank you, Angst," Alloria said, huskily. "For staying true."

"Uh, sure," Angst said, wiping her passion from his lips.

"Angst said we could party with you guys tonight," Bella said, nodding at Angst.

Karina was nodding too, her eyes pleading.

"Oh," Angst said, slow to pick up the hint. "Yeah, if you don't mind. They seem fun."

"We love fun," Karina said, brightly.

"Yeah," Bella said, with slightly less conviction.

Angst worried for half a minute while Alloria pondered. She made eye contact. Maybe it was because he was looking at her and not the twins that made her face brighten, but whatever complicated equation she was working through came together.

"We'd love that!" Alloria said, springing up and turning around.

There was more hugging and kissing and squealing as introductions ensued. Angst had the impression that Karina genuinely enjoyed this, while Bella played along reluctantly. The ceremony was odd, as if Angst had landed on foreign shores and all customs had changed. This night was going to be full of surprises. He took another long drink of the sweet wine and braced himself for The Fette.

11

A string of curses followed Rose out of Potterton Inn like grotesque ducklings following a mother who ran away. Half the party winced and stared at the ground, while the rest blushed as their jaws dropped. Victoria took deep breaths, trying her best to block the onslaught of profanity while "what nows" roiled in her mind and stomach.

"What is it?" Victoria asked.

"They are already at the orgy," she blurted, crossing her tiny arms before her breastplate.

Victoria sucked in her lips while everyone else muttered. It would've been a lie to say that Rose's news didn't sting. Angst was supposed to adventure with her, not Alloria. She didn't want to be part of a gross orgy, but raucous, flirty fun was…well, that was supposed to be their thing.

Rose looked at her with large, dark eyes filled with distraught frustration. "My apologies, Your Highness," she said, finally. "They're a day's ride away on swifen. I was hoping we'd be closer."

Dallow approached from around the side of the inn, nodding in confirmation to Victoria. "They're a good distance away," he said, brushing blond bangs from his eyes.

"Is it too far?" Mirim asked.

"No, I mean that's a good distance to trail behind," Dallow said.

"I thought we were chasing him down," Rose said with a dark frown.

"Catching up to him is easy, especially when he won't be in a hurry to leave The Fette," Dallow said. "We don't want to strike unless he's already weakened from attack. It's the only way we can stop him."

"Is it even possible for him to be weak with two foci?" Jaden asked.

"We hope so," Dallow said, nodding at Victoria. "But if you have a better idea, it'd be welcome."

"Surprising him now would be better," Jaden said. "If we can get close enough."

"How close until he notices?" Mirim asked, looking at Victoria.

"I'm hoping within several miles," Victoria said.

"Hoping?" Mirim asked.

"It's my best guess. Nobody knows the reach of his abilities," Victoria said. "I don't have an Angst measuring stick."

"He's short," Rose said.

"Not helpful," Victoria said.

"But The Fette is a perfect distraction," Jaden grumbled. "How can you be sure he'll sense us coming?"

"How can you be sure he won't?" Victoria asked in frustration. "Our choice is a surprise attack when he's at full power or stopping him when he's weak and tired. I choose the latter."

"But—"

"My decision is final," Victoria said. "We'll ride most of the way to The Fette and camp nearby. Hopefully, he's busy enough to be distracted."

"He will be," Rose said, rolling her eyes. "At this point, why don't we just stay at the inn, or head back to Unsel and wait it out?" she asked sarcastically.

"Enough of that," Victoria said, holding up her hand. "We'll trail behind him at a normal pace and stop a mile or two away."

Rose looked like she was biting her tongue hard enough to draw blood. She made eye contact with Mirim.

"With some coordination, we've got enough power here to face down an army. We've even got an Al'eyrn," Mirim said with a nod to Rose. "Why wait?"

"We don't really know what Angst is capable of with two foci, especially if they're driving him mad...which I don't believe," Dallow said, taking a deep breath. "And Rose may not be completely ready—"

"I'm ready," Rose said, turning on Dallow, her cheeks red with anger.

They stared at each other. Dallow's eyes were apologetic, but he didn't back down.

"Not to interrupt," Nikkola said. "But why isn't Rose ready?"

Dallow cocked his head, and Rose sighed.

"Jormbrinder gives me a lot of power," she said. "And Dallow has taught me some spells, so I should be fine."

"But?" Dallow said.

"I hate you right now," she seethed. "Fine. My foci won't talk to me."

"Talk to you?" Mirim asked.

"Supposedly Angst's foci talk to him, in his head, through music," she said. "My daggers give me power, but I haven't heard a peep. Dallow thinks it's because Magic tried forcing Chryslaenor to bond with me. Whatever he did made it so I could bond with Jormbrinder, but my weapon doesn't talk."

"Through music?" Nikkola asked. "Sure, that doesn't sound crazy."

"Exactly," Rose said. "I think Angst is a liar, and I think I'm ready."

"Angst always joked about having a relationship with his foci," Dallow said, gently. "Maybe you just need to figure out yours."

"One is almost too many," Rose snapped. "I don't want another relationship."

"Angst used to say that too," Dallow said, under his breath.

"I'm not Angst," Rose growled but said nothing else.

"We should probably be cautious while you three work things

out," Mirim said, looking from Dallow to Rose to the large daggers stuck to her hips. "I'd like to send a scout ahead, so we're prepared."

"That's not necessary, Mirim," Victoria said, distractedly. "Enough of us have experience with this. We don't need to split up."

"But—"

"Birds will let Sean know if anyone's nearby," Simon said in a soothing voice.

"We're relying on birds," Mirim said under her breath. "Great."

"Let's ride," Victoria said, steering her pink unicorn to follow Rose into the woods.

She led them along a wide trail, riding two by two for an hour until the path became too narrow. After another hour of ducking under low branches and plowing through thicket, they arrived at a short, stone cliff.

"This can't be right," Jaden said. "Are we lost?"

"Nope," Rose said. "The Fette's always well hidden."

"Is there a clearing nearby?" Mirim asked. "It's a good time for a break, and I'd like a better view of the area."

Sean raised a hand and closed his eyes. Within moments, a redbird landed on his finger. He brought it close to his ear, a broad smile on his face. The bird sang for a short time before flying off. He pointed after it.

"That way," Simon said with a nod.

After ten minutes of riding, they found a ten-foot clearing of tall grass and decomposing logs. Everyone dismounted and dismissed their swifen.

"Sean," Mirim said, placing a hand on the young man's shoulder. "Would you ask your friends to keep an eye on our surroundings?"

He closed his eyes once again. Nothing happened, but he eventually opened them and nodded at the captain.

She would never say it out loud, but Victoria was bored. She missed Angst, a lot. Their adventure included monsters and flirting and lots of sighs from his friends for being inappropriate. There was always a sense of danger, but it was nothing he couldn't handle.

"Sandwich?" Jaden asked, handing over a mass of bread, meat, and cheese.

"Thanks," she sighed, taking it.

"I'm glad we have this time together," he said, quietly.

She said nothing as she took a bite of her dry meal.

"You're thinking of him, aren't you?" Jaden asked, his face tense as a string on a guitar.

"Aren't *you*?" she asked, turning on him.

"Well, yeah," he said, looking down.

"I don't get it. You once told me that you felt closer to Angst than anyone," Victoria said. "Why do you want to kill him? Is that out of jealousy?"

"I can't help my jealousy. You hold him so close," Jaden said. "When I agreed to come back, I didn't realize what a distraction you would be from my mission."

"Oh, so now I'm just a distraction?" Victoria asked.

"No, it's not like that," Jaden floundered. "I was just never told that I'd—"

"Incoming," Simon said, loudly. "Women with wings heading this way."

"Berfemmian," Victoria said, hopefully. "I wonder if it's anyone I know. Can you wave them down?"

"They seem to be ignoring Sean's birds," Simon said.

She could barely make out three specks in the distant blue sky. Hailing them by waving, shouting, and hopping up and down didn't seem to help.

"Is there a way to signal them?" Victoria asked.

"I think so," Dallow said, his eyes becoming white as he searched through the catalog of knowledge in his mind. He raised a hand and uttered some nonsensical words.

A tiny ball of light shot up and sparked in the sky like fireworks. Two of the Berfemmian veered toward them.

"I'd love to recruit them to help stop Angst," she said.

"They're tough, skilled fighters, and those wings of light make them fly fast."

"Sean says their wings are black."

"Black?" Victoria asked in surprise. "The birds must be mistaken. Berfemmian wings look like rainbows. Here they come." She waved a hand excitedly.

"Their wings look black to me," Jaden said, shading his eyes with a hand. "Oh no, not good. Hurry, back to the woods. Summon your swifen, now!"

12

The tent Alloria bought for an obscene amount of gold was about the size of a sock. He walked around it, in two or three steps, and sighed. A year ago, getting stuck in this sleeve of a tent with Victoria would've been a fortunate accident, and kinda fun. Now things were different. This wasn't a tent for sleeping and he wasn't a teenager looking forward to a late-night romp. Unfortunately.

"This is cozy," Angst said wryly.

"Right?" she asked, excitedly, apparently pleased with the situation.

The twins stood several tents over, hawking their every move. Karina giggled into her hand while Bella glared at him, her arms crossed. It was as if she'd spent time with Heather. He sighed.

"So, where do I sleep?" he asked, delaying the inevitable.

"You're silly," Alloria said with a wide-eyed smile. "It'll be fun."

He wasn't sure he wanted to know what that meant. Was she talking about the party, or the after party?

"Alloria," Angst said quietly, trying to be gentle. "I'm forty or something. You're only, what, sixteen?"

"Seventeen," she said, frowning in confusion. "The same age my mom was when she got married."

His heart skipped and he took a long draw of sweet wine. She didn't look sixteen or seventeen, but even *his* fascination with beautiful young women drew a line in the sand somewhere. No, not a line, a brick wall as tall as a mountain covered in fire. This would never have happened if Dallow, Tarness, and Hector were here. Their admonishing gazes and judgmental glares surely would have kept the young woman at bay. They would've been the barrier he needed. He wanted an out and looked at the twins pleadingly. Bella's eyes went wide, and she shook her head.

"You look so sexy, Alloria," Karina said. "I love your outfit, especially the tiara. Totally jealous. I would never look as good in that."

Actually, the twins would've both looked incredible in Alloria's outfit. He was barely sober enough not to say that out loud when he finally realized it was a distraction.

"Oh," Alloria said, her face a little brighter. "Thank you. Angst bought it for me."

"Do you like to dance?" Karina asked.

"I love to dance," Alloria said. She looked at Angst then smiled slyly. "Maybe we could dance together."

"We should," Karina said.

"You totally should show Alloria your dancing skills, Angst," Bella said, her gaze cunning. "I hear you put elephants to shame."

It actually wasn't a terrible idea. Nothing could turn heads, and turn off women, like his off-beat ostrich flailing. How had Bella known he was a terrible dancer? She flashed him a satisfied grin but was apparently surprised by his grateful nod. Karina and Alloria stepped aside to plan, talk, and giggle while Bella approached him.

"We aren't supposed to get involved," Bella muttered.

"You may have just saved my life," Angst said, gratefully. "I really don't want to end up in here," he nodded at the tent, "with her."

"After buying her that hooker outfit?" she asked. "Could've fooled me."

"I'm sure it looks that way," he said. "But that just sort of happened. I actually want to keep more from happening."

"I don't understand," she said. "Don't you want her?"

"Of course I do," he said. "Other than the fact that she should be with someone her own age and I should be with my wife. That's the weird thing. It's been six months, and Heather is gone, but I still feel like I'm married. Maybe it's because I'm planning to save her, I don't know. I still feel connected to my family. It probably doesn't make any sense, but even though I'm drawn to Alloria, I just can't."

"It makes more sense than you know," Bella said warmly. "It's said that she's even crazier than you were."

"We're all crazy, Bella," he said. "Some keep it locked up, others wear it on their sleeve, and a few carry it like a banner. It's part of what makes us who we are."

The boom of a drum made Angst jump, followed by another and then more until they created a sort of rhythm. It was loud and deep enough to reverberate in his chest.

"It's starting," Karina said, excitedly.

"Let's go," Alloria said, taking her hand and leading them through the maze of tents.

Angst held hands with Karina and Bella as he followed them to the open space around the giant bonfire. They joined a quickly growing crowd of mostly naked young men and women. Some wore clothes, like handkerchiefs or undergarments, but only barely. Almost every article of clothing appeared to have lost a fight with a rainbow. It was a celebration of life that smacked his eyeballs. In the midst of his dreary, chaotic, hero's journey, this was a crate of happy puppies. He couldn't hold back the smile.

Alloria squished herself between Angst and Karina, practically popping out of her gray, threaded corset. She giggled while she tucked things back in, earning him a disapproving gaze from Bella that once again reminded him of Heather's wife-look. He retorted with a broad grin that hurt his cheeks. Rolling her eyes, she turned to the fire, but the tiniest of smiles crept up her cheeks. Bella's reaction took him by surprise, as if she'd been around Angst in similar situations.

Angst jerked his head up when a boom from the largest drum

on stage shook the ground. The crate of puppies around him cheered, hopping up and down with more combined energy than both his foci could store. They suddenly spread out, making room for a large, olive-skinned man, who landed before the fire and began to dance. The man had muscle on top of muscle, without an ounce of fat. His pale-green loincloth didn't cover enough for Angst to feel secure about his own manhood. How was it even possible to be that muscular without eating?

Alloria and Karina were giggling and pointing as the man gyrated to the beat.

"You've obviously been to one of these," Angst said. "How long does this go on?"

"For a night or three," Bella said.

"What?" he asked in surprise.

She laughed, shaking her head, not once taking her eyes off the spectacle. After the longest five minutes of Angst's life had passed, the dancer stopped. He raised a hand to his mouth and howled like a wolf at the moon. A chorus of booms and snaps and cracks from the other drums made Angst's teeth rattle as everyone under the age of forty started dancing.

His best dance move was awkward swaying while desperately hoping nobody would notice that he was off time or that his cheeks were flush and burned hot like the sun. There was no swaying at The Fette. This was dancing like he'd never seen.

Some of them hopped up and down like they were standing on a hot skillet. Others gyrated, humping the air unnaturally as if their joints didn't work like his...which they didn't. Alloria and Karina's dance made his jaw drop. They rocked forward and back, rubbing against each other, their legs intertwined. It was pretty much sex, and he wanted to pull up a chair and enjoy his drink. This was sweaty hedonism at its best.

That familiar, school-dance feeling washed over him. Angst didn't want to be the only one standing still and tried his best to sort of dance. Desperate to fit in without being noticed, he swayed back and forth like an old man on a child's rocking horse. Where was his grand confidence now? He was Al'eyrn, a killer of elements, a hero, and…he was still too sober. The awk-wardness of every party he'd attended crept up his spine and stiffened his body. This was not what he'd meant when he'd wished to be younger.

Alloria beckoned him over with a sensual gaze that made his heart race. Karina took a half step back to make room for Angst, her pale cheeks flushed with heat, and her long lashes weighing down her eyelids as she continued making love to the air. Moving between them seemed to be an excellent idea and he took a step toward their lusty display.

"Wait," Bella said, holding him back with a hand on his shoulder. "Look."

Angst followed Bella's finger up to the sky. He squinted to make out a shape through the smoke from the bonfire, swooping around high above. Something about the shape set him on edge. Even at this distance, he could tell it was too large to be a bird, yet too small to be a dragon. Was it a cavastil bird? He thought he'd killed all of Air's pets in Unsel shortly after bonding with Chryslaenor. Maybe there were more.

"What do you think it is?" he asked.

"We'll find out soon," Bella warned. "It's coming closer."

"I should get my swords," he shouted over the pounding beat of the party.

"No time." Bella rushed to her sister.

The creature dove unnaturally fast, landing hard enough before the bonfire to make the ground shudder. Flames blew down and spread out in its wake, making everyone leap away. The music stopped, and the crowd watched as it stood.

"Stay behind me," Angst shouted over his shoulder as he pushed through the crowd.

'It' was actually a she, and he sighed in relief. With the fire-light behind her, it was almost impossible to make out her face, but he would've recognized that petite frame anywhere.

"Marisha," he called out, rushing forward. He shouted over his shoulder, "It's okay. She's a friend."

"Angst," Alloria said. "Are you sure?"

"Of course. Marisha was Faeoris's best friend," he explained, facing the Berfemmian. "I'm so sorry I haven't come to tell you about Faeoris. I was injured, and now I'm trying to fix things."

She inched back toward the fire but really had nowhere to go. He stepped in for a hug, and she moved to the side.

"Marisha?" he asked. "It's me, Angst."

She stared down, shaking her head, but said nothing.

"Please don't kick me in the head," he muttered before speaking up. "Are you okay?"

She hunched over as if someone had punched her in the gut and let out an unnatural moan. Black wings with greasy feathers spread from her back with a wet, crunching sound. Marisha stood tall, arching her back as they unfolded. Her torso was now covered in motley black feathers and she reached for him with talons.

"What...what happened to you?" Angst said, taking a step back.

"You did," she said, her voice like nails on a chalkboard.

"How did I do this?" Angst said looking her over.

"You killed my *essent*!" she screeched, wrapping her arms around him and flying high into the night sky.

13

Maarja braced against a strong wind that kicked up dusty snow, temporarily masking her vision. Jintorich stood on her shoulder, long hair from his eyebrows brushing gently against her cheek. He held on with his bare feet that gripped like monkey paws, his armor-thick nails digging in surprisingly hard.

"How will we see anything in this weather?" Bryymel grunted. The stubby Nordruaut crossed his broad arms. "It feels like a trap."

"Says the man who looks for spies under his pallet before bed," Gose said with a chuckle. "You're more paranoid than anyone I've known."

"It's kept me alive this long," Bryymel said, peering up at the taller man. "And I don't trust any from the East. Tarness could be leading them here as we speak."

Maarja looked over, raising one eyebrow dangerously. She was only taller than him by several inches but leaned forward menacingly enough that he took a wary step back.

"Not on purpose, of course," Bryymel said. "He is only human."

"This is one of those times you should not be talking," she said.

Bryymel nodded and said nothing more. Gose shot her a sidelong glance that hinted at a smile. He looked as tired as she felt. Exhaustion, hunger, and anxiety was all that remained after the battle with the Eastern Nordruaut, with the Fulk'han, and with the monsters. Their thin herd of rebels had been decimated. Their leader and king, Jarle, had the charisma to inspire greatness. His core belief in doing right was enough to rally their pride and discard sense, but even Jarle hadn't expected the Fulk'han. He couldn't have predicted the power wrought by Niihlu, Angst, and the monster Lurp. And then there was Fire.

The element had appeared from a fireball created by Angst. Fire had been hot enough to melt all the nearby snow, and Angst's great blast of lightning had turned the ground beneath to glass. The battle left a wake of death that killed many from the East and more from the West. The Fulk'han had simply vanished through another portal. The battle was over, Angst had won, but they had lost. All that remained of the Western Nordruaut was a meager tribe, a band of insurgents that could've been wiped out in a breath. Worst of all, Jarle, their courage, was missing.

Gose, Jarle's nephew, had reluctantly taken command. The Nordruaut was a headstrong annoyance with more bravado and less experience than Maarja. He was cocky, but smart enough to back it up, which made her want to smack him. If only Tarness was Nordruaut so he could take the lead. He was respected by all, despite being human.

When the battle was over, there was a silent understanding that both sides needed time to bury their dead. Gose had successfully led them to find most of the bodies. Months later, Jarle remained missing, and only Tarness continued searching for him every day. While she worried over his newfound obsession, others admired his determination.

Her husband should've returned hours ago. It wasn't the first time he was late, but never before had he asked her to gather the others. Their consensus was that Tarness had found Jarle, and that their leader was probably dead. If so, why hadn't he asked her to help? It made no sense, even for a human.

She squeezed her longbow, making the wood creak. She glanced at it and smirked. Tarness hated this bow; the string was so tight he could barely draw it. It had actually been their first argument. He had lashed out in frustration, accusing her of taking up the weapon to mock him. Maarja had tried to explain why it would be best for her to stay a good distance from any battle, but he was so upset, he wouldn't listen. The argument made him angry enough to draw the bow. He later apologized and made it up to her. His frustration over the bow, his obsession at finding Jarle and the secret lessons with Jintorich made her wary. She'd decided to save the explanation for another day.

Jintorich's grip on her shoulder loosened as the wind subsided. He gently tugged at a platinum braid and pointed. She followed his finger, squinting to make out distant shapes.

"Tarness is not alone," Maarja said, tensely. She held out an arm to keep the other Nordruaut from advancing. "It's hard to make out through the snow. Jintorich, can you see anything with your magics?"

"No, my friend," Jintorich squeaked. "But my foci, Maehtikyn, tells me that one of them is not quite Nordruaut, nor human."

"Niihlu," Maarja growled.

"Or worse," Bryymel scoffed. "I told you this was a trap."

"And I told you to shut your mouth," Maarja said.

"Weapons at the ready," Gose called out, hefting a barbed spear.

"Fools, keep your weapons down," she shouted, whipping around to face him. "I will break anyone who harms Tarness. You know better, Gose. Of all Nordruaut, you were first to call him brother."

"Yes," Gose said, reluctantly, as he lowered his spear. "There are only three, and they approach slowly. This is obviously not an attack."

"It only took three monsters to destroy our army," Bryymel said, sniffing deeply. "Be wary."

"You may be Gose's brother," Maarja said, "but if you harm my husband, I will remove your head and apologize to Gose."

"Apology accepted," Gose said.

Bryymel swallowed hard.

Gose winked at her, and she nodded once in return. They'd both agreed that Bryymel was a necessary annoyance. The Nordruaut was tactically fit and robust with ideas, but the runt of the litter was filled with conspiracies that had to be filtered.

"No," Maarja said as she took a step forward.

"Hold," Gose said, grabbing her arm. "Look who he's with."

"Leave be," she snapped, pulling free. "They aren't here to fight.

Tarness carried the frozen remains of a body twice his size. Her husband was a large, muscular man. Easily a head taller than most humans. The pale furs that covered his armor made him almost appear as one of them. His dark skin glistened with sweat as thick, angry eyebrows hovered over a distraught gaze. She knew, they all knew, he had found Jarle.

"I'm sorry," he shouted. "They found him. They wanted to talk."

King Rasaol followed closely behind Tarness. Rasaol seemed as upset as her husband, his face stoic but his eyes filled with despair. The old king finally looked his age, as if war and loss had drained life from him. Beside Rasaol stood a tall, muscular Nordruaut whose skin was almost as pale as the snow. He wore leather boots and a loincloth that only covered what it was supposed to, as if the cold had no effect. His face was gaunt, and his sunken eyes were missing some sanity. A gold choker around his neck sparked and popped noisily, making the Nordruaut twitch. The giant, frozen axe over his shoulder cracked like ice on an unsure pond, making him jerk his head once more.

"Niihlu," Maarja said in shock. "You've changed again. What happened?"

After Niihlu had bonded with the giant axe foci, Ghorfjend, he'd become something unnatural. Ice covered his entire body, continually dripping off into slushy piles. The weapon had brought him great power and worse pain. Now he looked strong and whole, and very, very dangerous. He replied with a sneer.

"The hero returns," Bryymel said, smiling at Tarness. "You bring back our leader, and prisoners."

"You may call us prisoners, if you wish," Rasaol said, nodding at Niihlu.

The pale Nordruaut reached for the giant axe hovering over his back, which hissed as if freezing the very air it touched. Before anyone could attack, or defend themselves, he rested the foci on the snowy ground. It remained upright on its hilt as Niihlu slowly lowered his head.

"They brought me his body," Tarness said, gasping as he laid the frozen corpse on the ground. "They want to talk. I swore they wouldn't be harmed."

"Then they won't," Maarja said.

"Speak your words and leave," Bryymel snapped.

"It's not your place to make demands, brother," Gose said. He pointed to the tents. "Take your leave until morning."

"But," Bryymel said, his eyes wide.

Maarja took a step toward the small man, which was enough to send him stomping away.

"There is still much anger and passion in the west," Gose said to Rasaol.

"Rightfully so, brother," Rasaol said, solemnly. "We come to make things right again."

"How so?" Gose asked. "Returning the body of Jarle is not a sign of peace."

"A fair assessment, if we had killed him," Rasaol said. "But even as we bring you your fallen leader, our army marches south to hunt the man who killed him."

"And I should be there," Niihlu said, snapping his head up to glare at Rasaol. "I'm the only one who can stop Jarle's killer. The Angst will die by my hands."

"What?" Gose asked.

"No," Maarja said, looking at Tarness.

If Tarness had seemed tired from carrying Jarle's body, it was nothing compared to the weight he seemed to bear now. He closed his eyes and took a deep breath. "It's true," he said in a low, quiet voice. "Look at the body."

Jintorich hopped to the ground and trudged through the snow

to Jarle. He pulled back furs to reveal a hole burnt through Jarle's chest and lightning scars that covered his arms and legs.

"I believe Angst has finally gone crazy," Tarness said, so quiet he was hard to hear. "He needs to be stopped, and we have to help."

"We are on the hunt for him," Rasaol said, somberly. "We could use your help."

Gose looked at Maarja. She nodded reluctantly.

"Let's eat and discuss in my tent," Gose said to Rasaol and Niihlu. "Please, join me as guests."

Niihlu picked up his hissing axe and returned it to his back. The gold choker sparked again, making him twitch. He patted Tarness roughly on the shoulder and gave him that same sneering smile before following Gose and Rasaol.

"I will follow them, and share what I learn," Jintorich said. "Tarness, I'm sorry."

Tarness nodded, staring at the ground.

Maarja couldn't imagine what her husband was going through and struggled to find the right words. He'd regaled her with stories of his best friend. The look on his face hadn't been exhaustion from carrying Jarle's body. It was the heavy weight of guilt and betrayal, as though Angst's transgressions were his fault. Maarja wrapped her arms around him, but he was slow to return the affection. When she looked down into his eyes, they were glassy with tears.

"That must've been hard, husband," she said. "I'm proud of you. You did well."

"No," Tarness said, covering his eyes with a hand. "I failed. I failed everyone."

14

"Where's Rose?" Victoria shouted, barely ducking the loch-aber axe in time.

Several hairs drifted slowly to the ground. It had been that close. Victoria leaped back, barely able to keep up with her premonition. It was infuriating. She'd trained to know what opponents would do in enough time to counter attacks. She could beat most, if not all, humans in a duel on any given day. Berfemmian, not so much. Her opponent's speed was surpassed only by her strength. It was no wonder Faeoris had struck Angst hard enough to skip him across mountaintops like a stone on a lake. And he was Al'eyrn.

"No sign of her after the other, uh, bird-lady knocked her away," Simon shouted, inching forward with a small dagger that might as well have been a toothpick.

The Berfemmian squawked at Simon, making him jump back. The poor man shivered, unable to move. She looked more bird than woman, covered in greasy black feathers from sternum to calf. Eyes like dark blue marbles glared with hate. Her legs ended in talons, ideal for rending meat from bones. Slick, oily sweat coated her deflated breasts. Worse of all, she reeked of garbage and spoiled meat. There was no sign of the flattering armor the Berfemmian typically wore. Something had changed her from a warrior to a predator. But still, she was almost recognizable.

"Alyss?" Victoria called out.

CHAPTER FOURTEEN

The Berfemmian reeled as she looked about, the whites of her eyes returning like milk poured into a dark blue bowl.

"I'm not your enemy," Victoria said. "I was on Angoria and visited with your people. You spent...time with Tarness. We parted as friends. Something has happened to you. Please remember."

Alyss leaned over as if kicked in the gut. She gasped for air, fighting a battle Victoria didn't understand.

"Please," Victoria pleaded. "Let me help you."

The woman shook her head. Alyss was losing to whatever held her mind, and she lunged forward. It was a slow, clumsy attack for a Berfemmian. Victoria stepped aside easily. Her words must've been distracting, for now.

When those dark eyes returned, Alyss licked her lips, peering at Victoria. The princess brandished her short sword as they inched along an invisible circle like wrestlers on the verge of fighting. There was no indication of what the bird-woman would do next, and Victoria's heart raced painfully.

"Any luck with those three?" Victoria asked. She jerked her head toward the still forms of Jaden, Dallow, and Nikkola.

"Alive, but out cold," Simon said, shakily kneeling beside Nikkola. "Whatever spells Dallow and Jaden cast knocked them out."

"Where's your useless brother?" she asked, straining to sense what would happen next. It was almost impossible to focus.

"He's not useless," Simon snapped. He took a deep breath. "I'm sure he ran off for a reason."

"Stop making excuses and heal Jaden," Mirim commanded, pushing herself up.

"Not Jaden," Victoria said. "Heal Dallow. That's an order."

Mirim glared at her before rushing forward, slamming her shield into the feathered woman. Alyss grabbed both ends of the shield, ripped it from Mirim's hands, and threw it aside. She leaped into the air and spread her wings, rising until her talons could reach Mirim's face. The captain struck out with her long sword while ducking the grasping claws.

"Tell her more about your visit," Mirim said. "That seemed to distract her."

"Alyss. I remember your city. It's timeless, and filled with strong, beautiful women," Victoria said. "You were turned away from the tribes during your mating cycle. I...I remember you with Tarness. Do you remember Tarness? You two were, uh, intimate for a day or so."

The Berfemmian slowly lowered her axe and rubbed her face. Mirim carefully moved behind Alyss as the Berfemmian stared drunkenly at Victoria, waiting for more words.

"Keep going," Mirim said under her breath.

"I was there. You accepted us as friends," Victoria said in a pleading tone. "Angst became very close with whats-her-name... Faeoris. You remember Angst?"

Alyss snapped upright as if struck with a whip. Any hint of white in her eyes was gone entirely, and she gripped the wicked lochaber axe hard enough to make the wood handle creak.

"Not good," Simon whimpered.

The Berfemmian stared up at the sky and let out a piercing squawk that made Victoria wince.

"Definitely not good." Simon called out, "Sean, hurry!"

Victoria jumped back as Alyss lunged forward. She hit something solid and ducked just as the axe whizzed overhead and lodged into a tree.

"Strike now," Mirim commanded.

Victoria swung her sword across the dark Berfemmian midriff as Mirim chopped down on her back. Victoria's hands hurt as if her sword had struck a stone wall. Several black, greasy feathers fell to the ground, but there was no blood. The Berfemmian scowled as if irritated by the sting of a mosquito.

"What is she made of?" Mirim asked, chopping down again and again.

"Definitely not feathers," Victoria said.

Alyss jerked her weapon loose from the tree and regained her footing. She swung the long axe around and around, keeping both women at bay. Mirim turned and ran to her shield as Victoria dove beneath the swing and rolled to safety. Victoria scrambled to stand and turn around. The Berfemmian swiped at her with the axe, faster than a gasp, faster than thought. Mirim rushed to block, almost in time. The hilt struck Mirim's shield while the blade careened off Victoria's chest plate with a ringing *thunk*. Both of them were knocked to the ground. Mirim had softened the blow, but Victoria couldn't catch her breath. Her chest hurt so much that stars filled her eyes. There weren't seconds to waste, she needed to get up, but was distracted by too many possibilities. How could she not know? That was her thing.

"Thanks, Mirim," she wheezed, pushing herself up.

There was no reply, and she glanced over her shoulder. The captain was unconscious. Victoria's lungs were on fire, and her mind was a battle of what-ifs and could-happens. She was better than this. Captain Tyrell had told her she could be the best. Images flashed through her mind of Rose's mangled body lying still in the woods. Angst dancing with her half-naked cousin. This Berfemmian monster feeding on their corpses.

The dark woman twirled her axe before raising it high into the air. Victoria rolled to the side as the weapon struck hard on the forest floor, again and again. They were surrounded by a cloud of dirt that seemed to coat her lungs. She pushed up to a knee and made eye contact.

"Why are you doing this?" Victoria said weakly between coughs. "I'm not your enemy."

The Berfemmian let out another squawk that sounded more bird than human. Victoria tried scrambling away but was too slow. The axe struck her armored ankle with a loud crack. She screamed in pain and tucked into a ball. Alyss swung down, slamming the axe into the ground hard enough to make it shake. How strong was this crazy bitch?

Victoria's mind reeled, she couldn't catch her breath, and the trees tilted the wrong way. How could it end like this? The ground shook again with a roar. The ground was roaring? That wasn't right. It didn't matter. She had nothing left, except too many visions to know which she should choose.

There was a thud that fortunately wasn't the lochaber axe splitting her head. She glanced over to see the blurry form of a wolf the size of a small house. Was that a dire wolf? They were supposed to be a myth. You know, like dragons.

"Oh, now what?" she wheezed, collapsing to the forest floor.

15

Breathless. Angst was completely breathless as Marisha lifted him high over the The Fette. He instinctively reached for his swords, which were helpfully guarding the tent city entrance with the two pretty boys. Really, though, he needed his armor more than the swords. Her bone-crushing grip made it almost impossible to breathe, which may have been a good thing since she smelled of garbage. There was far more going on than her being upset about Faeoris's death, and it wasn't good.

Berfemmian were the most powerful creatures on Ehrde. A tribe of warrior women who were stronger than the Nordruaut, fought better than their Vex'steppe tribesmen counterparts, and were tougher than dragons. Oh, and they had wings that were typically made of light. They also had a temper. Angst had learned right away how quick and dangerous that Berfemmian temper was. Shortly after arriving at their island, Marisha had been the first to greet him, with her foot upside his distracted, gawking face. She'd knocked him out cold. Since then, he'd tasted Faeoris's fury several times.

He needed to calm Marisha and work this out. Talking to Faeoris had always ended in hugs that usually didn't break ribs. With a wince and a nudge of focus, he willed the minerals in his ribs to not break—barely in time. He also, carefully, drew her arms apart slightly, just enough to minimize his bruising.

"Marisha, I'm sorry," he pleaded. "Please, let's talk. I loved your *essent*. I promise I didn't kill her. She sacrificed herself to save me."

Marisha paused, looking at him with a startled expression. "Angst," she said, her high-pitched voice quavering. "What's happening to me?"

"Bring me to the ground," Angst said. "We'll figure this out, together."

The bright moon illuminated her face, and it was filled with confusion and panic. She looked so unsure he worried she would let go.

"Something is terribly wrong with you," he said. "Let me help."

"No," she squawked, suddenly diving to the ground.

They crashed hard, knocking the air from his lungs and the sense from his head. He should've died, but at the last second, Marisha had rolled to her back and taken the brunt of the blow. She was fighting whatever was changing her. Angst had to hurry and snap her out of it before she snapped him. He pushed himself away with a wheeze as she struggled to sit.

They were back at The Fette. With the bonfire blazing behind him, he could see what was wrong, and it was very wrong. Her wings were now shiny black, with fleshy claws protruding from the ends. Her feet, that his jaw had great experience with, had been replaced with vicious talons. And those beautiful, muscular, tanned legs he'd been so fond of were now covered in oily feathers all the way up her torso. Under any other circumstances, he would've been distracted by her bare breasts, but instead he was focused on her steel-clawed fingers. It was as if all that pent up Berfemmian anger had been entirely unleashed and wrapped in an ugly package.

"How did this happen?" Angst asked, reaching for her.

"I'm a monster," she cried, looking down in horror. "I just wanted the feather so I could revenge my *essent*. Please help me, Angst." Marisha looked up at him with her stunning green eyes that begged for a hero.

"Felking Angorian harpy," Bella shouted, drawing a large

mace from nowhere and swinging it at Marisha's head. "I'll tear off your wings!"

"Stop," Angst shouted. "I was just getting through to her."

Marisha's hand blurred as she caught the mace in her steel-clawed hand and bent it. Her green eyes went glossy black, as all her humanity washed away. Arrows whizzed by Angst's ear only to be batted away by black wings.

"Bella, we've got to go," Karina shouted. "There's no time."

"We can't leave Angst," Bella said, desperation in her voice as she wielded another mace.

Marisha's wings spread in a dangerous arc around Angst, striking Bella with a crack. The twin crashed into her sister and they rolled to a stop. She shakily pushed herself up with one arm, her eyes wild with a fury that matched Marisha's.

"Angst," Bella said. "I'm so sorry. We stayed too long, and I promised we wouldn't."

Karina reached for Bella's hand.

"We love—" But before Bella could finish the sentence, they were gone in a flash of light.

"Don't mind me," Angst said to no one. "I'll be fi—"

Marisha wrapped her arms around him in a crushing hold once again and flew into the sky so fast he lost his breath.

"Get her, Angst," Alloria cried after him. It didn't help.

The Berfemmian flew so fast, he wondered if she'd been turned into a swifen. He could've crushed her bones or created an air shield for her to fly into, but the last thing he wanted to do was hurt her. She was Faeoris's best friend. He'd liked her before she was covered in greasy, black feathers and smelled like she'd never bathed. Angst tried shouting, and pleading, but Marisha continued diving up into the clouds. There had to be another way to distract her, to grab her attention and reason with her. He had to bring her back again, and only one thing came to mind.

Angst turned his head to take a deep breath of fresh air, puckered his lips, and kissed her full on the mouth. Her eyes went wide, but she didn't pull back. Instead, she met his lips with a

119

burning passion. Marisha's hunger went far deeper than he'd expected, and that was when he remembered. The Berfemmian were stuck in their mating cycle.

Whatever dark magic had overtaken Marisha hadn't quashed her base instinct to procreate. In another world, in another lifetime, this could've been amazing. Except, it wasn't. This Berfemmian, this harpy's desire was instinct. His physical reaction was instinct, but he didn't want to be with her every bit as much as he didn't want to be with Alloria.

They'd stopped high in the clouds while he tried to think as she made love to his face. There was no keeping up with her hunger, and he was grateful no one could hear his comical moaning noises. She clawed at his back, digging into his skin. It burned and felt wet. She pulled away to smell the blood. Now the moaning was less funny.

"Bring us to the ground," he muttered, gently. "Where we can be together."

She drew back long enough to screech, "Yesssss." It was far less sexy than any fantasy he would've had of Marisha. Not that he'd fantasized about her. Nope.

He'd hoped to come up with a plan during their slow descent but spent most of his time dodging her pointy, bird-like tongue that darted at his mouth like an attacking wasp. Any time he'd pull back for a breath, she'd jerk his head forward with a painful grip. Without warning, Marisha threw him to the ground.

The landing jarred every bone from shoulder to hip. The sudden ground and lack of air made him dizzy. They had landed by the fire once again. Her clawed feet held down his legs as her steely fingers slashed away his shirt and cut into his chest. Would she actually sex him to death like Faeoris had initially planned to do? It wouldn't be the worst way to die. Though, with this version of Marisha, it might.

A steely hand grasped the back of her neck and drew Marisha off, throwing her to the ground. The silver flash of a blade swung back and forth in a blur, reflecting firelight in burning arcs. Dark feathers flew as though a pillow had broken its seams, and Marisha rose into the air. Her eyes went from black to green and then black again as they looked at Angst with hurt and betrayal. With a final screech, she flew away into the night.

"Marisha," Angst called, reaching after her. "Let me help you."

That same, armored hand grasped his and pulled Angst to standing. The tall man removed both gauntlets, dropping them on the ground before removing his helm.

"No," Alloria gasped.

"Yes," Ivan said, his snide tone resonating in Angst's head like a bad chord.

Angst reeled in shock, looking from Ivan to Alloria. The tall knight grabbed him by the remains of his tunic and slapped him across the face.

16

The raven-feathered Berfemmian launched at the giant wolf and struck it across the mouth. Her lochaber axe met bone with a *crack*, and the wolf yelped. A bloody tooth flew out, and globs of red dribbled from its chin.

The tooth landed with a thud mere inches from Tori. She gasped at the size of it, breathing in the gamey copper scent of the wolf's wound. The fear that kept her from moving also held in the contents of her stomach. Victoria didn't want to be anywhere near the battle between these two predators. Even if she survived their fight, she had no interest in being next.

She pushed herself up, and both creatures took note. Alyss screeched like a hawk, raising the axe high over Victoria. The wolf's ear-ringing bark stopped the dark woman. Alyss looked from Victoria to the wolf and then the sky. The Berfemmian leaped up and turned to flee, her black wings reaching wide. The giant wolf lunged, its jaws clamping hard around Alyss's tiny waist, pulling her back to the ground.

It shook its head back and forth violently, like a dog winning tug-of-war. Blood splattered nearby trees as feathers drifted in the air. There was a gurgling scream and a crunching sound. The great wolf wagged its tail and eyed Victoria. Lowering his enormous head, he let the Berfemmian's body roll out with a stream of red slobber. It landed next to the giant tooth.

Her heart raced, but the beast just stood there, smiling. His tail wagged excitedly as if he'd just delivered his favorite stick.

"Good...dog?" Victoria squeaked between breaths.

A head peeked out from behind the dire wolf's ear. Sean waved, his teeth shining in a broad grin. The young man grasped handfuls of white fur as he climbed down the wolf's shoulder. He patted the beast and nodded slowly. After a few more tail-wags, the wolf ran off with its prize.

"Thanks," Victoria said, clutching her ribs. She struggled to catch her breath. Fortunately, the pain in her ankle kept her from passing out. "Sean, can you...see to the others." Gasp. "Try waking them."

He nodded, rushing to his brother. That made sense; Simon could heal. She dragged herself to a satchel lying near a tree and fumbled for a flask of water. Mead would've been better. After gulping generous quantities of not-mead, she coughed and hacked her way to Mirim. The dark-skinned captain was moaning, pressing her palms against her temples.

Victoria reached out, handing over the flask.

"This better be mead," Mirim grumbled.

She shook her head. "You okay?"

"More frustrated than hurt," Mirim said as she capped the flask. "We lost that fight and have a lot to cover, Your Majesty."

"Later," Victoria said.

"You look pale," Simon said shakily. "Let me heal you."

"Just the ankle," Victoria said, braving a smile. "Let's make sure you have enough energy for this mess. Why don't you see to the idiots next? Probably Dallow. I think he can heal too."

At one end of the clearing, Jaden lay flat on his back, his arms spread wide as though he'd lost a drinking battle with a bachelor party. At the other end, Dallow had collapsed after body-hugging a tree. His eyebrows and bangs had been completely burnt away, and ash covered a face of burn scars. After repairing Victoria's ankle, Simon made his way to Dallow and placed a hand on his chest.

"This sort of healing isn't my specialty," Simon said, his hands glowing blue. "I never know how much..."

There was a flash of light followed by a loud pop. Dallow gasped as his body writhed. The scars washed away, and hair sprouted from his brows. "What was that?" Dallow said, his body still jerking. "Did you give it to me all at once?"

"Sorry," Simon said. "I was nervous."

"You did great," Victoria said, coughing out a chuckle. "Please heal Jaden too. I think he's more injured, so try a little harder."

"If you're sure." Simon looked at Victoria warily.

"I insist," Victoria said with a wry smile.

As if struck by a tiny bolt of lightning, Jaden went rigid. Before the young man could speak, his body convulsed in that same wiggly dance Dallow had done. He then sat up straight and shouted, "Don't you ever heal me like that again. And you…" He shakily pushed himself up and stumbled to Dallow. "I told you to wait. Those two spells, cast at the same time…you almost killed us all!"

"Me," Dallow said, pointing a trembling finger at Jaden. "I made it perfectly clear what I was going to do, and you still—"

"Enough," Victoria shouted. Her lungs protested with a vengeance of bloody coughing that silenced everyone. The rest of her words came out in a whisper. "Another word, another spell, and I'll command Simon to heal you again. Understand?"

Both men nodded, their anger replaced with concern.

"Don't touch me," Mirim said, dodging Simon's glowing hand. "I can handle pain. Not sure I can handle your cure."

Simon looked exhausted as when he finished healing Nikkola, as if he was pouring his own life into the others.

"Sean," Victoria said. "Can you have your, uh, friends help us find Rose?"

Sean began chittering and squeaking. Dozens of squirrels leaped from nearby trees and brush, rushing off into the forest.

"Found her," Simon said, patting Sean on the shoulder.

"So quick?" Mirim asked in surprise.

"Lots of squirrels in the forest," Simon said. "She's in bad shape. We should hurry."

CHAPTER SIXTEEN

After ten minutes of chasing squirrels, they found Rose. She lay very still on a pile of branches and sticks as if dropped from the sky, which she probably had been. A dark-feathered Berfemmian lay in a small clearing nearby with the two foci daggers lodged in her chest. Rose had won the battle at a terrible cost. Her body was a sprawling mess of blood, held together by her armor. Everything bent wrong. Her arms and legs appeared to have new joints, some of the bones jutting out from between her armor. The branches that had probably slowed her fall had taken their price by gouging any skin not protected by plate or chainmail.

"No," Dallow called out, rushing to her. Rather than holding her dead body close, he straightened her limbs as best he could. He bowed his head in concentration and grasped Rose's hand.

"He's going to try and heal her," Jaden whispered to Victoria, shaking his head. "She may be Al'eyrn, but she's only human."

"He loves her, and that's enough reason to try," Victoria said. "Would you give up so easily?"

"No," Jaden said sincerely. "I would never give up." And with that, he made his way to Rose's other hand.

There was waiting, and more waiting as the two men did their best to revive her. The bleeding slowed but didn't stop. Victoria felt like she was waiting for Rose to die. They needed time. Was it possible for Dallow to try poisoning Death again?

"Simon, get over here," Jaden snapped. "Maybe your...unique healing will help."

Simon stumbled over and knelt beside the young woman, squeezing his eyes shut in concentration.

"We need to...we need to..." Dallow was stuttering, his eyes wild. "Simon, try harder."

"I did," Simon said, pulling his hands away.

"Everyone quiet," Jaden said. He shot a look at Sean. "Everyone."

The forest quieted.

There it was. Rose gasped for breath like a fish out of water. Victoria wheezed and winced as she knelt beside the young

Al'eyrn. Placing a hand on Rose's forehead, Victoria concentrated. Was it possible to save her? Did she even have a future?

Victoria struggled to concentrate. Everything was a distraction. She couldn't catch her breath; her own wounds had taken their toll while getting to Rose. There was still time. Somehow, Rose lived. Deathly futures blurred by as Victoria sought that one glimpse of hope. The sight of what could be had passed almost too quickly, but there it was. There was one possibility Rose would live out of the many, many futures she saw. And it was so obvious, she was almost embarrassed to share.

"She needs her daggers," Victoria whispered.

"How?" Nikkola asked. "Nobody here can pick them up."

"Everyone help move her to the clearing," Victoria commanded. "Get her off those branches as gently as possible."

"Rose will die if we move her," Dallow said.

Victoria shot Mirim a look. The captain nodded once and bent over to pick Rose up. Dallow tried pushing her hands away, but she gently shoved him over. Mirim struggled to find a part of her that wasn't damaged as she lifted Rose's tiny body. Nikkola helped, and together they rested her on leaves near the Berfemmian. Mirim set Rose's hand on a dagger and stepped back. Breathless moments passed.

"You killed her," Dallow said, his lip trembling. "You killed her!"

"Wait for it," Victoria whispered.

A grotesque crunch of bone was soon followed by the slurpy sound of muscle and skin knitting together. Her calf straightened as her foot twisted around until it was facing the right direction. Rose's body began to glow a cool green as the other leg righted, and her spine stretched out to its proper length. Magic happened, and Rose became whole once again.

"Al'eyrn," Jaden said in reverence.

"That bitch," Rose snapped, opening her eyes. The dam broke, and a flood of curses poured from her mouth.

"Good," Victoria said in relief, gripping her side. She nodded once and collapsed.

17

Angst struggled to recapture reality. Ivan continued slapping him across the mouth. *Smack.* Marisha was now evil and wanted Angst dead. *Smack.* He couldn't see straight; he just needed to get his footing. *Smack.* The twins were here, weren't they? Had he imagined that? *Smack.* How could Ivan be alive after Angst had already killed him? *Smack.* Distant songs warned him of something. Were his foci finally singing to him again? *Smack.* More than anything, he just wanted this to be over. He wanted his children back. He missed Heather desperately.

"Stop," Alloria shouted, grabbing Ivan's hand.

The knight backhanded the young princess, knocking her to the ground. That moment, that breath, gave Angst enough time to regain his senses. Reality would be something to deal with later.

A sudden anger welled up in him, hungry to feed on this enemy he'd already killed. Lightning sparked about his arms before spilling from them, reaching out, crawling across the ground in all directions. The blue and red strings of power carefully danced around Alloria as Sir Ivan let go and shuffled away.

"No," Ivan cried out, trying to slap sparks away like a nest of killer bees. He took a step back, and his foot sank knee-deep into the ground. "Stop this, Angst. You deserved to be slapped. You beat me to humiliation, hunted me down, and killed me. I was a god."

"You were nothing more than a bully," Angst said, his voice practically a growl. He willed the lightning to form a circle around Ivan.

"I was sick, and you forced me away," Ivan said, jerking away from every threatening pop. "I thought heroes were supposed to have compassion."

"Other heroes," Angst said, grasping the man's armor with his mind. More than anything, he wanted to squeeze this overripe banana until everything oozed out the top.

"Angst, stop," Alloria pleaded. She was suddenly at his side, tugging at an arm. She kissed his cheek, and then his lips, whispering. "Please. Please, stop. Magic sent him."

"I'll send him back," Angst shouted, his voice loud enough to shake the ground.

Alloria winced, turning away and covering her ears. "Magic sent him," Alloria shouted, her voice desperate. "He knows the way to Prendere. We need him to save your family."

His family. Heather, Thom, and Eila. Their faces flashed in his mind, breaking through the red fury of his anger.

"We need Ivan alive," she said, her voice calming. "To save Scar, and Kala, and Faeoris."

She was right; he had to save his friends. That was why they were doing this: to save them all. Deep breaths calmed his thundering heart. The red fury subsided, and reality slowly returned. So did feeling. His cheek, his entire jaw was sore from Ivan's attack. It would've been humiliating if he'd cared. He didn't. Nothing was more important than saving his wife and kids, than saving everyone. His wasn't a life of pride and acceptance. Getting beaten was just another day. Just another misstep toward winning the battle.

Angst let go, and Ivan gasped for breath. The knight wiggled free from his dirt prison and dusted off his leg. Surprisingly, it only took a few breaths for the dead knight to regain his sneer. He towered over Angst, looking down his prodigious nose as if he'd stepped in dung. Ivan's judgmental gaze studied Angst with disgust. It was definitely the man he knew. But how?

"Why are you alive?" Angst snapped.

Ivan reached under his silver breastplate and removed a large, red ruby ring. It dangled from a chain around his neck. Angst wanted to smack that sneer across the tent city.

"It seems I can't be killed, now," Ivan said.

"I wouldn't be so sure," Alloria said with a frown and shudder.

Angst rested a hand on her shoulder. She would know death better than most. Magic had offered Alloria a similar ruby ring, saving her as Cliffview collapsed into the ocean. She'd done the element's bidding as Queen of Unsel. When Magic was done with Alloria, he'd destroyed the ring. Death had appeared as a dark vortex to claim her, sucking the young woman in one appendage at a time. Angst had refused to let that happen and willed her whole, pulling her together piece by piece.

"Magic will keep me alive," Ivan said, swallowing hard.

"Says the knight who hates wielders," Angst said. "Weren't you a tree?"

"I'm no longer a part of that carcass you created," Ivan said, glaring at him. "And won't return to that place."

Angst had once slapped Ivan senseless, and the knight had run away. It wasn't Angst's proudest moment, the exact opposite of being heroic, but Ivan was a bully, and he'd do it again. Despite hating the knight, his friends had spent half a day looking for Ivan without success, not realizing he'd stumbled into the Vex'kvette. That orange goo affected all non-magical creatures differently, either killing them or changing them. Ivan became a giant purple tentacle monster the size of Unsel's castle. When Angst killed him, Ivan had looked more like an enormous tree than a man.

"Fine," Angst said. "Give us a map to Prendere, and we can part ways."

"It's not that simple," Ivan said. "I need to guide you. It's the only way."

"Of course it is," Angst said, gritting his teeth. "I'll find it without you."

"Go ahead," Ivan said. "And five years from now, I'll make you beg me for directions."

"Or," Angst said, leaning forward and clenching his fists, "I could just turn you inside out again and again until you tell me."

"No, wait," Alloria said, standing between them and placing a hand on Angst's chest. "We need him."

"We need Magic," Angst said, doing his best to stare down the knight. The fact that his face was partly numb from being slapped didn't help. "Alloria, you said you'd bring me to Magic."

"He didn't want to come and sent me instead. I have little choice because he insisted I help you," Ivan said, looking down his long nose again. "For some reason, he thought you might try to kill him."

"Oh, there is no try," Angst said, lightning sparking from his fists. "I'll take Magic out like I did the other four elements. I'm happy to do you in again too. I'm surprised you came back for seconds."

Ivan shoved Alloria aside and leaned in, nose to nose with Angst.

"Angst," Alloria said, tugging at the sleeve of his tunic. "Please."

"Yes," Ivan taunted. "Listen to your young tramp."

Alloria reared around and punched Ivan in the face with such force that he stepped back. Angst was as shocked as the knight when she did it again. Blood sprayed from his mouth, and he sat hard on his rear.

"Wow," Angst said.

"I'll destroy you," Ivan shouted, struggling to stand in his full suit of armor.

Angst held Alloria's shoulders and gently drew her back.

"You deserve that and more," she screamed. The young woman was shaking, and her eyes were lost to a wildness that didn't feel completely sane. "I hate you!" Fury seethed from her as she gritted her teeth and gasped in short, feral breaths. She looked ready to claw Ivan's eyes out, tear out his throat with her teeth, or explode. "Hate!"

"Alloria?" Angst asked, wondering if this is how he'd reacted only moments ago.

She stopped, blinked several times in surprise, then turned to him with a loving expression. "Sorry, baby."

Angst sighed, shaking his head. She was probably more broken than he was.

Ivan burst out laughing. "I'm glad she's on your side," the knight said.

"Me too," Angst said in a small voice. It was true. He would've hated to be on the receiving end of that much crazy. "Fine, we go together."

"Let's leave tomorrow," she said. "After we rest."

"How can we rest with him lurking nearby?" Angst asked.

"Put your swords in front of the tent," Alloria said. "We'll be safe. You need your strength."

The look of worry on her face was justified. He was tired to the bone, and everything from cheek to back throbbed with pain. Or was that age? It would've been wise to leave The Fette tonight in case Marisha came back, but Alloria's eyes were a little frightened, or maybe desperate. He nodded, reluctantly, and she sighed. Her shoulders dropped, and she leaned into him.

"Fine," Ivan said, pushing himself up to standing. He opened his mouth and rubbed his jaw, peering at Alloria with calculating eyes. "Tomorrow then. I look forward to our...adventure."

Angst stared on in disbelief as the knight he killed wandered past the fire and into the distant woods. The man hadn't only died, his body had been completely destroyed. How could he possibly be here? The only way he could be alive was if Angst had gone to the past and reset everything, but that hadn't happened yet. It was confusing to his tired brain, and he decided that it was future Angst's problem.

"Bring me to bed, Champion," Alloria said, her voice a little too sultry.

"Sure," Angst said. "Lead the way."

Dying with Angst

* * * *

Despite exhaustion and confusion, he needed his swords. Angst slowly made his way back to the entrance of The Fette while Alloria readied herself for sleep. She'd said something about washing up, but he'd been more than distracted. The cool, night air smelled fresh, and the quiet was surreal compared to the attack. He meandered through the labyrinth of teenage sex-tents, letting his mind wander. It was the first time he'd been alone in recent memory, and he was grateful for the chance to think.

The beautiful twins had once again appeared and disappeared. They acted like friends, but he found them hard to read and could only hope their agenda was in line with his own. The twins always seemed too ready for something to happen, on the edge of their seat, even when sitting on the edge of his knees. They sought a foci, yet another foci to deal with, but were vague about why. And then there was that little thing about them being from the future. They were going back in time, apparently to right a wrong like he wanted to. That made his head swirl with whens and what-ifs that were better understood by the Dallows of the world.

And now he had to deal with Ivan. The haughty, self-important dead man he'd hated more than anyone was suddenly alive. How was that possible? Worse than that, Angst now had to team up with the knight to save his family. It made his stomach churn.

All of this, and now Marisha had somehow been transformed into something dark and smelly. One of the most dangerous, beautiful creatures on Ehrde wanted him dead. Marisha had ac-cused him of killing her *essent*, Faeoris. If she knew the truth, she'd be fighting by his side, preferably downwind.

This wasn't the hero story he'd planned all his life. His goal of becoming a knight had become a complicated mess of living elements, women from the future, too many loved ones lost, and an ache in every joint. What else had happened during his months of healing, and mourning? It didn't matter; he was tired of everyone's crap. All he wanted was to drop Alloria off on a secluded island where she was safe and harmless, get knighted, and retire drunk and happy with his wife and kids. Everyone else could go felk themselves.

The swords were waiting patiently, and he set them in place to hover over his back. It would've been better if they sang, but their presence was still comforting as he struggled to find his way back to Alloria. He grimaced in frustration at being lost, and barely stopped before plowing through a tent. With a calming breath, Angst reached out and summoned a globe of light. It was much brighter than he'd intended, but at least now he knew where—

"Hey," a young man called out from the tent he'd almost stomped on.

"Turn it off," a woman shouted from another.

Angst extinguished the spell immediately. The tent city was less empty than he'd expected. The silence was soon replaced by the moans of passionate, humping teens. Had they actually run in fear from the battle, or run for covers? The sounds distracted him from his frustration, and he couldn't help but smile at the youth. Sex was far, far more important than pending doom, right?

He rushed as carefully as he could, eventually finding the tent. It seemed even smaller than before as he set the swords by the entrance. He peeled off the remains of his tunic and tried using it to wipe away a thick layer of salty grime. It was moist enough from sweat that he'd undoubtedly just rubbed it in. He had taken the time to heal his wounds, but should've taken a bath too. Even though he felt over-warm, he kept the leggings on, hoping they'd be a layer of protective humility in the dark.

"Hey," he whispered, trying not to bump her as he crawled into the tent. He awkwardly found his spot and wiggled under the blankets.

"Hey," she said huskily, in a sleepy voice.

Sleepy was good. He was too tired to deal with more 'poppa'

issues.

She rolled over to snuggle next to him and placed a hand on his chest. He gasped as her large breasts squished against his side. They were covered in something silky, and she smelled like wildflowers. He didn't and was very aware of his personal stench of old-man-sweat, alcohol, and fear. Closing his eyes, he concentrated on grass, and rocks, and dead cats. It wasn't enough as she snuggled closer.

"Thanks for having my back," he said, clearing his throat several times. "You stopped Ivan long enough for me to defend myself."

"Anything for my champion," she said. Her hand slid down to his stomach.

He didn't notice. Really, he didn't notice. Why had he eaten so much cake throughout his life? Would it be too obvious to suck in his gut right now? Definitely. Not that it mattered. He wouldn't do anything foolish. Despite her hunger and perfect body, and that smell that wafted into his brain, she was far too young. When had he first started enjoying sex? Sixteen? Seventeen? It didn't matter; this was different.

"We make a good team," he said, his heart skipping a beat. Teammates weren't lovers, and he hoped she was just stretching her fingers. "After a good night's sleep, we'll be ready to do more team…stuff."

Alloria shifted and rolled so smoothly that he could do nothing more than gasp before she was on top. She held his face as she leaned forward, placing her lips against his. They were full, and soft, and sweet. This was so much better than getting beaten by Marisha and Ivan.

Her want, her need, her softness was incredible. For a moment, he let her. He couldn't help it. She kissed, he kissed, their tongues danced, and a fire burned inside him. That fire swelled in him like everyone else who remained at The Fette. He wanted this, he deserved it, and there was nothing to stop him.

Tori had slept naked next to him, but it had seemed nothing more than an inappropriate tease. Faeoris had crawled into their tent and taken off her clothes because she didn't enjoy wearing them. Well, and it was mating season for her. They were both friends, or something. Sex seemed an impossibility with either of them. Those flirtations had threatened his wall, kicking and striking with every bit of heat, all uncomfortably deflected by marriage. That one thing had kept him from doing what he really wanted, and that one thing was now gone.

Now, hovering over him was youth in perfection. Every fantasy he'd ever had was here and now. Alloria's hips ground against him, and he reacted like a teenager ready to go, writhing with her every gasping breath as she suckled his neck. Her hunger was raw and full of need. It had been a very long time since he'd been wanted that way, and he longed for the outcome. She would ride him like a pony until all that desperation, all that lust and desire, was completely extinguished.

It would take nothing, absolutely nothing, to give in to that hunger. His family was gone so there were no more walls. There was nothing left to lose, but somehow, a part of him knew he would lose everything. Was he becoming numb to the sight and feel of beautiful women? Nope, not even a little. Maybe he was just more prepared for it now. A little. This teen in all her beauty with her soft body and large breasts and firm nipples begging for attention was grasping for something that wasn't hers. And despite everything his body wanted, his mind reeled.

He clasped both her wrists in frustration and rolled over, making her squeal in fear or pain. With a gasp, her mouth met his again, even more desperate than before. She didn't wince away from his roughness; she welcomed it. Alloria would do anything for him. Anything.

The tent city was distracted, and they were just another couple. Nobody would know, nobody would care. It was infuriating because there was only one thing he really wanted. And he wouldn't take no for an answer. He had no choice but to follow his instincts.

18

The decision to combine forces with Eastern Nordruaut was unanimous. Paranoid Bryymel was the only one to complain, but even his reservations were minimal, and nobody listened anyway. Now convinced that Angst had killed Jarle, the East and West happily combined forces to hunt for him. There's nothing like having a common enemy to rally behind, and Angst's transgressions were bad enough to ultimately end their civil war.

Guilt rolled over Tarness like an avalanche that never quite seemed to stop. He'd lied to Maarja about training with Jintorich. He'd lied to everyone about searching for Jarle's body. And now, he'd lied to the Nordruaut about Angst killing Jarle.

When Tarness accepted the ring, he hadn't expected that it would make him lie. All he wanted was to get to Angst and help his friend through this new disaster. Not that he felt like much of a helper. Or even a friend. So far, his help had inspired the entire Nordruaut nation to hunt him down. He now spent a lot of time staring at his feet, trying to figure out how to pull himself free from that avalanche.

They were fast approaching the Rohjek border. The Nordruaut had run for four days, stopping six times for food and three times to sleep. At this point, Tarness needed a solid eight, or maybe twenty, hours of sleep. The Nordruaut woke refreshed after four. Despite riding swifen, Tarness and Jintorich spent more time exchanging yawns than talking, even though yawning meant taking in gasps of sweaty Bokeen stench. The enormous, pungent mounts must've been made of wet hay. Their scent coated his mouth with an earthy flavor that scratched his throat and made his nose run.

Eventually, to the chagrin of his wife, Tarness trailed far behind everyone. She reluctantly gave him space, but not without cost. Nobody could cold-shoulder like a Nordruaut who'd spent most of her life living on an iceberg. Jintorich did not give him space. He was like the neighbor kid who wanted all your toys. The little Meldusian rode close beside him, glancing over expectantly but saying nothing. No matter how small Jintorich was, four days of his discerning gaze was impossible to ignore.

"What?" Tarness finally muttered.

Jintorich continued staring.

"I feel like you want something, or like I'm in trouble," Tarness said. "Why don't you just borrow my dad's belt and give me a good wailing?"

"That belt is probably too large for me to swing," Jintorich said with a smirk.

"Heh." Tarness was unable to hold back the chuckle and wished Angst, Dallow, and Hector were here. Their irreverent humor could lift him up on his worst day. All these days felt like his worst.

"You didn't spend all those months searching for Jarle's body," Jintorich said, tugging at a wispy eyebrow.

"How did you know?" Tarness asked, once again staring down at the avalanche. It felt like the snow was beginning to pile up a little higher.

"You had no reason to bring Rasaol and Niihlu to us unless they had Jarle's body. They could have brought it at any time. I deduct that they were waiting for something," Jintorich said. "So, what have you been doing?"

"I've been collecting body parts and bringing them to Magic," Tarness said.

"Body parts?" Jintorich asked.

"Lurp's body parts," Tarness said with a shudder. "The

enormous four-legged Al'eyrn that fought against Angst and Niihlu."

"Right," Jintorich squeaked. "How could I forget such a monster? Too many thoughts in my head, I suppose. Why parts?"

"Lurp was too large to bring all at once," Tarness said. "And Magic refused to come out in the open himself. It took a month to chop off giant, frozen body parts and carry them to the cave where we met."

"Gross," Jintorich said, his tall ears twitching. "Did you say it was Al'eyrn?"

"Magic said a couple of humans, or a human and an animal, must've gotten caught up in the Vex'kvette," Tarness said with a grimace. "That they must've absorbed a foci when the orange goo combined them."

"That must've been a nightmare for those poor creatures," Jintorch said.

"Yeah," Tarness said. The thought made his stomach churn. "What are the chances?"

"Normally I would say it was impossible," Jintorich said. "Foci seem to be very particular. This would have to be very well planned."

"Which makes me wonder why Niihlu is whole and not an ice statue," Tarness said.

"His necklace." Jintorich gasped in surprise. "It must be another foci."

"He did look uncomfortable wearing it," Tarness said. "And I noticed sparks jumping back and forth from the necklace to the axe."

"Now you know why Magic wanted Lurp's remains," Jintorich said. "He was looking for the foci to repair Niihlu."

"I hate elements," Tarness said. "But wait, I thought Al'eyrn couldn't wield more than one foci. Isn't that why Angst is supposed to be going crazy?"

"Yes," Jintorich said, tapping his chin with a finger.

"I don't even understand how Niihlu became Al'eyrn," Tarness said. "Angst can pick up other foci, but when we first met

Niihlu, he couldn't even budge Angst's sword."

"Magic must've made Niihlu an Al'eyrn," Jintorich said, his voice squeaking with the excitement of discovery.

"He tried making Rose an Al'eyrn," Tarness said. "We found him in a cave near the underwater mage city. That's when Angst merged with his second foci."

"I hadn't heard this story," Jintorich said.

"Jormbrinder is a foci made of two daggers. Rose had one of the daggers. Angst had bonded with Dulgirgraut but was still able to pick up the other dagger. He said it dampened his magic, whatever that means," Tarness said. "We found Rose in a cave lying on a stone table. Chryslaenor hovered over her, and Magic was doing something that made it shock her with black lightning." He winced at the memory. "She was screaming in pain. Angst thought the only way he could save her was to bond with Chryslaenor. The battle was a mess, but he made it to Rose and the sword…and then he exploded."

"What?" Jintorich said, pulling his watery dragonfly swifen to a stop. "How is that possible? He'd be dead."

"You're asking me?" Tarness asked. "The blast blew the cave wide open. No one should've lived through that. It was enough to kill Air. According to Dallow, between the dagger dampening the other foci, the two swords, and Rose's healing, they both survived."

Jintorich closed his eyes and held onto his staff with both hands. A blue glow emanated from Maehtikyn for several minutes until Jintorich sighed deeply.

"You don't look very good," Tarness said.

"That's how I feel," Jintorich said, rubbing his bulbous temple. "Once again, an unlikely event that could only be planned. It explains how Angst now wields two foci, and that Magic can possibly force the bond of a foci with a host."

"Sort of," Tarness said.

"What do you mean?" Jintorich asked.

"He said my ring was a sort of foci," Tarness said, nodding at the ruby ring on his finger. "If that's so, he's bad at making them because it doesn't work for me like the swords work for Angst. Maybe he's bad at making Al'eyrn too. That has to be why Rose was in so much pain, and why Niihlu used to look like a slushy snowman. It's like Magic can only do it halfway."

"Which is why he needed a second foci for Niihlu," Jintorich said excitedly. "The two foci make him full Al'eyrn."

"I guess." Tarness shook his head. "Makes me wonder who else he's tried to bond with a foci."

"If he has tried again," Jintorich said, "it would only create more nightmares."

They stared at each other as a chill overtook Tarness, and it wasn't from the pleasant Nordruaut weather.

"So is that it?" Jintorich asked. "We've learned a lot from what you've shared. Is there anything more you want to tell me?"

In his mind, Tarness screamed the truth. That he'd killed Jarle. That Angst was innocent. His mind cried and pleaded, but the words wouldn't come out. Instead, his face became stiff, and the finger that wore the ruby ring burned.

"I can't share anything more," Tarness finally said.

"Yes, but there is more, isn't there?" Jintorich said, his dark-marble eyes intense. "Won't you tell me?"

He tried again. His head throbbed painfully, and his eyes felt like they would explode from his skull at any moment.

"I believe you, Tarness," Jintorich said with a nod. "I'm sure you've told me everything you're able to."

Tarness gasped for air as if he'd been drowning in a lake and finally broke through the ice. Slowly, ever so slowly, the pain subsided. When his eyes could focus, when his mind could reason, he made out Jintorich looking back and forth between his face and the ruby ring. He nodded.

"This guilt you carry, the lies you've told," Jintorich finally said. "They are not you, my friend. I realize you have little choice, but I worry they could be your end."

"Yes," Tarness said, a tear trickling down his cheek. It wasn't just the physical pain, he could deal with that. He hated what the ring was doing to him, what it was making him do, what it was making him become. He wasn't a liar. His wife deserved better, and his friends deserved better. The avalanche of his guilt was covering more of him by the minute, and he worried it would swallow him whole.

They rode forward slowly, following the broad path left behind by the Nordruaut. The blinding white snow was becoming darker. Winds had carried Rohjek ash miles past the Ruautu river, eating away at the Nordruaut border like hungry fungi.

"There is one thing left we can do," Jintorich said, nodding once again at the ring. "Something that may set your mind free."

"Really?" Tarness asked, wiping his nose.

"Have faith, my friend," Jintorich said. "I have an idea."

19

Angst woke with the dawn, despite the long night and lack of sleep. Grabbing his swords, he rushed through the camp toward the smoldering bonfire. The great fire had burned down to charcoal remains that emanated a gentle heat in the early morning coolness. The kids were all asleep in their tents, and this space was ample enough for what he needed.

He set both swords on their tips and stepped back. Angst took a deep breath, reaching high into the air before bending over to touch his knees. His feet were really far away. He grunted as he stood, listening to his back pop noisily. Shaking out his gimp knee with a crack and rolling his neck with a noisy crunch made him wonder if he was growing older or turning into a set of drums. Hector had always told him to stretch first, so he stretched.

Even though he was still bonded to Chryslaenor and Dulgirgraut, their connection was like a paper boat in an ocean storm. Bonding to both swords simultaneously, in an effort to save Rose, was too much for all three of them. They were disgruntled at moving in together and tended to be poor roommates in his mind. While the swords appeared physically identical, they were more like brothers with a grudge. The foci were, more or less, alive in a way beyond his understanding, and they eventually made peace. Once resolved, that symbiotic relationship had made him feel whole.

CHAPTER NINETEEN

When Angst had decided to go back in time and save his family, they'd set aside their differences to stop talking to him. They still gave him power to spare, but their companionship was gone. Angst didn't just need their power, he needed their guidance. He only knew of one way to make that happen. Sealtian.

When Angst was much younger, Hector had tried to teach him sealtian—the dance of swords. At the time, Angst had thought it merely calisthenics with blades, and was quickly bored after learning a handful of movements. Thirty minutes of bending and weaving slowly with swords hadn't been his idea of adventure.

After losing Chryslaenor the first time, Angst had become ill. Bonding with a reluctant Dulgirgraut kept him alive, but the sword refused to speak with him. In an attempt to connect with Faeoris, they'd agreed to do sealtian together. For him, sealtian didn't come naturally, or from years of practice. He'd started by following her movements, and the sword guided him through the rest. When it was done, Dulgirgraut sang in his mind.

He couldn't stretch out his years and gave up grinding his bones with a deep sigh. Angst reached for the two giant swords hovering upright before the glowing embers. Chryslaenor and Dulgirgraut buzzed noisily in his mind, anticipating the upcoming exercise. They were like children waiting to open gifts.

Angst let go of these thoughts and focused, lifting the swords vertically over his head with both hands. The red and blue lights surrounding the foci now covered his forearms. His mind was emptied, and with a deep breath, he concentrated and lowered the swords until they were horizontal to the ground. His movements became a dance, bending like a reed, crouching like a tiger, stretching like a swan ready to take flight. The sweat was cleansing and the cool morning breeze that rolled over his bare arms exhilarating.

Heather's beauty filled his mind. He thought about her smiles—the beautiful full-lipped smile on her face, and the one in her eyes. Her curly brown hair teased a few grays and she had some smile lines, and he drank it all in. She was often frustrated with him, or angry with his choices, especially since taking the swords, but the love in her eyes never went away.

He'd lost track of time and didn't care. The sealtian fulfilled their need in a way that left him whole. This wasn't the success from a battle barely won, or getting away with something he shouldn't have; this felt more permanent. Angst didn't know when the music from his foci had started accompanying his sealtian, when it had begun to flow to the rhythm of his movements, or when it stopped being just music. The swords' glow grew in him, and out from him. The music became information and power. He squeezed the tears from his eyes, and let it happen.

Angst envisioned the memory of when he first held Thom and Eila in the Unsel infirmary. Thankfully, they both looked like their mother. Thom had been quiet, looking around and taking in the world. Eila grasped his cheek roughly as if to ensure he was paying attention. They both held tight to his heart.

When he finished, the swords quieted and remained still in his mind. That connection was apparently only for the sealtian. All he'd accomplished was to build up a thick sheen of sweat and a loss of breath. It left him feeling silly. Part of him wanted to apologize to the swords, the other part wanted to argue about his plan and convince them it would work.

The visions of his family had made him dizzy. Had that just been a daydream, or some message from the swords? More than anything, he wanted to believe they were still alive and whole. They weren't.

A quick glance around the vast campsite showed no movement, and he allowed himself a moment to weep. He had failed them. Not only his wife and kids, but everyone who had died under his watch. No matter how many times he had gone over everything that had happened, he wouldn't have made any different choice. It felt like the whole universe had conspired against him, and he was sick of it. The moment eventually passed because he had hope. He knew what he had to do.

Angst threw the swords on his bare back and cursed in frustration, tromping noisily to the tent. With a deep sigh, he peeked in.

"Yum," Alloria said, eying him.

Angst grimaced a smile and wanted to reply, "Yuck." Not only to her response but to his extra thirty pounds of yum. Maybe forty, but who was counting? She leered at him in a way that he tried not to with the twins, and Alloria, and Victoria…it was a long list of not-leering.

"I meant what I said last night," he warned. "We aren't going to have sex. My family may be gone, but not in here." He tapped his sternum. "I'm going to save them. Being with you that way would be wrong."

She looked at him, her eyebrows furrowed seriously, and said, "Can I go pee now?"

"Oh, right," he said, feeling embarrassed.

She'd been like a starving octopus last night, and he hadn't known what to do. After rolling over, he finally decided to use magic and anchored her bones to the ground. There'd been a lot of cursing and a few tears, but she'd eventually fallen asleep inside the tent. He'd tried sleeping outside on the bare ground, not daring to go back in. It wasn't his best night's sleep.

He released the hold, and Alloria scrambled from the tent. She almost bounced out of her red, silky lace shirt-thing that didn't have enough cloth to blow his nose on. He sucked in his breath. She stood there for a moment so he could see before rushing off.

He took advantage of her absence to don his armor, finishing just in time. She sort of skipped toward him, and he tried not to gawk at the show.

"It's cold," she said.

"I noticed," he muttered.

Alloria winked before crawling into the tent, and he turned around until she finished dressing. Though, at this point, what difference did it make? He'd seen almost everything, that red thing covered nothing in the best way. Alloria crawled out of the tent in her barely-there gray leather. Her outfit said party, but her face was suddenly a torrent of worry and pain.

"Now that you're wearing clothes," Angst said, begging his eyes not to leer since they weren't really clothes, "we need to find Ivan and go."

"But...I really need a brush, and some makeup," she said, tugging at a long, honey-brown curl. "I know a town—"

"Alloria," he said. "It's time. You said you'd bring me to Magic after we got you clothes. I agreed to put up with Ivan, but no more delays."

She pulled so hard at the curl, he thought she'd tear it out. When she winced, he took her hand and held it.

"What's going on?" he asked.

"He scares me," she whispered, looking at the ground.

"I promise," Angst said, "he won't hurt you."

He stepped forward and drew her into a hug. She buried herself in his shoulder and cried. The moment he patted her hair, she looked up with pursed lips. Alloria looked more vulnerable than a newborn puppy. Instinctively, he licked his lips before realization struck and he pulled away.

"No," he said, releasing her. "No."

She peered at him, her eyes momentarily calculating as a smile crept up one cheek. Was it all a game? He may never know.

"What's for breakfast?" she asked. "I'm starved."

Angst shook his head in disbelief. She was like a weathercock in a hurricane. "There's some bread in the satchel. We can probably rummage up something more if the vendors left anything behind."

"Eww, bread makes you fat," she said with a pout.

"You don't eat bread?" he asked.

"Of course I do," she said.

"Then that's obviously a myth." He winked.

"Wait," she said, peering again. "Was that a compliment?"

"That was flirting," Ivan said. "The type you would expect from an old man."

His whiny tone crawled across Angst's flesh.

"I think it's nice," she said in his defense.

"What are you wearing?" Ivan asked, looking Alloria up and down. "You look like you're for sale."

"Shut it," Angst said, darkly.

"What?" Ivan said with a wry smile. "I suppose you picked it out for her."

"He helped," Alloria said, her tone full of innocence. "And then bought it for me."

Angst sighed deeply. How did this stuff keep happening to him? He wished Dallow and Tarness were here. They'd understand. Actually, no, they wouldn't.

"I like your taste," Ivan said, drinking her in with his eyes.

She crossed her arms and stepped behind Angst.

"Do you like your arms?" Angst asked. "I'm pretty sure you don't need them to guide us."

"Uh," Ivan stammered.

"Let's make a deal," Angst said. "You lead the way, as quietly as possible, and I won't spread your body parts all over Ehrde."

20

Victoria woke the next morning to breakfast cooking, birds chirping, and bickering. The others must've set up her tent and tucked her in. Someone should get a medal. Despite feeling better, she hid from the conversation in her cocoon and pretended to sleep.

"Where have you been?" Jaden snapped.

"Scouting," Dallow said. "Not that it's any of your business."

"Fine," Jaden said. "What do we do now?"

"We should find Angst and warn him," Nikkola said. "If there are more dark Berfemmian, he could be in danger."

"I thought we wanted him dead," Rose snapped. "Shouldn't we just let the Berfemmian monsters kill him?"

"Harpies," Jaden corrected. "I just never realized that the harpies from my future originated as Berfemmian."

"Whatever," Rose said. "It would save us the trouble. No, I'll just say it, it will save *us*. Angst is the reason we're here. He's the reason I almost died."

"We're here because the elements went to war," Victoria said, reluctantly crawling out of her tent. "No matter what he thinks, Angst has been caught up in this like we were."

"I agree with Nikkola," Dallow said. "If he's in danger, we should warn him."

"Knowing Angst, he probably kissed their leader and she flew away," Rose said. "Isn't that what he does?"

"What? No," Victoria said defensively. "Not that I'd know."

Everyone stared at her, and all of them looked like they were biting their tongues.

"You're probably right," Victoria said, her cheeks warm. "That he's fine. Not the kissing thing."

"Rose's armor is pretty beat up," Dallow said, graciously interrupting the painful silence. "If we aren't going after Angst, maybe we could head back to Potterton, or find her something to wear at The Fette."

Victoria and Rose burst out in laughter.

"What did I say?" Dallow frowned, looking back and forth between them.

"The clothes they sell at the Fette are for bedrooms. A different type of adventure," Rose said, kissing him on the cheek. "That's for thinking of me."

"We should stay on Angst's trail," Victoria said.

Everyone nodded reluctantly, except Mirim, who crossed her arms and glared at the ground.

"What's wrong?" Victoria asked. "What do you think we should do?"

"We should head back to Unsel," Mirim said, curtly. "Your Majesty."

"What?" Rose asked. "Why?"

"Why is the question," Mirim said. "Why am I here?"

They all looked at Victoria, except Mirim, who continued staring at the ground like it may attack.

"Because we need your knowledge of working with the zyn'ight," Victoria said. "We need a tactician."

"A tactician," Mirim scoffed. "You mean someone who coordinates. Like when I told Rose to fall back. Like when I told Jaden and Dallow to stand together and cast fireballs to burn their wings. Like when I told you to fight by my side."

"But we lived. We even won. Sort of." Victoria looked at the others. Now they were staring at the ground. "Go on."

"None of you listened to me," Mirim shouted. "We almost died. We would've died if not for your magics. There were only two Berfemmian harpies. Only two. How many do you think are out there on the hunt? And if the harpies are looking for Angst, who else is? You didn't fight like trained warriors. You were a funny carnival who accidentally survived. I don't care to die, and I don't want to watch you die."

"You're right," Victoria said with a grimace. "What do you want?"

"Either let me lead during battle," Mirim said, "or send me home."

"Done," Victoria said with a nod.

"That's not enough," Mirim snapped.

"It should be," Victoria said.

"You're right," Mirim said. "It should be, but it isn't. You're ready to lead, but don't want to offend anyone. Rose is too independent to follow orders. Jaden and Dallow seem more interested in killing each other than the enemy. As I see it, Sean, Simon and Nikkola were the only three even interested in working as a team."

The brothers bumped knuckles and nodded to each other.

"I told you we should leave them behind," Nikkola said.

"I don't want to kill him," Jaden said, nodding at Dallow.

"That's one of us," Dallow said in a droll tone.

"I know more about battle magic than he does," Jaden said. "I correct him so he can do better."

"You don't correct me," Dallow said. "You insult me, so I feel foolish."

"I can't help that you're foolish," Jaden said, standing tall. "It's not my fault if you don't want to learn."

"Stand down, Jaden," Rose said, drawing her daggers and moving between them. She looked at Dallow with softer eyes. "You too."

"Exactly what I'm talking about." A grimace overtook Mirim's face. "Dallow was busy creating a white ball filled with lightning…"

"My most powerful spell," Dallow said, smartly.

"…while Jaden summoned a giant snowball," Mirim continued.

"It was to slow her down," he grumbled.

"Apparently water and lightning don't mix," she explained. "But two fireballs would've grounded them. Then I would've sent Rose in to hamstring them with those daggers."

"I didn't know," Rose muttered.

"That's my point," Mirim said. "It's not your job to know. It's your job to do."

"What about us?" Simon asked.

"You're not here to fight monsters like those," Mirim said. "And Sean is my backup plan. In these woods, he's probably more powerful than anyone else."

Jaden and Dallow gasped as if punched in the gut. Sean seemed oblivious, nodding politely at a blue songbird on his finger. The bird sang and chirped excitedly.

"You're right, Mirim," Victoria said. "You're in charge for battles moving forward, and I'll deal with the other issues in due time."

Mirim nodded curtly as if she'd been fed a snack instead of a full meal. Victoria sighed and looked at Dallow.

"I believe they're still at The Fette," he said.

"That's not surprising," Rose said with raised eyebrows. "I can only imagine what those two spent their night doing. Something about that place makes you feel like you can get away with anything."

"Yes," Victoria said, unable to mask her worry. "Yes, it does."

21

Angst's favorite pastime was admonishing himself for failing—but there was no way he could have failed at killing Ivan. Was there? One doesn't just stop being a husked-out glowing tree. Ivan's very presence just felt wrong. Even the knight's horse was slow and sickly as if reluctantly dragged out of the same death hole Ivan had escaped.

Alloria seemed to be as frustrated as Angst. He had wanted to spend this quiet-time continuing his mental quest to befriend the two swords, but it was impossible with her constant fidgeting. What began with sighs evolved into grinding teeth, itching, and finally some hair pulling.

"What's up?" he asked, discarding a clump of her hair that had landed on his leg. "Are you okay?"

"You think I'm ugly," Alloria muttered under her breath.

"What?" Angst asked in surprise. "What on Ehrde would give you that idea?"

"You wouldn't have sex with me," she said.

"Oh?" Ivan asked.

With a surge of will and a wave of his hand, Angst knocked Ivan from his mount. He landed with a loud crash and a sharp curse. Angst considered grabbing his armor and bouncing him off several trees, but that should've been enough to make his point. They stopped as the disgruntled knight remounted his weary stallion.

"I don't want to discuss this in front of him," Angst muttered. "Now isn't the best time."

"When is it the best time?" she shouted, tearing off her tiara and throwing it to the ground.

A flock of small blackbirds left their tree to find a quieter, safer home.

"I'm in mourning," he said, softly. "And you're sixteen. I'm forty-one." He scratched his scalp that wasn't a bald spot. "I think I'm forty-one. What month is it?"

"I'm seventeen," she snapped. "Don't treat me like a child. After what I've been through, it shouldn't even be a question. And don't change the subject."

"I'm sorry," Angst said. "I shouldn't dismiss your age as if you don't have feelings. It's just...it's just more complicated than that."

"Like I said," she huffed. "You won't have sex with me. You think I'm ugly. That's not complicated."

She tensed as he wrapped his arms around her waist and dismissed the swifen. They dropped to the forest floor, and he pulled away. Alloria continued facing forward, away from him, refusing to turn around.

"Really," Ivan said. "Now?"

Angst dragged Ivan's armor to one side until he fell off the mount once again. He rolled over several times until Angst was done.

"Stop that," Ivan snapped.

"After you've remounted, why don't you ride ahead?" Angst said, flippantly. "It will keep you from falling off again."

"Why don't I leave for good?" Ivan said.

"Sure, and then you don't get whatever it is you want," Angst said. "I know you're here for a reason beyond helping us. Ride off, and we'll find Prendere on our own, or ride out of earshot and wait like a good dog. Your choice."

"You should leave her here," Ivan said.

"Not an option," Angst said, sharply.

Ivan mounted his horse in a huff and rode off.

"I'm not talking to you," Alloria said, sniffing deeply.

"Let me know when you're ready," Angst said.

It may have taken her an entire minute of arm crossing and corset tugging before she finally spoke. "Fine." Alloria spun around, her eyes a little wilder than normal. "Why can't we do it?"

"I don't cheat on my wife," Angst said.

"Ha," she said mockingly. "Ha."

"You only get one ha," he said.

"You had sex with my cousin," she said, leaning forward.

"Part of me wanted to," he said. His cheeks warmed, but he maintained eye contact.

"Everyone knows it," she accused.

"Only Victoria and I know," he said. "And Heather. She would've known immediately if I'd cheated. I couldn't keep anything from her. Victoria and Heather's opinions are far more important to me than jealous rumors."

"And your pretty bird-lady-friend," she said, pointing a finger at him. "How could you not have sex with her?"

"It was almost impossible," he said. "She was one of the most beautiful women I've ever met. Faeoris was in her mating cycle and would've had sex with a tree just to quench her fire. I'm a bad tree. I wanted her, I wanted both of them, but wouldn't."

"Why, Angst?" she said. "I don't believe you."

"It's not in my nature," he said. "I enjoy being friends with women. It's often misconstrued, but I don't feel the need to explain or apologize for it. I love Victoria, I loved Faeoris, but I'm *in* love with Heather."

"I don't understand," she said.

"That's because you've never been *in* love with anyone," he said. "Love isn't a measurement. You either do, or you don't. But being in love, that's something else. Heather and I, we had our struggles, all of them, but we never gave up. That's what this entire trip is about. I refuse to give up."

"But they aren't here, now," she said with a frown. "If this thing we're doing is going to kill you, what difference does it make?"

"That's just the point, isn't it?" he asked. "If I gave up on what I believe now, for even a second, why bother doing any of this?"

Alloria looked off into the distance as if considering her next chess move. After long consideration, she finally said, "You think I'm ugly."

Angst sighed and waved his hands until the ram swifen appeared. "I think you're fun to look at," Angst said. "I also think that there is beauty buried deep inside of you that I find a lot more attractive than lace-up-leather."

Angst hugged her tight until she pulled away.

"So," she said. "You don't think I'm ugly?"

"I never did," he said. "If I were young and single, you'd be way out of my league, but I'd still try."

"You still should," she said.

"I'll keep that in mind," he said with a laugh. He bent over and picked up the tiara. "Where did you say you got this?"

"It was a gift from my cousin," she said, blowing dust off and placing it back on her head.

"Right. I wonder—" He was cut off by a distant cry. "What was that?"

"That's you telling me more about how I'm not ugly," she said.

He shushed her, making her gasp, but at least she was quiet. For some reason, his hearing hadn't improved with age. In crowded bars, ambient sound destroyed all hope of conversation. That was just the thing, there was no ambient sound. No birds squawked from nearby trees, leaves weren't rustling from busy squirrels. Nothing. Except Alloria.

"I'm a princess," she snapped. "Don't shush me."

Angst leaned forward, his lips practically against her ear. Her body stiffened, and she quieted.

"Alloria," he whispered. "I think there is something dangerous nearby. Please, I need to keep you safe. I'm your champion."

She nodded.

"Angst," Ivan called out. "Hurry."

"Wait here," he whispered, once again dismounting the ram. With a deep breath, he wielded both swords and blurred toward Ivan.

In his infinite, long-winded wisdom, Hector had often warned Angst about rushing in. It was so crucial to his mentor that he'd brought it up enough times to bore Angst. "Know your surroundings. Know your opponents. It may be your only advantage when you face insurmountable odds." He was almost glad Hector wasn't here. The old man must've been laughing at him from behind death's door.

Ivan sat on a stump in the middle of a field, surrounded by a dozen Vex'steppe tribesmen. Dark, glistening skin covered their taut muscles, and they had plenty. Towering over them were two enormous red dragons. Three of the tribesmen stood behind Ivan with their spears against his throat. They looked impatient. The others were poised to leap at a breath, and Ivan was one mistake away from losing his head.

The dragons made his heart skip. Sure, he was Al'eyrn times two, but they were large and powerful. Their intelligent golden eyes looked him up and down as liquid-fire drooled from their fierce teeth. The dragons looked hungry, the tribesmen looked ready, and he should've followed Hector's advice.

"Let me go," Alloria said from behind him.

Two tribesmen dragged the flailing princess to Ivan and shoved her to the ground. If words were weapons, they would've all been dead. She lashed out with a round of cursing that made them jump back while a dragon cocked its gigantic head to one side. Rose would've been proud. A sick-looking dagger to her temple forced her tantrum to hide behind gritted teeth. Alloria looked at Angst with a surprising ferocity, leaning into the blade until it drew blood. The tribesmen jerked the weapon away as red trickled down her cheek. She laughed maniacally.

22

Victoria and her party were back on Angst's trail, following at a proper distance, according to Dallow. Rose shared bawdy stories about her frequent visits to the endless party known as The Fette. Dallow's incredulous expression only encouraged her, and, while they weren't her stories, Victoria felt a sense of nostalgia.

Young Victoria wasn't allowed to leave the castle, which was like a handwritten invitation to the princess that said, "Get out." She was caught the first time, and her mother watched as Tyrell lashed her with a belt. The humiliation wasn't the harsh lesson her mother had hoped for. Instead, it infuriated Victoria enough to try again, after some preparation. An unsuspecting Dallow, still new to the library, was more than happy to show her around. It took weeks to find the book she needed and even longer to learn an actual spell. Changing her long, black hair to a strawberry-blond bob, and throwing on a few un-princess-like clothes, was just enough to free Victoria from the confines of royalty. She almost didn't go back. It seemed that her happiest moments were adventures outside the castle. Except, maybe, for this one.

"Rose," Dallow said, sounding aghast.

"Too much?" she asked, innocently.

Everyone nodded, and Victoria was glad she'd been daydreaming. Rose tried leaning over to kiss Dallow. It was hard to tell if he pulled away to be funny or was genuinely concerned where Rose's mouth may have been.

"Jaden and I will scout ahead," Mirim said, her back stiff.

"Is that necessary?" Victoria asked. "Sean has birds and such that will warn us of danger."

"I could use some fresh air," Mirim said, lifting her nose slightly while glancing at Rose.

"Of course, Captain," Victoria said.

Jaden and Mirim rushed ahead on his Bokeen swifen, shuffling around trees and jumping over branches until they were soon out of sight.

"Prude," Rose muttered.

"You go too far, Rose," Victoria said. "It's like you feed off other people's discomfort."

"You didn't stop me," Rose said, flippantly.

"I wasn't listening," Victoria said.

Dallow glanced between Rose and Victoria. This was a growing problem that she'd have to deal with. Rose despised authority. Victoria had known that when she asked the young woman to be her champion, but there was a time and place to hate. Rose's behavior was making it more challenging to lead every day. Dallow was torn between trying to appease the woman he was puppy-loving and being there for his future queen. There was also the growing rift between Dallow and Jaden. She needed both of them, but Jaden was working way too hard to stand out. But the verbal or physical beatings would have to wait. It was more important to learn what had happened at The Fette.

They fell into single file as Rose led them along a thin, winding trail that deer would've struggled to follow. Twenty minutes passed when they came upon Jaden and Mirim towering over two frightened young men. A man with olive skin and long hair huddled close to his muscular, dark-skinned companion. Both were covered in dirt and soot and smelled like a party that had ended days ago.

"They're so pretty," Rose said in wonder.

"They're so naked," Dallow said.

"You're just in time," Mirim said, her tone as sharp as the sword in her hand. "I'm trying to find out if Angst came through, but Kale and Gahn here won't tell us a thing. I'm about to teach them what it means to spill your guts."

The boys now shook as if the only thing keeping them warm was a blanket made of fear.

"Stand down," Victoria said, waving her captain off. She dismounted her pink unicorn swifen and petted its neck.

"She's beautiful," Kale said.

"Come see," Victoria said, beckoning them over.

Like puppies who knew they were in trouble, the two young men slowly stood and inched toward her. They jumped back when the unicorn swifen snorted and pawed at the ground with a golden hoof.

"Cowards," Jaden snorted.

"Why don't you let that huge horn skewer you?" Rose said, defensively.

"Hush," Victoria said over her shoulder. She turned to smile at the men, every bit as warm and gentle as she'd been taught. "It's okay. She's perfectly safe."

The two men took turns petting the swifen's feathery neck or stroking its long nose. The unicorn lowered its head for more attention, making the men smile.

"Didn't you used to have lighter colored hair?" Gahn asked, braving a glance at her. "You were here several years ago. The life of the party."

"See," Rose said. "I told you guys."

"Shush," Victoria said, her tone falling somewhere between embarrassment and admonishment.

"You've been gone a long time," Kale said. "We were all hoping you'd come back."

"She's been busy ruling Unsel," Jaden said. "Soon to be queen, you know."

"What?" Gahn asked. He elbowed Kale, and they both fell to a knee.

Jaden let out an evil chuckle and stopped when he realized

Dallow was laughing too.

"And this is why I prefer traveling with Angst." Victoria shook her head. "Better company, and better at sticking to the plan."

Jaden froze, practically choking on a gasp. It was hard to tell if he was more upset about her preference of traveling companions, or if he suddenly remembered her title was to be kept secret.

"Speaking of Angst." Victoria faced the two half-naked men. "Have you seen a man in his forties traveling with a young blond woman. She would've looked like a tramp. He's stocky, handsome, and very charming."

"I'm going to throw up," Dallow whispered.

"We can share a bucket," Rose said, not whispering enough.

"That sounds like a lot of people," Kale said, looking sideways at Gahn.

"He was…different," she said, hopefully. "Two giant swords on his back…"

They looked at each other, their eyes wide and their faces pale.

"Your Highness," Gahn whispered. "You know we're not supposed to say who comes and goes."

"Tell me," she shouted. With a snap of her fingers, the unicorn disappeared. Both men cowered, now completely unsure where to go. With her thumb pressed against her middle finger, she raised her hand before their eyes and glared at them. "Don't make me snap you away, too."

"We saw him," Kale stuttered.

"Who was he with?" Victoria asked.

"A woman, she was much younger, and pretty with honey blond hair," Kale said. "They went shopping, and then she did look like a—"

"Of course she did," she said. "Go on."

"He was also with two young women," Gahn said. "Twins, both beautiful like you."

"What?" Victoria asked. "Twins?"

"He's made new friends," Rose said.

"Not a surprise," Dallow said, rolling his eyes.

"Where did they go?" Mirim asked

"We were at the back of the party when something attacked," Gahn said. "We ran until we couldn't. We've been lost in the woods ever since."

"You were right, Your Highness," Dallow corrected. "You knew right where to find him."

"Her," Victoria corrected. "Angst isn't always predictable unless he's flirting. Alloria has changed, but it was obvious for her to fall back on her old ways."

"What do we do with these two?" Mirim asked.

"Rose, please give them some food," Victoria said. "Sean, can you help them find their way back to town?"

Kale and Gahn devoured a loaf of bread, some cheese, and a flask of water while Sean stepped away. He returned after several minutes, followed closely by a gray rabbit.

"Bunny," Kale said, pointing to show Gahn.

"Follow it." Simon nodded at the rabbit. "He'll lead you to safety."

And without a bow or dismissal, the two men chased the rabbit through the woods.

"This place doesn't change much." Rose shook her head and smiled. "There's a candle in the window, but no one is home."

"Rose," Victoria said, coolly. "Please lead us the rest of the way."

Rose guided them on foot to The Fette. After ten minutes, the trees opened to a clearing. Rose covered her mouth with a hand and looked back at Victoria in shock.

Somewhere within the unrealistic fantasies of Victoria the teenager, she'd hoped to find Alloria and Angst amidst the party. After ceremoniously dismissing her traitorous cousin (which came in many different forms, from sending her back to prison to beating her senseless), Tori would release her traveling companions from their duties and proceed to enjoy The Fette with Angst. It was the best fantasy because it meant things were somewhat back to normal, at least between her and her best friend.

Victoria the soon-to-be-queen, the leader of this group preparing to go to war with her best friend, was reluctantly becoming a realist. The Fette party must've ended in chaos that frightened away the attendees. A stampede path led from the bonfire through a patch of tents and trampled right over her fantasy.

"Looks like Angst was here," Dallow said.

"You don't understand. It's worse than that," Rose said. "When the party moves, nothing is left behind."

"The Fette leaves no feet," Victoria said.

"What does that mean?" Sean asked.

"They try not to leave a footprint," Rose explained. "Not only taking care of nature as best they can but making it hard for others to locate them if they come back. This is bad."

"Your Majesty," Mirim said. "If I may?"

"Go ahead," Victoria said, conceding command. Her heart was heavy enough to distract her focus. Even as a young teen she'd felt safe at The Fette, and now it was tainted by the scars of war.

"Rose, stay with the princess. Sean, tell your friends to let us know if anyone's coming," Mirim commanded, pointing around the camp's edge. "Everyone else dismount and check for survivors. There are plenty of tents still standing."

Victoria headed straight to the bonfire, delicately traversing the tent maze, hoping she wouldn't stumble over a body. Mirim and Rose followed closely. The dry smell of ash filled her nostrils as they reached the fire pit. It didn't take long to find several oily, black feathers.

"I guess they found him," Rose said.

"Rose, go tell the others to hurry," Victoria said, stiffly. "I don't want to be here if any Berfemmian come back."

A short while later, they gathered at the bonfire.

"There are no bodies amongst the tents," Mirim said, her tone very formal. "I consider this good news and suspect they all escaped."

"Can we be sure?" Victoria asked.

Sean nodded.

"Animals don't exactly keep track of humans," Simon explained. "But there was nothing here for them to, uh, eat after the battle was done."

"Gross," Victoria said. "But good, I guess."

"How did the harpies find Angst?" Rose asked. "Unless he's showing off with lightning, he's just a guy with two giant spatulas on his back."

They all looked at each other for answers. Before Victoria could speak, Jaden let out an uncomfortable cough.

"In my future, harpies are considered the best trackers," Jaden said.

"That would've been good to know," Dallow chided. "Do you know how they track someone? Are they tracking Angst's swords?"

"No," Jaden said, rolling his eyes. "You can't track something magical, like foci. I'm surprised you don't know that."

Dallow grimaced and took a step forward. Victoria held out a warning hand that was enough to stop him, for now.

"In the future, harpies are more bird than human. I once witnessed someone torture a harpy," Jaden said with a shudder. "She eventually explained that they can sense a connection to their prey. Especially lust and love."

"Well, I'm safe," Rose said in a winning tone.

"Liar," Victoria said.

"But really, any strong emotional bond will do," Jaden continued.

"Like hatred or anger," Dallow said.

"Top marks," Jaden said. "You'd make an excellent student."

"It's at least a comfort to know that if the harpies were hunting me," Dallow said, "they'd kill you first."

"Boys," Victoria said with an exhausted sigh.

"Is there any way to throw them off the scent?" Mirim asked.

"None that I'm aware of," Jaden said.

"Do you know how the Berfemmain became harpies, or why they track emotional bonds?" Mirim asked.

"Unfortunately, no," Jaden said.

"Useful," Dallow scoffed.

"Considering how many of us feel something for Angst," Victoria said, looking around, "if they are on the hunt, why aren't they swarming?"

"Sean thinks that if their change happened recently, it might not be complete." The brothers were both nodding.

"Maybe they aren't all instinct," Dallow said. "Maybe they still have free will."

"For now," Nikkola said. "But how long will that last?"

23

Angst had faced more Vex'steppe tribesmen at one time, but that was alone, and there was no risk in throwing caution to the wind. This was different. He couldn't harm Alloria, shouldn't harm Ivan, and the tribesmen hadn't killed anyone. The dark-skinned, scantily clad men with sweat-painted muscles and nervous faces twitched with his every breath, as though he was going to steal the last morsel of food on Ehrde.

The two young dragons glared at Angst hungrily, licking their lips. They were smaller than most he'd seen, only half the height of nearby trees. It would take them several chews to swallow any one of them whole. The warriors standing beside the red-horned beasts shuffled away from the pooling lava that drooled from their mouths.

The poor tribesman in charge of Alloria was menacingly trying not to pierce her temple with a dagger. Blood tricked along her jaw and dripped from her chin. Every time he'd step away, she'd stand and bite at him. It was laughable, but she was doing a much better job at maniacal laughter than Angst ever could.

"Let's see you get us out of this one, hero," Ivan said. He winced as his captor poked the back of his neck with a knife tied to the end of his long staff.

"Don't you dare do that again," Angst said to the tribesman.

The knight jerked as the tribesman jabbed him again.

"Please, stop," Angst said in a deadpan voice.

"I hate you," Ivan said with a flinch as his captor stabbed his ear.

"Well, I guess that means you're serious," Angst said, loudly enough for them all to hear. He slowly drew the swords from his back, and to the awe of every tribesmen, rested them on their tips and let go. They watched in anticipation, waiting for the swords to fall.

"Hi, I'm Angst," he said, rubbing his hands together. "Who's going to die first? My bet is you." He nodded at the one nearest Alloria. The man's eyes darted between Angst and the not-falling swords. "Oh, you're wondering about my foci. I don't need those. At least, not to kill a handful of guys and two little dragons."

"They aren't little," a man near the dragons said defensively.

"Smallest ones I've killed lately," Angst said, placing his fists on his hips.

"Enough," said an older man from the back.

This tribesman was probably Angst's age. It was hard to determine from his physical perfection, jerk, but his calm voice, receding hair, and tired expression were telling. He walked halfway across the clearing and rested his knife-ended staff on the ground, followed by three daggers, a short sword, and a smallish hatchet. As naked as these men were, Angst was shocked at how many weapons the man carried. A bow and three daggers later, he opened his arms in a welcoming gesture.

"We're not hugging," Angst said.

"You aren't very good at this," the man said. "We took your servant and mistress without effort."

"I'm not his servant," Ivan grumbled.

"She's not my mistress," Angst said.

"Not yet, baby," Alloria said.

Angst rolled his eyes. "What is this about?"

"We had to be certain you are the Angst," the man said. "We feared you would attack if we merely approached you, so we took precautions. Even with your power, you couldn't save them and kill us at the same time. We will now parlay while on top of the hill."

"First of all, don't call me the Angst. I sort of like it, but it's pretentious," he said. "Just Angst, now and always."

The man nodded once in acceptance.

His opponent was right about being bad at this. Ignoring Hector's advice to think before attacking was a mistake. Another, often repeated bit of advice from his old mentor was to negotiate from a point of strength, from the high ground, or the top of the hill.

"Second..." His timing had to be perfect, so they understood. With a deep breath, Angst drew enough power from both swords to move as fast as he could.

He blurred to Alloria while simultaneously blasting her captor with air. Even before the man crashed against a nearby tree and crumpled to the ground, Angst had returned to where he started, releasing Alloria, who collapsed. The other tribesmen took a step back while both dragons stood tall and drew in air.

"My hero," she said, hugging his leg and rubbing her cheek against his thigh. "This is why I lo—"

"Ugh," he said, shaking his leg until she quieted. He returned his focus to their leader. "Second, I don't parlay from the bottom of the hill. You're outnumbered."

The other tribesmen laughed; the middle-aged man did not.

"Stop, all of you," he shouted, raising a hand. "What do you mean, outnumbered?"

"Boys," he shouted.

Twenty gamlin of all sizes dove up from the ground as if they were dolphins leaping from water. The hedgehog/porcupine creatures with human faces and practically indestructible hides ranged from two inches to three feet tall. A nervous tribesman threw a dagger that bounced off a larger gamlin. It horted with annoyance. The dragons inched back nervously, surprising every tribesman nearby.

"The gamlin are yours?" Ivan asked, looking around in stunned silence as if the creatures would steal his gold.

"They're so cute," Alloria said, clapping her hands.

"My gamlin eat dragons for dessert. Do we have an under-standing?" Angst asked. "Because it's taking everything I've got to keep them from coring your pets like apples."

"Weapons down," their leader said, an almost-smile creeping up his cheek.

The tribesmen lowered their weapons, and the gamlin turned to look at Angst.

"You did good, kids," Angst said with a nod. "Back into hid-ing, but stay close."

Several of the smaller ones waved before diving back into the ground, leaving nothing more than a small wake of dirt behind.

"Who are you?" Angst asked. "And what's this all about?"

"I'm SMyket," the older man said. "And you're in great dan-ger."

"That would've been news a year ago," Angst said, waving Ivan over. "You're already boring."

Jaws dropped, and SMyket grimaced, gripping his staudauf so hard that the wood handle strained. Maybe it was a bit harsh, but Angst really didn't have the time, or patience, to be cordial.

"If this is how you treat allies," SMyket said, "It's no wonder most on Ehrde hate you."

"Allies?" Angst said. "Allies don't kidnap and threaten my companions."

"We didn't kill them out of respect," SMyket said, looking perplexed. "You apparently do not understand the tribes if you saw that as a threat. Your companions live. That is our gift."

"Sorry I missed something so obvious. It's been a long life, and I seem to have misplaced my courtesy along the way," Angst said, rolling his eyes. "You were going to warn me of something. Please share so we can move on."

"Warbands are after you," SMyket said. "Not just one, but many."

"Who?" Angst asked. "How many?"

"So far, we have counted five parties of twenty to thirty fight-ers," SMyket said. "They are comprised of Fulk'han, Nordruaut, and others from the tribes."

"So, what about you and your friends?" Angst said. "Why all of this?"

"We believe our leader ANduaut is evil," SMyket said. "He is not aware, but we are not with him."

"ANduaut?" Angst asked. "Not the guy Faeoris kept thrashing for turning the Berfemmian away?"

Many of the tribesmen chuckled, a few laughed out loud.

SMyket remained stoic. "You are correct," he said. "ANduaut rejected her, and all Berfemmian, during the mating cycle. He is a fool."

"He really is," Angst said. "She was stuck in her mating cycle when we met and almost sexed me to death. It was everything I could do not to—"

Alloria's glare caught his eye. It was so furious that he took a step back.

"But actually, I didn't even notice her, at the time, when it happened," Angst said, rubbing the back of his neck. "What was ANduaut thinking?"

"ANduaut chooses to lie with men," SMyket said.

"Oh," Angst said. "Well, that's a reason not to have sex with her."

"Yes," SMyket nodded. "But he turned the Berfemmian away from all of us. Only some are like him. The rest are as locked in the same mating cycle as the women. It was a mistake."

"Huge. Huge mistake. No wonder you think he's evil," Angst said, lifting his swords. Blue and red lightning sparked between them, covering his arms and hands. "But that doesn't absolve any of you for what happened in Rohjek."

"No. No, it doesn't," SMyket said, looking at the others.

The tribesmen all bowed their heads in shame. Several covered their eyes, either fighting back tears or the horror of what they'd seen. The entire nation had been wiped out and fed to dragons, so they could nest. It was a horror beyond comprehension.

"Our small group of rebels saw many to freedom," SMyket said. "But it wasn't enough, and too terrible a burden to live with."

Angst understood, because he lived with that same burden of never enough. He let go of the power until the lightning dissipated and rested both swords behind his back. After approaching the warrior slowly, Angst placed a hand on the man's shoulder. SMyket looked up, staring into Angst's eyes, pleading for...something. It was a something that Angst couldn't give himself, but maybe he could help these lost tribesmen.

"No matter how hard I try, despite my best intentions, I always seem to fail," Angst said. His breath caught, and he swallowed it down hard. And then, he lied. "If I didn't forgive myself, if I didn't climb to the top of that hill, if I didn't use all this might for right, then all I'd struggled for and lost would be for naught. You saved some, and you should be proud of that."

It was what SMyket needed to hear, and his pleading eyes became those of a friend. In another life, in a life with time to spare, he would've liked to know this man.

"Thank you," SMyket said, pulling back. "You are truly Al'eyrn."

"There's still a chance we can fix this mess," Angst said. "I may call on you for help."

"We will be with you," SMyket said.

"I'm going to be ill," Ivan snarled. "What about the warbands?"

"In this forest alone, we've seen many Fulk'han and Nordruaut," SMyket said. "If we are able to sneak up on you so easily, you don't stand a chance."

SMyket was right. Had he been so distracted by Alloria's boobs that he'd discarded all sense of precaution? Yes. He'd been so busy shopping for her almost-clothing and flirting with the mysterious twins that he hadn't even considered sending the gamlin on patrol. Hector would've admonished him in the worst way for this, and his cheeks warmed. This was an obvious mistake and one that could've cost him. He'd made assumptions that his power would keep them safe but trying was still necessary.

"Thank you." Angst bowed his head. "We'll find a path or

make one if we have to."

"Are you just going to kill them all?" SMyket asked.

"Yes," Ivan said. "That's what they deserve."

"No," Angst said, staring down the knight. "That's not my way. I want allies, not enemies. Now that SMyket has shaken some sense into me, I'll be on the watch to avoid them. My friends underground will alert me to everyone traveling on foot."

"Not in the air?" SMyket asked. "There are dragons, cavistil birds, and bird women dressed in black feathers with dark wings."

"Harpies," Ivan said.

"Harpies?" SMyket looked at Ivan quizzically.

"No, not harpies," Angst said. "Berfemmian."

The tribesmen all became more attentive, tense, looking at each other with wary eyes. Angst had hoped it was just Marisha, but whatever dark spell had changed her had apparently changed all of them. They were his greatest danger right now. The gamlin could warn him of anyone on the ground, but not in the sky. Without the help of his swords, he may never sleep again.

"Please tell me this is one of your human jokes," SMyket said.

"I wish. Faeoris's *essent* attacked me. She'd been changed into something dark and evil," Angst said. "I didn't realize the change had affected all of them."

"Like the dark that has taken over ANduaut," SMyket said with a deep sigh. "They must be stopped."

"Yes," Angst said. "But try not to kill them. A part of her was still Marisha, like she hadn't completely changed. It's hard to explain, but I won't kill them either. That said, they're more dangerous than ever."

"We will be fine," SMyket said. "They don't hunt for us, just for you. But…our mates… Can you save them?"

"Maybe," Angst said. "If I can do it, my plan will save everyone."

Ivan let out a "*pfft.*"

"Good," SMyket said. "I'm glad we didn't kill you."

"Me too," Angst said with a chuckle. "Are you coming with us?"

"No," SMyket said. "That would just attract attention from the other tribes and put us all at risk. We will die for our beliefs, but we will save that dying until it counts. We will pretend to be on the hunt for you and hopefully guide others away from your path."

"Thank you, SMyket," Angst said. "You know, I think Faeoris would've preferred you to ANduaut."

"Really?" he asked, his eyes so wide it was like Angst had handed him a cookie.

"Yeah," Angst said with a smile. "Hey, can I ask a small favor?" Angst whispered into his ear.

SMyket smiled broadly, nodded once, then raised his hand in a fist. When he opened his hand, the dragons whooshed into the sky, and the Vex'steppe tribesmen were gone like steam on the wind. Angst reached out, searching for minerals, and could sense their bones. They bounded through the woods like antelope. He could feel them but couldn't hear a thing.

"Welp," Angst said. "Everything just stopped being easy. Go figure."

* * * *

The woods were shrouded in shadows by early evening, and Victoria struggled to make out their surroundings. The day's ride had been quiet. Not only was it uneventful, but the threat of a harpy attack made everyone focus on staying alive instead of talking. They probably should've stopped sooner, but she was enjoying the silence. Everyone's fear was her relief from the childish bickering. She'd have to remember that.

"We need a clearing to make camp before it gets too dark," Victoria said, breaking the silence and making a few of them jump. "Sean, can you find us something?"

Sean pointed sleepily from his ferret mount. It was odd, compared to the other swifen. Despite its great size, it looked like a normal ferret with fine brown fur. Maybe it was because he was so close to animals, but Victoria found it disconcerting. The ferret was just too real. The long, slinky rat rode close to the ground, wrapping around corners and scampering up hills. Victoria wasn't a fan of rats, especially giant ones that could bite off a hand.

"Sean says we're close," Simon said.

"Why are the woods so quiet?" Captain Mirim asked.

"Sean says we're safe," Simon said.

"Sean says a lot for not saying anything," Nikkola said.

The almost-bickering was enough to tighten the knot between Victoria's shoulders. She really wanted a hot rose-petal bath in her favorite copper tub. The hotter, the better. At this point, she'd be happy to be cooked in a stew with an apple in her mouth if it meant relaxed muscles.

Minutes later, they crested a hill to find Sean's clearing. It was the perfect amount of space for a campsite, and Victoria's sigh was deep enough to reach her chafing thighs. She'd spent plenty of time riding, and flying her swifen, but not in armor. Still, she looked pretty and fierce, making it easy to deal with the discomfort.

"What's that?" Jaden asked, drawing his Bokeen mount to a halt. He pointed at a dark, unmoving mass in the middle of their future campsite.

"Dallow," Victoria said. "Would you mind creating some light?"

"Wouldn't that attract attention?" he asked, warily.

"It would be better than falling into a giant, open mouth," Rose said.

"A what?" Dallow asked.

"I've seen things," she said. "So have you. Remember the flying holes on our way to Fulk'han?"

"Right," he said. He whispered something in Acratic.

Victoria had expected something akin to torchlight, but instead, Dallow impressed. The clearing was completely visible, as though flooded with light from a white sun. Like sunlight, it was everywhere, but the whiteness gave an eerie, unnatural sheen to everything it touched.

"Neat," Jaden said.

"Dragon," Sean said, leaping from his ferret and rushing ahead.

"Now he talks?" Nikkola asked.

"He doesn't stop talking," Simon said, rolling his eyes. "At least not to me."

"Shouldn't we be fleeing in panic?" Mirim asked, her voice shaky but her sword at the ready.

"I'm pretty sure it would've eaten us already," Jaden said, sliding off the side of the Bokeen swifen. "If it were alive."

The dragon was much smaller than the mother Victoria had seen Angst kill. This one was only the size of a barn. Several spears protruded from its shoulders and wings. Even as Sean patted its triangular head, it didn't move. Didn't breathe.

"Is anyone else concerned that a bunch of someones killed a dragon in our new campsite?" Rose asked. "Maybe we should find somewhere else to make camp. Like twenty miles from here."

"I'm okay to keep riding," Nikkola said. "I don't think I ever need to sleep again."

"There's nothing to be afraid of," Jaden said. He approached the beast and set a foot on its shoulder, placing his fists in a heroic pose against his waist.

"If you say so." Victoria giggled. He was being cute, which was frustrating when she was supposed to be angry at him.

Mirim dismounted Jaden's swifen and walked around the dragon several times. "It's not breathing, Your Highness," she said, jerking a spear from its wing. She looked at it quizzically. "That's odd. It wasn't actually in the dragon."

"Eye," Dallow said, pointing. "Eye."

The dragon blinked, and its broad mouth pulled back in a toothy grin.

"Dragon," Sean said once more, patting its wing.

The monster reared up, making everyone leap away. It stood to full height, looked up at the sky, and let loose a bellow of dragon fire.

"Mirim," Victoria said, her heart pounding. "Mirim. This is it. This is your moment. What do we do?"

"Run!" Mirim shouted.

Mirim, Jaden, and Sean ran to their swifen and scrambled to mount them.

"Where to?" Victoria asked.

"Anywhere," Mirim said. "The Fette, Potterton, just go!"

And they did go, as fast as they could while the mighty dragon blasted fire high into the night sky. As they were leaving, Victoria heard something. Or did she? She couldn't have. It sounded like a man—no, men—laughing at them as they rushed away into the night.

24

Waiting was his favorite, and Alloria loved making him wait. She'd left to take care of business and would be back in "a few." According to his internal Alloria clock, "a few" should've ended by now. Leaving him with Ivan only made it seem longer. Thirty minutes alone with the knight had been as entertaining as cleaning a chalkboard with a nail file.

"If I have to listen to you sigh one more time, I might tear off my ears," Ivan said. "Rather than knocking me off my horse again, why don't you go find your girlfriend?"

"Fine," Angst said, not-sighing.

He'd been reluctant to go looking for her. Chances were she was chatting with squirrels and rabbits. There was a greater possibility her clothes had "fallen off," and she was pretending to drown in a shallow pond. That would lead to another argument he didn't have the energy for. Ivan tearing off his ears sounded more fun.

Reaching out with his mind, he sought the immediate area for bones. It took several minutes; the forest was busy with deer and fox and more than a few critters. A quarter-mile away, he finally sensed the bones of something substantial beside something small. The more massive creature could've been anything from a baby dragon to a giant red bear.

"Always something." He grunted, drawing both swords and blurring to them.

CHAPTER TWENTY FOUR

It had been a while since he'd seen a Vex'kvette monster wandering through Ehrde. This one wasn't any prettier than the others. The orange river created by Magic must've merged two men, made them a giant, and, of course, given the creature a third arm. Its legs and torso were human-like and dense with muscles and two autonomous heads were set evenly between broad shoulders.

The heads could've easily come from brothers—their eyes, noses, and ears were similar. One had a rounder face and gray hair while the other was bald. Both men had kind faces, leaving Angst reluctant to break up the party until he saw Alloria.

The third arm was apparently attached to its back, because monster. It reached over the two heads, dangling an angry princess between them. She swung wildly with a small dagger, spinning around and screaming in frustration. The arm moved toward one face, and then the other, as though undecided who got the snack.

"It's my turn, Brent," the bald one said, licking his lips.

"But I'm hungry, Scott," Brent said, urging the arm over.

"We have the same stomach," Scott said with a frown.

"But I like chewing them," Brent complained.

Alloria rocked back and forth as the third arm struggled to find a home. Apparently, they both had some control over the appendage—or maybe lack of control.

The last time he'd fought a monster like this, he'd cut its stomach open and been showered in guts. Rushing in to cut the monster in half could leave him in a similar state. Plus, if they dropped Alloria from that height and Angst didn't catch her in time, she would die. Based on his recent run of luck when rushing in, he considered another approach and set down his swords.

"Whoa, whoa, whoa," Angst said as he stepped toward them, holding out both hands. "Whatever you do, don't eat that one."

"But I found her," Brent said. "I get to eat her."

"You didn't find her," Scott said, reaching up with the arm on his side and smacking his brother's face. "I found her!"

Brent's head lolled to one side as he reeled from the strike.

The third arm holding Alloria moved closer to Scott's mouth.

"She'll make you sick. She's way too much for you to handle," Angst said. He muttered, "I think she's too much for me to handle."

Scott held her before his nose and sniffed deeply. "She smells fine."

"Good," Brent said. "Then she's safe for me to eat."

Alloria continued taking wild swipes with her dagger, her blows bouncing off harmlessly. So far, Angst had been equally effective. There had to be another way.

"Isn't it Scott's turn?" Angst called out.

"Yeah," Scott said, the arm jerking to his side. "My turn."

"But Brent," Angst said. "You found her. Don't you deserve to eat her?"

"She's mine," Brent shouted, forcing the arm in his direction.

"Don't take that from him, Scott," Angst said, trying not to laugh. He cleared his throat and waited a moment before saying, "Brent, are you going to let him talk to you that way?"

Brent swung, his fist connecting with Scott's cheek just as the other fist struck Brent's nose. The hands grappled and slugged as the two fought like angry siblings. The third arm seemed confused, torn between what to do with Alloria and which head to smack.

The monster stumbled, and the third arm tossed Alloria aside. Angst rushed forward to catch her and blur back out of reach. Now free from holding the princess, the third arm took turns with the two heads, poking eyes and tugging on ears.

In a final attempt to win dinner, both hands reached up to clutch their brother's neck. Angst set Alloria down, unable to hold back laughter as the Brent-Scott monster collapsed to its knees. They both gasped for air, unwilling to give up their hold. After several long, gurgly minutes, it fell forward to collapse on its faces.

"That was great," Angst said. "I don't think I want to kill them."

Alloria faced away, holding herself and rocking back and

forth. She must've been scared out of her mind, and he admonished himself for not checking on her immediately. He approached her slowly, gently placing his hands on her shoulders.

Spinning around, she lashed out with her dagger, slicing deep across his chin. Angst leaped back as she swung again and again. The young woman roared in fury, her eyes wild.

"Alloria, stop," he shouted.

She continued her wild attack, finally overreaching enough to provide him an opening. Angst slapped her across the cheek, and she collapsed, dropping the dagger.

"What was that?" he yelled, grasping his blood-slick chin.

"What?" she asked weakly, shaking her head. Her eyes widened as she looked up. "Angst, you're hurt. What happened?"

Alloria drew a pink, silk handkerchief from nowhere and pressed it against the wound. When her eyes fell on the two-headed creature, she jerked back.

"Did the monster do this to you?" she fumed. "I'll kill it."

"It's okay. I'll heal," Angst said, torn between fright and concern. "It was a monster, but we'll leave it alone. Not all monsters should be killed."

25

The Nordruaut practically sprinted through their own nation, but the dire wastelands of Rohjek slowed them to a brisk jog, and eventually a stiff walk. As their pace faltered, so did their banter, as if the ashen wasteland had coated their tongues.

Thick layers of soot and grime covered the ground like sand in a desert. It was deep enough for Jintorich to get lost in and spongy enough to make Tarness's calves sore if he had to walk for any distance. The ash that closely followed their wake had the tangy, familiar taste of death. Most Nordruaut remained perched on their hairy Bokeen, enormous six-legged hippos with moppy brown hair. Even though the ash was hardly an obstacle for them to trudge through, it plumed into the air, forcing them to spread out so those in the back could breathe.

By the third night, they came to realize the importance of stopping early enough to dig out camp. Each of them looked like thieves that had snuck down the chimney to try to steal fresh air. Masks of cloth kept them from coughing, but nothing could protect their eyes.

"Can't you magic something, Al'eyrn?" Rasaol snapped at Niihlu. "Make all of this go away!"

"The foci tell me nothing," Niihlu said, shaking his head and creating a small cloud of ash. "They merely give me power."

"Fah, two foci and still useless," Rasaol barked before turning on Maarja. "Where are you leading us, woman?"

"Show my wife respect," Tarness said, glaring at the king, "or I will teach you."

"Is that a challenge, man-child?" Rasaol said, flexing arms that could've carried his Bokeen.

"Show my husband respect," Maarja said, "or I will teach you."

Maarja smiled at Tarness and nodded. He was still learning their code of chivalry. In Unsel, knights would fight to protect the honor of fair maidens. In Nordruaut, they simply had each other's backs. You don't hold the door for a woman just because, you hold the door open for the person whose arms were full because it was right. Threatening Rasaol wasn't just about Nordruaut honor. His short time with the Eastern Nordruaut had been filled with more than a little coddling. He'd enjoy the opportunity to bloody a nose or three.

"A challenge here and now is a waste of time," Gose said. "But I will champion Tarness if needed."

"I'm ready to champion myself," Tarness said. He dismounted his swifen and landed solidly in the ash, which almost reached his waist. It didn't help his temper, and that familiar resolute power of his magic began to swell inside. His strength and immobility increased with his anger, and Rasaol's size wouldn't matter. "Let's go."

"Majesty," Niihlu said through a sneer. "This human is powerful with the magics. He bested me in a challenge."

"And we all know how incapable you are," Rasaol thundered. "I've wanted to teach this pig a lesson since—"

That was enough to make Tarness snap, and with little effort, he shoved the king's Bokeen over. The beast bleated as it tipped over. There was a loud snap as it landed on Rasaol's leg, and those watching grimaced in pain. A plume of ash drove everyone back.

Tarness sighed and shook his head. After walking around the Bokeen, he pushed it upright, patting it firmly before offering Rasaol a hand.

"We can war with each other, here and now," Tarness said.

"Or we can march to the drums and bring war to our enemies."

Rasaol stared at Tarness, his hand, and the mount. A waiting silence hung in the air for everyone who watched. Tarness reached out once again, meeting Rasaol's eyes. The king's sigh ended in a cough.

"This ash is not natural, or healthy," Tarness said. "Lead us through this so we can save Ehrde and return home."

Rasaol looked at Tarness as if he'd just met the man. With a nod, he took Tarness's hand and stood on one foot. Niihlu smiled in approval as if his loss had been vindicated. Tarness grimaced. He was angry enough to challenge both of them at once. They still deserved a good bending.

"You are indeed Nordruaut, son," Rasaol said, sounding kingly once more. "And I am an old man distraught with what has happened to our neighbors. We had great respect for those of Rohjek, but I wouldn't wish this on our enemies. Not even the Fulk'han."

"Probably not," Tarness said with a smirk, his anger slowly seeping from him.

Several nearby chuckled. Rasaol nodded to Maarja, the best apology that could be expected from royalty. It was enough.

"We will continue south to the dragon nest," Maarja said. "One more day if we push hard."

"And then?" Rasaol asked.

"We head to the border of Melkier and search for your army," Maarja said. "Or Angst."

"Lead the way," Rasaol said, looking up at the Bokeen warily.

"If I may, Your Majesty," Jintorich squeaked. "Allow me to fix that leg. I used to be a physician."

"Amongst other things," Tarness said.

"I am one," Jintorich said with a wink. "One of many."

* * * *

On the fourth day, they approached the dragon's nest with

caution. From several miles, it looked like a clump of red grass in an empty tundra, shrouded by foul clouds of death. Like a distant mountain, it was farther away than expected and much larger up close. Dull red crystals of various sizes jutted out, as though breaking free from the ground's confinement. The crystals were three times taller than any Nordruaut and clearly formed a complex, circular shape.

"What happened here?" Rasaol asked, his voice tight.

"When our party reached the edge of Unsel, we were surprised that Rohjek had become a land of ash. Angst and I scouted ahead to learn what had happened," Maarja said. She turned to Tarness. "Your little friend flirted the entire way."

"Heh." Tarness shook his head. "Sounds like Angst."

"This doesn't bother you?" she asked.

"He's harmless," Tarness said, knowing his friend's charm wasn't for everyone.

"Hmf." Maarja raised her chin. "We discovered this nest and heard moans from inside. Angst wanted to investigate even though I told him we should leave. It was obviously a trap, but he insisted. That man can be very frustrating."

"You've noticed," Tarness said.

She nodded. "I threw him over the side, and he landed on an egg, killing a baby dragon. In an attempt to climb out, he discovered humans alive. They were imprisoned in the crystals, food for the baby dragons. That's when their mother arrived. She wasn't happy."

"I guess Angst wasn't either," Tarness said with a nod.

Maarja led them to the damaged section of the nest. The crystals along the side were singed, and then melted, and then gone entirely. From this angle, the round nest now looked more like a horseshoe. The layer of ash was low enough to reveal twenty leathery eggs—each the size of a Nordruaut. Tarness and Jintorich dismounted and made their way to a baby that hadn't made it, its decomposed head leaning over the edge of the egg. Tarness whistled.

"Angst sent me to gather the others," she said. "When we arrived, the mother dragon was already dead, and he was facing down a hundred tribesmen."

"It must've been a small dragon," Niihlu said, haughtily. "I'm surprised the human didn't become food like the rest of Rohjek."

Jintorich's staff glowed as he held a hand to his mouth and blew a kiss toward a distant mound of ash. Wind cleared a path toward the mound until finally reaching his target. Within moments, the ash was gone, revealing the enormous, diamond-shaped head of the mother dragon. The head was larger than four Bokeen, and everyone gasped or took a step back.

"He...killed that, and then fought the tribes?" Niihlu swallowed hard. "That's crazy."

"That's a lot of power," Rasaol said, his voice shaky.

"That's Angst," Tarness said with a nod.

"Why did you bring us here, woman?" Niihlu snapped. "We are in a hurry, and don't have time for this."

"It was not out of the way, man," Maarja said, her tone dangerously calm. "And you have to know what we're dealing with. You all have to know. Angst is not just a human. Al'eyrn are dangerous, and he has two foci."

All heads turned to Niihlu, and then Jintorich.

"Don't look at me," Jintorich said, his tall ears twitching. "I only have one."

"What chance do we have if he truly has gone mad?" Bryymel asked, rubbing sweat from his bald head.

"That's the question, isn't it?" Tarness said, loud enough for everyone to hear. "If my friend has gone crazy, we may all die trying to stop him. But this? This wasn't the act of a crazy man. The dragons here were killed by a hero." The ruby ring on his finger burned, and his tongue slowed. Unable to say more, he looked to Jintorich for help.

"I believe my friend's concerns should be ours," Jintorich said. "Do we stop a madman, or help a hero?"

"He killed Jarle," Bryymel said. "The answer is obvious."

"I didn't see him kill Jarle," Jintorich said, looking at Bryymel. "Did you?" He looked at Rasaol. "Or you?" His large navy marble eyes fell on Tarness. "Or even you, my friend?"

Tarness could barely shake his head, and the rest remained silent.

"I don't wish to remain here," Rasaol finally said. "Or anywhere in Rohjek."

"We are three days march," Gose said. "It's possible to cross over to Fulk'han in two or Unsel in one. But if we are met with resistance, it will slow our progress."

As the others conferred, Jintorich bounded over to Tarness. The Meldusian's head barely peeked out of the ash. His thick eyebrows may have been frowning, it was hard to tell.

"Are you all right?" he asked.

The heat surrounding Tarness's finger was gone, and he moved his tongue around his mouth. Finally, he nodded, swallowing down the shame that he wasn't strong enough to break this shackle.

"We should go," Jintorich said. "Now is the best time."

"What do I say?" Tarness whispered.

"You could try the truth," Jintorich said. He was definitely frowning now.

"I doubt the ring will let me," Tarness grumbled, "and I don't feel like being pummeled into dragon food."

"What are you two planning now?" Maarja asked. "More training?"

Tarness looked from her to Jintorich. The little man sighed.

"Yes, my friend," Jintorich said. "As a part of Tarness's training, I must bring him to the Mendahir."

"Oh?" Maarja asked. "When do we leave."

"It should be just the two of us," Jintorich continued. "If you recall, they didn't exactly invite you back to visit."

Maarja stared at Jintorich for a long time before her distrusting eyes fell on Tarness. It was unfair that he had such a hard time reading his wife yet felt transparent before her gaze.

"Is this what you wish, husband?" Maarja asked.

"It is best this way," Tarness said, his throat dry, but not from ash.

"We won't be long," Jintorich said.

"How will you find me when you are done?" Maarja asked.

"I used to be a tracker," Jintorich said. "It will be easy."

"Hurry back to me," Maarja said, giving Tarness the barest of kisses. She turned away, crossing her arms.

"You're in trouble," Jintorich said.

"You can tell?" Tarness asked. "I was hoping that was worry."

Maarja made her way back to the group, roughly shoving Bryymel with a shoulder. He took a step back and cowered.

"Nope, not worry," Jintorich said. "We should hurry, before she changes her mind."

26

The fall air was crisp enough to clear Angst's head. The near-by trees were just starting to change color, and he had plenty of time to appreciate it. They rode slowly through the woods, held back by the speed of Ivan's stallion and wary of surprise attacks. Angst was paying attention now, a little more than less, and hopefully the gamlin would warn them of impending doom.

Ivan led the way, only several paces ahead. His head leaned back as if looking down his nose at the world, and his silence made him seem haughty. It grated Angst's nerves but was still better than the knight falling off his horse and continuously getting sick all over himself like their first outing.

Angst wanted to ask Ivan questions. How had he come back? Why was he willing to work for Magic? Why wasn't he a tree? He appreciated the knight's silence far more than answers he probably wouldn't have liked anyway.

"Can you wish for more wishes?" Alloria asked, her voice a little dreamy.

Ivan let out a "*pfft*" that Angst tried to ignore.

"I don't really know how it works," Angst said, smiling at the thought. "That sounds nice, but I doubt it."

"Why not?" Alloria asked.

"Just a theory," Angst said, "but I'm sure there are rules. If not, an element could wish to always win. I can't imagine one of them haven't tried."

"Well," Alloria said, pondering. "Maybe you could wish that I get a wish."

"I will certainly try," Angst chuckled.

"Really?" she asked, turning her head to try to look at him.

"Sure," he said.

She squeed a little, and Ivan's head rolled forward as he sighed.

"What would you wish for?" Angst asked. "Other than more wishes."

She leaned back into him, placed her hand on the back of his head, and pulled it down so she could whisper in his ear.

"Alloria!" he said, his cheeks and ears burning.

She laughed and laughed as he awkwardly cleared his throat. As always, she was more shocking than flattering. Those fantasies were supposed to be his and not whispered into his ear by someone else. She was all walls and no boundaries and far beyond his ability to manage. It took her a long while to compose herself.

"Or," he said. "If that wasn't an option. Ever."

"Don't get old on me," she said. "Poppa."

"Gross," Ivan muttered.

"Never," Angst said. "Not a 'poppa' and not getting old. So, about your wish…"

"I'd have my revenge," she said very calmly.

"Oh?" he asked, a little concerned.

"I would wish that Magic experienced everything he put me through, and worse, for the next two thousand years."

Ivan sat upright and cocked his ear toward them.

"Torture, humiliation," she said, her voice singsonging despite her shaking hands. "I would pour all my hatred into that wish so he could suffer like the elements have made everyone suffer. Like he made me suffer."

Angst took Alloria's hands in his, and her breathing caught. He couldn't even imagine what the beast had put her through, and he squeezed gently. No wonder the poor thing was crazy.

"He deserves that and more," Angst said softly. "And when I

destroy him, I'll do everything I can to make it hurt."

She nodded, pulling his arms around her in a hug.

"What about you, Ivan?" Angst said, wishing to change the subject. "Would you wish for your life back?"

"No," Ivan said. "No, I'd wish for everything to be set right."

"What does that mean?" he asked.

"I want peace," Ivan said. "A paradise like none have seen."

"I've seen your paradise," Angst spat. "I saw what you did to the Fulk'han women. You twisted them all into something obscene."

"Into something magnificent," Ivan said, proudly. "You can't tell me you didn't like what you saw."

Of course he'd liked the women. They were sex walking. Large breasts and full lips and shapely legs were Angst's favorite, even if the fur and tail were inhuman. The men, however, were practically identical, with pale gray skin, protruding ribs, and turtle-shell armor that grew from their bodies.

"But that's not what *they* wanted, is it?" Angst asked. "They didn't ask to be twisted into your dark fantasy. They were already perfect in their own way."

"Humans aren't perfect," Ivan said, his tone disgusted.

"By definition, nothing is perfect. Not humans or elements or Ehrde," Angst said. "It's our imperfections that make us amazing. The gift of life, the innocence of youth, the struggle to become something better. That will to survive and achieve is something pure. I would call that perfection."

"And is that what you want to waste your wish on?" Ivan said.

"I just want to save my family," Angst said quietly.

"Your family?" Ivan asked.

"Fire killed them. I'm surprised you didn't know," Angst said. "I would've assumed that Magic told his minions everything."

"That fool," Ivan said, almost too quietly to hear. "No, I wasn't aware. I'm sorry for your loss. This may surprise you, but out of respect, Magic wouldn't have done that."

That did surprise him. Ivan had no reason to say it. He was rarely kind.

"I don't believe you," Angst said. "Magic will do anything to win."

"The elements typically disregard humans as ants, but they respect Al'eyrn," Ivan said. "Most wouldn't do something so rash as to encourage their wrath."

"How comforting," Angst said, dryly. He didn't believe a word Ivan said. The elements used humans, and despite the power Al'eyrn wielded, they were still human.

"Believe what you will," Ivan said. "But Al'eyrn hold great power, and now that you wield two foci, even you don't know—"

"Stop," Angst said, holding up a hand and willing his swifen to halt.

"Oh, now what?" Ivan scoffed. "Do you two need more time in a tent?"

"Yes," Alloria said, hopefully.

"That would be a lot more fun," Angst whispered. "Gamlin are warning me that there's a war band of Nordruaut ahead."

"How many?" Ivan unsheathed his sword.

"Gamlin can't count," Angst said. "But I can sense quite a few. "

"Kill them," Ivan said. "Use those two big knives of yours to dice them so we can move on."

"Yeah, baby," Alloria said. "Can't you make a path?"

What had he gotten himself into? He wasn't a murderer. Even if these Nordruaut wanted to stop them, even if they were enemies, that didn't mean they deserved to die.

"Maybe I could just knock them out," Angst pondered.

"And maybe I could just ask them to leave," Ivan said, rolling his eyes.

"Ha." Alloria laughed and then said. "That wasn't funny."

"Let me go see," he said. "You two wait here."

"You're leaving me with him?" Alloria asked, gripping Angst's arm.

"He knows the consequences of even looking at you funny," Angst said, staring down the knight with a raised eyebrow. "Don't you, Ivan?"

"I could care less about this one," he said with a sneer. "I won't do anything that gets us, or me, attacked."

"Be careful." Alloria kissed Angst on the cheek.

He smiled and nodded, grateful it wasn't followed by sappy declarations of love or overdramatic pleas. Sane Alloria was his favorite Alloria. He dismounted his great steel ram and drew both swords from his back.

The gamlin had, sort of, indicated that there were 'many biggies' nearby. Their descriptions were as vague as they were alien and didn't translate well. At least the gamlin had warned him, but his plan of attack required more. Was Tarness there? Could he possibly be traveling with Maarja? Or was it the other guys?

If it was Niihlu and friends, Angst would, indeed, carve a path. He blamed Niihlu and that Lurp creature for Hector's death. Sure, heroes were supposed to seek justice, but the wave of revenge and remorse that struck him washed away any consideration of heroics. Niihlu was evil, and death was coming for that Nordruaut and any who rode with him.

The cold of hatred passed as the familiar buzzing from the gamlin led him to the giants. Like painting, hiding his feelings, and walking in a straight line when he was drunk, sneaking wasn't his gift. He half-considered giving up and announcing himself after the first five steps, each one crunching leaves and sticks like he was a herd of cows. His armor had never been louder and needed oil like he needed a bath. He was downwind, of course, and these natural-born hunters were probably sniffing him out already.

Angst stumbled on the camp and hurried to hide behind a tree. They were heart-skippingly close. Despite having spent time with the Nordruaut, especially Maarja, there was something about their size that was disconcerting. Their proportions made them appear like any other human, except they were two to three times his size. They were covered in furs and leathers earned from their hunts. Every Nordruaut had long platinum hair, dark tans, and war paint on their faces. Sure, he could probably take them being bonded with both swords, and with the help of gamlin, but that was still a probably. While the Berfemmian and Vex'steppe tribesmen were the two most dangerous races on Ehrde, Nordruaut came in a very close third.

Sweat trickled down his cheek as he counted ten. The small number meant some Nordruaut could be out hunting. Waiting around to be prey seemed like a bad idea. No Tarness, no Jintorich, and no Niihlu meant that these were innocent bystanders—innocence being relative. According to Ivan, this was the direction they needed to go, so he had to get rid of them without starting World War Ehrde.

"C'mon, guys," Angst whispered over his shoulder. "Foci know everything. Can't you help me a little?"

Nothing, not even a spark. Angst sighed. The two swords were acting like children upset at having to go visit the crazy aunt who pinched cheeks too hard and made lousy food. He really needed to hash out this silent treatment with them before reaching Prendere, but now was not the time.

The familiar buzz of gamlin filled his mind. They were ready to fight, but he didn't need murder, he needed the Nordruaut to leave. He had an idea.

* * * *

"That was surprisingly easy," Angst said, with a smug smile as he returned.

Alloria was facing away from Ivan with her arms crossed. Her cheeks practically glowed red. Ivan peered at her and said nothing, as if biting his tongue.

"I said, that was surprisingly easy," Angst said more firmly. His simple solution deserved at least some recognition.

"My hero," Ivan said, tearing his eyes away from Alloria.

"Thanks," Angst said, dryly, looking back and forth between them. "But I think that's her line."

"Heh," Alloria said, readjusting her tiara.

"Did he hurt you?" Angst asked as he approached her.

"I'm fine," Alloria muttered, her tone dark.

"I could break him," Angst said, placing his hands on her shoulders. "If that'd make it better."

She spun about, buried her face into his shoulder and wept. Angst looked for blood or bruises but saw nothing. He glared at Ivan, who stared at the ground with a self-satisfied smirk. She gasped for breath, and he petted her hair until she was done.

"We should hurry," Angst said. "The Nordruaut won't be gone long."

"Then let's go," she said suddenly, looking up at him with wide eyes and a broad grin.

Those eyes were far, far too old for seventeen. How much of that smile was crazy, and how much of it hid everything she'd gone through? Angst brushed a strand of honey brown hair from her face, and she leaned her head into his hand.

"Shall I scout ahead?" Ivan asked. Angst could practically hear his eyes roll.

"You can shut your dumb mouth," Angst snapped.

He pulled away slowly and mounted the ram before offering Alloria a hand. There were times that she felt like a crate of shaken eggs, perfect on the outside with a messed-up center. Even if he didn't know what to do about it, he had to keep reminding himself of that center.

They rode slowly toward the Nordruaut camp, trying to minimize their noise.

"Wow," Alloria said when they arrived. "How many were there?"

"I counted ten," Angst said. "There may be more. They like to hunt."

Ivan hopped off his mount.

"What are you doing?" Angst asked. "We need to get out of here."

The knight grabbed a giant leg of cooked something and placed the heavy end in his satchel. Enough meat and bone stuck out that Angst half expected it to fall back to the ground. Ivan mounted his stallion and nodded. "It'll feed us for days."

"Fine," Angst said. "Anything else? Did you need a blanket or some pillows?"

"Ha," Ivan said. "But you are correct. From the size of their camp, we should move on. I'd hate to deal with that mess of Nordruaut. How did you get rid of them, anyway?"

"Well," Angst said. "It's funny you should ask…"

* * * *

The first day's silence was welcome, but after encountering the dragon, Victoria longed for the quick banter of Angst and his friends. Rose led the conversation with this group, and it was always biting and snarky. It was as if the power from bonding with a foci, or her position as champion, had gone to her head. While Victoria shared the occasional exhausted glance with Mirim, poor Dallow looked defeated.

"Stop," Sean said, bringing his ferret to a halt.

The second time Sean spoke to the group wasn't the goofy dragon-love he'd expressed earlier.

"I think I liked it better when he didn't talk," Nikkola said nervously.

Captain Mirim slid off Jaden's Bokeen swifen and placed an ear to the ground.

"Something's coming fast," she said. "Can you feel the—"

The ground shook as leaves on the forest floor began to hop. Without warning, a gamlin leaped from the ground and landed in Victoria's arms. Its cute frown made her smile, and she immediately wanted to hug the creature but was wary of its knife-edged spines.

"Hi," she said. "Are you okay?"

It opened its mouth, letting out a hort. The creature's face contorted in frustration.

"Angst must be near," Victoria said. "I'm sure he's sending us a message. What is it, little guy?"

After some sort of internal struggle, the gamlin finally said,

"Run."

"They talk?" Mirim asked, her eyes wide.

"No," Victoria said as the gamlin dove back into the ground. "At least, they didn't used to."

"And they used to be cute," Nikkola said. "Now they're creepy."

"Nordruaut," Simon said. "Sean says they're chasing gamlin and heading this way."

"Felk," Rose said.

"What do we do, Mirim?" Victoria asked.

"Run," Mirim said, scrambling back up onto the giant swifen. "By the Dark Vivek, run!"

And once again, they ran.

27

When the border of life and death that separated Unsel and Rohjek came into view, they sighed in relief. Tarness and Jintorich looked at each other, nodded once, and pushed their swifen faster than any horse could've traveled. Tarness glanced over his shoulder to see a cloud of ash following them like a trail of signal fires pointing anything hungry their way. It was worth the risk. Long, depressing days through the ash-ridden wasteland were finally behind them, and Unsel was merely a swifen stride away. Unsel was safe. Unsel was home.

They raced past the border until they reached a field of grass barely touched by ash. Tarness dismissed his obsidian stallion before it came to a full stop and landed in a sprawl. He breathed in the sweet smell of life before rolling over and closing his eyes.

"Are you all right?" Jintorich asked, delicately sliding off his watery dragonfly swifen.

"Getting there," Tarness said, gripping handfuls of warm, sweaty grass.

"What are you doing?" Jintorich asked.

"I'm loving everything green," Tarness said, making the word green last as long as his breath. He rolled over again, just because he could, and stretched. "I can't tell you how much I've missed green. Between the constant Nordruaut winter, and the ashen fields of Rohjek, it feels like it's been forever."

"Are we going to roll around in the grass naked now?" Jintorich asked. "I love being naked."

"Nope," Tarness said, sitting up quickly. "Uh, allergies."

"Oh," Jintorich said, his tall ears drooping. He took several deep gulps of air before letting out a tiny, rabbit sigh. "This beauty is almost worth the lies."

"Yeah, those," Tarness said, his stomach clenching.

"I'm not a liar," Jintorich said, softly. "And yet I lied to your wife, my best friend."

"I'm sorry," Tarness said as the joy washed away, leaving behind something bitter.

"It's going to take a lot of apologies," Jintorich said. "From both of us."

"I hear flowers are good," Tarness said.

"And pie." Jintorich nodded, his ears perking a little. "My wife loved rubunberry pie."

"I didn't know you were married," Tarness said, sitting up and leaning back on his arms.

"I... Well, yes, I..." Jintorich cocked his head to one side and frowned.

"What was her name?" Tarness asked. "Tell me about her. That is, if you feel like it."

"I don't... I—" Jintorich's body seemed to stiffen, and he tugged at his ears frantically. "Remembering is hard."

"Uh." Tarness didn't know what to do. Jintorich looked like he felt when Magic's ring kept him from speaking. "Maybe just tell me what she looked like."

"No," Jintorich shouted. His body convulsed, slowly at first until he vibrated unnaturally fast. Ghostly Meldusian faces peeked out from his bulbous head, each of them looking around before returning. A dozen blurry arms reached out from his chest and back. His ears grew then shrank then grew again.

"Jin?" Tarness asked, not sure if he should hug him or run away before the explosion.

Jintorich opened one mouth and let out a glass-breaking scream. His staff glowed brighter and brighter. Tarness could only cover his ears and squeeze his eyes shut as the maddening pot boiled over and over into his brain.

Silence. A silence so abrupt it was jarring. Tarness shifted his jaw until his ears popped then opened his eyes to see Jintorich inches from his face. The deep blue orbs were intense enough to make him jerk back.

"What was that?" Tarness asked.

"I am one," Jintorich said, calmly. "One of many."

"One of too many," Tarness said. "You care to explain what that means?"

"I care," Jintorich said, holding himself and staring at the ground. "But I can't explain."

"It's okay, Jin. Maybe the Mendahir can help you too," Tarness said.

Jintorich merely nodded. His eyebrows were frazzled, and his ears drooped.

"Things are weird," Tarness said, hoping to calm his friend. "I'm married to a woman twice my size, the elements are now living beings, or were, and my best friend thinks he's one of them."

"Is he?" Jintorich asked, his head popping up. "Or is he going crazy?"

"Not my boy," Tarness said, resolutely. "Not Angst. I believe in him. He always wanted to be a hero, but you don't always get what you want. He's just in over his head, like usual. That's why I came back, to help him sort it out so we can save the day."

"He sounds like a good friend," Jintorich said. "Someone who would always be there for you."

"No, that's impossible," Tarness said, leaning back on his arms. "Too much can go wrong for someone to always be there. But Angst has been there when it counts."

"When I traveled with Angst, he was always polite, but also distant," Jintorich said.

"Don't take it personally." Tarness chuckled. "He doesn't have many friends who are men."

"He certainly liked Faeoris," Jintorich said.

"Doesn't everyone?" Tarness asked, raising his eyebrows.

They sat in silence for a moment, taking in the green. The leaves were just starting to change color and the air was cool without being cold. It was his favorite time of year.

"Didn't you have a six-legged-dog swifen?" Tarness asked.

"That was before I died," Jintorich said. "I'm certain this one reflects the change in me."

"What does that mean?" Tarness asked with raised eyebrows.

"I am one, one of many," Jintorich said.

"Right," Tarness said. "I don't even know how you ride something made of water."

"At least my swifen isn't of fire and ice," Jintorich said.

"That sounds painful," Tarness said with a wince.

"Less painful than what you'll face at home," Jintorich said, his brows furrowed. "Maarja didn't take our departure well."

"Not so much," Tarness said. "Fortunately, she took it out on Bryymel. She'll end his game."

"I don't trust him," Jintorich squeaked. "Do you know where they are heading?"

"Potterton," Tarness said. "But I feel bad not being there. Things are going to get hairy."

"We don't have a choice," Jintorich said. "We can't continue to let that ring lord over you."

"I feel like my transgressions are a never-ending story," Tarness said.

"There is no wheel of time to roll back mistakes," Jintorich said, wisely.

"I just want to be free," Tarness said.

"Didn't you recently get married?" Jintorich said with a wink. "Sorry, I used to be a comedian."

"It's okay," Tarness said, standing and brushing himself off. "I like being on the road with you. It's like a show."

"Uh, what's that?" Jintorich asked, pointing to the sky with his staff.

Several dots circled overhead, like vultures waiting for their meal.

"Too big to be birds," Tarness said. "Hopefully Berfemmian. I liked them." He waved.

"I don't think that's wise," Jintorich said. "Maehtikyn says they are dangerous."

"We'll find out soon. Here they come," Tarness said, blocking the sun with a hand. "Whoa, and fast. Jin, get down!"

"I am down," Jintorich said.

The world flipped and turned as Tarness rolled with his attacker, tumbling heel over head. There was no time to pull away and see what he was dealing with. It was strong enough to squeeze the air from his lungs through plate armor.

The somersaulting finally stopped, but he was too disoriented to attack. The creature drew back and let out a piercing squawk. It was a bird woman, but not like any Berfemmian he'd seen. Maybe if you took away their pretty, rolled them around in sticky garbage, and covered them in black feathers. Oh no.

"What happened to you?" he asked. "It's Tarness. I'm a friend."

"You smell of Angst," she screeched.

"I do not." He pushed and shoved, but she was so strong.

"Where is he?" She wrapped a talon around his neck and squeezed.

There was a noisy *tunk* of metal hitting bone as Jintorich's staff met her temple, batting her away. She smashed against a nearby tree with a loud crack and collapsed to the ground.

"Can you stand?" Jintorich asked. "There are more coming."

"I can run if it means staying away from that," Tarness said, scrambling to his feet. He summoned his swifen. "Was that a Berfemmian? What happened to her?"

The ground shook as another dark Berfemmian landed then felt like an earthquake when the other six arrived. They looked at their fallen comrade and let out a war cry that froze Tarness's blood.

"On your swifen," Jintorich shouted. "Ride!"

28

"Oh, now what?" Ivan asked, dismissing Angst's shush. "More giants you won't kill? More tribesmen to befriend? I'm exhausted from your—"

"Then please, you lead the way," Angst whispered. "We'll wait here."

"Yeah," Alloria said, not quite whispering. "After you."

Ivan pulled his horse around and looked at them warily. "What's up there?" he asked, jerking his head in that direction.

"Why, your people," Angst said with a broad grin. "I'm sure they'd love to see their Takarn."

"You're so funny," Alloria said, barking out a laugh.

Ivan stared at him, waiting for an answer.

"According to the gamlin, there are a lot of Fulk'han ahead," Angst said, immediately holding up a hand. "Don't ask me how many. They don't know."

"Yeah," Alloria said in a high-pitched tone. "Don't ask."

Angst sighed. This was a different crazy than the others she'd expressed, and he was already annoyed.

"Maybe you can talk them into letting us pass," Angst said.

"There's a greater chance they'd kill me for being an imposter," Ivan said, swallowing hard.

"Good," Angst and Alloria said at the same time. She barked out another laugh that made him grimace.

"Have it your way," Ivan said, rolling his eyes. "We go

around the animals."

"It's not that easy," Angst said. "They're everywhere."

"You could just kill 'em," Alloria said, excitedly.

"Maybe," Angst said.

"What's that?" Ivan asked, looking up.

Dark shadows rushed overhead, just beyond the tree line. Angst had no doubt who they were.

"Marisha," Angst said, in awe. He hadn't seen her specifically, but she was their leader, and he could only assume she was in the search party.

"Mean Berfemmian," Alloria said, ducking and covering her head. "So many."

"Now what, hero?" Ivan asked. "That's a lot of killing."

"Yeah," Alloria said. "Them killing us."

Angst grunted in frustration, wrapped an arm around Alloria, and dismissed his swifen. She cooed as they dropped to the ground. As gently as he could, he shoved her aside to give himself room for pacing. Was the entire universe conspiring against him, again? All he wanted was to get to Prendere, and every path he took was met with another delay. First a warning from the Vex'steppe tribesmen, then Nordruaut, now Fulk'han *and* Berfemmian? Way too many were on the hunt for him to call it coincidence.

"Why?" Angst asked, stopping before Ivan. "Why are they all converging on us?"

"I would assume you've upset everyone," Ivan said. "It shouldn't be a surprise. They all hate you."

Angst drew in his will until his hands glowed blue. He grabbed Ivan's arm and pulled him from his saddle. The knight landed hard on his back. Angst straddled him and raised a fist.

"Tell me, you idiot," Angst growled. "You're Magic's lackey. You should know what's going on. Tell me!"

Ivan laughed, and Angst punched him in the face over and over until he stopped.

"I didn't lie, you fool," Ivan said, spitting a glob of blood off to the side. "They do hate you, all of them. Magic made certain of it."

"What?" Angst asked. "How?"

"The longer we take to get to where we're going, the more armies amass at Prendere," Ivan said. "Berfemmian, Fulk'han, tribesmen, Nordruaut, the Melkier and merpeople all think your wish will destroy Ehrde. Magic provided them directions, and they are all on the march to keep you from reaching your prize! He even helped Unsel's army along so you'd have them to trip over too. With so many armies, it will be that much harder for you to reach the beam of light."

Angst looked at him in surprise, blinking several times before bursting out in laughter. Ivan's face contorted in confusion, which made him laugh harder. Finally, Alloria started laughing for no reason. It was disturbing enough to calm him. She continued laughing as they both looked at her.

"Sorry," she said, finally. "Are we done?"

"We are," Angst said, winking at her. He stood and offered Ivan a hand.

"I don't get the joke," Ivan said, standing without Angst's help.

"Magic apparently can't get into Prendere without me, or he'd have done it already," Angst explained. "Slowing me down only slows him down."

Ivan's face was a blotchy red; the man looked ready to scream. Alloria laughed uncomfortably as they watched the knight. His overreaction was baffling, but at least he'd shut up so Angst could concentrate.

He wouldn't lose much sleep over killing a handful of Fulk'han, but based on what he'd seen on the battlefield at Nordruaut, it would be almost impossible. After Ivan had changed the zealots of Fulk'han into gray men and pastel-colored women, they became strong and feral. They'd continued to evolve and now healed from wounds almost immediately. Faeoris had to cut off Guldrich's head in order to kill him. There were a lot of heads in the surrounding woods. He couldn't remove them all *and* fend off the Berfemmian.

He also didn't have much help. Despite Ivan's prowess as a knight, he wouldn't be a match for either race. Alloria's job, apparently, was to look pretty during fights and cheer him on in the most embarrassing way possible.

They needed a way around the mess. The gamlin told him about a large lake to the east. They wouldn't go near it since they were vulnerable to water, but apparently neither would the Fulk'han.

"Got it," Angst finally said. "Let's see what I can do to disappoint your boss." He summoned his steel ram swifen and helped Alloria mount.

Ivan wiped blood off his mouth and mounted his horse. He frowned when Angst didn't join Alloria on the ram. "Are you staying behind? Oh please, tell me you're sacrificing yourself so we can live."

"Funny," Angst said.

"Ooh," Alloria said as two gamlin dove up from the ground.

"My buddies here will lead you to a lake several miles away," Angst said. "I'll meet you there when I'm done."

"But—" Alloria said, biting her lip and glancing at Ivan.

"If he threatens you, makes eye contact, or says something mean, the gamlin will eat him," Angst said.

The gamlin nodded and glared viciously at Ivan. The knight raised his chin but kept quiet.

"Boys," Angst said. "Go slow. This is the first time someone else has ridden my ram alone. If it disappears, she'll have to walk."

"Yessir," they squeaked with a salute.

"Ooh, they talk now?" Alloria asked.

"Pretty soon they'll be smarter than Ivan," Angst said, trying not to let his concern show. It had been disconcerting when the gamlin had warned him to stay away from Rohjek by saying "danger." But this sounded even more human. They were connected to his mind. And while he'd never been good at understanding what they tried to tell him, maybe they were beginning to understand him.

"They've become an aberration." Ivan looked at them like something ugly on the bottom of his shoe.

"Now they'll be able to tell me if you say anything you shouldn't, Ivan," Angst said. "Alloria, go ahead and say anything you want."

"Oh, goodie," she said, clapping her hands.

Ivan's groaned as the gamlin led them to the lake. Without the distraction of his traveling companions, Angst could focus enough to sense the mass of bones several miles away. The gamlin were right: this was a large camp of Fulk'han. They even had guards surrounding the vast perimeter. He needed to be close to the middle for his plan to work. A portal would be ideal, but he was no element. Running at top speed like a blur would only attract the Berfemmian. There was only one other way.

After a twenty-minute, sweaty, knee-popping hike of not-sneaking, he was as close as he could get. A brief rest sounded nice, but guards were approaching fast. Angst drew in as much magic as he could and took a deep breath.

* * * *

"Hi. Remember me?" Angst blurted as he popped out of the ground. He gasped for breath, desperately hoping the stars in his eyes would go away before he passed out.

The Fulk'han sitting around the campfire screamed in fear as they leaped back. Four of them ran, but two men and one woman remained. Angst looked up as they reached for weapons. Berfemmian darkened the sky. Luck and timing had never been worthy companions, but this could work. He just needed several rocks, or maybe a boulder.

Angst's knees folded as an enormous gray man tackled him low. Another leaped at his chest, knocking the remaining air from his lungs. Only pure will kept him conscious as several more dog-piled him. Why had Ivan made the Fulk'han so heavy? It had to be the men; they were obscenely muscular and covered in bone armor. Bone armor. Armor made of bone.

"I don't have boulders," Angst wheezed at a Fulk'han whose eye was right next to his. "But you'll do fine."

The power he'd summoned before diving into the ground was still there, and with a grunt, he threw the dog-pile high into the air. Even as he stood, more gray men and colorful women ran toward him. They all experienced flight for the first, and last, time as he tossed them into the air. It became easier after catching his breath, and he was able to throw them directly at the Berfemmian.

"That should start a fight," Angst said, glancing up to see bodies falling and Berfemmian diving to attack the Fulk'han camp.

A young, pale blue woman stood at the edge of the campsite. She looked around for help, but the others were gone.

"C'mon," he beckoned. "C'mon."

She shook her head and tried running away, but he held her bones. Her unnaturally large eyes were filled with fear, and she screamed for help that didn't come. More than anything, he wanted to toss her like a stone into the abyss. The hunger to kill was almost overwhelming. They wanted to kill him. Didn't they deserve the same? But there she stood. Young. Afraid. Beautiful. And those large eyes were something to get lost in. It was his greatest weakness, and despite his screaming common sense, he approached her.

"Do you know who I am?" he asked.

"You...you're The Angst," she said, so scared her voice was barely a peep.

"No, just Angst," he said.

Her head cocked to one side, and she looked at him with distrust.

"What's your name?" he asked.

"Teesha," she said, warily.

"Not, The Teesha?" he asked.

She laughed nervously and shook her head.

"I'm not the enemy you think I am," Angst said. "I'm not the bad guy."

"Lies," she spat. "You killed Takarn Ivan."

"I did, but I didn't want to," Angst said. "He wasn't the Takarn you thought he was. Ivan was just a man, changed like you were changed."

Teesha looked down at her body in confusion. "I don't understand," she said. "He was not Takarn and you are not killing me like you killed them."

"You didn't attack me, but they would have," Angst said. "I couldn't think of another way to get past all of you."

"I understand," she said.

Angst let go, and to his surprise she not only stayed, but looked up at him defiantly.

"You will not kill me?" she asked.

"Only if you don't kill me first," he said. "But we only have minutes. Maybe seconds."

"Liar," she said, leaning. "They say you are crazy and only live to kill Fulk'han. You taunt me before killing me because you are The Angst."

He couldn't help the tears that came out. There was no reason to hate the Fulk'han as much as he did. Most of that hate came from their connection with Ivan. The knight had reformed them into his twisted vision, and they worshiped him for that change. It wasn't their fault, or their choice. Looking away, he tried composing himself. Some hero. Completely vulnerable, he expected a knife in his gut, but instead she placed a hand on his shoulder.

"Are they wrong?" Teesha asked.

"I've made terrible mistakes, but I don't know what I could've done different," he said, taking her hand from his shoulder and holding it. "Your people are wrong about me, and they were wrong about Ivan. I'm trying to fix all of it."

All around, he could hear war as Berfemmian screeched and Fulk'han roared their war cries. The crashing of weapons and the crunching of bone surrounded them. He'd done it. He'd created his distraction, but once again, at a terrible cost.

"What do you want of me?" Teesha asked, sharply.

"Go home," Angst said. "If I fail at this, Ehrde still needs a future. Go home, get married, make babies, and teach them the terrible things you've learned about war so it never happens again. I'm not your enemy. You are not my enemy. We need to stop fighting. So please, just go home."

"I was vulnerable, and you could've killed me." Teesha slowly drew her hand away, looking him up and down. "You were vulnerable, and I could've killed you."

"Yes," he said.

"I believe you, Angst. Maybe you are a hero. Maybe, I'm a hero too." She pulled him close, kissed him on the cheek, and ran off into the woods.

"Run, Teesha, run," he called out. And while war raged around him, he wondered, and hoped. Maybe he was a hero. And with a deep breath, Angst dove into the ground.

* * * *

"Are we going for a swim?" Angst asked as he approached Alloria.

"Angst," she said, wrapping her arms around him. "You did it."

"Just another day of great heroing," he said. That moment with Teesha had actually given him a little hope that this was possibly worth doing.

"He's no hero," Ivan said. "He's an accident with two giant swords, breaking everything on Ehrde that he trips over."

"Pardon?" Angst said, his self-appreciation deflating. He pulled away from Alloria and approached the knight. "Is the cowering getting to you, Ivan? For a knight, you're the first to run away from these battles."

"And you don't know what you're doing," Ivan said.

"Angst?" Alloria asked, her voice filled with worry. "I think something's wrong."

That obvious statement would've made his eyes roll back far enough to see his brain. They'd snuck past hordes of war parties from almost every nation, and despite this brief moment of safety, she still thought something was wrong.

According to the gamlin, and a quick glance up, there was nothing on land or in the air that could harm them. This meant she wanted a sandwich, or a hairbrush, or a bath, or something else distracting. All of which he was losing patience for. Something was always wrong, and he wasn't in the mood for distractions, especially when he was ready to kill an enemy he'd already killed once before.

"One minute," he said, holding up a finger in her direction while glaring at Ivan. "I'm about to slap a dead knight senseless."

"I'm not weak like I once was," Ivan said, his face stoic. "Do you think I'll put up with your hands striking my cheeks again?"

"Who said I was using my hands?" Angst said, jerking a thumb over his shoulder. Both swords sparked anxiously.

"Right, and without your foci, you're useless," he said. "And I still say you don't have a clue what you're doing."

"Probably," Angst said with a grimace. "But since I have these foci, idiots like you have to listen to me."

"Angst?" Alloria asked. "There's something in the lake."

He dragged his eyes away from Ivan long enough to look at Alloria and the lake behind her. She held herself tight, probably cold from her poor choice of travel clothes, that he really liked.

The lake was large, stretching out beyond his vision. Fir trees lined the shore, their roots reaching out from eroded walls of dirt to drink deeply. Steam rose from the lake's glass-smooth waters, wafting into the cool, evening air. The water below was still and the only bones he could sense were critters and fish. On another day, when he wasn't balancing on the fine line between panic and fury, it would've been a nice picnic spot.

"You're fine," he said. "Just give us a moment. This won't take long."

"You're bad at this, aren't you?" Ivan asked.

"Do you have a point?" Angst asked. "Because if you don't have a point, we should keep moving."

"My point, Al'eyrn, is that you don't understand how absolutely unheroic you really are," he said. "Everything you do is by accident, which is why people close to you continuously get hurt or killed. You're no great hero. You are a user of people and you use them until they die. You used your friends to become a hero. You're using Alloria to find Prendere. It's a long list of using."

Angst winced at Ivan's piercing words. It was the type of thing someone who really knew him well would say if their intent was to hurt. That was the odd thing, he had never been close to the man. The old Ivan was a name-calling bully. This new Ivan was far more calculating and malevolent. Maybe Angst just hadn't known him that well, but something felt different. Or maybe he was just on edge in this man's presence. Maybe. Regardless, this Ivan wasn't completely right.

"Sure, I'm not a great hero. People keep getting hurt and killed, but that's because of this war, which was started by uncaring monsters who are the embodiment of the elements. They obviously don't care about humans, or any race on Ehrde, but I do. I've made terrible mistakes, done things I'll regret, but there's nothing I could've done differently. None of it is my fault," Angst said. He took a step back and covered his mouth with a hand. "Uh, hey, did I just forgive myself?"

"Angst?" Alloria said, her voice filled with desperation. "Something's on me. She's—"

Angst spun around. Alloria was gone. There was a small wake in the dark waters, but he hadn't heard any splashing.

"Alloria?" he called out.

"Let her go, Angst," Ivan said. "Alloria is far more broken than you realize, and she just slows us down. It's not like you have feelings for her."

"I do," Angst said, wielding both swords. "I'm out of threats, Ivan, and you're out of time. Where is she?"

"Where else could she be, you fool?" Ivan said, hastily, pointing at the water. "And the mermaid that took her has probably finished her meal already."

29

Angst called out for Alloria again and again without success. Ivan's laughter didn't help his irritation. Why hadn't he listened to her? He was so used to dodging her affections and questioning her sanity that she'd slipped through his fingers. Frustration welled in his churning gut as Angst wielded both foci and drew in power.

Hopefully Alloria was bait and not dinner. No longer distracted by Ivan, Angst reached out with his mind, seeking those bones that apparently weren't fish. If he was right, there was a school of merpeople 50 to 100 yards out. They were there, incredibly still, as if waiting for him to come into the lake. He'd be at a huge disadvantage trying to battle merpeople underwater.

Power was easy, but a plan wasn't. He could use air to create a path through the water, but that might push Alloria and her abductors farther away. A fireball would get rid of the water, the merpeople, and Alloria. The only other thing he really knew was earth. Forcing the entire floor of the lake to rise sounded exhausting. What he really needed was a net. Angst smiled.

The ground about him complained as the tranquil lake rocked with the fury of a squall. A wall of stone and rock rose from the end of the inlet, easily four hundred yards across. Waves crashed against the shore as he pulled the wall to them.

"Fool," Ivan spat. "You're going to drown both of us."

"Shut up," Angst grumbled. "It's not a wall; it's a net. There

211

are holes large enough to let water through, you just can't see them."

The stone net closed in, and several merpeople tried climbing over it. He anchored their bones to his wall and continued drawing everyone closer. Sweat tickled his brow and dribbled down his cheeks. This was harder than he'd expected, and there was no way he could keep all of them from escaping.

"*Stop,*" a high-pitched voice rang in his mind.

The mermaid was mostly nude, with long strands of red hair covering her firm breasts. Her pale blue face was long, with high, ruddy cheeks that came down sharply to her jutting chin. She had large eyes that were blue like ice and thin, pursed lips. While not nearly as attractive as Moyra, the sight of her brought back all those memories. The mermaid took several steps forward, and held Alloria up by the back of her neck.

"*Face us in water, or we eat your mate,*" she warned, sounding more nervous than brave.

He winced. It had been a while since Moyra had spoken to him in his head, and rarely so loudly. "Is she alive? Did you breathe for her?"

"*I did,*" she said. "*Your hooman lives.*"

"Kill them," Ivan whispered loudly. "It's the only way to save her."

"*We kill you first,*" she said. "*Hooman with two foci.*"

"I won't fight you." He released the merpeople from his rocky net and returned the swords to his back.

Eight mermen and three mermaids approached on legs, each holding a wicked harpoon or long dagger, looking as vicious as sharks hungry to feed. The mermaid released Alloria and balled up her fists. The princess collapsed to the ground, hacking roughly. At least she was breathing.

"Why do you attack me, and mine?" Angst asked, holding out his hands.

"*You are hooman who killed Moyra,*" she said. "*You will use Prendere to steal our water forever. You will kill us all.*"

"Who told you that?" Angst asked, frowning. "I didn't kill

Moyra. I…I loved her."

"What?" Alloria asked between gasps. Her glare was a mixture of hurt and fury.

"You've got to be kidding me," Ivan said. Angst could almost hear the eye roll as the knight mockingly said, "I'm a lover, not a fighter."

"*But…you could not love her,*" the mermaid said. "*You killed her.*"

"Moyra brought me deep, deep underwater, breathing for me the entire time," he said. "It was the most frightening thing I've ever experienced. At any time, she could've let me die. But we trusted each other, and you should trust me like Moyra did."

The mermaid looked perplexed, glancing at her party of soldiers. "*How do we believe you?*"

"She showed me her eggs," he said. This struck a chord, and they all shared a curious look.

"The eggs are precious, are secret," the mermaid said, looking around at the others. "She would not have shared this."

"*I thought she, uh…*" His cheeks warmed, and he rubbed the back of his neck. "*I thought she wanted me to mate.*"

The merpeople all burst out in gurgly laughter that made his ears burn. Ivan was laughing too, which made it worse. This was a time for humility, and honesty, and not a time to bury everyone up to their necks. That would be bad, right?

"Moyra laughed at me too," he said, taking a calming breath. "And then I learned about the curse. I learned how the men were locked in the mage city forever. I broke the curse."

"*No,*" she gasped. "*Our Moyra broke that curse, and then we attacked Unsel.*"

"Were you there?" Angst asked. "Were you at Unsel during the battle where I fought the oldest living creature on Ehrde?"

"I hate that thing," Ivan grumbled.

"*We were all there,*" she said. "*We saw you destroy her.*"

"What else did you see?" he asked.

"*She pressed her lips against yours,*" a merman said. "*I thought she would eat you, but it was more like breathing for you.*"

"Hoo…humans call that kissing," Angst said. "We do it with people we love."

"You kissed her?" Alloria roared.

"Alloria," he snapped. "Tell them what it means to us."

She shook with anger, standing beside the mermaid, and took several deep breaths. "It's true. We kiss for love."

"Then why did you kill her?" the mermaid asked.

"Water killed her," he said, swallowing hard. "She did it because she hated me. Water blamed me for killing a human she loved and killed Moyra for revenge."

"That sounds like Water," she said.

"I didn't kill her, but it was my fault," he said, his voice catching. "I couldn't save her. I destroyed Water, but that didn't bring Moyra back. I'm sorry."

He covered his face. It was one of his least favorite bandages to rip off. Moyra should've been alive, and free, and roaming the ocean not eating hoomans. Angst was running out of tears, but his heart hurt in a thousand different ways. To his surprise, cold hands grabbed his shoulders. She stared at him with those ice-blue eyes. He brushed her cool cheek with the back of his hand. She didn't jerk away, or try to eat him, and sighed.

"I'm sorry I failed her," he said in a strained voice.

"I believe you, hooman," she said. *"I sense your pain. It is the same as ours."*

"Now what do we do?" he asked, looking around at all of them.

"We talk," she said, waving a hand into the air, *"and eat."*

"Eat?" he asked, taking a cautious step back.

They all laughed again. It was less embarrassing this time. A little.

Two mermen and a mermaid leaped high into the air, their legs forming into tails as they dove back into the lake.

"I'm going to make the wall of stone go away," he said. "I promise, I won't attack anyone."

She nodded, and he willed his net back into the ground.

"Ivan, please collect some firewood," Angst said. "They'll eat their fish raw, but we'll need to cook ours."

The mermaid and Alloria both looked at him as if he'd said something disgusting.

"You okay?" he asked the princess.

"No," she grumbled.

"*I promise,*" the mermaid said, "*we didn't harm her.*"

"I believe you," he said. "Hi, my name is Angst."

"*Hi, An-gst,*" she said. "*I'm Lyda.*"

"Why am I the one going to collect firewood?" Ivan asked.

"Because if you don't," Angst said, "I'm feeding you to the merpeople."

"*We are very hungry,*" she said with a broad smile.

Ivan paled and scrambled off into the woods, making Lyda laugh.

"I'll help," Alloria grumbled, storming off into the woods in a different direction than Ivan.

Angst and Lyda sat cross-legged, knee to knee, as Ivan brought firewood and her people brought fish. A lot of fish. He told her everything about Moyra, from finding her in the trap to her death at the hands of Water. Despite the pain of those memories, Angst was grateful to tell their story. Few could understand their connection who wouldn't judge it, so he'd kept it all in. Sharing it seemed to purge his heartache. She listened patiently, only interrupting when she didn't understand.

A merman handed Lyda a bottle. She uncorked it and took a long draw that made Angst lick his lips.

With a curious smile, she offered it to him. "*You may not like it,*" she said. "*It is strong.*"

"My favorite," he said, raising the bottle to toast.

The merpeople looked at each other quizzically as he sniffed, took a cautious sip, and smiled. He'd expected something salty, or fishy, and was surprised by the rich tang of oranges. He took several gulps before she gently pulled the bottle away with concern in her eyes. The bitter aftertaste made his lips purse. Raising a finger, he drank more.

"Beautiful," Angst said as warmth spread through his body. His lips and the tip of his tongue were already numb. "You could get rich selling this stuff. What is it? Or, do I not want to know?"

"*Aberbrou,*" she said with a smile. Looking into his eyes, she took the bottle and drank.

They talked and feasted long into the night. He explained his plan, promising not to take away the water. Alloria came back from the woods a different Alloria, without wood, but happy. She spent most of her time sharing Angst's bottle or flirting with a helpless merman.

"*We came to kill you. Now what do we do?*" Lyda asked. "*If you had not taken up your swords, my people would still be prisoners in the mage city. If your plan works, they will remain trapped.*"

"True," he said, "but they'll live until someone else lifts the curse."

"*How do you know it will work?*" she asked.

"Because he's my champion. He is the killer of dragons, destroyer of elements, strong enough to fight Death and win," Alloria said, placing a hand on his shoulder.

They all looked at her. Angst was embarrassed but appreciated her encouragement.

"What?" she asked. "Angst can do anything."

"No, he can't," Ivan said. "I'm told only an element can enter Prendere to make a wish."

"Has an Al'eyrn ever tried?" Angst said, leaning against Alloria as the ground tilted. "Nope. You can hate me for that too."

"*I do not trust that one, An-gst,*" Lyda said, darkly. "*Moyra said hoomans are not food, but we could still eat him.*"

"Ha," Angst said. "I'm tempted to leave him, but he knows how to get there. Maybe just nibble around the edges?"

The merpeople thought this was pretty funny. Ivan apparently didn't and stomped off to find more wood.

"*I will talk to my people,*" she said. "*I will tell them I believe in you. Maybe they will help.*"

"Thank you, Lyda," Angst said with a broad smile.

"Tonight, we will stay with you, An-gst," she said. *"And to-morrow we will part as friends."*

"Good," Angst said. "We should be friends. Hey, how much of that Aberbrou do you have?"

"A lot," she said with a broad smile.

"I may have a favor to ask," he said.

They continued talking late into the night about Angst's adventures, and fish, and elements. Eventually, Angst lay down with a full stomach and settled conscience. Heroing wasn't always bad.

30

"There," Tarness cried out, pointing at a grove of enormous gray trees with his sword.

A piercing squawk barely gave him enough time to duck as Berfemmian talons raked the top of his bushy black hair. They wrapped around the blade of his broadsword and jerked it from his sweaty grip.

"My sword," he said.

Jintorich shouted something in Acratic, and a beam of white light erupted from his staff, blasting the Angorian. She flew against a tree, dropping the weapon.

Tarness wanted to swing his obsidian stallion around and retrieve it, but a glance over his shoulder shocked some sense into him. Dozens of dark figures trailed them, inching closer with every racing breath.

"Faster," Tarness shouted.

"This is faster," Jintorich said.

"How can they keep up?" Tarness said, hunching closer to his swifen's neck. "It's not like they're Al'eyrn."

"Just about there," Jintorich squeaked.

"And how will being there help us?" Tarness asked.

"The Mendahir don't like Berfemmian," Jintorich said. "I'm hoping they won't follow."

"You're hoping?" Tarness said. "That's pretty weak, Jin."

His friend said nothing, and his mind raced for something

other than hope to save them. The trees were large enough and thick enough to slow down the flying women, but they'd eventually have to slow down too. There was no way he could fight them off, and Jintorich had to be tired from pushing their swifen to run at this speed.

When the giant trees were several hundred yards away, Tarness braved another glance. To his surprise, the Berfemmains kept their distance. They hovered like a swarm of gnats—very loud gnats who screamed in frustration.

"Jin, you were right," Tarness shouted. "You're a genius."

"I am one," Jintorich said. "One of many."

"That's a lot of geniuses," Tarness said. "I love all of them."

Crossing the threshold of Grayhollow Forest was like entering another world. Not only did color wash away like caked-on dirt in a hot bath, but the dark Berfemmian refused to enter. Even though Jintorich was right, they continued at their breakneck pace until it became too hard to dodge trees.

When they finally stopped, Tarness had to let his pounding heart and gulping breaths calm before dismounting. The race had gone on for hours, and the abrupt end made him dizzy enough to sit down. He needed food, mead, a nap, more mead, and another nap.

"Wow," Jintorich said.

"Yeah," Tarness said. "A lot of wow. What do you think happened to them?"

The tiny Meldusian hadn't been referring to the Berfemmian. He gawked at his colorless hands as if their frantic race to live had never happened.

"I don't think I'll ever get used to this," he squeaked, turning them over and squeezing tight. "Are you okay?"

"Yeah," Tarness said. The chase had left him exhausted, and the loss of color made him uneasy. He grabbed a loaf of bread from his satchel and tore out a large bite with his teeth. Nordruaut bread was as plain and hearty as those who made it. Not his favorite, but he was happy to be eating. He held out the loaf to Jintorich. "Wan sumb?"

"No thanks," Jintorich said, looking around in wonder.

"What next?" Tarness asked around another mouthful.

"I believe I'm next," a whispery voice said.

A sharp blue glow emanated from the forest flor, surrounded by vertical lines of white and blue light. Tarness swallowed hard as the Mendahir ghost appeared before them. He hadn't seen the Mendahir Rise during his first visit to Grayhollow and had almost laughed when Angst recounted the story. Dallow had called them a phenomenon, like a rainbow. It had sounded unreal, and seemed unbelievable even now.

After rising from the ground like mist from a lake, the Mendahir solidified into a less translucent cloud. Tarness wasn't in the habit of calling other men beautiful, but there it was. He was tall, thin, and had glowing blue eyes. Bright vapors around his face revealed a long nose, strong chin, and pointed ears. Tarness felt like bowing, which wasn't possible from his sitting position. Without knowing what else to do, he reached out with the half-eaten chunk of bread.

The Mendahir leaned forward and took a deep breath as though trying to smell it. "I miss the satisfaction of eating," he said. "Is Nordruaut bread as hearty as I remember?"

Tarness nodded and shoved the bread back in his satchel.

"What can I do for you, one of many?" he asked, turning to Jintorich.

"We seek your wisdom, great Kitecor," Jintorich said, pointing at Tarness's ring.

Tarness held up his hand for Kitecor to inspect. The Mendahir frowned in concentration, leaning over close to study the ruby ring.

"It is almost a foci," he said, his voice like a distant breeze. "But not one of our creations."

"Can you tell us how to remove it?" Tarness asked. "Please, uh, sir."

Kitecor flicked it, his finger passing through Tarness's hand, leaving behind a brief chill.

"We must seek counsel," he said. "Follow me."

Tarness scrambled to stand and rushed to follow the glowing

apparition.

"You have strong magics, young wielder," Kitecor said.

"I do?" Tarness asked. "Well, I guess I do, sometimes. It doesn't always work when I want."

"It could," he said. "Jintorich, from where does this faux foci originate?"

"From the element Magic," Jintorich said.

"That fool?" he said. "Then war is upon Ehrde once more. Or is it over? This would explain your Angst bonding with two foci."

"Over?" Tarness asked. "How do you not know?"

"We no longer belong to time," he said. "Time now belongs to us."

Tarness looked at Jintorich, who shrugged.

"For us, the war is now," Jintorich explained. "And Magic is the last remaining element."

Kitecor stopped and looked around. "No, he is not, or all would be lost to his chaos."

Without further explanation, he pressed forward, leading them to a clearing. Four other Mendahir apparitions floated toward them, every bit as beautiful as Kitecor. Three women and one man smiled at them, so kindly that Tarness didn't want to leave. Lights danced around his periphery. He pulled his gaze away and gasped.

"Uh, Jin?" he asked.

"I see," Jintorich said. "More wow."

"A lot more," Tarness said.

The forest had become a city of trees. Some trees were homes, where children peeked out from high-arched doorways. Others were shops or libraries connected by long, pale branches that became a complex pathway of bridges. There were hundreds, maybe thousands of Mendahir floating from building to building. This city of supposed-to-be-dead was too much for Tarness to grasp, and he forced his eyes back to things that almost made sense.

"You're becoming stronger," Jintorich said.

"Angst was right," Kitecor said. "Our return is nigh. Has he destroyed Ehrde yet? Or has he saved it?"

"That's two futures, friend Kitecor," Jintorich said.

"Angst has many to struggle with," the Mendahir said. "What do you think of this, my sisters and brother?" Kitecor pointed at the ring, and Tarness raised his hand.

The four additional Mendahir took turns studying his ruby ring before circling to discuss. What must've been speech sounded like a choir to Tarness. It was eerily beautiful and hard to comprehend. When it finally stopped, his heart sank at the loss.

"Destroying the ring will invite Death to visit," Kitecor finally said.

"Yup," Tarness said. "We've seen that."

"Have you tried removing the arm?" Kitecor asked.

"No," Tarness said, firmly. "And we're not going to."

"Of course." Kitecor smiled, knowingly. "A foci created by an element is wrong. We created foci to *stop* elements. They cannot even touch our gifts without great pain."

"But Magic tried forcing a foci to bond with one of my friends," Tarness said.

The Mendahir looked at each other with concern.

"That would have cost the element much," Kitecor said. "And if it were even possible, curse the unfortunate person who bonded with that foci."

Tarness let out a low whistle.

"Did it work?" Kitecor asked.

"No," Tarness said. "I think it has with others, but they all were pretty messed up as a result."

"That makes sense," Kitecor said. "Bonding is a sacrifice. You agree to give a part of yourself to the foci, and the foci becomes a part of you. Terrible things can happen if it is forced."

"What about my friend?" Jintorich asked.

"Did you agree to bond with the ring?" Kitecor asked.

Tarness nodded as the guilt welled in his chest.

"I'm sorry," Kitecor said. "We cannot remove it and keep you alive."

CHAPTER THIRTY

"Isn't there something you can do?" Jintorich pleaded. "Magic controls him with that ring. Angst needs his friend. We all do."

The Mendahir sang their beautiful song again as the council discussed. Tarness wanted to cry at the beauty of it and looked away. The city was gone, the trees were trees, and their light was dimming. It felt like last call at the Wizard's Revenge.

"In this form, we do not see time as you do," Kitecor said. "While Angst has many paths, there are two that change everything. He could lead Ehrde to darkness or peace. His choice hinges on you, young wielder."

"Me?" Tarness asked. "Why me?"

"You are his friend," Kitecor said. "And you will decide for us all."

This didn't help at all, and Tarness couldn't have been more frustrated. That frustration became anger as power flowed through him. He stomped his foot, shaking the forest floor.

"Much power, indeed," the fading Mendahir said with a smile.

"How do I help Angst? Tell me," Tarness shouted. He reached out to grasp a handful of light. "I don't even know how to get out of this stupid forest. We're stuck here, surrounded by Dark Berfemmian, and have no chance of getting back to help Angst choose the right path. Can't you do something?"

"A portal would help us greatly," Jintorich said.

"There is one thing I can do," Kitecor said with a nod. "If it still works."

"Still works?" Tarness asked.

There was a loud pop, and Tarness screamed.

31

After three days of riding as fast as Angst could push, they finally crossed into Meldusia. Ivan had kept their pace slow so Magic had time to maneuver his chess pieces. Mocking that plan seemed to be a catalyst for their speed. Miraculously, Ivan's horse no longer needed a sluggish pace or frequent rests. Angst did his best to nudge it along without putting the poor beast in its grave.

There were no further signs of warbands, which was a worrisome relief. While it was nice not being hunted, the lack of attention made him wonder if they were going the right way.

Two more days passed, and those concerns sweated out through his pores. The forest slowly became a jungle the likes of which Angst had never seen, and never wanted to see again. The vine-covered trees seemed to hover over their path, practically choking the life out of the very air. Even breathing was a chore as the humidity weighed on his lungs.

The nights were almost worse than their days. Instead of the cool relief of a fall wind, it rained hard and nonstop. The evening storms imprisoned him in a tent with Alloria, who insisted on being naked for fear of getting overheated. She would laugh herself to sleep at his discomfort while he lay on his side, smacking bugs. Bugs. They only bit him, entirely avoiding Alloria and Ivan. When this was over, his life goal may just be to kill all of the bugs. Then he'd be the true hero of Ehrde.

On day six, Ivan abruptly stopped.

Angst reached out to the gamlin, but none were close. It made sense. The soppy ground and thick humidity would probably kill them. "What is it?" he asked.

"A butterfly," Ivan said, looking back with a sneer.

"Where?" Alloria asked. "I love butterflies."

"I'm sure you'll find plenty here in Garathou, the Meldusian jungle," Ivan said, sounding frustrated. "I'm assuming Angst will want to stop and make peace with them."

"What are you talking about?" Angst asked.

"You didn't kill the Berfemmian, you kissed her," Ivan said. "You didn't destroy the war band of tribesmen, you befriended them...and the merpeople. You're a fool."

"He's a hero," Alloria shouted, defensively. Her voice became dreamy. "He's my hero."

"Of course I tried to befriend them," Angst said. "Why do you think that's bad?"

"Because you've let your guard down. Because you've shown your weakness," Ivan said. "You'll soon be at war with all of them at Prendere as they fight for the prize."

"Most of them want the same thing. A safe Ehrde," he said. "Why fight, when we can work together?"

"You think they'll help you win the prize?" Ivan asked. "They all want it, and will kill you to win it, which makes you an idiot."

"Just do your job, and take us to Prendere," Angst snapped.

"It's not that simple," Ivan said. "To enter, you will need the key."

"Fine," Angst said, rolling his eyes. "Then take us to the key."

"We're already here," Ivan said.

Angst followed him through an opening in the jungle and gasped. A vast sea of vines covered the ground like a pit of snakes, reaching for miles beyond his vision. This gardener's nightmare coalesced into a mound the size of a city, reaching high into the sky, arcing in the shape of a dome.

"Is this…" Angst looked around, taking it all in. "Is this a mage city?"

"Welcome to Gyldorane," Ivan said. "The richest of all mage cities."

"Ooh," Alloria said, leaning forward.

"No," Angst said, his shoulders barely able to hold up his armor.

"Is something wrong?" Alloria asked.

"I was expecting Prendere." He struggled to keep the defeat out of his voice. The hope that had driven him to this point, past the warbands, and through that awful jungle was gone. "I thought I was close to seeing my family, not this."

"I'm sure we're just passing through," Alloria said, her voice still filled with hope.

"I'm sure we're not," Angst said, with a deep sigh. "Why are we here?"

"At the end of the last war, an Al'eyrn cast a spell. She created an impenetrable shield around that beam of light," Ivan said. "The foci she used to create that shield is in this mage city."

"A shield that elements can't get through?" Angst asked.

"You aren't the only fool to utter the words, 'at all cost'," Ivan said.

"That would work," Angst said with a shudder.

"That foci is the key to taking down that barrier," Ivan said. "All you need to do is find it. It's a—"

"Horn," Angst said.

"How did you know?" Ivan asked, his eyes wide.

"Some friends told me," Angst said. The twins had been looking for the horn foci, and it only made sense that it was in this mess of a mage city. He sighed.

"This is the last step, hero." Ivan's voice, his demeanor, became unnaturally respectful. "Your journey is almost complete."

Angst gathered what was left of his reserves. There weren't many, but what choice did he have? "Lead the way."

It wasn't the lengthy trek through the vine maze that Angst had expected. The dead knight led them flawlessly along the tops of thick vines. All the while, Angst's frustration grew. Where was this helpful tracker when they'd skirted the warbands? Where was this respectful leader when he'd made peace with his enemies? Suddenly, Ivan was adept, kind, and even useful.

"Is that our way in?" Angst asked.

A wide, almost welcoming, stone pathway was mostly free of vines. It led to a large doorway that looked more like a mouth than a mage city entrance.

"We could go that way, but it's a complicated entrance," Ivan warned.

"I want to see," Angst said.

"As you wish," Ivan said.

Angst and Alloria immediately dismounted when they arrived. The limestone road was well kept and refreshingly sturdy underfoot. Sets of stairways and plateaus led to enormous double doors, also carved from stone. It would take magic to open those doors. There was probably a puzzle here that Dallow would've loved to solve. His intelligent friend had translated Acratic to enter Gressmore. He longed for his friends to be here; he needed them now more than ever.

"You say there's an easier way in?" Angst asked.

"Yes," Ivan said. "We aren't far."

"Let's go," Angst said with a nod. "But I'd like to spend a private moment with Alloria. This is a special place, and I'd like to make it memorable."

"Uh, sure," Ivan said, rubbing the back of his neck. "Ride along the biggest vine over there. I'll wait for you out of earshot."

She frowned and squeezed her hands several times nervously as if she'd lost control of their sexual tension. Her sexual tension. He wanted to laugh but didn't know how she'd react, so he held it in. Alloria looked ready to say something. He set a finger against his lips until Ivan was gone.

"Go ahead," he said.

"You're not going to ask me to leave," she said. "Are you?"

"No way. We're in this together," Angst said.

Her shoulders dropped. "Memorable, huh?" she asked, licking her lips. And the sexual tension was hers once again.

"Not like that," he said. "I have a favor to ask."

* * * *

The jungle nightmare ended at a vast field of thick vines reaching farther than they could see. At the distant center of the growth was an unfathomably large dome of vines. Dallow referred to it as the mage city Gyldorane. According to her visions, it was time to face Angst. She paced through her anxiety, looking for words that would inspire the exhaustion out of everyone, but found only curses as she stumbled over spongy vines.

"This doesn't make me feel better about that jungle," Rose said, looking over the field.

"At least there are no bugs," Nikkola said.

"Or animals," Simon said. "According to Sean."

"So, what do we do?" Nikkola asked.

"We save Ehrde," Victoria said. She pointed toward Gyldorane. "This is where it happens. I've seen it. He could be waiting for us at the entrance, or inside the city, but there will be a battle here."

"I'm ready," Rose said with determination.

The others nodded in agreement. It wasn't exactly a pep talk, but she would accept any form of encouragement, even the little ones.

"Do we have to kill him?" Dallow asked.

"I don't know," Victoria said, swallowing hard. "We'll do what we have to. What's the best way through this, Captain?"

"We ride along the tops of the largest vines," she said. "He'll be able to see us from a distance, so we'll have to ride fast. Listen to my commands when we get there. Mount up."

"Dallow needs to lead the way," Victoria said. "He knows exactly where we're going."

They all looked at her quizzically, but she provided no further explanation. Dallow mounted his polished, hardwood gazelle and bounded to a great vine taller than him. Waving for them to follow, he rode forward at an incredible speed.

Victoria was acutely aware of her pounding heart, gasping breath, and time as she followed Dallow's lead. They were close, but it was already taking too long to get there, and her mind raced the swifen to Gyldorane. Would Dallow's swifen stumble over a vine, forcing them all to crash in a heap? Would they have to dodge Angst's attacks while preparing their own? Did she have it in her heart to order his death?

As they reached a wide limestone patio, all fears and concerns were lost to a new problem.

"Where is he?" Jaden asked.

Victoria dismounted her unicorn and knelt to pick up Alloria's tiara. She handed it to Dallow, who took it with a sigh.

"Well," Dallow said. "It got us this far."

"I don't understand," Jaden said.

"We discovered a memndus when visiting Gressmore Towers," Dallow said. "It was a giant glass map of Ehrde that you could use to view people. It was unfinished, and when Angst pushed it a little too hard, the memndus shattered. We learned that you could use the memndus shards to track other shards, one of which is in this tiara Alloria's been wearing."

"I didn't think magic could be used to track magic," Jaden said.

"I know," Dallow said with a smile.

"Why didn't you tell us?" Mirim asked, frowning irritably.

"Angst and I used to speak to each other through stone," Victoria said. "That stopped when Earth was destroyed, but Dallow and I were concerned he could still listen in."

"He left the tiara here for us to find," Dallow said. "He must've figured it out."

"Yes, a while ago," Victoria said.

"I find that hard to believe," Rose said with a sniff.

"It doesn't matter. He's here, and so are we," Jaden said in disbelief. "What do we do now?"

"We figure out how to open that door," Victoria said.

32

"Here we are," Ivan said.

The three of them stood on a weatherworn, stone terrace easily the size of his small house. Angst stared at the alcove of vine walls before him in confusion. A thick drapery of leaves hung from drooping branches and vines wider than his legs. The few openings were windows into darkness and shadow, the natural habitat for everything that crawled, slithered, and bit. This wasn't the doorway he'd expected. It was as welcoming as coming home at 2am from a late night of drinking, smelling like someone else's perfume. That door usually ended up in his face.

"Gosh," Angst said. "Thanks for bringing us nowhere. How did you even become a knight? Do you just suck at everything?"

"Oooh," Alloria said, her eyes darting back and forth. "Fight!"

"It's here, Angst," Ivan said, still polite. "All you have to do is push through."

"Or this is a trap," Alloria said, studying a fingernail.

With a growl, Angst grabbed Ivan by the breastplate, spun him around, and shoved the knight against the vine wall covering the mage city.

"No, wait," Ivan said, arms flailing. "You don't know what you're—"

The explosion blasted them to the terrace edge. Angst landed on his back, rolled over his shoulder to stand, and drew both swords. Alloria applauded his quick recovery. Part of him wanted to bow, the other part wanted his vision to clear.

"No," Ivan moaned, gripping his stomach, his face locked in a grimace. The man lay on his side, gray smoke rising from him like he'd just been taken off the grill. Ivan melted, slowly reforming into the shape of a tall, awkward-looking bald man Angst knew too well.

"Magic," Angst shouted, rushing over to the element.

"Hi," Magic wheezed, trying to push himself up.

Both foci buzzed with power. Blue and red lightning crashed around him, sparking noisily on the stone floor. They sang in his mind, a rare harmony that said very clearly, "Destroy the element."

"You'll never save your family if you end me," Magic said, turning his head to look at Angst.

"I should destroy you for what you did to Tarness," Angst said. "For what you've done to Alloria."

"Would you rather they were dead?" Magic asked. "This is a poor way to thank me."

"Then Marisha," Angst said. "Whatever you did to her—"

"To all Berfemmian," Magic said nonchalantly. "Faeoris's golden feather is a foci. I'm surprised you hadn't figured that out. It's different than your swords. When she bonded with it, all Berfemmian got their wings of light. When I forced the foci to bond with Marisha…well, needless to say, I need a little more practice."

"Monster," Angst shouted.

"Your wife and children…or me?" Magic asked. "Without me, you'll never find Prendere, and you won't be able to save any of them."

The swords were practically begging, so loud in his mind that his hands shook. Lightning bit at Magic's arms and legs, making the element jerk with every strike. Angst's foci wanted this more than anything. This is what they were made for. Their hunger, their songs, were almost uncontrollable. He had to mentally shush them to consider.

This could be it: the death of the last element. Angst would win. Everyone on Ehrde would be safe for another two thousand years, and he could just walk away a hero. The hero they all needed, the hero everyone wanted, the hero he had longed to be.

But then there was the plan. His crazy plan to save his family and friends. If there was a chance, even the smallest chance he could keep this war from ever happening, wasn't that his responsibility? And what if his plan failed, letting Magic win and leaving Ehrde in chaos?

"Do it, baby," Alloria said. "Kill him. Please."

It was the wrong sort of encouragement, and with a deep sigh, he said, "No."

The swords went silent so suddenly it was if he'd gone deaf. The impressive pyrotechnic display of lightning stopped abruptly as well. Alloria sighed. Magic laughed.

"When I end you," Angst said with a forced calm, "it won't be out of petty revenge. I'll do it with my family at my side, and I'll be saving everyone I love."

"Sure," Magic said in a coddling tone, pushing himself up to a sitting position.

"Why?" Angst asked, returning his disgruntled foci to his back. "Why this? Why Ivan?"

"To throw you off," Alloria said. "He's been taking different forms from the beginning. A Fulk'han woman. A—"

"Bitch," Magic shouted, raising a clawed hand that seemed to be sucking in dark shadowy bubbles like a sponge.

"No," Angst said warningly. He drew Chryslaenor and pressed the tip to Magic's forehead. For a brief moment, his swords were happy again. "I may not kill you, but I can make things very uncomfortable."

"Whatever," Magic said, lowering his hand and pulling away.

"Why do you hate humans so much?" Angst asked.

"Because you're a virus," Magic said, his voice seething with hatred. "You get in the way and make it harder to fight our war. And then this happened… You happened. We've always worried there would be an aberration, that the virus would be too much for us to handle. We should have rid ourselves of you long ago, but the Vivek likes humans, so there are rules."

Angst was going to sheath Chryslaenor but thought better of it and gently *thunked* Magic on the forehead instead. The element yelped, and Alloria barked out a laugh. He returned the blade to his back.

"Since we aren't allowed to completely wipe out the human race, we use them like tools," Magic said, rubbing his forehead. "They always fought back, but it never seemed to go their way. Two thousand years ago, it came dangerously close. The Mendahir created foci that made wielders more powerful than ever. Those wielders created mage cities with protections that made it impossible for us to enter."

"That's why you were thrown back from the wall," Angst said.

"Clever human," Magic said, rolling his eyes.

"If the mage cities kept wielders safe from the elements," Angst began. "Why are they gone?"

"He cursed them," Alloria said.

They both looked at her in surprise.

"What?" she asked, tugging at a lock of hair. "He talks a lot."

"She's right," Magic said with a smirk. "I sank Azaktrha and trapped the mermen. I had Fire send dragons after Gressmore. I cast a spell that would slowly kill anyone returning to the Nordruaut mage city Enurthen."

"I can't wait to kill you," Angst said, licking his lips. "What did you do here?"

"Why would I tell you?" Magic spat.

"If I don't survive, no foci, and no prize," Angst said. "And you're too proud not to boast."

"Good points," he said with a malicious grin. "This was one of my favorites. After millennia of experimenting on humans, I have come to realize that you're all slightly unhinged. Some far more than others. But you also need your crazy. You can't live without that tenuous balance. I don't completely understand, but I accept it for whatever it is. This weakness inspired the perfect curse."

"You're boring me," Angst said. "Get to it."

"Everyone who enters Gyldorane is immediately shadowed," Magic said with a broad grin.

"You mean followed?" Angst asked.

"In a way," Magic said. "The moment you enter, a shade of yourself will begin to form. With every passing hour, a bit of your sanity will leak out, strengthening that shade until it's saner than you are. And then it kills you."

"So everyone murdered themselves." Angst shook his head.

"More or less," Magic said.

"Why is he just telling us?" Alloria asked, tugging on his cloak. "I don't trust him."

"Magic wants us to be prepared," Angst said. "He needs us to live long enough to escape with the foci. Neither of us can get into the light without it."

"So you believe him?" she asked, her lip quivering. "How will we survive?"

"He's hoping my foci protects me," Angst said, staring at Magic for any sign of disagreement. "And I'm sorry, Alloria, but you're already a bag of squirrels."

"Thanks," she said, sticking out her tongue. She sighed deeply. "I like squirrels."

Angst couldn't help but chuckle.

"She'll be better off than you are," Magic said, standing up and brushing himself off.

"Probably," Angst said. "But she's right. That was too quick, too honest. What aren't you telling us?"

Magic waved his arm in a vertical circle that twisted color and light until it formed a shadowy portal. "I'll be here when you escape," Magic said, disappearing through the dark window. "If you escape."

The portal was gone with a pop, and they were alone.

"What next?" Angst asked. "And how do we get in?"

Alloria reached between branches, deep to her shoulder, sticking out her tongue in concentration. Her eyes went wide, and she grabbed at him with her free hand.

"Help," she said. "Angst, something's got me."

Angst wrapped his arms around her and gently pulled. Her arm freed immediately and seemed completely unharmed. He turned his head to look at her in confusion.

"My champion," she said, planting a kiss on his mouth.

He tried taking a step away, but his back was against jungle wall. She clung to him like an octopus and planted her lips on his. He didn't want to beat her away. She was kissing him, and Angst didn't have it in him to be mean to a beautiful woman kissing him.

Angst tried pushing and took a step back, and then another. He opened his mouth to admonish but was immediately accosted by tongue. His useless mumbling was overwhelmed by her moaning, which made his cheeks flush hot. She bit his tongue and giggled as she reached for his crotch.

"Alloria," he shouted, practically dancing backward.

Leaves brushed his ears and vines tickled his arms as he tried cowering into the blanket of jungle.

"This armor isn't exactly easy to get off, is it?" she asked, grabbing a handful of steel.

"Stop," he said, trying harder than ever to move away. "I warned you. We aren't going to do this. I'll make you stop."

"You don't want me to stop. You love this," she said, squeezing tighter with her octopus arms and legs. "Give me one kiss, and I'll leave be, for now. Just one, Angst."

She went in for the kill, and he relaxed his face enough to barely kiss her back. Those full lips pressed against his were intoxicatingly delicious, and for the briefest moment, he was drawn into her hunger. His heart raced like a teenager's. She was so filled with passion that he just wanted to throw her to the ground and…and… It took a moment to come to his senses and un-suction himself from her.

"Thank you for finally kissing me," she said, releasing him from her grasp. Alloria wiped off her mouth. There was a faint blush on her cheeks, and she was gasping for breath. "Good job."

"Oh, uh," Angst said, his ears now burning too. He looked down, scratching the back of his sweaty neck. "You're, uh, good at kissing too."

She burst out in laughter, which did absolutely nothing for his confidence.

"This is exactly why I love you," she said. "Your kiss was nice, but I meant for getting us here."

"Here?" Angst asked.

Alloria swept her hand in a wide arc that presented the city before them. "Welcome to Gyldorane."

33

Tarness stopped screaming five minutes after the Mendahir sent them on their way. Jintorich's request for a portal had turned into something else entirely. Rather than magically appearing somewhere, an invisible harness jerked them through Ehrde at an unfathomable speed. The first tree they passed through made Jintorich cheer and Tarness panic. The ride became less fun when they suddenly dove underwater before shooting straight up the side of a mountain. Hither and fro were apparently directions as they were roughly sent down both paths. It was like a complex labyrinth of invisible highways that only the Mendahir knew about. Riding a wild, bucking horse down the side of a cliff would've been a better time.

Tarness's stomach had either been left behind or just given up. *He* had given up, with the understanding that he was dead and being punished for his transgressions.

"If we make it out of this, Jin," Tarness said, "I swear I'll tell the truth from now on."

"Me tooooo," Jintorich squealed.

After too long, they were spun around like a bolo until slowing to a halt. Their tethers released with an audible pop and both men collapsed to the forest floor.

"It's an attack," Bryymel said, leaping back and grabbing for the two sturdy axes at his waist.

"Not a very good one," Maarja said. "Husband? Jintorich?

What is this?"

Tarness could only moan and wait for the world to stop spinning. He hadn't felt like this since his first night drinking with Angst. Maarja gently patted his shoulder, and he rolled to his side to see Jintorich leap from the ground.

"That was fantastic," the Meldusian shouted, raising a fist in the air.

"What was fantastic?" Rasaol asked with a growl.

"Did you learn how to create a portal?" Maarja asked, warily. "I didn't realize you had the power."

"No, my friend," Jintorich said, calming a bit. "It was the Mendahir."

"The Mendahir?" Rasaol asked. "They were ended long ago."

"No, not entirely," Maarja said. "A story I have not yet shared. Mendahir still appear as ghosts in Grayhollow. I faced them on my return trip to Nordruaut with Angst and Jintorich. They were going to kill me, along with that Berfemmian, for our people's parts in their deaths. They accepted our apology and asked that we leave. I do not remember them offering to make portals like elements or Al'eyrn."

"It was so much more than a portal," Jintorich said, his ears pointed in excitement.

As Jin went on to explain their wild ride, Tarness's brain finally caught up to his body. He sat as best he could in armor and looked around. Dusk had fallen on the Nordruaut camp, and distant fires dotted his vision. Maarja and the others around this small fire had just finished roasting a large buck. The delicious smell made his mouth water, even if his stomach hadn't completely forgiven him yet. They'd undoubtedly make amends soon.

There was also tension around the campfire, as if he'd accidentally walked in on his parents arguing. Rasaol and Gose were aggressively questioning Jintorich, while Maarja stood on and watched. She didn't defend Jin or show any affection to Tarness. Bryymel and Niihlu ignored the inquisition, staring at Tarness with hands on their weapons.

He stood, brushed himself off, and approached the feast. Tarness grabbed a bone, pulled off a chunk of meat and offered Jintorich a bite. The Meldusian shook his head, his tall eyebrows furrowed with concern.

"Mmmm," Tarness said, chewing the bland meat slowly. He choked it down, approached Niihlu, and nodded at the flask in his hand.

Niihlu threw it to the ground and kicked it over. With a calming breath, Tarness lifted it and took a draw. His stomach flinched at the bitter ale, but he could manage. After that ride, he could probably handle anything.

"You don't all usually camp together," Tarness said, pointing at them with the venison. He hurriedly took another bite. Who knew how this would go down, and they appeared unlikely to share more food. "What is this?"

"Rasaol and Niihlu have told us you are a servant of Magic," Maarja said. "I don't believe them, but..." She glanced at his ring.

Tarness swallowed hard. He had hoped to explain everything to his wife in private, assuming the ring would let him. She deserved to understand why he'd done what he had before telling the others.

"We just need your story, brother," Gose said.

"I—" His words instantly cut off as the ring burned his finger. Nothing came out of his mouth, and he shook with rage.

"He cannot speak what is on his mind," Jintorich said, glancing at Tarness. "But if I may? Tarness and his friends discovered a mage city in Nordruaut. They were stuck in a blizzard with no way in until friend Dallow created an entrance. It was small, and just enough for Tarness to throw them through to safety before the doorway closed. As Tarness was dying in the cold, Magic appeared and offered him that ring for his life."

Tarness gasped for breath. Whatever trap had locked his jaw and frozen his tongue was suddenly gone. The anger and power seeping from him were quickly replaced with guilt.

"I can talk, Jin," he said.

"Then talk, my friend," Jintorich said. "Hurry."

"I took it to help Angst," Tarness said, staring at Maarja.

"I believe this," Maarja said, her downcast eyes briefly glancing up to his.

"Jintorich has been trying to help me remove it without success," Tarness said. "That's why we sought out the Mendahir."

"They couldn't do anything," Jintorich said, defeat heavy in his voice.

"So you remain a servant of Magic," Rasaol said coldly. "You were almost dead from cold when we took you in. We would have killed you had we known."

"We still should," Niihlu said, wielding Ghorfjend.

"I would suggest standing down, friend Nordruaut," Jintorich said, his tiny staff glowing brightly.

"I have two foci, little man," Niihlu said.

"I only need one," Jintorich said, crouching low to the ground.

"Wait, there's more," Tarness said. He wasn't the only one working with Magic. The element had delivered him to Rasaol and brought Jarle's body to them. If it was the time for truth, they should hear everything. "Let's put all the dice on the table. I... I..." His jaw locked in place as the familiar burn of the ring returned. It was as if Magic knew exactly when to stop him from speaking. He looked around desperately from Jintorich to Maarja and finally Bryymel. The short, bald Nordruaut stared at him malevolently. All he could say was, "No."

"Yes," Bryymel said. "King Rasaol, please tell everyone what you told me."

"Tarness killed Jarle," Rasaol said, his voice as cold and dead as Jarle's body.

"No," Maarja wailed.

"Is...is this true?" Jintorich asked, his large blue eyes were wider than ever.

"I think so, yes," Tarness said, "but..."

Maarja's fist moved so fast and struck with such force that everything went dark before Tarness hit the ground.

34

After two minutes of Jaden and Dallow arguing, Rose's snarky chiding, and Captain Mirim's tired glances, Victoria decided it was time.

"Rose and I are going to scout the area," she said.

"We are?" Rose asked.

"Is that wise?" Mirim asked. "I would be more than happy to join you."

"I will soon be Queen of Unsel," Victoria said, coolly. "So it is wise."

"Oh," Mirim said, her eyebrows raised. "Yes, Your Highness."

"Nikkola, if Jaden or Dallow say anything insulting to each other," Victoria said as she summoned her swifen, "I would like you to blast them both."

"Okay," Nikkola said. Her hands turned black, and bubbles of dark power floated around them.

"Simon," Victoria said, sweetly, "be a dear and heal them so she can do it again."

"Gladly." Simon bowed to her and smiled.

Dallow and Jaden stared at her in surprise. Jaden was about to say something, but Dallow shook his head and nodded toward Nikkola.

"Come along, Rose," Victoria said. "This won't take long."

"What are we doing again?" Rose asked, mounting her red

sapling buck.

"Girl stuff," Victoria said.

"Ugh," Rose said. "As long as I don't have to brush your hair."

Having seen the clearing on the way to the mage city entrance, Victoria led them across enormous vines. She took deep, calming breaths while Rose whined and prattled on like they were sisters—venting about lousy food, sweaty jungles, dumb boys, and her sore back.

Victoria cleared her head of Rose's noise. She let her worries for Angst, her people back home, and all of Ehrde wash away. Just as Captain Guard Tyrell had taught her, she focused on this moment. It had a lot of possibilities. Victoria could see all of them like an old apple tree with many branches. In her mind, she plucked a few of the ripest fruits and set them in a pile. When they arrived at the clearing, she dismounted her unicorn, ready for whatever may come.

"What's this?" Rose asked.

"I took much of what my mother taught me for granted, but I always listened," Victoria said. "You see, she wasn't always a nice person, or even a good mom, but she was a great queen."

"She wasn't *my* favorite," Rose said, dismounting at the opposite side of the clearing. "But, now that she's dead, it doesn't matter anymore. What's your point?"

The dig was easy to dismiss. After this trip, Victoria was numb to Rose's barbed tongue. She smiled calmly at the young redhead, and Rose flushed.

"Our queen taught me that subjects either lead, follow, or are dealt with. The leaders become needed advisers and champions of Unsel. The followers become patriots," she said. "I'm here to deal with you."

"Oh," Rose said, fondling the daggers on her hips. "And how do you propose to deal with me?"

"A duel, you and me," Victoria said, brandishing her sword and setting the tip on the ground, directly before her foot. "Everything on the table. If I win, you go home—or wherever you want—and leave your daggers behind."

"And when I win?" Rose asked.

"What do you want?" Victoria asked.

"I get to decide what we do with Angst," Rose said. "And you renounce your throne."

"Oh, is that how we're playing it?" Victoria asked, holding that fruit close. She drew her sword, and her voice became dark and cold. "Let's go."

Rose didn't go, or come, or blur toward her. She stared at Victoria, her jaw agape and hands shaking.

"This is a trick," Rose said. "You know the future, but I'm Al'eyrn. You can't beat me."

"I'm waiting," Victoria said. She crouched slightly, set the tip of her blade on the ground, and extended her free arm behind her back to balance.

The wind blew, a bird cawed overhead, and Victoria smirked with confidence.

"You're not afraid, even a little," Rose said. "You'll win, won't you?"

"You promised to be my champion but have been nothing more than a painful growth that I need to be rid of," Victoria said. "Let's get this over with. I have a world to save."

Rose dropped the daggers, collapsed to her knees, and sobbed. Victoria glanced up at the bird before walking over to her.

"Get up," she said, sheathing her sword. "We're done here, and we have work to do."

"How can you just let it go?" Rose asked, tears pooling in her large, dark eyes. "Angst hurt us. He hurt me. How do you get over that?"

"Because I'm a queen," Victoria said. "Of course I was hurt. Angst is my closest friend. He's also a man desperate to save his family. I don't agree with his methods, but I understand his decisions. It would've taken nothing for him to kill us. Instead, he stopped us the only way he could. You don't even realize that he protected us during our journey to this awful place."

Rose sniffled deeply and stared at the daggers. Victoria turned her back on the young woman and summoned her unicorn.

"You have been a poor friend to Angst because you're faithless. You are a worse champion to me because you're selfish," Victoria said, mounting the beast. "We are not family. We are not friends. Either be my champion and follow my lead or stay here and rot in your tears."

Rose looked up, gasping through her sobs. Her breath caught, and she stared at Victoria in shock.

"If you do choose to stay here," Victoria said, "stay out of Unsel, forever. You will no longer be welcome there."

As she rode off, Rose called out to her. Most of her pleas and apologies were incomprehensible, save for one moment of clarity.

"I don't understand," Rose said. "When did your swifen get armor?"

* * * *

Victoria returned alone to wary, yet respectful glances. Since arriving at this nightmare of vines, they hadn't seen a single animal, not even a bug. When she'd faced down Rose, there had been a bird overhead. She had no doubt Sean was watching and had Simon tell them everything.

"I see the boys standing," Victoria said to Nikkola. "I take that as a good sign."

The woman nodded quickly.

"And the door?" she asked Captain Mirim.

"Dallow figured it out," she said, smiling proudly. "Ready when you are, Your Highness."

"Are we…" Dallow stared down the path behind her. "Do we wait?"

"You can stay behind after opening the door," Victoria said coolly. "We need you, but the choice is yours."

"No," Dallow said, closing his eyes and letting out a deep sigh. "No, there is no choice. This isn't about me."

Jaden and Dallow walked to opposite ends of the enormous double door. Both men looked at each other, nodded, and placed their fingers against small copper disks in the wall. Their hands sank through to the elbow.

"You were right," Jaden said.

"We were right. We make a good team," Dallow said. "On my mark. Three...Two...One."

Simultaneously, they twisted their arms in opposite directions. The noisy rattle of chains was soon followed by a painful wrenching of rusty steel. The doors opened with a gasp as the city took a breath of fresh air. Everyone stepped back as they swung wide.

Light from the doorway revealed a vine path into darkness. Victoria dismounted her armored unicorn and dismissed it before leading the way. Inside, she whispered something to Sean. The young man smiled and nodded.

As the doors slowly closed, Dallow watched on, the hope fading from his eyes.

"Everything works out eventually," she said, resting a hand on his shoulder. "You'll see."

The tall man nodded as they heard a resounding slam and darkness enveloped them.

35

"This place smells like rotting vegetables," Alloria said, clutching her stomach.

"Exactly why I avoid salads," Angst said, trying not to breathe through his nose. "They're dangerous."

She let out the barest of chuckles. "I don't feel very good."

"That's what happens when you kiss old men," Angst said, placing a hand on her shoulder. "We have cooties."

"Not funny," Alloria said, wincing. "I don't want to be in here."

"We'll hurry," he said.

"To where?" she asked.

The light that spilled through tiny cracks in the vine-covered dome was as useful as starlight on a cloudy night. Asking the swords for help was like asking a teenager to clean their room. His pleas were reluctantly met with just enough light to see Alloria's worried face.

To make it worse, the ruins of this mage city weren't much different than being in the jungle. The thick air was stale and made everything feel close. Alloria nudged up against him, and he jumped.

"Sorry," she said, her face gaunt. "I'm just so tired. It's like this place is eating my strength."

"It's got to be part of the curse," he said. "I feel it too."

The curse Magic had warned them about wasn't supposed to

act so quickly, assuming he'd told the truth. But the element couldn't come in here, and who knew how strong, or hungry, the curse was after so many years.

"Can't you do anything?" she asked.

Magic had said that the shadows absorbed their sanity. He felt tired not crazy. Not to mention, it was too dark for shadows, so that couldn't be the problem. Burning away the vines overhead was a welcome thought but would probably bring down a rain of fire. Definitely a bad idea. Even if he made a shield to protect them, the fire might destroy what they'd come for.

"I wish Dallow were here," Angst muttered. "He'd know what to do."

* * * *

"No wonder Angst hates vegetables," Victoria said. "This place stinks."

"I feel like I ate a bad turnip," Nikkola said, clutching her stomach.

Sean collapsed into a heap and began convulsing. Simon rushed to his brother, a blue grow surrounding his hands.

"I can keep him alive, but it's like his life is being sucked out," Simon said. "We need to do something."

"Can you make us some light?" Mirim asked. "Dallow, Jaden, both of you?"

"I know the spell you cast in the forest," Jaden said in rushed words. "The one that revealed the dragon."

"Go," Dallow said.

The flash of white light that filled the entrance was quickly swallowed by darkness.

"That should've worked," Jaden said in frustration.

"We're too weak. This city must be cursed like the others," Dallow said. "No offense, but I wish Angst were here."

* * * *

"I need a sun," Angst said to his foci. "Now."

Nothing. Not even a hum. He was desperate for their help; he couldn't do it alone.

"Fine. It's over," he said, pulling both swords from his back and setting them flat on the ground. He lay down beside them. The vines were cold, and hungry, and absorbed his life even faster than before.

"Angst," Alloria said, her voice shaky. "What are you doing?"

"Giving up," he said. "Without the foci, there's nothing left for me. The swords can rest here for an eternity and enjoy watching me decay."

"Why are you doing this?" she said, dropping to her knees beside him. She pounded on his chest, weakly. "We can leave and be together. That would be better than this. Anything would be better than this."

"I said I was going to save my family," Angst said. "If my foci won't help, then it's over. You can leave or stay."

"Please, no," she said, her voice an even higher pitch than normal. Alloria lay across his chest, giving into exhaustion. "So tired."

"I'm sorry, Alloria," he said, struggling to breathe. "I didn't mean for it to end like this."

"'S okay," Alloria said. "All I wanted was you, and now we're together."

Her voice trailed off, and he shut his eyes. Maybe it truly was over, and what did it matter? Heather was gone. His children were gone. If he died here, would he see them again or was it only darkness? And darkness came in cool, slithering tendrils, creeping like vines over his entire body.

"I love you," Alloria whispered.

"I know," Angst said.

The familiar dirge of Dulgirgraut the Defender filled his ears, soon followed by Chryslaenor's excited tune. They went back and forth until the foci found harmony and shared a spell. Angst muttered the words, barely lifting his hands and waving them as directed. It was enough.

Light blared overhead, far too bright to sleep through. He opened his eyes and immediately squinted. Whatever that spell was, it hadn't only created sunlight inside the dome—his energy slowly returned. He lay there for long moments, taking deep breaths and petting Alloria's hair.

"Thank you," he said to his foci in a scratchy voice. "Just what we needed."

Angst shook Alloria gently, but she didn't move. He sat up and rolled her over. She wasn't breathing. Was his gamble a fatal mistake? Had the swords taken too long? Chryslaenor reminded him of how he'd revived her after escaping the Unsel prison. He took a deep breath, parted his lips, and saw...something. Was that a pucker?

"Nice try," he said, flicking her nose.

"Ouch," she said, covering it with a hand. "That's no way to treat a lady."

"I'll keep that in mind when I find one," he said. He shoved Alloria off and stood, dusting himself off before helping her up.

"You made a sun," she said, shielding her eyes as she glanced up. Her voice became sultry. "You could help make a son with me."

"At least you're consistent," he said, rolling his eyes. "I'll take that as a sign you're better."

Alloria held her hands behind her back, thrusting out her chest and twisting about so he could fully view her bodaciousness.

"I see that everything is okay," he said with a wry smile. "We should move quickly in case something else goes wrong."

"What could possibly go wrong now?" she asked, innocently.

"No wonder everyone hates it when I say that," he said with a wince.

* * * *

"Angst," Victoria said, picking herself up from the ground. "He's here."

"Took him long enough," Mirim muttered, vigorously rubbing her arms.

"Maybe he wasn't affected like the rest of us," Jaden said. "If he's on the move, we need to hurry."

"Hurry where?" Nikkola asked, groggily.

Simon knelt beside her and placed his glowing hand on her forehead. After several moments she nodded and was able to stand.

"Maybe there?" Jaden asked, pointing to a building at the center of the city surrounded by large pyramids.

Dallow circled everyone slowly, looking down the entire time. He took cautious steps, pausing to stare at everyone's feet.

"Maybe he hit his head?" Nikkola asked.

"Something's not right," Dallow said, finally looking up.

"What is it?" Victoria asked.

"Our shadows," he said. "They're falling in the wrong direction."

36

"Wow," Alloria said with a twirl. "This place must've been something else."

She tripped, somehow falling into Angst's arms. Rather than chiding her, like he probably should have, he instead dipped her like they were at a fancy ball. She giggled in surprise as he lifted her, reaching out so she could twirl off his arm.

"You can dance?" she asked, excitedly.

"I cannot," he said. "Have you ever seen a foal stand for the first time? Imagine that to music."

"Ha," she said with another spin. "I used to be a good dancer, but I forgot. Hey, I stopped spinning, but my shadow added another twirl." She bent over, eyeing the shadow suspiciously.

"It's the curse," he said. "We should hurry."

"To where?" she asked.

Gyldorane was vast, even by mage city standards, and must've been home to tens of thousands. Few structures remained, most of them fallen away to time or eaten by vines. Five keep-sized pyramids circled a slightly larger building in the shape of a hexagon. He had optimistically hoped to find the foci dead center, but it would take a lifetime and a half to search them all. A little direction would help. Maybe after teaching him how to cast sunlight, the swords were willing to share more.

"You awake back there?" he asked, rapping a knuckle on the side of Chryslaenor. The sword responded with a blue spark that

251

singed his hand like stray charcoal from a campfire. "Ouch," he said, jerking his hand back and sucking the wound.

"They don't seem to like you much," she said, gently taking his hand and blowing on the burn. At least she wasn't licking it.

"They don't like my plan," Angst said. "And apparently will only help if we're dying."

"We need a map," she said. "You should do your blurry, running thing and find one."

"Good idea," he said in surprise. Why hadn't he thought of that? "Will you be okay?"

"Maybe leave one of your friends behind," she suggested, nodding at the swords.

"Right," he said, wielding Dulgirgraut and setting it to rest vertically on its tip. Pointing a finger at the sword, he said, "Behave yourself."

"He won't burn me," she said, resting her cheek against the flat of the blade and petting it like a kitten. "I'm not a mean, old man."

"Hey, I'm not old," he said with a wink. In the back of his mind, Dulgirgraut played a quiet chord that almost sounded like a distraught sigh. With a chuckle, he said, "Be right back."

Drawing in magic with a breath, he ran in a blur to the nearest ruin of a building, and then the next. He quickly learned to run across the top of vines that were wide enough to carry him instead of continually stumbling over the smaller ones. Every ten minutes, he sprinted past a bored Alloria before returning to his search.

A sweaty, heart-racing hour later, he found it. An obsidian obelisk stood at the center of what could've been an intersection. It was identical to the one that had led him and his friends to Gressmore Towers. The monolith stood four feet tall and pointed straight up, which wasn't the direction he needed. Pushing on it only made him sweat more, and kicking it made his knee pop painfully.

He growled and stomped around as frustration slowly became rage. The shadow beneath his feet grew and jerked about wildly.

Was this the curse or was it the madness that would make him break Ehrde? Insanity was a horrifying concept, and it approached like a wild boar. Panic overwhelmed him, and he crouched, ready to run back to Alloria and hide behind Dulgirgraut.

A puppy yipped behind him then barked until he spun around. Scar. His black lab puppy, killed by Fire, bounded toward him. Scar's tail wagged hard enough to make his butt rock. Angst collapsed to his knees, tears pouring from his eyes as the dog leaped into his arms and bombarded him with puppy licks. This was a crazy he could handle. If he could see his dead dog, he might get to see his family too.

"I missed you so much," Angst said, petting Scar over and over, knowing if he stopped, his dog would be gone.

Dizziness overtook him, and he leaned back, squeezing his eyes shut. Opening his eyes made the vertigo worse and his stomach churn. A silent explosion of light flashed so bright he could see it through his eyelids. Scar barked loudly enough to boom like thunder. He licked Angst's face once more, and then there was nothing.

Like jumping into an icy lake, clarity returned with a shock that made him stand. He gasped for breath, brushing away tears and a runny nose with his cloak. His shadow had returned to normal, along with his sanity.

"Scar," he whispered.

It hadn't been Scar—it was the madness of this place—but the memory of his old friend had brought back his senses and his resolve.

"Thank you, Scar," Angst said. "You may have just saved us all."

He approached the obelisk and studied it. The Acratic etchings along its side were useless to anyone but Dallow and his less-than-helpful swords. Anderfeld, the Al'eyrn leader at Gressmore Towers, had somehow planted obelisks around Unsel to provide Angst and his friends directions. Maybe he was overthinking this, because shoving and kicking is a way of overthinking, right?

"Direct me to the foci," Angst said.

With a grinding shudder, the obelisk slowly pointed to Angst.

"Funny," Angst said. "Yes, my sword is a foci. Show me the other foci."

The grind sounded more painful this time as the stone directed him to Alloria.

"Right," he said. "Got to be smarter than a rock."

It was impressive that the spell powering this obelisk had lasted so long, but it didn't sound healthy. He may only have one or two questions left and needed to be more specific. What did he know about it? The foci's name was the key he didn't have. The twins had mentioned that it was a horn. It was worth a try.

"Direct me to the horn foci in Gyldorane," he said.

The obelisk reluctantly leaned away from him, eventually grinding to a stop. His eyes followed the pointer to distant rubble, just beyond one of the pyramids. It wasn't a lot, but it'd have to be enough.

"Thanks," he said, before realizing he'd just thanked a rock. As he was leaving, an idea struck him. "Direct me to Prendere."

The obelisk leaned forward and back several times before rising over the ground. Angst stepped away as it shuddered violently until there was nothing left but sparkling dust.

"That would've been too much luck," Angst said.

A final glance around him revealed no signs of his dog. It had been so real. He shook his head, grateful for the memory, and blurred to Alloria.

* * * *

Angst stopped beside Dulgirgraut and watched in amazement as Alloria danced. Unlike the spinning and falling, this was surprisingly elegant. She rose on her toes, held her elbows straight out with her hands against her chest, and spun before leaping into the air. He couldn't imagine the leg strength it took to jump so high. The landing was so quiet, she must've been on invisible feathers. Arching back wincingly far, her hands touched the floor. She smoothly lifted a leg overhead before lithely setting her foot on the ground beside the other. Raising her hands high, she took a deep breath and froze. Her eyes were wide and she covered her mouth.

"Oh," she said, blushing as she slowly rested flat on her feet. "Um, hi."

"That was...entrancing," Angst said, in genuine awe. "I've never seen anyone dance like that. I can't imagine how much you trained. How long did it take to learn?"

"Mom always said I was a natural," she said, brushing honey blond hair from her damp cheek. "I took some lessons, but then she died, and Father had other plans."

"I'm sorry," Angst said, frowning. "But to me, it looks like you should be teaching, or performing."

"You really liked it?" she asked, her eyes pleading.

This was a very young Alloria, surprisingly insecure and hungry for praise. He sensed no mischief or even her voracious sexual appetite. This was a side of her he'd never seen, and he really liked it. She was both artistic and humble in her abilities.

"I did," he said. "What inspired you to suddenly do...that?"

"I was dancing with my shadow," she said with a full-lipped smile. "It was like dancing with myself. I've never had a partner before."

He tried his best to hide his worry and sadness behind a smile. She was like a shattered mirror, and the curse had found a long-buried shard. The broken piece he'd spent the most time with was an out-of-control party girl in desperate heat. He'd barely glimpsed the other shards, which seemed to have weight and meaning. Inside that mess was a person who cared, and another who was wise, and now this one, the humble woman who danced like she'd been performing her entire life.

Alloria deserved those shards to be made whole so she could choose which path to live. Not even his great foci had an answer or spell that would glue the young woman back together. Magic had broken her, and Angst didn't know what to do. All he could think of was to encourage the good Alloria. Maybe that would help. Maybe.

"I only wish I could dance as well as your shadow," he said, smiling softly. "You deserve a partner who could compliment your grace and talent."

"Really?" she said hopefully. Alloria blinked several times and shook her head. Her voice transformed from innocent to something far sultrier. "But, honey. I'll dance for you any time you want."

She shimmied up to him, spun around and gyrated. Grasping her shoulders, he gently turned her about to face him. She licked her lips, readying for a kiss. Instead, he leaned his head to one side and pulled her into a firm hug.

She stomped. "Hugs are boring," she muttered into his shoulder.

"Should I stop holding you?" he asked, kissing the top of her head.

"No," she said, relaxing into his embrace.

Without warning, Alloria began sobbing, and he wished his hug was the cure she needed. Her shadow was tiny, as if the curse had given up and was hiding beneath her feet. He wouldn't give up. After a long time, she pulled back, wiping her cheeks and sniffing away her sadness.

"Thanks," she said, almost too quietly for him to hear. She whispered, "I love you."

"Alloria," he said, lifting her chin with a finger. "I love you too."

"Really?" she asked, hopefully.

"Really," he said, staring into those big, beautiful eyes. "Maybe not the way you want, but hopefully the way you need."

"I understand," she said, looking slightly defeated. A mischievous grin crept across her face. "But I still can't wait to have sex with you."

"What?" he said in shock, taking a step back.

She winked, spun about, and ran toward the pyramids, laughing the whole way. He couldn't help but smile and chase after her. Alloria deserved to be chased. Everyone does.

37

"This place must've been amazing," Victoria said, taking it all in.

Jaden stood beside her, more interested in imminent dangers than the distant pyramids. It was cute that he felt the need to protect her. He was cute. When Jaden had first arrived, he couldn't remember much—just his name and that he was from the future. She'd been drawn to his mystery and intelligence. It didn't take long for their flirting to become something more...until he remembered. Jaden had spent months unconscious in the infirmary. When he woke, his memories changed everything.

Conversations with the man now ended in frustration and shouting, because she refused to believe him. In his future, Angst's wish at Prendere had cracked Ehrde, leaving a wide gap between the halves. The loss of life was beyond her understanding. Humanity had survived, but it had become something twisted. Two dystopian nations had grown from the ashes to rule their side beyond the crack. War had become a way of life as countries found new ways to cross the divide.

His stories of floating ships, machines of war, science warriors, steam, and the fact that most could wield magic was an overwhelming fantasy. She could comprehend most of his narrative and had wanted to believe, until he admitted the truth. He'd been sent back to kill Angst so that none of those horrors would happen. When Jaden had told her who'd sent him, she'd been filled with uncontrollable rage. She knew in her heart that they had to be lies.

It just didn't add up. More than anyone, she understood how change affected the future. The fact that he was here and had already dipped his toe in the pool of time should've created enough ripples to affect everything, but he refused to accept her argument. If she was willing to believe his future, he should've believed what she saw. It was a tough sell when Jaden's future wasn't a series of straight lines but a jigsaw puzzle with missing pieces.

Yet, here they stood, in the last mage city before the end of all things. She had given up so much and was on the verge of losing more. Her mother was gone, Tyrell was gone, and Angst was lost to her. Was Jaden all she had left? Maybe they couldn't be lovers, but it was still possible for them to be something. Friends would be nice. More than friends would be better. And, he was cute.

"Are there mage cities in your future?" she asked.

His head whipped about as if stung by a wasp, and a hopeful smile crept up one cheek. "Actually, there is one," he said. "Not far from your castle. It has a sovereign leader, separate from the western empire. That city is a haven in the middle of a nightmare. If you can find your way in, they'll teach you wielding. That's where I learned, before being caught and slaved to the arenas…" He trailed off as his tone darkened.

She didn't press for more and placed a hand on his.

"Are we…?" he said, his face pained.

"Friends or something," she said. "That's a good place right now."

"Friends works," he said, facing her with glassy eyes. "Or something."

"Are you going to try to kill Angst?" she asked.

"I promised I wouldn't," he said, staring at her hand. "I don't think I could, anyway."

"Those two swords make him a lot to handle," she said.

"That's not what I meant. I don't think it's in me to try," he said, now looking into her eyes. "When I was sent back, I planned to be ruthless like in my arena days. I promised myself I wouldn't fall in love with you, but—"

"Do you ever shut up?" she said, gripping the back of his neck and pressing her lips to his.

Thirty seconds of passion and wet lips and dancing tongues wasn't enough to quench her longing. They needed a room, not a city. Victoria's heart raced to satin sheets and a steamy night as she forced herself to pull away. It wasn't her first choice or even her hundredth, but it was the right decision. They laughed with foreheads pressed together and her hand still holding the back of his neck.

"I...I just want you to know," he said, slow to release her. "I understand if you have to choose another, but my feelings will never change."

That sacrifice broke Victoria's heart. He would give up everything to save Ehrde, knowing she would give anything to save her best friend.

"They're coming," he said.

"Thank you," she said. "I needed this."

"Me too," he said.

Their team approached, and both stood tall and looking on as if life hadn't just happened.

"Why are you upset?" Victoria asked, reaching for Dallow's hand. He sighed as she took it. "Oh no."

"Yeah," he said, his shoulders slumping in defeat.

"What?" Simon asked, looking around nervously. "Did you guys find something?"

"An obelisk that gave me directions," Dallow said, his eyes downcast. "There are libraries everywhere. Maybe thirty or forty."

"I'd expect you to be jumping for joy," Jaden said in a snide tone.

"Normally, yes. This would be a great find," Dallow said. "But we don't have time to search them all."

"Did it tell you where to find Angst?" Simon asked.

"Sort of," Dallow said. "I think he's headed beyond the farthest pyramid."

"Helpful," Jaden said, turning to Victoria. "Can't you just tell us where we end up?"

She concentrated on the future and immediately reeled with vertigo. Jaden grabbed her arm, and she held on until it passed.

"Nope," she said, swallowing bile, several times. "I'm limited here. I get sick when I try to see the future."

"Then we follow Dallow's lead," Jaden said. "The libraries are a waste of time."

"Libraries are never a waste of time," Dallow said, his eyes flashing white.

"We need to stop Angst," Jaden shouted. "I'm already giving up everything, I refuse to give up Ehrde."

"We need direction," Dallow snapped. "We don't even know why we're here."

The argument simmered to a boil as everyone vomited out vile anger. Nikkola's hands bubbled with dark power, and red lightning spewed from Jaden's fists. Victoria leaned in so everyone would hear, the sword in her hand rattling against Mirim's. Fury and rage blurred her vision. She raised her sword, preparing to swing...

An explosion of sound struck them, making everyone grab their ears and take a step back. It was a fierce, growly, bark of a noise that cleared Victoria's mind like a splash of cold water. She wanted to cheer, and cry, and vomit as sanity and focus slowly returned.

"That sucked," Nikkola said, grasping her belly. "What happened?"

Sean turned away and leaned over as the contents of his stomach emptied onto the vines.

"A curse," Dallow said. "All mage cities seem to have them. This one is bad."

"Your shadows," Mirim said, pointing at the ground between Dallow and Jaden.

The shadows beneath the two men were larger than the others

and jerked about in an invisible tug-of-war. They both stared down with wide eyes. Jaden poked his with a sword while Dallow lifted one foot, and then the other. They took calming breaths and nodded at each other as their shadows subsided.

"It'd be best to split these two up," Mirim said, looking at Victoria.

"Agreed," she said with a nod. "We go find Angst while Dallow and someone go to the libraries."

"Nikkola," Mirim said. "He needs offensive support."

"That's me," Nikkola said, raising her hand. "I'm offensive."

"Not what I meant," the captain said, rolling her eyes.

"But which one?" Dallow asked. "There are so many, I don't even know where to begin."

"Why so many libraries?" Mirim asked. "Are they all the same?"

"These people may have been crazy," Dallow scoffed. "Our libraries back home have books on everything. Here, each library specializes on a theme."

"Like what?" Mirim asked.

"Cooking, art, elements, history, geology, magic," Dallow said. "It's a long list."

"Is there a library that tells you where to go?" Mirim asked.

"Sort of," Dallow said. "The history library is also cartography, or guidance. It didn't translate well."

Mirim raised an eyebrow and smiled.

"You're a genius," Dallow said, his face brightening.

"I am," Mirim said, lifting her chin proudly.

"Jaden was right, pointing to the farthest pyramid isn't helpful. Let me try something," he said. Kneeling, he whispered something into his cupped hands and blew. A blue orb floated from his hand and stopped five feet away. As it emanated a dim light, a second orb appeared five feet beyond the first, and then another. The path soon led well beyond view.

"Wow," Nikkola said. "Nice hands."

"Thanks," Dallow said with a wink.

"Be careful," Victoria said, placing a hand on Dallow's

shoulder.

"You too," he said. "Hurry, they won't last long."

"Dallow," Jaden said, with a strained effort. "I, uh…"

"We'll figure it out," Dallow said with a nod. "Let's get out of here first."

38

"Go away," Maarja said. She sat against a large oak, staring down at her flask of wine. "Go away, or I'll punch you too."

"You broke his face," Jintorich said, settling down beside her.

"Good." The large woman snuffled into some furs and took a draw from her flask. "He broke our marriage."

"I was able to heal him while he was still unconscious," Jintorich said. "I don't think he'll remember much."

"Then I'll do it again," she said, baring a fist.

"I doubt there will be time," Jintorich said. "Rasaol ordered Niihlu to 'take him to the woods' tomorrow morning. I don't know what that means."

Fear washed away resentment, and her eyes met his for the first time. "Nordruaut are fond of small pets, like bears and frost lions."

"Small?" Jintorich asked, his ears rising tall.

"As with all things, pets become old," Maarja said. "We give them a quick death in the woods rather than making them die slowly from age."

"I understand," Jintorich said, respectfully. "Referring to Tarness as a small pet is quite the insult."

"I will correct Rasaol in good time," Maarja said. "But I understand their decision. Nordruaut kill traitors."

"And you're okay with that?" he asked.

"He lied to me," she shouted, slamming the ground with her

fist.

Jintorich popped up like corn on the griddle and sat again when the forest floor calmed.

"Tarness was unable to tell you the truth," Jintorich said.

"*You* lied to me," she said, darkly.

"For that, I am sorry," Jintorich said, spreading his hands out. "But it was not my truth to tell. I knew little of Tarness's story, only enough to get him killed. I would not be a friend to put him or you in that position."

"Fine, I won't hit you," Maarja said with a sigh. "Even if you idiots thought you were doing the right thing, he still killed Jarle. There's no way to fix that."

"What if he didn't kill Jarle?" Jintorich stood, placing his staff foci to rest on its tip.

"You're trying to fix that," she said, rolling her eyes. "Rasaol told us that Tarness killed Jarle."

"And Tarness?" Jintorich asked, resting his tiny hands behind his back. "What did he say?"

"I don't remember," she muttered. "I was too angry."

"Your husband said, 'I think so,'" Jintorich said.

"What does that mean?" she asked. "You either kill someone, or you don't."

"What if he was tricked into killing Jarle?" Jintorich asked. "Or worse, tricked to believe he had killed Jarle?"

"He is no fool," she said in a half-hearted defense. "Unless I'm upset with him."

"I love Tarness. He is a good man with more common sense than anyone I know," Jintorich said. "But he is also just a man, and susceptible to being tricked by an element like Magic."

Maarja looked at the Meldusian with a hint of hope in her eyes.

"Look at what Magic has done to the Fulk'han, to my people and me," Jintorich said, his ears drooping slightly. "And they burned Rohjek to ash."

"Yes, but those are nations," Maarja said in an unsure tone. "My husband is just one human."

CHAPTER THIRTY EIGHT

"He is also Angst's best friend," Jintorich said. "I couldn't imagine a better tool to manipulate Angst."

"It makes sense," she said. "What do we tell the others?"

"I've spent the last six months helping Tarness try to remove that ring," Jintorich said. "A man completely under Magic's control would not be able to try. If Magic couldn't keep him from trying to remove the ring, Magic could not make him kill Jarle. What do you think?"

Her blue eyes became wet with tears, and her lower lip trembled. "I broke my husband's face?" she sobbed, burying her face in her hands.

Jintorich bounded over to her shoulder and patted her long, platinum hair. They were an odd couple, the giant and the mouse. He was small enough for her to eat in a bite, but the Al'eyrn had incredible power and uncanny wisdom. What had happened to all Meldusians was unexpected, but with his foci, Jintorich was a danger to be wary of.

Moments and tears passed before she leaned her head against him. When she finally nodded, he hopped back to the ground.

"It's the worst argument ever," she said with a sad laugh. "I think you are right and I should have believed in my husband. But the others will never agree. With Rasaol as king and Niihlu his right hand, few would stand up for Tarness."

Jintorich paced the length of her leg several times before stopping to look at her.

"We have no choice," she said, sitting up and pulling her hair to one side. "We need to break him free."

"That will be a challenge," Jintorich said. "He is bound on the tallest hill at the center of camp."

"Can you create a distraction that will draw the others away?" she asked.

"Several," he said. "But we will have to be quick."

"Agreed," she said. "Then where do we go?"

"We find Angst," Jintorich said, his long brows furrowing. "And we help him end this."

Bryymel smiled as he pulled back to the shadows of tree and

brush. The Nordruaut and Meldusian's simple escape plan would be easy to foil, and with Niihlu's help, he may even be rid of Jintorich. That tiny aberration was far more dangerous than he'd anticipated. When so many of his plans had failed, it was a relief that this one finally worked to his liking.

* * * *

Tarness shifted in his restraints, rocking from side to side in an attempt to find some semblance of comfort. After sitting for hours with his arms bound behind him and his mouth gagged, everything itched. His full suit of plate armor was stifling in his stress and anxiety. Sweat dripping down his back felt like they had set him on an anthill. It almost angered him to the point of breaking free, just to strip naked and roll around in pine cones.

But what would be the point? Niihlu would be here soon enough to ice him with that giant foci war axe. The ring Tarness had accepted from Magic was supposed to keep him alive, but hopefully, he wouldn't live without a head or chopped into pieces. It may be funny at parties but would make it tough to eat.

At times like this, right before facing the next big bad, Angst would cringeworthingly utter the words, "What could possibly go wrong?" If Angst were here, and Tarness could've spoken around the rope gag, he would've shouted, "This!" Tarness accepted that phrase as the darker side of Angst's humor, but here and now, he wondered if there was more to it. It was like accepting that everything *was* going to go wrong and they'd have to face it anyway. That would be profound, even for Angst. He'd have loved to ask his friend, but that wasn't going to happen now or two thousand years from now if he couldn't break free.

"I'm sure you're thinking of a way to escape," Bryymel said as he crested the hill. "I would be."

Tarness looked away in a weak attempt to ignore the Nordruaut. Ever since he'd appeared, seemingly out of nowhere, Tarness had tried avoiding him. Gose's younger brother was the runt of the litter with something to prove. He was the only bald

Nordruaut Tarness had seen, shorter even than Maarja—though the only person this seemed to bother was Bryymel. The Nordruaut was capable enough on good days, but full of distrust and poisonous conspiracy on bad. His brother's rise to power had emboldened his tongue, and on more than one occasion, Tarness had wanted to remove it.

"But escape would be useless, wouldn't it?" Bryymel said. "Even if you could fight through the horde of Nordruaut surrounding this hill, I'm sure you wouldn't be hard to track."

Tarness looked at the man in surprise. Was he referring to their innate ability to track or the ruby ring that tethered him to Magic?

"The knowledge of your transgressions has spread to the other camps like a leaf on the wind," Bryymel said, reaching behind Tarness to remove the gag. "It will be nearly impossible to wash away your sins."

"Who are you?" Tarness asked. "I know you're Gose's brother, but he thought you'd died in battle."

"There's nothing suspicious about surviving," he said.

"Right, but what you just said," Tarness peered at him. "You don't even talk like the other Nordruaut."

"You have other concerns, Tarness," Bryymel said. "Your friends are coming to break you free tonight and don't expect anyone to be here. They will be surprised."

"Why are you telling me this?" Tarness asked. "Are you just trying to torture me?"

"Yes," Bryymel said with a full-lipped smile. "And I want you to think on it. You have…what, four hours to ponder all the possible outcomes? If Rasaol and Niihlu were to catch Maarja and Jintorich, they would also be put to death."

"Don't do this, Brymell," Tarness pleaded. "They don't need to die trying to save me. I'll tell them to leave."

"I don't think so," Bryymel said, replacing the gag. "Their treachery must be revealed."

Tarness shouted through the gag, attracting two Nordruaut guards from the bottom of the hill.

"What's going on here?" a towering woman asked.

"He was trying to free himself," Bryymel said. "You should check the restraints."

"I'll get more rope," another guard said, lumbering back down the hill.

Tarness could do nothing but glare as the Nordruaut woman lifted him to check the ropes. She dropped him roughly onto his side, and Bryymel kneeled beside him.

"I told you to stop trying to remove the ring," Bryymel whispered. "You should never have gone to the Mendahir."

Tarness's eyes went wide, and his blood ran as cold as a Nordruaut winter.

39

"This can't be right," Angst said as they approached their destination.

"What do you mean?" Alloria asked. "I can see the foci from here. Angst, we found it."

They had, indeed, found the horn. The foci rested on a four-foot tall pedestal, light from Angst's makeshift sun reflecting off its silver bell like a sign that said, "I'm right here. Just pick me up." The excitement of the discovery was tarnished by the enormous pile of bones that led to the horn. The skeletal hill stretched out for fifty yards in all directions with no clear path to the center.

"Yeah, but how do I get there?" he asked. "This has to be some sort of trap."

"Can't you turn them to sand like you do with metal doors?" she asked. "Or maybe brush them away to make a path?"

He should've thought of that. Like bad hair dye he would never admit to using, the insanity cure at the obelisk was fading. Fortunately, the reason that dripped out of his mind seemed to pour into Alloria's.

Willing the bones into dust didn't work. With an effort, he drew in power from his foci and pushed. The pile didn't budge. He kicked the nearest rib cage and was grateful for steel-toed armor, even though it still stung.

"I don't know if it's me, or this place," he said with a discouraged sigh. "These bones aren't going anywhere."

"What about rushing in and out?" she asked, her voice filled with encouragement. "Like a blur."

"Yeah, I guess," he said, removing his swords and setting them beside her.

"You're leaving both to protect me?" she asked. "I don't think there are any monsters here to eat me, honey. Maybe just leave one to keep watch."

"Sure," Angst said, struggling to understand. "Wait, no. I don't know what will happen if I hold the horn and another foci."

"What are you going to do after you grab the horn?" she asked. "How will you carry all three?"

"I dunno. I'm still working on that," he said. "Hopefully they'll get along. I'll ask when I get back."

He warily placed a foot on the first skull. To his surprise, he didn't burst into flames, the dome didn't collapse, and Ehrde didn't explode. Alloria pulled him back before he could take another and gently kissed his cheek.

"For luck," she said.

He nodded his thanks and pressed forward. Blurring there and back sounded great, but there was no telling if all the bones were as sturdy as the one he'd kicked. After fifteen sweaty, ankle-twisting minutes, he found a rib cage intact enough to balance on. The horn foci was only ten yards away. Behind him, Alloria violently tugged a lock of honey-blond hair while wearing a fake princess-smile. She looked more nervous than he felt.

"Almost there," he said. "I'll grab it and blur back like you suggested."

"Be careful," she said.

He turned around and took a gentle step forward. The ground beneath him fell, and darkness swallowed him.

* * * *

Dallow's guiding orbs led Victoria and the others on a path as logical as their caster. They followed a pathway without vines before stair-stepping up rubble to end up on an enormous vine that crossed a sinkhole. It would've been nearly impossible to cross this labyrinth of terrors without his guidance.

"How powerful is this guy?" Jaden asked, assisting Victoria with a hand.

"Angst once told me that Dallow knew so many spells, he probably didn't require a foci," Tori said, shuffling down the large vine back to solid ground.

"Glad I didn't fight him," Jaden said. "I've treated Dallow poorly. I'm used to defending myself and standing out in battle. It's tough to change, but you're right, we're on the same side."

Victoria stopped and kissed him full on the mouth. Everyone around them did a poor job of pretending not to notice. She pulled away and smiled.

"What...what was that for?" he asked, touching his lips.

"For growing to be the person I know you can be," she said with a mischievous smile. "And for telling me I'm right. I like to encourage good habits."

Jaden smiled dumbly, nodding in agreement.

Sean and Simon were the last to arrive, and the brothers held each other for dear life.

"Are you two okay?" Victoria asked.

They looked at each other before coming to some unheard agreement. "Simon isn't well," Sean finally said, his voice quiet and dry as if he'd spent a lifetime inhaling campfire.

"Sean?" she asked, looking between them. "Simon?"

Simon looked down as though ashamed.

"We don't have long," Sean urged.

"Do you hear that?" Captain Mirim asked, holding up a hand to quiet everyone.

Distant shouts for help reached them.

"My cousin," Victoria said, unable to keep the disgust from her voice. All eyes fell on her. "We spent a lot of time together growing up. She was always calling for some boy to save her. I'm guessing just so the little tramp could reward—"

"It sounds like she's calling for Angst, Your Highness," Mirim said, adulting the young woman with a steady gaze. "Either she's in trouble, or he is."

"You're right, Captain," she said, taking a deep breath. "Aside from being manipulative, my cousin is either the sweetest person you'll meet or one of the most dangerous. Be prepared for anything. She's crazier than this place, so don't turn your back on her."

The blue orb directly beside them popped out of existence and the five rushed forward as carefully as they could. Alloria stood atop a pile of bones, leaning over and calling after Angst. They stopped beside his two giant foci at the base of the hill, and Victoria drew her sword.

"Hello, cousin," Alloria said, turning around. "You're just in time."

Her face was calm and cool as a mountain lake, making Victoria grit her teeth as everyone else took a step back. She really wanted to race up the hill of bones, behead her cousin in a fit of rage, then giggle it off as curse madness. Angry, bitter, resentful Victoria might do that on a bad day. A queen would probably have someone else do it. Since there were no mercenaries nearby, she let it go with a shudder.

"Where's Angst?" Victoria asked. "Did you kill him?"

"Don't be foolish. He's the only one who can save us," Alloria said, waving them up. "He fell down a pit and isn't moving. Come to me, and hurry. None of the bones will give way."

"She seems saner than I feel," Jaden said, rubbing his temple.

"You said expect anything," Mirim said. "I wasn't expecting this."

"Sean, Simon, stay by the swords," Victoria said.

They both collapsed to the ground. Sean leaned against the giant blade and held Simon close.

Alloria hadn't lied. The footing was stable, and they reached her quickly. Victoria stared at her cousin in awe. Aside from the gray leather hooker outfit that filled her with jealousy and rage, Alloria had an air of serene calm about her. Someone had poured a pitcher of awareness into her eyes, followed by a shot glass of regret.

"I have too much to apologize for in the time we have here," Alloria said. "But I suppose there isn't enough time to make up for all I've done. If I could go back and undo it all, I would," she said, tears welling in her eyes. "I believe Angst can, so I'm helping him save everyone and undo my own mistakes."

In all their time together, Victoria had never seen this side of Alloria. The young woman was regal beyond measure. If it had been possible for this Alloria to escape Gyldorane, she would make a fine queen.

"Where is Angst?" Mirim interrupted.

"He fell into that pit," Alloria said, pointing to the nearby ledge. "He's lying still on a pile of bones. I can't tell if he's alive—"

"He's alive," Victoria said. "His swords won't let him die."

Victoria, Jaden, and Mirim leaned over the edge for a peek. The light Angst had created cast a small spotlight on his still body. Jaden uttered something and reached out. A focused beam of light shot from his clawed hand, revealing the great bone pile Angst lay on and some of the interior around him.

"I think he's moving," Victoria said.

"How do we get him out?" Captain Mirim asked. "This pit is like a hollowed pumpkin."

"We could cut one of the smaller vines and lower it to him," Alloria said.

"On it," Jaden said, looking around.

"Alloria?" Mirim asked. "Where is your shadow?"

While Victoria, Mirim, and Jaden's shadows took turns slap-fighting and playing patty-cake, Alloria's was entirely missing. She lifted a foot, revealing a brighter light beneath it.

"I think my shadow is afraid of me," Alloria said, blushing prettily.

"I know I am," Mirim said with a shudder.

"Ugh," Angst moaned. "Who hit me? Was that Magic, or another dragon? Are they dead? I might be dead."

273

Victoria's eyes met Alloria's, and they smiled in relief. Then she realized who she was smiling at and looked at her cousin sternly. Gray leather? Really?

"I'm here, Angst," she called out.

"Tori?" he asked, pushing himself up to stand. "You're really here?"

"Every brave knight needs a princess to save them once in a while," she said.

"You've been saving me for a long time," he said. "I don't feel well."

"We don't either," she said, her heart swelling.

"Isn't he wonderful?" Alloria said.

"Shut up," Victoria snapped over her shoulder. She turned back to Angst. "Jaden is looking for a vine we can drop down to pull you out."

"Are there any vines along the walls you could use?" Mirim asked.

"Plenty," he said. "But I can't get to them."

"Why not?" she asked.

"Because," he said after a long pause. "I'm not alone."

40

Dallow and Nikkola followed a second path of floating balls. These glowed with a gentle red hue so they could be easily distinguished from the blue path. The trail was more efficient than he'd expected, leading them around obstacles and down clear pathways.

He was grateful for the time to glimpse the wonder of these ruins. The five pyramids were surrounded by squat, rectangular buildings—each 150 to 200 yards wide. Thanks to the perpetual white light from Angst's spell, even the obscene overgrowth of vines couldn't completely hide the interconnecting highways. Like uptight mathematicians, the architects had labored to create a city of 90-degree angles and straight lines. It was logic in design he'd never seen and would have to take note to research one day. To think that—

"Ouch," Dallow said, jerking back the hand Nikkola had been squeezing.

"Sorry." She stopped and covered her mouth, the white light almost masking her blush. "You weren't replying to me, and I was getting scared."

It was his turn to blush. The mage city had absorbed so much of his attention that he'd ignored her. This place may have been an archeologist's dream, but it was also an adventurer's nightmare. Her shadow was slightly larger than his and hopped around more. Hopefully, that was her fear and not something worse. Either way, he had to calm her.

"It's okay to be scared. I am," he said, stretching his fingers until blood and feeling returned.

"Really?" she asked. "But you've been to mage cities before."

"I've been fortunate enough to visit four," Dallow said. "I believe there were five at one time, maybe more. My history books at the library didn't have much to say about them. I'm hoping the books I've been able to collect from the cities will teach us more. I just need more time to translate them."

"Oh," she said with the interest of a student on the last day of school.

Boring also seemed to be calming, and the erratic movement of her shadow began to subside.

"Sorry, I didn't mean to ignore you," Dallow said, offering his hand, which was only a little numb.

She took it and gave him a full-lipped smile so genuine he was taken off guard. This thirty-something wielder with unkempt black velvet hair, high cheeks, and piercing dark eyes was quite pretty. Her dusky zyn'ight armor hinted at a demure figure. While trying to decide if she was taller than five feet without the metal boots, he realized that she'd been sizing him up too.

The red ball beside them popped out of existence, and he jerked his head toward their destination. She nodded, and they walked, hand in vice-locked hand.

"So, you and Rose are…" Nikkola said, waiting for Dallow to fill in the blank.

"Something," he said. "You're direct."

"Is there time for anything else?" she asked. "We can talk more about this place if you prefer."

He hesitated. His relationship with Rose had weighed heavily on him for months, and this trek had created a divide he was wary of crossing. Maybe sharing his concerns with a receptive companion would shed light on his woes. Nikkola had been pleasant on this trip, even funny at times, but he didn't know her at all. Normally he would go to Angst. That wasn't possible, and he could use a friendly ear.

"I was still married when Rose and I first started flirting," he said.

"Nothing wrong with a little flirting," she said with a mischievous smile.

"My ex-wife wouldn't agree," he said, clearing his throat. "But this wasn't Angst-flirting, which is a lot of bark. She flirted with intent, and I loved the attention."

"I'm sure," Nikkola said. "Rose is pretty."

"Yes," he agreed. "When I lost my eyes to dragonfire—"

"Oh no," she said. "You poor thing."

"Thanks. It was awful," he said. "I had a lot of time to think in the dark. My marriage had been broken for a long time. The realization that my wife would leave me because of my scars and blindness was enough to make me end it."

"I get it. I had to end mine too," she said, taking a deep breath. "My ex-husband didn't like that I weighed more after giving birth to Kala. He also didn't like that my face bruised easily. He hit me on the wrong day, and I bruised his face with my power. It was a shame, but he never woke up."

"Really?" Dallow asked, stopping to turn around.

"Yes," she said.

"Good," Dallow said, hesitant to say more.

A brief moment of awkward silence was immediately pushed aside when she asked, "Why did you stop talking?"

"My concerns seem insignificant in comparison."

"No," she said with a frown. "Even if someone else has problems worse than you, that doesn't make yours go away. I was the one who asked."

"You're right," he said. They continued following the path. "With my divorce final, we became a thing. It was great at first."

"Until you learned more about her after the sex," Nikkola said with a nod.

"Yeah," he said with a sigh. "She's crass to the point of being vulgar, and bonding to those daggers didn't help her attitude. I don't like how Rose treats Victoria, but how she's turned on

Angst is worse. He's been a good friend to her, and she wants to destroy him. If he really is going crazy, that just means he needs our help. I guess…I just don't know. What do I do?"

"You've already answered that, Dallow," she said. "I'm sorry. It's not what, but when."

He nodded and kept quiet until the catch in his throat went away.

"What about you?" he asked. "I've been curious why you volunteered."

"Because my daughter is alive," she said with no quaver or hint of sorrow in her voice. "I believe Angst will save her, and I'm going to help him."

"You mean…this whole time," Dallow said in surprise.

"Team Angst. Woohoo," she said, twirling a finger in the air. "I won't let anyone kill him, and neither will you."

"Yeah," he said, nodding in agreement.

"Hey," Nikkola said. "We're here."

"Thanks," Dallow said, turning to look at her. "That helped."

"That's what friends are for," she said, tapping his nose with a finger. "You're welcome to call on me when you've got things sorted out."

"Oh," he said, his cheeks warming. "I, uh…"

"You're cute when you're speechless," she said. "Let's go in."

Dallow spun about to follow the remaining orbs down a broad flight of stairs that led under the building. The vast structure was only neck high above the ground, making it seem more appropriate for Jintorichs than tall Dallows. To his wonder, the stairs they followed into the library were steep enough that he didn't have to duck on entry. Stealing his hand back from Nikkola, he cast the same light spell that had revealed the dragon.

"Ooh," Nikkola said.

"Yeah," Dallow agreed, stumbling over a tiny vine.

The entrance was a grand, white marble affair held up by cracked pillars. Vines had stopped just steps beyond the doorway, as if fearing the knowledge inside. The room smelled of decaying wood and moist parchment. Rows of wooden desks had long ago collapsed to rot. On each side, walkways of bookshelves had dominoed under the weight of time.

"Oh no," Nikkola said. "Dallow, I'm so sorry."

"Don't be," he said, unable to hold back a smile. "Libraries have a sort of magic that never leaves. We just need to find it."

She cocked her head to one side and frowned.

"C'mon," he said, leading her further in.

The magic of this library smelled dank and moldy. Humidity-trapping vines of the city had done nothing to help preserve the tomes held in this subterranean basement. The first book they found squished at the touch like thick, wet cake. The remaining books had become giant mold spores or mushrooms you wouldn't feed to your worst enemy.

"So much lost," Dallow said with a sigh. "Maybe I can convince Angst to go back in time a little further and save all of this."

Nikkola patted his shoulder then squeezed gently. "Hey, what's that over there?"

At the back of the room stood a long table surrounded by a steel railing.

"That's what we're looking for," Dallow said, excitedly.

Walking over a thick carpet of growth and dodging puddles of black something were enough to make Dallow squeeze Nikkola's hand too tight. It felt like they were in the lung of a sick giant, and she met his firm grip.

The waist-high black marble table was twenty feet wide and four deep. The top faced them at a thirty-degree angle, too steep to hold books or parchments. Smooth, steel rails surrounded it, coming together at a steel plaque with two hand-shaped indentions.

"Most of the mage cities have had similar devices," he said, nodding at the plaque. "It should activate whatever this thing does."

"Handy," she said with a wry smile.

"Cute." He tried to not roll his eyes at the pun.

"What does it do?" she asked, leaning close.

"I believe it removes your fingers," Dallow said.

"What?" she said, jerking back and gripping his arm.

He laughed, and she struck him in the shoulder. "It is weird, though," he said. "The ones that I've seen always require a flat palm. This one has holes for each finger.

"So, you just finger it?" she asked, waggling her eyebrows.

His eyes went wide, and it was her turn to laugh.

"I think you're right," he said, reaching out with two clawed hands.

"Wait," she said. Reaching to some hidden compartment along her thigh, she drew a thin dagger and proceeded to poke the holes. "This is my bad-date dagger."

"I think you need to date better guys," he said, warily.

"I'm trying," she said, returning her dagger to its sheath. "Nothing squishy. You're good to finger."

He flashed her a quick grin before facing the plaque. With a deep breath, Dallow cautiously placed his fingers in the holes. Moments past and nothing happened.

"Maybe you need to wiggle them," she said.

"Some women are too impatient," he said.

Holding his breath, Dallow drew in magic as if preparing to cast a spell. After a loud wrenching sound, the plaque vibrated until the grips beneath his hands slowly formed into domes. He could move them around within the confines of the plaque and even lift them slightly, but something kept them tethered to the table.

"Oooh," Nikkola said.

A gentle ivory glow appeared across the angled top of the long table like fuzzy moonlight. Wonder and excitement swelled in Dallow as the light came into focus. Discovery was his favorite part of any adventure. Thin black lines stretched horizontally across the table like ledger lines on sheet music. The center-most line turned sky blue growing wide enough to reveal Dallow's name in dark letters.

"It knows your name," she said, walking the length of the

railing.

"Clever," he said, studying the lines for clues. "I would've preferred instructions."

Shifting the dome-shaped handles around the plaque interrupted the lines, creating jerky vertical breaks on the far left of the table. Those jagged lines slowly flowed across the table until they disappeared on the right side as if falling off a waterfall. When he stopped moving, the jagged disruptions flattened again.

"It's hard to tell, but I believe the lines are moving from left to right," he said. "Except for my name."

"If it knows your name," she said. "I wonder what else it knows about you?"

That was the right question. Even as he thought about Nikkola's words, images from his life replaced ledger lines on the left side of the table. The horizontal lines remained to his right.

"Is this you?" she asked, leaning over the railing.

Nikkola poked a finger at an image of ten-year-old Dallow reading a book. The ripples that spread across the table steadied within seconds.

"There has to be a reason the image is roughly a quarter of the distance from the far left edge. My history's on that side of the table, and nothing is on the right," he said, speaking his thoughts out loud. That's when he realized what this table could do. "Oh, my."

Dallow tried willing the image closer. Nothing happened until he began shifting the handles. After several minutes of distorting visions of his history by moving them about, he understood how to operate it. Lifting the domes an inch above the plaque and setting them back down on the left side created a white, vertical line over his ten-year-old self. Dallow gently drew the handles over until the image was directly before him.

"Did your, uh, portrait get bigger, or am I seeing things?" she asked.

"I think you're right," Dallow said. "Moving these handles across the table is like rubbing ice cubes together. It's tough to keep them steady."

His hands were already together, so he pulled them apart to the opposite corners of the plaque. The image grew and ten-year-old Dallow flipped a page, his eyes running along the lines of text.

"You were cute," Nikkola said.

"I still am," he said with a grin. "If I'm not mistaken, this is when I discovered my magic."

The younger image of himself slammed the cover shut in frustration and let out a deep sigh. His eyes flashed bright white and frustration was washed away by wonder. A curious smile crept up his cheek as he finished absorbing the first book and quickly reached for another.

"That was a late night," he said, pulling his hands back together and stilling the vision. "Now, the scary part."

"Scary?" she asked, moving closer to him.

"I misunderstood the obelisk description of this place," Dallow said. "This library doesn't only contain history, but future as well."

Dallow moved the handles across the plaque until the horizontal lines were directly before them. Spreading his hands apart revealed an image of Nikkola kissing him on the cheek.

"I don't remember that," she said. "Are you teasing me?"

"No, this hasn't happened yet," Dallow said. He pulled back from that future and focused on another line, revealing an image of Rose and Dallow kissing on a mountaintop overlooking a vast field. "That hasn't happened either."

"Good," she muttered. "What does all of this mean?"

"This table sort of works like Victoria's abilities to see futures," Dallow explained. "Our lives don't have just one path. We have free will to decide which path to take. Combine that with random events, and we end up with multiple futures. This device presents them in a way that could help us choose which one to take."

"It sounds like cheating," she said. "I'm made up of my success and failures. I wouldn't be the same person if I knew what to do all the time. It also sounds boring."

"Agreed," Dallow said. "Though, I think these are more like 'what ifs' and not 'what will bes.'"

"How can it help us?" she asked. "Instead of focusing in on one portrait, is there a way to see everyone's?"

He lifted the handles and placed them on opposite corners before drawing them together. The label changed each time he repeated this, from Dallow to Gyldorane, and then to Meldusia, and finally to Ehrde.

After thirty minutes of glimpsing various futures, Dallow finally removed his hands. The light along the tabletop faded as the plaque handles flattened.

"What a mess," he said, rubbing his eyes. "If we help Angst win, his timeline ends. I can only assume that means he dies. If Magic wins, his future vision of Ehrde is madness—we'd never survive. I just wish I had more time to sort through these futures. I don't understand how Victoria does it."

"What if Angst doesn't pick up the horn at all?" Nikkola asked. "Magic will never get to Prendere, and the two thousand-year cycle of element wars would end."

"That could work," Dallow said, turning to the device. "Let me check."

"There's no time," Nikkola said, tugging at his sleeve. "We'll have to leave this one up to chance or luck."

"Right," he said with a final, longing gaze at the table.

Nikkola kissed him on the cheek. He placed a hand on it and smiled.

"That's the future I liked," she said with a wink. "Now let's get out of this stinky library."

41

Angst wiggled a pinky and winced with pain. Everything hurt like he'd been chased twenty-six miles before jumping off a cliff into a stampede of wild boar. Age caressed his wounds like an angry teacher with her favorite smacking ruler. Dying felt like a much better idea than standing, sitting, or lying still.

But Victoria was here, and her warm voice encouraged him to stand. He would gladly be the hero that Unsel deserved, after a month of Rose's healing, several weeks of drinking at The Fette with the twins, and another month of healing. With every movement he took to stand, Angst's bones popped and hissed like a blacksmith beating iron to a pulp in the rain. Except, bones weren't supposed to hiss.

"I'm not alone," he called out.

"Dropping some light," Jaden said.

A golden orb lowered slowly, revealing far more of this husked-out sinkhole. He stood dead center in a spider web of bone-laden pathways that reached into darkness. Shadows darted from one cave to the next as if crossing roads in a nightmare city.

Instinctively, he reached for the orb only to have it grasped from his hand by something that chilled his heart.

"What was that?" Jaden asked.

"Just the monster," Angst called out. "Got that vine yet? I'm ready to leave."

"Don't be in such a hurry, young Al'eyrn," said a voice so low he felt it in his chest.

"Calling me young doesn't make me like you," Angst said, turning around to follow it.

The darkness surrounding him seemed to move and breathe as though fear itself had taken form. Angst grasped for power and spewed lightning from his extended arms again and again until his breath had to be caught.

"Feed us more of your light," the voice said. "There are many Al'eyrn here for you to meet. Just relax and let it happen."

"Sounds nice, but I've got plans tonight," he said between gasps. "Who are you?"

"Who are you?" "Who are you?" "Who are you?" echoed through the distant shadowy caves, every time coming faster and rising in pitch.

"Scary," Angst said, unsure if it was pee or sweat dribbling down his leg.

"I am the spell that freed shadows from their bodies. Call me The Cursed," it said. "Welcome to my home."

"Most housewarming parties include pie or cake. I don't feel welcome," Angst said. He looked up and shouted, "Vine!"

"Your welcome is over," The Cursed said.

Dark fingers clawed around the circle of light beneath his feet and squeezed. The light surrounding him shrank an inch for every heartbeat and another inch for every drop of panicked sweat.

"Just give it to me," Alloria shouted. "Stop arguing."

"Get out of here," Angst cried out. "I don't know if I can stop it. Tori, I'm sorry."

Their sudden silence was calming. Hopefully, it meant that they'd left and he could throw everything at the monster. It felt like the time he'd attacked the oldest creature on Ehrde, beating it again and again with his swords. He may have bruised it, it was hard to tell. Angst had learned much since then, and when his friends were clear, this Cursed would understand the full power of a mad Al'eyrn with two foci.

"Angst?" Alloria called down from above.

"You were supposed to run," he cried. "I'm trying to do hero stuff."

"My turn," she said.

Somewhere between a heartbeat and a breath, Alloria fell beside him with a dead-on hero landing that made jealousy pool in his heart. A blurry dream of pure light emanating from her made The Cursed reel back and let loose a maddening scream.

"Grab the vine, champion," she said, nodding at the one around her waist. "We've got this."

Holding onto the vine over her head, Alloria kissed him once before pulling away demurely. Twenty-year-old Angst would've fallen in love with this princess who was saving him from this nightmare. Forty-something Angst waited for his heart to stop trying to escape and finally said, "Thank you."

At the edge of the hole, Angst and Alloria grasped at skulls and hipbones to pull themselves free. Sprawled on his back and gasping for air, Angst looked up to see the beautiful face of his best friend.

"Hi," he said.

Victoria fell on him in a hug that made most turn away. Jaden watched, and to Angst's surprise, his gaze wasn't filled with jealousy. He winked at the young man, and after the princess pulled free, accepted his arm to stand. Before Angst could say anything, Jaden pulled him into a hug.

"I, uh," Angst floundered for words.

"Sorry," Jaden whispered, patting his chest plate. "Just glad you're safe, old man."

"I'm fine," Angst said, pulling away. Where had that come from? He would've expected Jaden to lash out at Victoria's affections, but instead, he smiled.

"What now?" Mirim asked.

"We grab the foci," he said, pointing at the distant horn. "And get out of here before that nightmare figures out how to crawl out and eat our brains."

"Foci?" Victoria asked.

"It's a key, of sorts," Alloria said. "Prendere is guarded by a barrier, and playing that horn lowers it."

"You seem to know quite a bit about this," Mirim said, warily.

"I spent a lot of time with an element who's planning to win," she said.

"So, if we leave it here," Mirim said, "Magic can't get through the barrier?"

"And I can't save my family," Angst said, resolutely. "Not an option."

"Then we fight?" Jaden asked.

"Here? Now?" Victoria said, exasperated. "We're all exhausted and fading fast. Can't we just step outside and discuss after our heads clear?"

"What about rock-paper-scissors?" Angst said with a sigh. "Did anyone bring dice?"

Tired smiles and shaking heads made him wonder if they were just going to stand here. The last thing he wanted to do was hurt his friends, and it took so much concentration to keep his focus that they could've beaten him down with a feather duster. He had to get over this nightmare pit with Alloria, grab the foci, and escape this place before losing his mind. What he needed was a distraction.

"Stop," Dallow called. Everyone turned to watch the tall man stumble toward them with Nikkola close behind. He was gasping for breath and hard to understand. "Don't fight Angst. No need…just keep him from…"

"Thanks," Angst called out. Holding onto their escape vine with one hand and wrapping his arm around Alloria with the other, he swung over the pit to the foci.

It wasn't that easy or that smooth. Alloria was light enough to lift, but he was physically exhausted. With little magic and willpower remaining, he anchored her bones to his armor and pushed that armor to the other side. His toe barely caught the lip as shadows darted hungrily beneath them. Another nudge of will pushed them forward. He released Alloria and tripped over bones to land on his face.

With a groan, he pushed himself up to see the beautiful, silver horn. The bell wasn't larger than his hand, and the neck extended to an oval the length of his forearm before stopping at a mouthpiece. His friends' shouts were lost to the excited thrumming of his heart.

"Angst, don't do it," Dallow cried.

"Do it," Alloria said, licking her lips.

Holding his breath, Angst took the foci in both hands and lifted it. **Cornuclav** blared through his mind, the song of a hundred horns. It was a beautiful, proud introduction that befitted this key to the gateway of wishes. He could sense its great power that felt so different than his own foci. Cornuclav served one purpose, and it was time to put the foci to use.

"See," he said turning around, holding the horn up high for his friends to view. "What could possibly go wrong now?"

The light from his sun popped and went dark, returning the city to shadows.

"Felk."

42

As a youth, Maarja had once snuck up on a pride of sleeping frost lions. Few her age were adept enough to attempt the feat, and less were willing to try. Frost lions had the propensity to be extremely sensitive to their surroundings, and unforgiving to intruders. Seeking a cub to raise as a pet, she'd brought a satchel to carry it home, but no weapons to speak of other than a small dagger.

On arrival, she immediately realized her mistake. Foliage and stone outcrops shadowed the entrances to a dozen or more dens. Grabbing a cub would wake its mother and alert them all. She'd come prepared to deal with a single cat, but not a pride.

Turning away from the sleeping lions, she found a lioness waiting on her path. The great white cat was much larger than she'd expected, and its hungry licking made her freeze. Running would only bring chase that could wake the others; fighting most certainly would wake them.

Wiping away tears of frustration, she unsheathed her dagger and crouched to attack. The lioness took this as a cue and pounced.

Jarle grasped the back of the lioness's scruff mid-leap and held it at a safe distance. After a tumultuous battle of biting and swiping at the air, the great cat finally gave up, hanging limply from his hand. Jarle brought it around until they made eye contact, and the lioness cowered. He thwapped it on the nose and tossed it far into the woods.

Jarle quietly waved Maarja over. With a frown, he grasped the back of her neck, not unlike the lioness, and marched her out of the forest. The talking to had been stern. He was equally upset that she'd put herself in danger and put the frost lions in jeopardy. If the lions had eaten her, the Nordruaut would've had to kill the entire pride.

The first lesson learned was simple. Don't sneak up on a pride of sleeping lions or you will spend a month scrubbing pots and skinning game. The second lesson took longer to understand. "Do not kill the pride for a cub," Jarle said. She'd originally taken this as, "Don't be greedy," but over the years had come to understand it as, "Selfish choices will cost you everything."

She often reflected on the memory when sneaking through woods, and longed for Jarle's wisdom now more than ever. Waking this den of lions would cost her everything, but saving Tarness was only a little selfish, and she had grown to become a more formidable hunter.

Jintorich's feet gripped tight to her shoulder as they rounded a large tree to find her husband. Tarness lay on his side, bound tight like a package ready to be shipped. Jintorich hopped to the ground and quickly made his way to Tarness while she searched nearby for guards.

The sounds of Jintorich's bird-call-whistle and her husband moaning brought her back after a quick pass. Tarness was rocking back and forth, his eyes wide as he sputtered around his gag.

"Shush," she said, holding him still while Jintorich untied him.

"Tarp," Tarness mouthed around the loosening gag. "Ith a tarp."

"What's a tarp?" the Meldusian squeaked quietly.

"I don't know," she said. "Humans are so odd."

Tarness rolled his eyes. When Jintorich finally freed his mouth, Tarness blurted out, "Trap. I said it's a trap, not a tarp."

"I saw no one," Maarja said, rolling him to his stomach. She wielded her knife to cut him free and eyed the ring. He would not be unattractive with only nine fingers.

"Hurry," Jintorich said. "They're coming."

Maarja gave up on the finger idea and sawed the ropes until her husband was free. He pushed himself up and climbed out of leftover restraints. They looked at each other for several breaths.

"Later," Jintorich said. "We need to go."

"Please, take your time," Bryymel said as he entered the clearing, followed closely by Rasaol and Niihlu.

"We can take them," Jintorich said, his staff glowing brightly.

"No, we can't," Maarja said. "That's not Bryymel."

"I'm impressed," Bryymel said. His body shrank and re-formed until all signs of the Nordruaut were replaced with a tall, bald, awkward-looking man.

"How did you know?" Magic asked.

"Bryymel was paranoid," Maarja said. "He was never intelligent enough to be devious."

"Clever," Magic said.

"Run or fight?" Jintorich asked.

"Neither," Maarja said. "They could alert the others before we escape. Had they intended to fight, they would've already attacked."

"What do you want now?" Tarness asked, standing before Maarja.

"Come with me to fight Angst," Magic said, "or your family dies."

"My family," Tarness said. "You mean Maarja and Jin?"

"Tarness, he means me," she said. "And our child."

"What?" he asked, turning around. "I didn't know...you never said."

"It seems we have both been less than truthful," she said. "I am sorry, husband."

"I'm sorry, too," Tarness said, tears brimming in his eyes. "I think I can fix this."

"I believe in you," she said. "I will never stop believing in you again."

"I believe in us," Tarness said.

"I believe I'm going to be ill," Magic said in a snide tone. "I enjoyed it more when everyone was lying."

"How do I know you'll keep your promise?" Tarness asked.

"They are only useful to me alive," Magic said, swinging his arm round and round until colors swirled together into a dark, vertical pool. "It's time we leave."

"Take care of her, Jin," Tarness said as he approached the portal.

"I said nothing about saving the Al'eyrn," Magic said, shoving Tarness through the dark hole. "Leave the woman but kill the Al'eyrn as many times as it takes."

As Magic disappeared through the portal, Maarja realized that she was not the hunter, but the lioness. The element had no idea how much this would cost him.

"I will not strike down a pregnant woman," Rasaol said, holding up both hands.

"That will make this easy," she said, leaping forward and tackling the large man.

She punched his gut and elbowed his chin as they rolled down an embankment, leaving behind explosions of light. Jintorich let out a high-pitched war cry as two foci met with an ear-jarring *crack*.

There was no way Jintorich would survive that battle alone. Niihlu was a mountain taller and now wielded two foci. She had to dispatch the old king quickly to save her friend. Maybe together they could stop Niihlu.

"Enough," Rasaol shouted, grasping her shoulders and holding her down. "This war is almost over. You and your child will enjoy a peaceful Ehrde when Magic wins Prendere for Nordruaut."

"You old fool," Maarja said, struggling to free herself. "Magic wants Prendere for himself, not for us. He would destroy us all for his greed."

"And you do not know Magic as I do," he said. "He has helped us for years. The element wants what is best for

Nordruaut. He provided us with our champion, Niihlu, and led me to Jarle so I could end this war."

"You killed Jarle?" she asked.

"I had to, he found me with Magic," he said. The wild look on his face, outlined by the flashing lights of the ongoing battle between Jintorich and Niihlu, was horrifying. Rasaol grabbed a long hunting knife from his thigh and raised it high overhead. "You leave me no choice. I cannot have you telling the others when we are so close to victory."

As King Rasaol rocked down, Maarja shoved her dagger into his neck. Hot blood splattered her face, and the king collapsed to his side. She scrambled away to see Gose's spear jutting from his back.

The young Nordruaut leader offered her a hand.

"You...you heard?" she asked, gladfully accepting his help up.

"Enough," he said. "Let's free your husband and hear the rest of this story."

"Tarness," she said in a panic. "Jin."

The battle on the hill was silent. She jerked the spear from Rasaol's back and rushed up the hill. Niihlu would see what a lioness could do. Reaching the top, Maarja leaped high with the weapon in both hands. She could only hope for a second of surprise before the Al'eyrn would defend himself. The surprise was hers.

She landed beside Jintorich and looked about the clearing in amazement. The Meldusian stood with his legs apart in a battle stance, the staff touching the ground before him. The white glow from his staff revealed hundreds of colorful ice shards spread around them. The axe Ghorjfend and the necklace foci lay amidst the shards.

"My friend, you are okay?" she asked. "What happened."

Gose crested the hilltop, followed by several others with torches, all eyeing the Meldusian with caution.

"In my attempt to help your husband, I've learned much about removing foci," Jintorich said. "My spells didn't work on

Magic's ring but did work on this necklace that had no desire to be worn by a false Al'eyrn. With the necklace gone, Niihlu froze."

"So, all of this ice…is Niihlu?" Gose asked, swallowing hard. "What about Tarness?"

"Magic stole my husband," Maarja said, her worry returning. "Jintorich, what do we do?"

"We save him," Jintorich said.

43

The light from Dallow's outstretched hand revealed shadowy figures boiling over the pit. Panic gave Angst enough strength to swing back on the vine with Alloria in his arms and the horn tucked neatly between his legs. Jaden caught them on the other side and pulled them past the brink.

"I don't believe you swung on a vine with her," Victoria snapped. "I should push you back in."

"Didn't you hear me?" Dallow asked. "If you'd left the foci there, Magic would never get to Prendere. It would've ended the cycle of element wars forever."

"Oh," Angst said, scratching the back of his neck.

"It doesn't matter," Captain Mirim said, pointing to the pit. "The Cursed is coming."

The dark monstrosity that slowly rose behind Mirim was hard to see in Dallow's faint light. Cold tendrils wrapping around their feet and the guttural, slavering sound of pure hunger introduced him to a new level of fear.

"She's right," Victoria said. "We need to run."

"What are you going to do with the horn?" Dallow said. "Those two swords have already made you crazy. You don't need a third foci."

Angst reached out, set the horn in Alloria's arms, and let go. To everyone's amazement, she didn't drop it.

"Pretty," she said in wonder.

"It makes sense," Victoria said. "Alloria was able to hold Jormbrinder, too."

"The only thing that makes sense is running," Mirim shouted. "Jaden, help me with the brothers. Angst, keep that monster off our tail while Dallow provides us light."

"Follow me," Alloria said. "I know the way out."

Angst grabbed his swords and jogged behind them, tripping over vines as he constantly looked over his shoulder. They were moving too slowly, and no amount of fear could push through their exhaustion. The hungry vines and the shadow curse were overwhelming. Angst hastily threw up an air shield that shattered instantly beneath a swiping blow from The Cursed.

"What is that?" Dallow asked. "What are we fighting?"

"Like the monster said, it's the curse," Angst said, gasping for air. "Everyone who lived here leaked sanity that formed shadows and killed them. The shadows never went away, and that's apparently their leader."

"That's horrifying," Nikkola cried.

"Air shields aren't stopping it, and my foci aren't telling me anything," Angst said.

"Shield us with another element," Dallow said. "Try all of the elements."

"I hunger for your shadow, and thirst for your life," The Cursed said in a booming voice.

Nikkola and Simon both screamed in fear as shadowy arms grasped through them.

"I will eat your body and cover my home with your bones."

"Oh, shut up," Angst said. "Everyone, faster."

Angst drew in what power he could from the foci, and created a barrier of everything and his grandma's old hat. A layer of air, fire, dirt from the ground, and sweat from their pores created what looked like a floating grease pit. The shadow king pounded on it again and again as it lumbered after them.

"You'd make a great foci, Dallow," Angst said.

"Gee, thanks," Dallow said. "How much further."

"Just ahead," Alloria said, pointing with the horn foci.

"It's a wall of vine," Victoria said.

"They'll give way when we push through," Angst said. "It's gross, but better than this."

The Cursed struck with such might that Angst stumbled. He somehow caught himself only to glimpse a thin crack in the shield. His source of water was drying up along with his tongue; they must all be getting dehydrated. Reaching out with his mind, he located an underground river that was too far down to access without stopping.

As they slowed along the city's edge, The Cursed struck his shield again and again. Cracks became a spider web, and soon gaps appeared that were barely held together by his exhausted will. Alloria pushed them through single file, every moment passing by slower and slower.

"I won't last much longer," Angst called out.

"You won't need to," Alloria said. "You did it, baby. It's done."

Her shadow had been completely replaced by a glow of golden light that surrounded her. She pulled him into that light, and into her protection. Despite every angry blow, The Cursed was no match for what this place had done to her. She led him through the shield of vines, with less kissing this time, until they were back at the patio.

While the exhaustion was still there—wasn't it always?—clarity returned like he'd just woken up. It wasn't only a relief; it was realization. Everyone was worried that he was going mad, but being in Gyldorane was the only time he'd felt his sanity slipping. Out here, he wasn't going crazy, and that was a relief. His decisions didn't always make sense to others, but they were still his and not some foci madness.

Screams from The Cursed were muffled by layers of vine as he pounded away in frustration.

"I said shut up," Angst yelled toward the mage city.

Everyone was sprawled around the patio like they'd been spilled from the city. Everyone. Tired was better than dead. He really wanted to get away from this place, but it was unlikely anyone would hop up, ready to go.

"You did it, baby," Alloria said, wrapping her tentacle arms around him and planting a juicy kiss on his cheek.

Apparently, the change in clarity that Angst had enjoyed had the opposite effect on Alloria. He gently detached the young woman to see Victoria glaring over her shoulder. Rather than apologizing to one princess and begging the other to stop, he held Alloria at arm's length and looked into her eyes.

"You did it, Alloria," Angst said. "You saved us. Because of you, I can save my family."

"I did?" she asked, twirling a lock of sweaty hair. "I don't remember."

"It's okay," Angst said, pulling her into a hug. "You did good."

When his eyes met Victoria's again, he saw sadness. She understood that something was very wrong with her cousin, and while that gaze wasn't forgiveness, it was a start.

"Angst," Sean called out, "help."

Angst whipped around to see the young man wrapped in shadowy tendrils, pulling him back through their escape. Simon leaped for his brother, grasping his hands as they were both pulled back into Gyldorane.

"No," Angst shouted, wielding both swords and storming in after them.

On the other side of the shield, the angry red and blue lightning from his foci revealed the brothers hanging mid-air. The Cursed held them by their necks and leaned forward to sniff his meal.

"Let them go," Angst said. "Please let them go. You can have me instead."

"No," he said. "I will have you all."

The Cursed let go, and trailing wisps of shadow escaped the brothers as their bodies fell to the ground. The dark echoes of Sean and Simon's faces screamed in silent horror until they were consumed by the giant monster. Angst staggered back, and then again, staring at the still corpses of two men who'd come to stop him. They had become zyn'ight to protect Unsel, and had chased Angst to save Ehrde. They were heroes.

"Delicious," the shadow monster said, reaching for Angst. "More."

Angst backed through the vines as a fury grew inside. It was the rage he'd felt when Fire killed his family, the anger that blinded him when Hector was killed, the loss he'd felt when Moyra died. That rage and anger and loss drew more power from his swords than he could handle...but he wouldn't need to handle it for long.

"Angst, the brothers, are they...?" Victoria asked. "Angst?"

"Run," Angst said.

As his friends scrambled away, Angst combined elements— all of them. He wrapped the entire city in a ball of water from the stream far below and a thick layer of earth. Fire came from his unmitigated rage, and Angst shook as he poured it into the city. Air from inside fed his flames and exploded, cracking the ball. His head pounded and the swords blared for him to stop, but it wasn't enough, the anger was still there. With a deep breath, he forced the city-sized ball to compress.

The brothers deserved to live. The ball shrank. His family deserved to live. It shrank more. This was his fault. And more. No one would die to this monster again.

"Angst," Victoria said, placing a hand on his arm. "It's done."

He let go and the grapefruit-sized ball that was Gyldorane fell into a newly formed crater. Angst collapsed and wept like a baby. Victoria was there, holding him close and rocking.

"I tried to save them," he said. "I should've died, not them."

"It's not your fault, Angst," she said, patting the back of his head. "We will finish this together. When this is done, you'll either save everyone, or we will mourn them like heroes."

"Wow, I'm not sure *I* could've done that," Magic said, slow clapping as he looked over the crater.

The element stood between an open portal and Alloria, who held the horn foci close. Angst leaped up with his arms outstretched, ready to kill Magic with his bare hands. The element blew him a kiss that threw him back in a gust of wind.

"Oh my, destroying that mage city must've taken a lot out of you," he said. A ball of lightning formed in his hand, so bright it was impossible to look at. "I should take the opportunity and end this now."

"Good idea," Rose said, as she blurred past Magic, slicing deep into his face with her dagger.

"Al'eyrn," Magic cried out, grabbing his cheek.

A dribble of night sky fell from his face and landed on the ground. Grass and flowers sprouted from Magic's blood before withering and dying. The element looked on in horror.

"Fine," Magic said, grasping Alloria by her hair. "This will be over in minutes."

"Never again," Alloria screamed.

The princess spun around, striking the element with the horn again and again. Rose rushed over and sliced across his stomach with both blades of her foci. Magic crouched down and abruptly stretched out. Alloria and Rose were knocked into the air, both landing hard ten feet away.

"Fine," Magic said, wiping his cheek with the back of a hand. "Plan B."

Looking at Angst with a malicious grin, he slipped through the portal and it closed with a pop.

44

It took several sleepless nights before Angst was ready to speak to anyone. He'd almost drowned in the raw power he'd summoned to crush the mage city. It left him with bone-deep fatigue that had squeezed out his very will. While the exhaustion would eventually pass, his fear might never truly go away. The haunting image of the brothers pleading in silent screams would take longer to bury than Gyldorane.

Almost more frightening was what he had done to the city. What had he done to the city? Aerella and Jaden's warnings that he would go mad and split Ehrde in half had always made him laugh in disbelief. But it wasn't funny anymore. Whether it be living elements, Viveks, or an Al'eyrn with two swords glued to his back, nobody should be able to wield the raw power he had. All Angst had wanted was to be a hero, a knight in shining armor. City crushing was never part of the deal.

On their slow trek to Prendere, everyone gave him the space he needed. He couldn't tell if they kept their distance out of respect, or fear, or their own need to mourn. The weariness in their faces and the tension in their shoulders mirrored his own.

A part of him wanted to rally the troops and help everyone find the hope they needed. Victoria took charge before that concern weighed on him for long, either keeping people busy or giving them space. Even more surprising, she'd taken Alloria underwing. After a change into less revealing clothes, Alloria spent time being healed by Rose or answering Dallow and Victoria's questions.

On the third night, they sat around the campfire and compared trips to the mage city.

"I'm guessing you had Sean send that bird to guide me back?" Rose asked.

"I did, though it was your choice to follow," Victoria said. "Just in time, too."

"Thank you," Rose said.

"Angst," Dallow said. "When did you figure out the tiara had a memndus stone?"

"Just outside The Fette. Alloria threw it to the ground," Angst said. "When I handed it back, she mentioned it was a gift from Tori. That's when I put it together. Smart." Angst nodded to his friend in respect.

"Thank you," Dallow said, with a gentle smile.

"I miss my tiara," Alloria said, crossing her arms.

"I'll get you a new one, honey," Victoria said. "Every princess deserves a tiara."

"Okay," Alloria said, her irritation washed away.

"Why didn't you leave the tiara behind at The Fette?" Mirim asked.

"Victoria wouldn't have given up so easily," Angst said. "It was a way to keep you safe without letting you get too close. Had we met up, you would have wanted to fight, and that would have attracted every war band straight to us."

"We were almost killed by Berfemmian," Rose snapped. "How is that keeping us safe?"

"I couldn't have known about the Berfemmian," Angst said. "When I faced Marisha, she seemed to be fighting whatever had changed her. I didn't realize it had affected all of them until Magic explained that Faeoris was Al'eyrn."

"What?" Jaden asked

"When Fire killed her, she left behind a golden feather. It was a foci that gave the Berfemmian their wings," Angst said. "Magic forced Marisha to bond with it. Like Niihlu, it didn't go well."

"In my future, we call them Angorian harpies," Jaden said. "They don't get less dangerous over time."

"Something else to fix," Angst said with a sigh. "Any other dangers I should know about?"

"We were chased by a dragon," Rose said, peering at him. "And don't forget almost being trampled by Nordruaut."

Angst met eyes with Dallow and Victoria, and the three laughed. Like removing the cork on pent-up anxiety, everyone joined in. Everyone but Rose.

"Now I feel stupid," she said, her cheeks as red as her name. "Want to let me in?"

"Angst set it all up to protect us," Victoria said. "I heard tribesmen laughing when the dragon chased us from that clearing. A gamlin warned us to run before the Nordruaut arrived. We walked through the aftermath of a battle between Fulk'han and harpies only to spend a night getting drunk with merpeople."

"Love me some merpeeps," Angst said, raising an eyebrow.

"Speaking of," Dallow said, pulling an aged bottle of Aberbrou from his satchel. "I wasn't sure if this was a good time."

"It's the best time," Angst said, licking his lips. He grabbed for it like a toddler reaching for cake. After uncorking the bottle with his teeth, he took several long draws.

"How is this a good time?" Mirim asked. "Shouldn't we be in a hurry?"

"Nope," Angst said. "No one can get into Prendere without Alloria's horn."

"Yay," she said, patting the silver foci in her lap.

"For the first time ever," Dallow said, taking the bottle back and drinking, "War waits for us."

"Good," Victoria said with a nod. "My army needs that time to get there, it'll be close."

"Uh, how much Aberbrou do you have?" Angst asked.

Mirim, Nikkola, Victoria, Jaden, and Rose all pulled out two full bottles of the delicious brew.

"Apparently the bottles don't break," Nikkola said, opening hers and chugging a good portion. "I'm glad you said something.

I needed that."

"Better allies than enemies," Angst said, raising Dallow's bottle to toast.

"You made friends along the way," Victoria said.

"I tried," he said. "A tribesman named SMyket warned us of the warbands and said he'd be willing to help. I met a young Fulk'han named Teesha and tried convincing her that we shouldn't be enemies. And, you've met Lyda of the merpeople. None of them want this war. They give me hope."

"Don't forget the twins," Alloria said. "I loved dancing with Bella and Karina. They are so beautiful."

"What?" Jaden asked, sputtering out drink. "They were here?"

"Yes, I've seen them several times," Angst said. "Karina was concerned for you."

"This is bad," Jaden said, corking his bottle and standing.

"Why?" Angst asked.

"They're from my future." Jaden covered his mouth and looked at Victoria. "If they're here, does that mean my future is inevitable? Does that mean I have to—"

"No," Victoria said firmly. "It absolutely does not."

The two stared at each other, their faces painted with concern.

Angst cleared his throat to interrupt the gaze. "This is sharing time now." He handed the bottle back to Dallow and stood before Jaden. Placing a hand on the young man's shoulder, he said, "Please, tell us."

"I was sent back in time to kill you," Jaden said, swallowing hard.

"Oh," Angst said, removing his hand and taking a step back.

Jaden sniffed deeply and smiled at his reaction.

"Who sent you?" Angst asked.

"I did," Victoria said.

"Right," Angst said. He took Dallow's bottle and drank until it was empty. "Go on."

"I found a message from Victoria," Jaden said. "She was the one who told me to come back. In those messages, she ordered me to kill you before you destroyed everything."

Dallow let out a low whistle.

"That's why you kept calling him a liar?" Rose asked.

"I would never tell anyone to harm you, Angst," she said. "I couldn't believe you'd destroy Ehrde. Nobody has that sort of power, but after what we just saw at Gyldorane, I'm starting to believe Jaden."

"Bottle," Angst said, dropping the empty in his hand.

Nikkola hugged hers like a newborn, but Mirim leaned forward to share.

Angst took it and drank slowly as things were starting to numb a bit too much. "And I thought Aerella hopping around time gave me headaches."

"How did you get to our time?" Nikkola asked.

"The twins brought him," Angst said.

Jaden looked at Angst with wide eyes.

"It's not only how they appear and disappear. They knew you, and they know m..." Angst grimaced. "It's not going to happen like that."

"Tell him the rest," Victoria said.

"No," Angst said, chopping at the air with his hand. "Sharing time is over."

"Why not?" Jaden asked.

"Because it's pointless," Angst said. "That's a future that will not exist. I won't let it."

"Is it pointless?" Jaden asked. "Victoria believes that by being here I've already affected time. But if the twins are still visiting from my future, doesn't that make it inevitable?"

They all looked at Angst. He took that moment to hide behind a bottle while emptying it.

"It's not decided yet, Jaden," Dallow said, steepling two fingers and pressing them against his chin. "A table Nikkola and I found at the library showed a lot of different possible futures. It reminded me of how you've explained your power, Your Highness."

"Which barely seems to work," Victoria said in frustration.

"The table wasn't hindered by Al'eyrn or emotional ties," Dallow said with an understanding nod. "I don't believe it would've shown other possible futures if none existed."

"True," Jaden said, reluctantly.

"The worst future we saw was Magic winning," Nikkola said. "There isn't enough mermaid booze to make that memory go away."

Dallow looked forlornly at his empty bottle, and Nikkola offered hers.

"Thanks," he said with a wink. He raised the bottle. "So we help Angst, and hope for the best."

Rose stood while everyone toasted. "I'm going to get more wood," she said. "I need to make dinner."

"I'll help," Dallow said, following her.

"Don't bother," she snapped. "I'm fine on my own."

* * * *

After twenty minutes of drinking, stories, and drinking, Dallow waved him over from the edge of the woods. Angst tipsily pushed himself up and set both swords on his back. He followed his tall friend until they were several minutes out of earshot.

"Everything okay?" he asked.

"I think one of us was supposed to go after Rose," Dallow said with a wince.

"Pretty sure that's your job," Angst said. "Are you two okay?"

"Probably not," Dallow said. "But we can deal with that after all of this."

"That's not the only reason you waved me over," Angst said.

"It's the future," Dallow said around a thick tongue. "It's not good."

"Oh," Angst said. "How does it play out?"

"You probably didn't know this, but I can juggle," Dallow said. "Three balls if I'm sober, four if I'm drunk."

"Really?" Angst asked. "I need to see this."

"The next time I see you dance," Dallow said with a wink. "I can handle three, maybe four futures—but I saw hundreds. Most ended with Magic swirling Ehrde into a bowl of rainbow porridge."

"After what he did to the Fulk'han," Angst said. "I can only imagine."

"My point is that you're our only hope," Dallow said, his face wrenching in pain. "But…"

"That doesn't sound like a good but," Angst said.

"No." Dallow shook his head for a long time, listing slightly. He finally looked up with tear-filled eyes. "No matter how many of your futures I saw, they all ended at Prendere. All of them. The table showed your life in a series of straight lines that just stopped."

"Hey," Angst said. "It's okay. We talked about this. Going back in time is going to kill me. But it's like starting over, right?"

"Sure," Dallow said, tears streaming from his eyes. "Losing Hector was the hardest thing I've gone through. You're my oldest friend. If this goes wrong, I just… I'm going to miss the felk out of you."

They embraced like only old friends can. When hidden tears and catching breaths passed, Angst grabbed the back of his neck.

"We're not done yet, old friend," Angst said, clearing his throat. "You didn't see all the futures, and we're far too young and beautiful to die just yet."

"Right," Dallow said, wiping tears from his eyes.

"Hey," Angst said. "We've broken all the rules so far. Why stop now?"

Dallow looked up.

"All my life I've been told what I can't do," Angst said. "I can't be a knight because I wield magic. I'm too old, too short, and too fat to be a hero. And here we are, Dallow. We've accomplished the amazing and are on the verge of the impossible. I won't give up if you don't."

"Not for a second," Dallow said, pulling back and gathering

himself. "I think I'm going to go finish one of those bottles."

"Save me some," Angst said. "In case I survive Rose."

"No promises," Dallow said with a smile, patting him on the shoulder.

* * * *

Rose sat cross-legged in the middle of a new clearing. Her two daggers rested at each side, glowing brightly enough to reveal their surroundings. Six or more trees had fallen away from her, as though trying to escape. A fresh, clean cut at each base could only have been made by an angry Al'eyrn.

"Glad I'm not a tree," Angst said, removing his swords and sitting across from her.

Despite her apparent fury, a hint of a smile crept up one cheek.

"Sorry," he said. "I know you hate when you're angry and I make you smile. Wait, you are angry, right?"

He reeled from her glare and held up his hands.

"Angry, right," he said. "I should send *you* after Magic. There's no way he could face that raw fury."

"Stop it," she said, now struggling to remain stoic. "I haven't forgiven you for hurting me."

"Are you still upset about the ankle?" he asked. "Break mine if it makes you feel better. I've been hurt so many times since this started, I feel like a pin cushion ready to give up its fluff."

"It's not just that," she said. "I think you're lying. I think you've been lying this whole time. I'm upset because I don't know what to do about it."

"Huh," he said. "I don't lie often. They're too hard to keep track of. What do you think I'm lying about?"

"You're lying that you sent those monsters to chase us just to keep us safe. You're lying about saving your family. I think you just want the wish so you can be a hero," she said. "You're lying about your foci singing."

"I see," he said. "Is that it?"

"That's a start," she said, crossing her arms.

"If I can prove that at least one of those is not a lie," he said, "would you give me a chance?"

"Maybe," she said.

"That'll do," he said. "My life is held together by maybes."

The clearing wasn't wide enough. Angst stood, hefted both swords, and drew in power. His mind sifted through the packed dirt and thirsty roots all around until he found a way to make it all fit. With a grunt, he pushed the trees and roots away until they had a clear fifteen feet of space all around them.

"Show off," she said, unimpressed. "What was that for?"

"Sealtian," Angst said, positioning himself. "Something Hector taught me. It's a series of movements, like a slow dance. My foci seem to like it. I bet yours will too."

"It sounds like a waste of time," she said.

"You said you'd give me a chance," he said. "Or would your time be better spent glaring at me?"

"Fine," Rose said, rolling her eyes more than an entitled teenager. She picked up her daggers and stood beside him. "What do I do?"

"Stand like this." Moving in front of her, Angst held both swords out horizontally.

"Won't this take forever?" she asked. "You're not even sober."

"I'm not a teacher," he said, "but your foci is."

"I don't understand," she said.

"When I did the sealtian with Faeoris, I reached out to feel her bones so I would know what movements to make," he said. "I relaxed and opened myself up to Dulgirgraut, and the foci guided me to complete the dance."

"I don't want to feel your bones," she said, wryly.

"Being a healer, I bet you can sense when someone is well, or ill," he said. "Concentrate, and you'll be able to sense my muscles, my breathing, and my movements."

To his surprise, she squeezed her eyes shut and tried.

"I can sense you," she said in surprise. "Oh, hey, your shoulders are tight, and your hair is falling out."

"Not news," he said with a sigh. "Follow my movements, and let your foci guide."

"Okay," she said, nervously.

Angst focused. The red and blue lights surrounding his foci covered his forearms and lit their clearing. Taking deep breaths, he concentrated, moving slowly so she could feel his movements.

"Felk," she said. "Start over."

More cursing followed as they restarted their dance several times. Eventually, the cursing stopped and within minutes were followed by a gasp. They moved together, mirror images performing the same beautiful dance. He turned his focus on his own sealtian and listened for his swords. With every movement, their harmony became louder and even purer. Two voices became a quartet, and then a choir eventually followed by a symphony.

Maybe they felt bad about what had happened at Gylorane. Or the foci realized if Angst didn't win, Magic would. The reason didn't really matter. When the dance was done, he took a deep and grateful breath of relief that his friends had returned.

He turned to see Rose hugging herself, tears trickling down her cheeks. Hers wasn't a sad cry, it was the cry of discovery and wonder.

"Jormbrinder's song," she said. "It's the most beautiful thing I've ever heard."

"I'm proud of you," he said. "Al'eyrn."

"I hate you," she said, wiping her eyes.

"I hate you, too," he said, pulling her into a hug. "And I'm sorry. I'm sorry for all of it."

She didn't reply, but what else needed to be said?

* * * *

Angst returned to the campfire with Rose in tow. She found the nearest bottle and proceeded to empty it. After an acknowledging nod to Dallow, he found a seat near Mirim and Nikkola.

Alloria sat next to him and rested her head on his shoulder.

The two women looked at him nervously, like he would suddenly sprout daggers and hug them to death. He nodded at the Aberbrau that Nikkola clutched, and she reluctantly handed it over.

"May I ask a favor?" he said, taking a small sip. "Would you tell me more about the brothers? I would like to know Sean and Simon better."

They both nodded, and with a deep breath, Mirim began to share stories.

45

When they arrived at the top of a mountain pass several days later, everyone gasped for breath in the thin air. Even those tiny breaths were stolen as the great field from Angst's dreams came into view.

Snow-capped mountains guarded the long, flat field that was easily ten miles across and five miles wide. From a thousand feet up, it looked like an oblong salad bowl filled with green silk.

Victoria had dismissed the others to let Mirot know they had arrived. They were finally alone, and Angst sat beside Victoria on the cliff's edge. His hand rested on hers, both out of friendship and concern. When she'd lean forward far enough that her long black hair covered her cheeks, he'd squeeze. Angst didn't hate heights, he hated others near heights, and she knew it.

"You look a little pale," she said. "I didn't think Alloria's champion got scared. At least, not according to Alloria."

She wanted to argue? Now? He took a deep breath and avoided the bait. Alloria would be a discussion for another time. Or perhaps she wouldn't.

"We argued last time we were here," he said. "Do you remember the dreams we shared?"

"As I recall," she said. "We were naked."

"Aren't dreams weird?" he asked.

"Yeah," she said with a crooked smile. "Weird."

"In most of my dreams of this place, Fire stood there," he

said, pointing to the left. "He was lobbing balls of lava across the mountains. Air was a large tornado creature on the same side. Across the way were Earth and Water. Magic was a dark beam that reached the sky, about where we are."

"So, what's that?" she asked, her voice trembling slightly.

Directly across the field from them was a beam of light so bright it was almost impossible to look at. He couldn't begin to guess its width from this distance, but the light stretched from ground to sky. Even this far away, the low hum of power was easy to hear. He felt drawn to it in a way he couldn't explain and didn't want to try to understand. It made his blood warm that his family's salvation was so close, and then boil that he had to fight his way to get there. Somehow, he also knew all answers were in there, that he would finally learn what this was all about.

"I dunno," he said with a sigh, attempting to release some of the tension. "I guess Prendere. That's where I need to go. That's where I'll make my wish and save everyone."

"And die," she said.

"That's what heroes do," he said with a winning smile. "I'll win, and everything will start over. Young Angst will be alive, you can still be friends, and he won't break everything next time."

"Sure," she said, not sounding very convinced. "I don't see the past. I don't think you can go back and change things. You can't take back an angry word, or a mistake, or a kiss. It doesn't work that way. At least, that's not the future Jaden says will happen."

"Hey, no worries," he said, not wanting to know more. "I've got this."

She sighed and shook her head. "Then why are you so worried? I don't need to read you to know something is bothering you, a lot. Your cheeks and ears are flushed, your jaw is jutting out, and you're a terrible liar. Are we going to be surrounded by angry elements?"

"No," he said. Something about her concern, her familiarity was comforting. She was being his friend, and he needed that now more than anything. "I'm worried that I'm going to fail again. That I won't go back in time and you all get killed in the process. I don't want to be stuck on an Ehrde mad and alone."

"Are you going mad?" she asked.

"I will if you're killed," he said. "Or anyone else I love."

"You keep talking about your failures," she said, pulling him into a side-hug. "You've saved countless lives and destroyed four elements. Dallow says that's never been done before, not by a human. I wouldn't call any of that failure."

"It's just so much more than I'd expected," he said, looking down. "I just wanted to be a knight."

"Hey," she said. "That could still happen."

"You're just saying nice things because I'm cute," he said, pulling back, but only a little.

"You're just holding on because you like my hugs," Tori said, pushing him away.

They both turned to look into each other's eyes. He tried to feign confidence, and her eyes tried to believe him.

"We could still walk away, Angst," she said. "There would be no war. We would be home. You could be whatever you want back at Unsel. It would be easy."

It was a tempting offer. He was so tired. The trek here was grueling, his plan was filled with unknowns that ended with his death, and his wish could destroy Ehrde. But giving up wouldn't bring back his family and friends. He closed his eyes and took a deep breath. His greatest challenge may not be Vex'steppe monsters or living elements, it may be his best friend. The last thing he wanted to dwell on was what-ifs that weren't his.

"My father once said I make things more complicated than anyone he knew. At this point, I'm not sure I'd even know what to do with easy," he said, trying to smile. "Not to mention, it looks like everyone showed up to the party. There are armies everywhere."

"Wh-what?" she asked, scanning the field. "I don't see—"

"They're too far away or hidden behind mountains," he said. "But I sense them. All of them. Tribesmen, Nordruaut, Fulk'han,

merpeople, Berfemmian, and I believe a pretty good-sized army
from Melkier. They're on paths, like ours, leading down to the
field." He laughed.

"Don't go crazy on me yet, old man," she said, her thin brows
furrowing in a worried frown.

"It's just that, in my dreams, I always thought this looked like
a giant bowl," he said. "It's not. It's more like a stadium."

"What are the armies doing?" she asked.

"Waiting," he said.

"For what?" she asked.

"For me," he said. "For us."

"How will we get through all of them?" she asked.

"No worries," he said with a broad smile. "I have a plan."

Her shoulders drooped, and she looked at him with a deadpan
gaze. "You're going to do something stupid, aren't you?"

"It's an old habit," he said, raising his eyebrows. "I'll try to
break it when this is over."

"Aren't you dead when this is over?" she asked.

"According to Dallow," Angst said. "But then my bad habits
will be gone."

"You think you're clever," she said, rolling her eyes.

"Let's hope so," he said.

* * * *

"That's not a plan," Jaden said, slashing the air with his hand.
"That's maniacal."

"He's right," Dallow said. "Going alone is idiotic. Everyone
should ride swifen across the field together. We'd be at the beam
before the armies were on us."

"Assuming Angst is right, the Nordruaut and Berfemmian are
too close to that light," Victoria said, staring off in the distance.
"Even the swifen aren't fast enough to beat them there."

"You lot would get boxed in," General Mirot said, tugging at
his long mustache. "I also don't like the idea of being split up.
Without the zyn'ight, our troops would be slaughtered."

They all turned to the magic-hating general in surprise, he replied with a harumph but said nothing further.

"What about flying there?" Victoria asked. "My unicorn could take us. We've done it before."

"Is your mount agile enough to dodge an army of Berfemmian?" Mirim asked.

Angst let this go on for several minutes, listening for anything he may have missed. They were dead set against his idea, so he'd have to prove it was the best way. Angst removed his gauntlet and reached out to Victoria.

"No walls or barriers," he said. "Just me, Your Highness."

Beads of sweat formed on Victoria's temples, and she licked her lips. Squeezing her eyes shut, she took Angst's hand. It was like watching someone read a good book filled with horror and then heroics followed by humor with a little death sprinkled in. Angst held her arm as she wavered. When the stories were done, she let go and gasped for breath.

"Maybe," she said. "I saw outcomes rather than events, some clearer than others."

"Can you cover it one more time?" Mirot asked, his ears red. "I'm an old soldier and not familiar with the magics. It doesn't all make sense."

"Angst is going to swim underground with four foci—his swords, the horn, and Rose's daggers," Victoria said, holding up a hand to keep Mirot from asking questions. "A wielder should only ever have one foci. Jormbrinder can dampen magic and should allow him to carry more."

"If I don't explode again," Angst said with a broad grin. It was supposed to make everyone laugh. It didn't.

"When Angst arrives, our troops will charge," Victoria said, her tone strained. "Hopefully our distraction will lead everyone away from Angst, giving him enough time to blow the horn and enter Prendere."

"It sounds pretty thin," Rose said.

"First time you've ever called me thin," Angst said with a wink, earning a quick jab to the shoulder. He looked at the others. "Any better ideas?"

"Home sounds nice," Dallow said with a smile.

"Ha," Angst laughed. "Right after we do this one little thing."

"So, you think this will work?" Mirim asked. "You've seen it?"

"That beam of light could be interfering, or it's possible other Al'eyrn are nearby," Victoria said. "But I believe there's a chance."

"Other Al'eyrn?" Mirot asked.

"Niihlu," Rose grumbled.

"Or Jintorich," Angst said, more hopefully. "Which could also mean Tarness."

"If he's on our side," Dallow muttered.

"What?" Tori and Rose asked, looking at Angst.

"He wears one of Magic's rings like Alloria did," Angst said, holding out a hand to calm them. "I trust Tarness. No matter what he's facing, he'll stand by us."

"You really think Tarness is out there?" Dallow asked.

"I'm counting on it," Angst said. "We need him now more than ever."

"I'm hesitant to charge so late in the day," Mirot said. "Wouldn't morning be better?"

"If the Berfemmian realize I'm here, the war will come to us," Angst said. "There's no waiting."

"I'll ready the troops," Mirot said. He looked at Angst for a minute then saluted before leaving.

His friends exchanged glances in an awkward moment of silence. Without another word, Angst pulled Rose into a hug.

"I told you," she said, her voice catching. "No more dying."

"Keep her safe, Champion," he said, nodding toward Victoria.

Rose took a few steps back and held herself.

Jaden reached out to clasp arms. "If this goes wrong…"

"I know, Ehrde split in half, blah blah blah," Angst said with a crooked smile. "Let's make sure it goes right."

Jaden smiled tersely.

"What about me?" Alloria said softly, hugging the horn and stepping close. "I'll fight for you."

"You already did," he said, placing a hand on her cheek. She leaned into it. "None of this could've happened without you. In spite of everything Magic put you through, you made this possible. In my opinion, you redeemed yourself. You're a hero, Alloria."

"Really?" she asked, licking her lips.

"Yes," he said.

As she pulled him in for a kiss, he turned away so it landed on his cheek. Rose barked out a laugh, and Victoria smiled broadly.

"A dozen guards will remain behind to keep you safe," he said, looking at Alloria sternly. "Let them protect you, and don't hurt anyone."

She rolled her eyes and stepped back.

"Uh, Dallow," Angst said, looking at his feet. "If I don't make it, would you mind..."

"I know," he said with a sigh. "Pay your tab at Graloon's. You shouldn't have been so generous with your tips to the barmaid."

"Do you blame me?" he asked with a wink.

Victoria was looking over the field. When she turned to face him, her eyes were keen and her face stoic. The lost teenage princess was long gone, and Angst knelt before his queen. Everyone followed his lead. He kissed her hand, and she set it atop his head.

"Let's go save Ehrde," she said.

They all stood. Angst looked into Tori's eyes, and they softened a bit.

"Tell young Angst to find me in the courtyard. I don't want to do any of this without you," she said, quietly. "That's an order."

"Yes, Your Highness," he said with a deep bow.

"What's that?" Mirim asked, peering out at the field.

A speck, a tiny dot had appeared a stone's throw from the beam of white light. Angst sent some gamlin to investigate before reaching out with his mind. He sensed no bones or anything else. The gamlin stopped several hundred yards from the dot, unwilling or unable to approach.

"Magic," Angst whispered under his breath.

"Element of humans," Magic said. His voice was so clear it was if he stood beside Angst.

"Did you hear that?" Angst asked.

Everyone nodded.

"Neat trick," Dallow said.

"Let's make this easy," Magic said. "Let's avoid this war and fight the duel you've always wanted. Man to man. Element to element. Come face me, hero of Unsel."

"Tempting," Angst said between gritted teeth. "I can't believe he's stupid enough to fight me alone."

"Don't be cocky," Rose said. "He's still an element. You're not."

"You're right," Angst said, taking a few calming breaths. "We should stick to the plan."

"Come to me, Angst," Magic said. "Or your best friend will die a most painful death."

"Tarness," Angst whispered. He suddenly sensed bones. It was too far to see, but someone was definitely beside Magic.

"It's a trap, Angst," Dallow said.

"Of course it's a trap," Angst said. "But if he's got Tarness...I can't let another friend die."

"But if he kills you, it's all over," Rose said.

"What a failure of a hero," Magic said, his voice winding its way into his frustration. "Are you too frightened to face my challenge?"

"If you're going back in time to change everything, would saving him even matter?" Mirim asked.

"It would if I fail," Angst said.

"Hold on, Angst," Dallow said, his eyes glowing white. "Give me a minute to block him out."

"Do you know what kind of person would let his best friend die a painful death?" Magic said. "The same one who would let his family die in fire."

Angst saw red as fury boiled his blood. With a roar, he leaped over the cliff's edge and landed on his steel ram swifen.

"Angst, no," Victoria called after him. "This is the wrong future!"

Blue and red lightning surrounded him as he rode straight down the cliff wall. The swords wanted this more than he did. It's what they were made for, and they fueled his power. He landed on the field and raced toward Magic in a blur.

"Get him," Alloria shouted.

46

Thunder echoed throughout the canyon as the fury of all nations poured onto the field. Victoria swallowed hard as plans and visions were run over in the stampede. Accepting a small telescope from Mirim, she viewed what she already knew. Angst was right; armies had been waiting along the field's edge. As Nordruaut, Fulk'han, tribesmen, merpeople, and the army of Melkier raced toward Angst on the ground, dark forms of Berfemmian took to the air. To make matters worse, watery gargoyles, dragons, and cavastil birds now littered the skies.

"He's moving so fast I can barely follow him," Jaden said in surprise. "How is that possible, even for an Al'eyrn?"

"He's Angst," Alloria said, hopping up and down.

"We should go after him," Rose said.

"Even at top speed," Dallow said, "the armies will be on him before we arrive."

"Keep talking," Victoria said as she watched Angst race toward Tarness. "Give me options."

"The field will be full by the time our army arrives," Mirim said. "We'd have to fight our way to him, which is a lot to ask considering some of our opponents."

"How will Angst and Magic be able to fight when they're swarmed by all of that?" Nikkola asked.

"The element won't want to be distracted," Jaden said. "He'll keep the armies from interfering with a shield."

321

"We have to beat them to Prendere," Dallow said. "To create a path for Angst when he wins, or stop Magic if he doesn't."

"Can we get there in time?" Victoria asked.

"Angst has his full rage on, and Magic is fighting for the trophy," Dallow said, looking up and tapping his chin. "I'd guess we have twenty minutes."

"An Al'eyrn can push swifen faster than normal," Jaden said, nodding to Rose. "Even skirting the battle, we could be there in ten."

"I can do that," Rose said proudly, her daggers glowing green. "Then what?"

"Even when Angst is an idiot, I believe in him," Victoria said. "He wouldn't just rush and leave us behind."

"You're right," Dallow said. "What does the future tell you?"

Angst's plan, and seeing a hint of his future, had given her hope. Without him, Victoria's visions of the distant future were a mix of unreliable and frightening. No matter how hard she sought the win, too many paths showed the worst sort of dead ends. Despite her fear, she desperately searched. All remained silent as she flipped through pages of books with bad endings.

"Victoria," Jaden said, placing a hand on her shoulder. "You don't need to see the distant future for us to trust in you as a leader."

"That's it," she said, gripping his hand. She was looking too far into the unknown. They needed to know what would keep them alive over the next few hours. Tomorrow was future Victoria's problem. With that, she smiled and opened her eyes. "Boys?"

Everyone jumped back and drew weapons as five gamlin popped out of the ground, shaking off dirt like dogs shake away water. Victoria couldn't help but smile. The hedgehog/porcupine creatures were adorable and dangerous enough to core dragons. The gamlin saluted her, and she nodded in return.

"Wow," Nikkola said.

"Aren't they cute?" Alloria asked, clapping her hands.

"How will they help us?" Jaden asked.

"Yes," General Mirot huffed as he rushed to them. "What's the new plan?"

"We're going around that edge of the field," Victoria said, pointing. "Some friends are waiting to help us, and the gamlin will get us the rest of the way. When we arrive, we'll send up a signal. Our army will ride in, and hopefully, provide enough distraction that we can create a path from Angst to Prendere."

"That could work," Mirot said.

"Mirim," Victoria said. "I want you to lead the zyn'ight as they charge in with the Unsel army."

"Yes, Your Highness," she said with a polite bow.

"Dallow, Rose, Jaden, and Nikkola," she said, summoning a swifen. She picked up the smallest gamlin and handed it to Alloria. "Each of you take one, carefully—their quills are like razors. Alloria, you'll ride with me. You'll need to keep hold of the gamlin and the foci."

Each rider carefully placed a gamlin on their swifen before mounting.

"I'm suddenly glad I've got armor," Rose said as her gamlin settled back. She sat up straight. "Ready."

"As long as we aren't riding down the cliff," Dallow said, "I'm ready."

"Thank you," Nikkola said, patting her gamlin on the head. "I can't wait to see Kala."

"Ready, my queen," Jaden said, proudly.

"General," Victoria said, facing Mirot. "Are our troops ready?"

"They'd expected to charge in with you and Angst," he said, tugging at his mustache. "They are ready, but—"

"Let's give them what they need," Victoria said.

* * * *

"There are so many," Victoria said, gripping the reins of her armored unicorn tight.

Thousands and thousands of strong men and women from

Unsel stood at attention. They were squared off into companies a hundred strong, each commanded by a stalwart captain. Dividing the two halves of her army stood forty knights on their war horses. A dozen zyn'ight adorned with dusky armor stood apart from the others, though every bit as formal in their waiting.

She didn't need magic to sense everyone's trepidation; the smell of sweat and steel permeated the air. Old eyes and young looked on with worry as the world went to war a spear throw away. This was a war no one had fought in recorded history, and they needed her words. Never had she felt so powerful and so frightened.

"How will they hear me?" she asked.

"Magic's trick wasn't so clever," Dallow said. He whispered a few words in Acratic and placed a finger on her throat. "Unsel will hear you."

"Thank you," she said.

The older soldiers jumped at her words while the younger turned to gawk. Several captains shouts of, "Attention" faced them forward.

With a wide-eyed nod to Dallow, she rode before the army of Unsel.

"I said thank you," she said, and all eyes turned to follow her. "Thank you for dying for Unsel. That's right. You're going to die. I'm going to die. But not today! We have never faced a battle like this. This war of giants and monsters that threaten Unsel and Ehrde is frightening. Every one of you is scared, and anyone who says otherwise is a liar. But you are heroes. A hero is someone who does the right thing even when they're afraid. You wonder if you'll be brave enough to face all of that. You will."

To her surprise, one man near the front shouted, "For Unsel!"

"Many of you are wondering why we don't race in after Angst. I didn't bring you here to die. We are outnumbered and overpowered, and rushing in will only make us a part of the mob. My mother, our queen, once told me if you can't be the strongest, you'd better be the smartest. I will not send you in to hunt the entire herd. You will go in like butchers and carve out the finest meat."

"For Unsel!" more soldiers cried.

"Angst has to make it to that light, or it's over for all of us. When you see the signal, ride hard and ride fierce. Charge forth with all your might and butcher that mob. You will give Angst the chance he needs."

"For Unsel!" everyone shouted, and her heart raced.

"This is a place that won't be seen again for generations. An event that only happens once every two thousand years. There will be stories about this day, and those stories will be about you. We have been a nation divided, of those who wield and those who don't. This day we fight together and make a new story. One people. One Unsel."

"For Unsel!"

"Angst is not the hero today. You are. I charge all of you to fight. I charge all of you to live. I charge all of you to win!"

"For Unsel," Mirot said, his voice as loud as hers.

"For Unsel," the army shouted.

"For Queen Victoria," Mirot said.

"For the queen," the army repeated.

47

Half a mile from his target, Angst glanced around the field to see lines of dust plumes avalanche down mountain paths as nations converged. Cavastil birds, gargoyles, and dark Berfemmian shot toward him like a thousand arrows. War was coming fast, and its cries were loud enough to hear through the rage that buzzed in his ears.

Five hundred yards to go, and he could make out Tarness grappling with Magic, either trying to break free or merely trying to break the element. His powerful friend stood no chance, but hopefully he was angry enough to hold Magic off, because Angst was angry enough to end this.

The first dark Berfemmian arrived when he was only three hundred yards away and bounced off his air shield like a rock thrown at a tree. Before she could recover, the long, steel beak of a cavastil bird punctured her chest. The bird opened its maw, splitting her in half. A second Berfemmian grabbed the bird's head. She placed two feet against its wings and pulled until the head snapped off.

Two hundred yards from Magic, Angst drew his swords. Tarness was alive and running toward him. Blood red waves of power cascaded from Magic's arms, reaching for the big man. Chryslaenor and Dulgirgraut's songs clashed as one blared warnings and the other begged for Angst to destroy the element. With Tarness free, all he had to do was rush past his friend, cut

Magic's head off, and rain the field with all the lightning he could summon.

He made eye contact with Tarness only a hundred yards away. Anger and pain wracked his friend's face, which was much better than dead. Angst flashed him a wild grin. Tarness leaped up with a roar and held out his arm, striking Angst in the chest. His ram swifen disappeared, and he cried out in pain as Tarness slammed him to the ground.

Everything hurt but his eyes, which couldn't seem to focus as his vision faded in and out. Tarness punched his chest again before pulling back and drawing a longsword. Angst blinked rapidly, desperately gasping for air. The swords forced power into him, but that wasn't enough. Even casting a shield or a healing spell would take time, and he was still reeling from that attack. His best option was to talk his friend down.

"Please," he wheezed, holding out a hand. "Please, stop."

Tarness held the sword high overhead.

"What are you doi—" Angst coughed, covering his chest piece in blood. "Let me kill Magic and save my family."

"I'm here to save *my* family, Angst," Tarness said. "Maarja is pregnant, and I won't give that up for anyone. Not even you."

"You're not thinking clearly," Angst said. "If Magic wins, he'll destroy everything."

Tarness turned to look at the element, giving Angst a moment to heal. The spell was a bandage so weak that it had moth holes and was frayed at the edges. At least he could breathe, a little.

"I command you to kill him," Magic shouted.

The ring on Tarness's finger sparked, making the big man wince. Why wasn't Magic attacking? As Tarness floundered with his fate, Angst looked about to see a dark shield overhead. The element was powerful enough to keep others from interfering, but not to attack him at the same time.

"He's using that ring to make you do this," Angst said. "Magic is weak. You can fight him!"

"I won't let my family die," Tarness roared, swinging down hard.

* * * *

They reached the base of the mountain and took to the field at full speed. Victoria led the charge as they raced forward, fast enough to make her eyes water. Now that Rose and Jormbrinder were on speaking terms, she had the knowledge to drive their swifen at stomach-clenching speed. What should've taken a harried forty-five minutes would now take ten without distraction. Like it would be that easy.

Within minutes, a flock of cavastil birds dove at them. Rose released the swifen, and they abruptly slowed from a hummingbird sprint to a turtle crawl. The jarring transition was just enough, and the birds missed their target. They swooped around, giving everyone enough time to wield weapons.

A dozen landed before them. They were ostrich-sized ravens with velvety purple wings and bright crimson chests. Thick, steel taloned legs and long beaks glistened in the light of the distant beam. A fan of feathers popped up from the bird's necks, covered in eyes that blinked in unison.

Nikkola let out a scream as she shot dark bolts from her hands. The attack blasted a hole in one cavastil bird, knocking the carcass into another. The others lifted, hovering several feet over the ground.

"We can take them," Jaden said. "Send the gamlin. They can drill right through them."

"We need to keep these gamlin alive," Victoria said. "Nikkola, hold your attack. Help is coming."

"They better hurry," Alloria said, holding the gamlin as tight as she could.

Twenty Fulk'han men and women leaped from a rocky outcrop, making everyone rear back in surprise. The gray men and colorful women tackled the cavastil birds, wrestling them far away from their path. A young woman with pale blue skin rushed over.

"Are you Teesha?" Victoria asked.

"I am," she said, her long tail flicking back and forth. "We fight for Angst. We fight for Ehrde. Now go." And with that, she let out a trilling scream, launched into the air and landed on the back of a cavastil bird.

"Ride," Victoria commanded.

Time seemed to slow as Victoria sought their next attackers. It felt like she was juggling in a hurricane. Not only was she riding with Alloria and their gamlin, but she was leading because she'd seen this future. She had to focus on what would happen next, and when. The hairs on her arms rose, and she knew it was time.

"Rose, stop," she shouted, rearing back her unicorn. "Dallow, Jaden, shield."

A furnace blast of dragonfire slammed against the air shield. They coughed as the air became too hot to breathe. An enormous dragon landed before them, shaking the ground on impact. While smaller than the mother-of-all-dragons, this was no whelpling. It's diamond-shaped head lifted, revealing a mouth large enough to scoop up the six of them and the ground they stood on. A thick armor of red scales covered the wyrm. The battle-weary monster glared at them with one fierce golden eye, the other deeply scarred and leaking dribbles of lava.

"I can't deflect another blast," Dallow shouted. "Not from that thing."

"You won't have to," a tribesman said, landing before them. He lifted his double-bladed staff and pointed it at the dragon. "End this creature."

A dozen perfectly sculpted dark-skinned men attacked the dragons with their staudouf. Each attack landing at a different point, striking joints with clinical precision. The dragon stumbled as lava poured from every wound. It attempted to draw in air, only to roar in pain as a staff went through its good eye. In unison, the tribesmen leaped from the beast and began yelling, drawing it away from their path.

"Tell Angst that SMyket and his tribe are with him," the man said. "Now go!"

With a loud grunt from Rose, they rushed forward even faster than before. While the shield surrounding Prendere was invisible, it was outlined by war and bodies. Soldiers from all nations had given it a wide berth, as if afraid that touching it meant death.

"Almost there," Victoria called out. "Just to the far edge."

"No more monsters?" Nikkola asked.

She looked over her shoulder and saw nothing. "I thought there were more, but…"

Their gamlin leaped from the swifen as cold water surrounded them. The watery gargoyle was large enough to absorb her, the unicorn, and Alloria. Desperate for air, she clutched at her throat. As her eyes closes, a mouth met hers, breathing air into her lungs. The mermaid gave her several breaths. Victoria opened her eyes in time to see a wink before she pulled away. The mermaid spun, forcing the gargoyle to release them. The spinning continued at an unbelievable speed until the gargoyle exploded.

Victoria coughed until she caught her breath. The others were hacking and gasping, having experienced similar attacks. A young mermaid waited patiently beside her, gently placing a hand on her leg.

"Lyda," Victoria said. "Thank you."

"*Tell Angst we are with him,*" the mermaid said with a nod. "*We will keep your path clear of the gargoyles.*"

Without another word, Lyda ran off, followed by a bevy of merpeople.

"Thanks for the booze," Nikkola said with a wave. She muttered, "I could use some now."

"Almost there," Victoria said, hopping off to grab the gamlin. "No more stops."

She could sense that their fear and exhaustion matched her own. The short race had been both frightening and gross. It felt like her dragon-singed eyebrows were covered in gargoyle snot. When they finally arrived, she was wary of telling them what was next. It was going to get worse.

"It's going to get worse," Nikkola said. "Isn't it?"

Victoria and her cousin dismounted before dismissing her swifen. The others followed, their expressions wary. Protecting her eyes from the beam's glare, she found what she was looking for.

"There's a shield surrounding that light," Victoria said. "The battle is staying away from it, but not far. We need to get to the middle and create a path to Angst."

They all stared at the mass of armies standing between them and their destination.

"How are we supposed to fight through all of that?" Rose asked, sighing before she added, "Your Highness."

"You got anything?" Jaden asked Dallow.

"Nope," Dallow said. "You?"

"Nuh uh," Jaden said.

"This will be the least fun part," Victoria said. "The gamlin will take us."

"Felk," Alloria said.

"What?" Rose asked.

"That means two miles of not breathing," Dallow said. "The gamlin can swim through rock and bring us with. We just can't breathe dirt."

"And we'll have to be ready to fight when we get there," Victoria said. "Dallow, you've got thirty seconds to teach Rose how to create an air shield around everyone's heads, or we're dead on arrival."

"Ooookay," Dallow said, turning to Rose. "You can do this."

"I guess we'll find out," Rose said.

48

Angst rolled to one side and then the other, barely in time to dodge Tarness's strikes. He spider-crawled back, and the longsword landed hard between his legs, a mere inch from anything important.

"Hey," Angst said. "Not cool."

Normally, his friend would've let out a chuckle, but there was nothing but hatred and murder in the man's wild eyes. This wasn't Tarness; this was Magic twisting him into something else. Angst could let loose and lightning bolt a hole through Tarness's chest, but that would be like crushing his own heart. That left him with only one idea.

"I give up," Angst said.

"What?" Tarness asked, staggering back.

"Too much has happened to be a coincidence, and I'm tired of being at the receiving end of fate," Angst said, pushing himself up to stand. "We've been lured, manipulated, and trapped by the elements and their stupid war." He looked up into his friend's eyes. "If we don't start making our own choices, nothing will ever go our way."

Tarness shook his head and looked around as if he didn't know where he was.

"I won't fight you," Angst said, lowering both swords. "I know in my heart that the decision is yours. Kill me, and Magic wins. Let me live, and maybe fate will be ours."

CHAPTER FORTY EIGHT

"Angst?" Tarness asked, lowering his sword.

"Kill him," Magic cried. "Or I will destroy you, and your family."

"Fight it," Angst said.

"I...but, my family." Tarness shook his head until the fury left his eyes. "No, I will not kill someone I love. I will not kill Angst."

"Tarness?" said a familiar voice.

They all looked over to see Maarja, her hands pressed against the element's shield.

"Please hurry," Jintorich squeaked. "I can't hold off so many for long."

"Maarja," Tarness said, taking a step toward her.

"I said kill him," Magic screamed. "Destroy Angst."

Tarness shuddered. He swung his fist, knocking Angst back against the far end of the shield.

"That's it," Magic said. "End this."

Angst was staring at the sky again, hoping the world would stop spinning in time.

"Magic is the enemy, Tarness, not Angst," Maarja pleaded. "I believe in you."

The big man collapsed to his knees as fury battled indecision. Glaring at Magic, he shouted, "My fate is my own." Resting his forearm on the ground, Tarness reached up high with the sword and swung down. He screamed as he pulled back, leaving his forearm and the ruby ring behind. Dropping the longsword, he grasped the bleeding stump.

"No," Magic said as he staggered back.

A dark void of power swirled behind Tarness as Death came for him. His dark skin and silver armor slowly twisted into the darkness like paint spilled in a whirlpool.

"I love you, Maarja," Tarness said. "Tell our child I was not a coward."

She could only nod as tears streamed down her cheeks.

"Angst," he said, turning to face him. "I did this for you. Now, make fate your own."

As he faded away into the void of Death, a blinding flash of light swallowed him whole. Tarness was gone.

"No," Maarja roared.

Before Angst could push himself up, Magic's shield disappeared, and the madness of war poured in.

* * * *

They erupted from the ground like new volcanos, each of them gasping for breath. Victoria was dizzy, desperate for air. She'd breathed too fast, using up her air during their panic-ridden two-mile swim through earth. Dallow, Rose, and Alloria were all conscious; the others weren't. The battle had already noticed them, leaving Dallow precious seconds to create a protective shield. Rose stumbled over and knelt beside her.

"I'm awake," Victoria said between coughs. "Rouse Jaden, and Nikkola—in that order."

"What do I do?" Alloria asked, pale with fear.

"Protect that foci with your life," she said. "Gamlin, will you stay and fight with us?"

The six creatures lined up and saluted, their tiny human-like faces scrunched in determination. It was a little too cute for war.

"Guard the person you rode with," she said with a nod. They quickly scurried into position. "Dallow, how are you holding up?"

He grunted, shaking his head. His shield was a small half-dome that fit around them glove-tight. Men and women from every army fought with their backs against the edge. The beam of light hummed with power fifty yards behind them, protected by an invisible barrier. A gargoyle slammed against Dallow's shield several times before flying away.

After waking the others with gentle healing, Rose approached. "What next?" she asked. "Dallow can't hold them for long."

"We need more space," Victoria said. "I'm hoping that when we signal the Unsel army, they'll draw attention from us."

"You hope?" Rose asked with a frown.

"If you've got something better than hope," Victoria said, "please share."

"Hope works," Rose said, taking a deep breath. "What's the signal?"

"Can you project a giant image of Angst's swords overhead?" Victoria asked.

"Let me see," Rose said, cocking her head to one side. "Jormbrinder says yes to the image but no to the swords. I'd have to be looking at them to make the projection."

"Hurry," Dallow grunted. His hands shook with the effort and sweat beaded his forehead.

"Jaden, help him," Victoria said. She turned to Rose, "What can we use?"

Rose looked her up and down. She smiled broadly and said, "Draw your sword."

* * * *

Guenther had always been fast. Whether on foot, horse, or sea turtle, he would always be there first. Some said it was a gift, others called it magics. When he'd enlisted as a soldier of Unsel, the wariness of those others forced him to slow down. He'd still be there first, but always within arm's reach. His speed and de-termination had helped him save many lives, eventually earning him a knighthood.

Despite having been a knight for so long, he felt out of place standing amidst the other soldiers. If what he could do truly was driven by magic, shouldn't he be standing with the zyn'ight? Shouldn't he have ridden out with Angst? More than anything, he wanted to help everyone—wielder and non-wielder alike. Angst was out there alone. There were too many armies to battle, even with those two giant swords. Maybe it was time to prove what he could really do.

He waited in nervous anticipation, drawing his hand over the tight, dark beard around his mouth. His short brown hair was already matted with sweat, making him reluctant to put on the steel helm.

A giant image of Princess Victoria rose above the far end of the battlefield. She brandished a longsword and pointed forward before exploding into fireworks.

"Wow," Mirot called out. "I mean, charge!"

Guenther charged. At first, he kept pace with his regiment, only inching ahead slightly. After having watched the zyn'ight train, he understood how they drew in will to wield their magics. It was almost identical to how he made himself or his mount move faster.

Their plan was working. As the Unsel army raced across the field, the mob turned to face them. Concentrating and drawing in his will to move faster, Guenther waited for that one break in the ranks. A path no wider than a deer trail opened up. It would have to be enough. With all his focus, he willed his stallion to ride fast.

A hundred yards ahead of his army soon became two hundred and more. He lithely dodged a spear before charging into the path. It was an obstacle course of ducking under Nordruaut axes and leaping over tribesmen staves. His watering eyes captured dust like a magnet as his sweat-soaked hands gripped the reins for dear life.

He finally slowed as the path became a clearing. Angst was on his knees, screaming for Tarness. A furious Nordruaut launched herself at a tall, bald man whose appearance began to change as he disappeared into the crowd. Unseen by all was a limping tribesman covered in burn scars heading straight for Angst. Guenther forced his stallion to a halt while leaping from his horse, hoping to tackle the sneak.

Mid-air, he landed in the gloppy gelatinous body of a gargoyle. The monster held him like a fly in amber. Swinging wildly accomplished nothing, and he futilely grasped for something solid to pull himself out. As precious air began bubbling from his mouth, a jarring pain expunged the rest.

The steel beak of a cavastil bird had punctured his chest, the monster flying him clear of the gargoyle. His first captor roared as it exploded. Guenther gasped for breath, coughing out blood and phlegm. At least he was still alive. The bird's head dipped low with the weight of his armor. Its claws pressed against his back as if trying to remove meat from a kabob. That was when things went bad.

The cavastil bird let out a muttered squawk as a dragon bit deep into its torso. The red wyrm landed hard and shook its head. Guenther flew off the end of the beak, crashing to the ground beside Angst.

"You look worse than I feel," Angst said, kneeling beside him.

"There," was all he could wheeze, pointing behind the chubby old hero.

Angst spun to see a husk of a tribesman approach. By all accounts, the man shouldn't have been alive. The side of his forehead was caved in, and most of his body was covered in burn scars. One good arm held firm a staff with blades at both ends. Despite appearing more beggar than warrior, his eyes were filled with hatred.

"ANduaut?" Angst asked. "You're alive? Sort of alive?"

"I'm here to take the prize from you, Angst," ANduaut said, limping forward.

"I think you'd have a hard time taking a copper from me," Angst said.

Without word or warning, ANduaut threw the double-bladed staff at Angst. Time slowed as Guenther drew in the last of his will, and the last of his life. He was fast, probably faster than anyone, and just fast enough to shield Angst as he launched from the ground. He roared in pain as the weapon sank deep into his stomach.

"No," ANduaut cried. He rushed forward, only to be tackled by another tribesman.

"SMyket," Angst called out.

"Get to the light, my friend," SMyket said. "This one is mine."

Angst turned to face the knight. After jerking out the staff, he knelt beside him, placing a hand on his chest.

"I'm sorry," he said. "There's too much damage to heal."

Guenther closed his eyes and nodded.

"What's your name?" Angst asked.

"Guenther," he said.

"Thank you, Guenther," Angst said. "Thank you for saving me. Die in peace knowing you may have just saved Ehrde."

49

"There are too many," Maarja said, swinging wildly to keep the mob at bay. "Can't you do something?"

"I don't want to kill them all," Angst said. "Too many are dying already, and they don't even know why."

She roared in fury, backhanding a Fulk'han into the crowd as she stormed to Angst. Grasping him around his dusky chest piece, she lifted the little man up so they were face to face.

"You will find a way into that thing to get my husband back if I have to throw you at it," she said, trying not to shake him too violently. "You will save my husband."

"Or I'll die trying," he said, glancing over her shoulders. "Look, right in front of the light. Victoria and some of the others are trying to make a path to us."

Maarja followed his eyes and took in their friends' helpless battle. Victoria directed Nikkola, Jaden, Dallow, and Rose like a ringmaster while Alloria cowered behind. They were maintaining an air shield that kept most opponents out. Dragons blasted the shield with liquid fire as gargoyles jumped up and down on it, shaking the barrier and the ground beneath. They would strategically let a part of the shield down long enough for Nikkola to let loose a volley of dark blasts. Some would strike, but many reflected off Melkier armor or dragon scale like light off a mirror.

"They are fighting too many to help us," Maarja said, glaring at Angst. "Either use those weapons, or I'll use you as a weapon."

"That won't be necessary," Jintorich said, landing on her shoulder. "I agree with Angst. We can't kill them all."

"What do you have in mind?" Angst asked.

Maarja set Angst down and held out a hand for Jintorich. He hopped over and faced her. The Meldusian had an unusually sad expression, his eyebrows and ears drooping.

"I understand now," Jintorich said. "My foci finally explained how I am one of many."

"What is this?" Maarja said, cocking her head. "You're going to do something dumb. All men do dumb things."

"You have been a wonderful friend, and our time together will not be forgotten," Jintorich said. He turned to Angst. "Thanks for the adventure. I believe you will make this right."

"What are you going to do?" Maarja asked. "What is it you have learned?"

"I'm not just one of many," Jintorich shouted. "I'm many of one."

Jintorich leaped into the air, landing between them and the beam of light. Anyone within ten feet was knocked away. He knelt, facing down reverently, his staff glowing so bright it was hard to look at.

"Jin?" Losing her husband had already been too much. She didn't know what she'd do without her best friend.

There was an audible pop as a second Jintorich appeared. Both of them struck the ground with their foci staves. Two new Jintorichs popped into existence. They did it again and again as everyone nearby scrambled away.

"One of many," Angst said, his face awestruck.

Within minutes, there were thousands of Jintorichs, each with their own foci. Together, they let loose a piercing battle cry that made anyone within earshot wince. The Meldusian spread out, either rushing to them or the beam of light. Size didn't matter to the little Al'eyrn as they batted away anyone in their path. Nordruaut, Berfemmian, and even dragons were all smacked away with a *tunk* as metal struck bone in a flash of light.

The Jintorich army had created a path. Acting like one person, they made a tunnel of air shields that led straight to Prendere.

"Run," they cried out in unison.

Without waiting, Maarja picked up Angst and sprinted to the others.

* * * *

"Go save my husband," Maarja said, tossing Angst against the barrier.

He bounced off, collapsing to his side.

"Tarness is dead?" Rose asked. "All of this to save him, and he...he's gone?"

"Now isn't the time," Victoria said, helping Angst up. "We need to get you in there so we can end this, one way or another."

"Use the horn to take down that barrier," Dallow said. "Jintorich's foci won't last long split up like this."

"Your turn, Alloria," Angst said. "Blow the horn."

"Okay, baby," she said. The princess wrapped her full lips around the mouthpiece and blew. The horn was silent, and the shield remained. She tried again, and again, but eventually lowered Cornuclav and shook her head.

"Try something else," Dallow pleaded. "People are slipping through."

Jaden raised a finger. "I could—"

A flash of light interrupted him, and two beautiful, young women appeared.

"Bella, Karina," Angst said. "But how?"

"No time," Karina said with a wink. "We're just relieved you finally found it."

"Hi, Alloria," Bella said, reaching out a hand. "May I?"

Alloria nodded mutely, handing her the foci. Bella pressed her lips to the mouthpiece and blew. She held the note steady for long moments, breathing through her nose as the horn blared. A visible crack appeared in the barrier that slowly spider-webbed all around until reaching high up into the sky. As she lowered the horn, gasping for breath, shards of the barrier fell into wispy smoke.

"You did it," Angst said, grasping Bella's arm as she wavered.

"Not done yet," she said between breaths. "We need to go open the other side."

"What?" Angst asked.

"Don't forget to save us," Karina said.

And with that, the sisters held hands and disappeared in a flash of light—taking the foci with them.

"Does it ever stop being weird?" Angst asked, shaking his head.

"So, this is it," Victoria said.

"This is it," Angst said.

"You should hurry," Rose said. "Before something else goes wrong."

"Fulk'han," Jaden said, pointing toward the light.

"I don't sense anyone," Angst said, following his finger.

A purple woman stood directly before the bright beam. As she looked back at Angst, a smile crept across her face. She grew a head taller and the purple faded to pale, revealing the tall, awkward-looking man he knew too well.

"Magic," Angst cried out. "No."

"Nice try, Al'eyrn," Magic said with a wink before entering Prendere.

Without hesitation, Angst blurred into the light.

50

Angst's heart thrummed in his ears. It was a good sign because it probably meant he was alive. Probably. So far, his immediate fears of burning on entry, being shot up into space, or simply disappearing into nothing hadn't happened. On the other hand, being inside the wish-maker was disillusioning. No wish in his mind had come true. It hadn't sent him back in time, washed away his exhaustion, flushed out his anger, or even made him younger—which he felt in his bones.

His first mistake was facing Prendere with eyes wide open because the blinding light did its job. Passing through the portal left him numb, like when your arm falls asleep from poor circulation, but all over. His ears were deafened by the constant low hum of power generated by the light beam. Even the swords were quiet. This wasn't the, "I'm being a big baby and am unwilling to help," quiet. It was more like, "We weren't invited to the party but good luck," quiet. All that remained was his sense of smell and witty internal dialog—certainly enough to battle a living element.

What had started as a brave rush into the light had become a blind-man's shuffle. The mystery of Prendere seemed to be its size because he'd walked far enough to reach the other side and back. Maybe Prendere had suddenly realized he was just a man entering an elements-only club? That wouldn't do. He'd fought too hard and sacrificed too much to be jailed in this white void.

"I've come for the prize," he shouted, standing still and placing his hands on his hips. The silent treatment fed his growing anger, and he drew in his will. Chryslaenor and Dulgirgraut may have gone quiet, but they still provided him with power. "I am here to stop Magic, end this war, and save my family. Give me the prize, now!" He reached up and released bolts of lightning into the light above.

The buzzing in his ears subsided and feeling slowly returned to his body. That sucked because he'd forgotten how much everything hurt. Tarness had really done a number on him, and he cursed himself for not getting healed before entering.

He took a deep breath of stale air as his sight slowly returned. A room appeared around him, and Angst shuddered in relief. Escaping that prison of numbing, blinding, deafening light made him want to cry. He couldn't imagine what Dallow had gone through being blind for so many months.

The round, jousting-sized room was the most unremarkable and beautiful thing he'd ever seen. Cracked ivory tile covered the open floor. Twenty-foot obsidian pillars stood every eight feet around the outside. Between each pillar was a statue or a black, arched doorway—apparently like the one he'd just passed through. The nearest statue was worn by time and practically featureless in the dim light that came from nowhere.

"If getting angry was my key to entering, this shouldn't take long," he said, cautiously approaching the center. "For something so mysterious and powerful, this room is as exciting as my bathroom—and I get more done there." He yelled, "I'm not impressed."

When the echoes faded, someone cleared their throat. Spinning around slowly revealed nothing but statues, doorways, and pillars. The second polite cough made him look up.

"I take it back," he said. "I'm impressed."

The ceiling in the middle of this pantheon opened up to a glorious night sky. Four living constellations, complete with lines between stars, stared down at him in curiosity or judgment. He recognized them all. Earth in her toga and thonged sandals nodded respectfully and smiled as if this were her plan all along.

"Thank you for your gamlin," Angst said. "They've saved me and my friends numerous times. I wouldn't be here without your gift."

Water leaned forward with arms crossed, her eyes two bright stars that glared at him.

"You blamed me for an accident," he said, feeling the familiar boil in his blood. "You intentionally hurt me by killing someone I love. I have no regrets about destroying you."

Fire was the most animated constellation, threatening him with starry fists and shouting silent curses.

"Come on down here," Angst said, his rage bringing him to a very dark place. "There will never be forgiveness for what you've taken from me. I would gladly live forever just to destroy you again and again."

When he faced Air, his anger blinded him more than the white light.

"Make room," Angst roared, his fists shaking. "There's one more heading up there. Now tell me. Where is Magic?"

Air smiled and pointed toward a doorway.

Another Angst spryly leaped through the dark entrance. It was him, but obviously not him. The doppelganger looked older, with thinner hair and more defined wrinkles. He seemed skinny in comparison and sported a gray goatee. The other Angst's armor was identical in design, but rather than his dusky black finish, this Angst's brushed silver armor practically glowed. When their eyes met, the older Angst looked at him with sadness and concern.

"Neat trick," Angst said, drawing both swords from his back. "First you show up as Ivan then you sneak in here as a Fulk'han woman, and now you look like me."

"It's not what you think," the older Angst said, holding out both hands. "I'll make this go easy. Just let me explain."

"I'm done with your lies, Magic. I'm done with you," he said, launching himself forward in a blur.

He swung down hard, embedding his two swords deep in the tile. Magic now stood at the other end of the room, wielding his mirror copies of Chryslaenor and Dulgirgraut.

"Coward," he called out, jerking his swords free. "You won't even face me as yourself!"

"You're not thinking straight," the older Angst said. "Just look closer. Tell me what you see."

"Another dead element," Angst cried as he rushed forward.

Magic met him head-on. The four swords collided in an explosion of light, knocking both men back. He slammed against a statue, breaking it in half and falling to his knees. The older Angst was already in the center of the room, looking about nervously. Angst followed his eyes to see dark figures running from one shadowy doorway to another.

"What is this?" Angst shouted. "More tricks?"

"Sure," Magic said. "But the fight is over here, hero. Are you giving up so fast?"

Angst blurred forward, swinging with all his might. One blow cascaded off another, showering the floor in sparks.

"Your stupid war killed my friends," he said, swinging down hard. Chryslaenor bounced off the fake Dulgirgraut. He flipped back, landing on his feet before blurring forward. "You killed my family." He drove Dulgirgraut at his opponent's chest, and the older Angst turned to one side, barely in time. "You killed my felking dog," Angst shouted as he spun around.

Both swords met Magic's ribs with a crunch. The older Angst flew back, slamming against a pillar and collapsing to the ground. Angst rushed forward and raised both swords high overhead.

"All clear," said a familiar voice. "Try not to hurt him too badly."

Angst turned to the voice. "Heather?"

* * * *

Hope. More than anything, Victoria was desperate for hope. The vast field before her was pure chaos. A thousand or more Meldusians barely kept the horde of armies at bay. Nordruaut and Berfemmian harpies, and merpeople, and Fulk'han and

Melkier battled mercilessly. The Unsel soldiers and accompanying zyn'ight seemed tiny and hard to find in the distance. Dragons and cavastil birds fought overhead while gamlin dodged gargoyle attacks. It was almost too overwhelming to fathom.

Victoria, Dallow, Jaden, Rose, Nikkola, and Maarja all watched in helpless awe. They were the last line of defense, keeping everyone from reaching the giant beam of light.

"Shield," Victoria shouted, pointing up to the right.

Rose, Dallow, and Jaden lifted their arms and created an air shield that deflected a barrage of liquid dragonfire. Dallow collapsed to a knee as five dragons flew away in a v formation.

"Tribesmen attacking our left," Victoria barked.

A dozen, tiny Meldusians with their foci staves blurred to the left, knocking back the attacking tribesmen.

"Melkier on our right," Victoria shouted, pointing.

Nikkola's dark blasts bounced off the dusky Melkier armor like pebbles off a boulder. Maarja picked up one and hurled him far into the battle as Rose blurred forward, finding open necks and exposed kidneys with her daggers.

"How long do we have?" Victoria asked Dallow.

"A half hour at most," Dallow said, standing on unsure legs. "It all depends on how long Jin's staff lasts being split amongst so many."

The ground began shaking, so gently at first it was hard to tell with the war around them. When Ehrde quaked violently enough to make everyone brace themselves, Victoria could only wonder when it would split in two.

"I take it back. Minutes," Dallow said. "If Angst had won, this would be over."

His words echoed her greatest worry. As she began thinking of an exit, there was a loud pop, followed by another. The Meldusian staves were blinking out of existence, as were the many Jintorichs. Every Jin that disappeared was replaced by a very vulnerable Meldusian man or woman.

"We are many," they said in unison.

"Get your many asses over here," Victoria commanded.

"I'm sorry I upset you," Jaden said, suddenly beside her. His eyes were full of love and apology. "I read every journal and note you wrote. They were like love letters, and I fell hard. The last one I read told me to kill Angst, at all costs. I was torn, and now..."

"I should have believed you," she said.

"I love you, Victoria," he said.

"I love you too," she said, burying her face in his shoulder.

"Need some help?" a young woman asked as she leaped from the beam of light. Her long black hair billowed about her tanned face. She reached out with her hands, and nothing happened. "Ugh, I forget, magic is different now." She scrunched her nose in concentration and muttered words that Victoria didn't understand. Black holes appeared beneath every attacker in a ten-yard radius, swallowing them whole before blinking out of existence.

"Who are you?" Victoria asked.

"Kala, Your Majesty," she said, her tone determined and fierce. "More are coming. This isn't over."

"K-Kala?" Nikkola asked, glancing over her shoulder. "It's really you? You're so big."

"Hi, Mom," she said, hugging the woman. "I missed you."

"Looks like I'm in time," a deep voice said from behind her.

"Tarness," Maarja said, rushing to him. She grasped him in a bear hug, unable to hold back tears. Setting him down, she gawked. "Your arm."

"Yeah, wait until you see what it does," he said, stretching it. The mechanical arm hissed and whined as metallic pullies jerked his hand into a fist. With a roar, he rushed forward, knocking a bevy of mermen senseless.

"Where is my *essent*?" Faeoris asked as she exited the beam. "Where is Marisha?"

The tall, beautiful Berfemmian was covered neck to ankle in form-fitting scale armor. Steel wings stretched out from her back, each rectangular feather serrated, and the ends of every joint a steel claw. One wing hesitated until she rapped it with a knuckle. The steam that whistled from between her shoulders made the Berfemmian grimace.

Victoria pointed to the sky, and Faeoris rocketed forward. She watched the Berfemmain in wonder until a puppy barked from behind. A small black lab with a scar along its ribs yipped excitedly as it exited the beam of light, followed closely by two children.

"A fight," a ten-year-old boy said. He had pale skin, dark curly hair, and intelligent blue eyes that looked very familiar.

"Dad said to be careful," a ten-year-old girl said snappily. She had those same blue eyes and an adorable round face. Her long brown hair was pulled back in a pony tail.

"Thom, Eila," Heather said as she exited the light, a firm hand on their shoulders. "Your father said to stay out of it."

"Right," Thom said, winking at his sister.

She raised an eyebrow and met his gaze with a mischievous grin.

"You're alive," Victoria said, throwing her arms around Heather. "How? I thought…"

"Scar saved us all and brought us somewhere safe," Heather said, meeting her hug. "It took a while for Angst to find us… He'll be here soon."

"Really?" she asked, pulling back. "I thought he lost. It felt like everything was…"

"Everything will be fine," Heather said with a gracious smile. "He just needs to make his wish."

51

Nations go to war. Companies of soldiers fight in skirmishes. Friends tussle. What do you call it when two beings with the power to destroy a planet go to battle?

"What did you do with Heather?" Angst roared. "Give me back my wife!"

Red and blue lightning shot from his hands, raking tile up like leaves and bouncing harmlessly off the older Angst.

"That's it?" he said, calmly stepping aside.

"Not a chance," the younger Angst shouted. Sheathing his swords, he reached up with two clawed hands and pulled.

The room shook as boulder-sized chunks of marble ceiling pulled away. With a grunt, he directed them at the old man. Every one landed with a crunch until the entire roof was gone, revealing an eternity of stars above them.

His heavy breathing caught with a gasp when the older Angst stepped free from the rubble like gamlin diving up from the ground.

"You can do better," the man said as he dusted himself off.

Freeing a slab from the floor, Angst shot up high into the starry sky while the other remained on the ground until they were just specks in each other's vision. He drew both swords and pointed them at his opponent. With a roar of fury, he dove at a blinding speed. The walls blew out on impact, leaving nothing but floor, doorways, and the other Angst.

"That's not possible," he cried, panting like a runner at the end of a race.

Young Angst's face was red and he shook with fury, his eyes filled with a wild madness. With a roar, he swung wildly again and again.

"I will save them," he roared. "I will be the hero!"

For what seemed like an eternity, he chopped and hacked and slashed only to be blocked and parried and dodged until there was nothing left. He dropped both swords and stared in disbelief, completely drained and dumbfounded.

"That's enough," the older Angst said, calmly. "Your rage that destroyed Gyldorane would also destroy Ehrde. I hate to put you through this, but you can be better. They need you to be better. You leave me no choice."

His first blow struck a leg, cracking the armor and bone beneath it. The younger Angst looked at him in stunned disbelief as he proceeded to perform surgery. He blurred around his opponent, striking with precise intent. Every blow would hurt, but none would maim or kill. After practically destroying the armor, he sliced an arm before jamming the hilt of his sword into the man's face. A swollen eye, a bloody nose, and an arm that bled freely left his opponent an angry, helpless mess.

"You're not Magic," the broken man muttered.

"Taken care of before you arrived," Angst said. "That's why I was late to the party."

"But why?" he asked. "I was supposed to win. I'm the hero."

"Being a hero is more than just power and fury," he said, grasping the man's armor behind his neck and dragging him. "I was hoping it wouldn't have to go down this way, but you're not ready yet."

They reached a shadowy doorway, and Angst grabbed the seat of younger Angst's armor, holding him like a bouncer ready to throw a rowdy drunk from the bar.

"Go see what your anger has wrought," he said. "Then find a better way."

With a heave, he threw the helpless man through the dark door. Angst picked up the duplicate Chryslaenor and Dulgirgraut, sighed deeply, and tossed them in after him. He crossed the room, picked up his own swords, and returned them to his back.

"Thank you, old friends," Angst said over his shoulder. He looked up to see the night sky, but the constellations were gone. "I'm getting too old for this. How long are you going to make me wait, Vivek?"

A warm, golden light flooded the room. This was it. This was everything he'd fought for. It was finally time for his wish. Wiping away tears and smoothing his goatee, Angst turned around.

* * * *

Marisha was surprisingly easy for Faeoris to find amidst the chaos. Some poor Vex'steppe tribesman was in the middle of a battle he was going to lose. On one side stood a haggard but formidable ANduaut. Burns covered most of his body, and the corner of his head was crushed. He simply shouldn't have been alive.

On the other side stood a wilted reflection of her essent, covered in dark feathers with a pained expression on her face—as though undecided if she would pounce or flee.

A circle of tribesmen had formed around them, keeping others at bay. The tribesman in the center held two broken pieces of his staudauf—pointing one at each opponent.

"You should never have turned against me, SMyket," ANduaut said, fencing playfully with his own double-bladed staff.

"You should never have made your deal with Magic," SMyket said. "Not only are you a traitor to our people, but your help in destroying Rohjek makes you a traitor to all of Ehrde."

Faeoris had heard enough and guided her mechanical wings to land her behind the circle. She picked up a tribesman by his shoulders and roughly tossed him away like trash.

"Essent," Marisha said, now appearing confused and frightened.

"You," ANduaut said, his tone filled with venom.

"Faeoris," SMyket said, looking as if he'd just opened a present. "I was told you were dead."

"You, cute one," Faeoris said, nodding at SMyket. "Keep ANduaut off us for a minute but leave some for me."

"I'm...cute?" SMyket said with a crooked smile.

"You're dead," ANduaut said, slicing down with his staudauf.

While SMyket deflected blows, Faeoris tackled Marisha. She knocked her essent to the ground and straddled her.

"Please, help me," Marisha said, making a weak attempt to struggle.

"My mother's feather was never meant for you, my dear one," Faeoris said, looking her in the eye. "This is going to hurt."

Closing her eyes, she placed a clawed hand between Marisha's breasts. The foci she'd bonded with after her mother died was there; she could feel it. The golden feather's tainted bond to Marisha was like a prison. It longed to be free.

There was an audible snap. Marisha let out a scream as the feather rose from her chest. Her essent was covered in sweat, breathing rabbit-fast.

"Yes," Faeoris said, tears streaming down her cheeks as the familiar bond returned. "I'm whole again, and so are my people."

Marisha's dark feathers whisped away like smoke from embers, revealing her beautiful, naked body beneath. She was unconscious but alive.

Several screams from above caught her attention as other Berfemmian lost their dark feathers and fell from the sky.

She stormed over to ANduaut, grabbed his throat and lifted him off the ground.

"Guard my essent," she said to SMyket.

"Anything," he said, rushing to stand over the Berfemmian.

"I would kill you with my bare hands," Faeoris said, "but this will hurt more."

Her metallic wings spread, curving forward as though ready to embrace ANduaut. The clawed tips of her metallic wings bored into the tribesman's chest. Before he could scream, the wings spread, tearing him asunder.

"I hope that ring keeps you alive," she said, spitting on the twitching hand that hosted Magic's ruby ring.

"So beautiful," SMyket said.

She approached, winking at him before turning away.

"These wings are fused to me," she said. "You will tear away bone and skin when you remove them."

"I...I cannot harm you," SMyket said.

"Hurry," she said. "The feather will heal me while the bond is new."

"As you wish," he said.

His first tug was an annoyance and the second felt like a small animal bite.

"I see the look in your eyes," she said, facing him. "If you ever want a chance to father my children, you will do this."

He grimaced in determination, and she turned around. SMyket placed a foot between her shoulders, grasping the inside of her metal wings. With a roar, he braced his foot against her back and pulled.

It was pain like she hadn't experienced since they'd been attached. Bone cracked, and muscle tore as flesh was ripped from her body. She collapsed, and he threw away the wings.

"Worth it," she said. With a grunt, wings of light grew from her back, washing away the pain.

"Find me in Unsel when this is over and we will mate," she said, delicately picking up Marisha. "Bring the wings."

"Okay," he said, dumbfounded.

She launched into the air with a broad smile as SMyket's cheers were met by the other tribesmen's.

52

Within a blink, the walls and partial ceiling returned as if no fight had taken place. A warm, golden light flooded the room. This was it. This was everything he'd fought for. It was finally time for his wish. Wiping away tears and flattening his goatee, Angst turned around.

"Mom... Dad?" he asked, his chin quivering. It was too much. They'd passed away years ago.

"No, Angst, we are Vivek," his mom said. "We chose these forms to make it easier for you to understand."

"This isn't easy. You're bad at this," he said, wanting more than anything to hug them both. They were everything he remembered. His mom's wrinkled, caring face. His dad's thoughtful blue eyes and thinning hair. Angst breathed in and remembered their scent. He took a step toward them, his voice shaky. "What are you?"

"I suppose you may consider us life," his father said, nodding to his mom.

"We're more than that, more complicated than that, but it's an explanation," she said, wringing her hands together as his own mother would have. "The elements you've been battling are our children."

"Your children are assholes," Angst said.

Vivek smiled, both of them. "And yours aren't?"

"No," he grumbled. "My children are perfect."

"Ours are too," Vivek replied together.

"Please don't talk at the same time," Angst said. "It's too much."

His parents looked at each other impatiently. Despite the turmoil burning a hole in Angst's gut, he felt the great need to hurry.

"You seem like nice...life...people." Angst stumbled over his words. The whole concept was so far beyond him, he didn't really want to think about it. "Why do you let your children do this?"

"For balance," his dad said. "There must be balance on Ehrde or all will be lost."

"Balance? There is no balance! I almost lost everyone," Angst yelled, slashing the air with his hands. "You've got an element for Earth, Air, Fire, Water, and Magic. Who is the element that protects life? If you are, you're doing a crappy job!"

"Six elements?" they asked in unison, looking at one another.

Their eyes flashed a color he didn't recognize, and thinking about that color made him reel, so he didn't.

"So, what is this?" Angst asked, looking around the room. "I fought myself. I fought through time." He pointed in some random direction. "I went through all of that and I still need to stop a war. Was it all for nothing?"

"No," his dad said, placing a hand on his shoulder. "You've been through much, son."

"We want to thank you," his mom said, "for bringing the balance we've always wanted. We are here to give you a gift."

They seemed so real his hands shook. He'd been close to his parents, which made it hurt all the more.

"What are you offering?" he asked, his voice shaky.

"A wish, for lack of a better word," his mom said. "You deserve a reward, Angst, for all you've done."

"A wish? Really?" he asked. After all he'd been through, it almost felt like a trap.

They both nodded with soft expressions and caring eyes.

"Hector," Angst said. "I couldn't find... He... Please bring Hector back."

"You know we can't," his father said. "Not Hector, nor any of the others. The dead are gone. I'm sorry."

Whatever he'd been holding back came out as he bawled like a baby on his mom's shoulder. She patted him gently, holding him like his own mom had. His heart ached from failure, but something about this felt like home and gave him strength.

"I'm sorry, Angst," his dad said. "We have little time."

Angst pulled away, smiling at his mom with gratitude. She placed an old hand on his cheek. He sniffed loudly.

"Well, I guess, it would be nice to be younger again," Angst said.

They laughed; they actually laughed. Angst had made life, the creators of everything, laugh out loud, which was great, and awful.

"It doesn't work like that," his dad said.

"Of course it doesn't," Angst said with a deep sigh.

"Hurry," he said. "You have a world to save."

He couldn't bring back the dead. He couldn't make himself younger. He already knew how he'd end the war. At this point, he just wanted some cake and a nap, but he could do that after battling hordes of armies from every nation on Ehrde. This wish couldn't be for himself, not really. He had to make a wish that helped someone else. After everything he'd been through, there weren't many left that he hadn't lost or saved, except...

"The twins," he said, hope rising in his heart. "I want the twins."

"Your children are already safely back in your time," his mom said.

"You know that's not who I'm talking about," Angst said. "I want Bella and Karina to come back."

"They are not from your time, son," his dad said, looking nervously at his mom as if he'd just asked to ride a pony into town for the first time.

"They don't belong—" his mom began.

"I want the twins to come with me," he said, irritation raising the hairs on his neck. "They deserve to be saved, just like the others."

"I don't think we can—"

"I want the twins," Angst shouted as loud as he could. Blue and red lighting reached out from his swords, the songs in his head screaming with his own frustration.

Everything stopped. Lightning froze in the air. His lungs didn't move. His heart didn't beat. He couldn't wiggle a finger. Mom and Dad were gone, replaced by a glowing thing in that color he couldn't recognize. His brain hurt.

"Don't test me," Vivek said. And his doubt was gone; this was indeed Vivek.

Angst wanted to plead for the twins. He would have begged. The incomprehensible light flashed, and he wished he could've closed his eyes because the Vivek was too much to understand. Before he succumbed to a new madness, his parents returned, and he could breathe once again. He did. Dropping to all fours, Angst gasped for sweet air. His entire body shook with fear. They let this pass before helping him up.

"You may have the twins," his dad said in a stern voice he recognized all too well.

"Thank you," Angst said.

"But there will be a price," his mom said with a familiar look. He felt like he was being sent to the corner of the room.

"Isn't there always?" Angst asked, sighing deeply. "Haven't I already paid it, over, and over, and over again?"

"They don't belong in this time, Angst," she said. "It's the only way I will agree to this."

"Anything," he said. They deserved it. "Just tell me, so I know what to expect."

They both leaned in and whispered.

"Oh?" he replied.

Vivek nodded.

"I'll do my best," he said.

"That's all we ask," they replied in unison.

CHAPTER FIFTY TWO

He heard squeals of delight behind him, and his heart leaped with hope. The twins ran from the doorway and wrapped their arms around him.

"Go," he said. "We don't have much time."

"Got it, boss," Bella said.

"Thank you, Angst," Karina said softly, kissing him on the cheek. "For whatever it is you did."

"Anything for you two," he replied. "Now hurry, and please be careful. Tell them I'll only be a minute."

The twins rushed off, and in a flash of light, they were gone.

"It's time, Angst," his father said. "This is it."

"We have many other worlds to manage," his mom said wisely. "Ehrde is just one, one of many."

"I have a selfish request," Angst said, looking at both of them. "Before we part ways."

They smiled like his parents, and he wrapped his arms around them. He hugged his mom, he hugged his dad, he hugged them both and then they were gone. It wasn't really them, or maybe it was. It didn't matter because the hugs were great.

Angst reached over his shoulders to touch both swords and smiled.

"Time to finish this adventure."

53

"Looks like we came at just the right time," said a young woman.

"Or the wrong time," said another.

Victoria turned to see two beautiful young women appear from the light. The identical twins were perfect enough that she wondered what Angst had wished for. The blond looked ready to party while the redhead was prepared for war.

"Angst's twins," Victoria said. "Where did you—"

"Call me Bella," the redhead said with a sincere gaze. "And I'm not Angst's."

"Speak for yourself," the blond said with a wry smile. "Hi, I'm Karina."

"I'm Victoria," she said. "Where is he?"

"He'll be here soon," Bella said. "The old man is just taking his time."

Victoria looked back and forth between the sisters as they spoke in a dialect she didn't recognize. It sounded made up, like a language only twins shared. The conversation ended with Karina blushing fiercely.

"I know you think she's a legend," Bella said, rolling her eyes. "Even legends like compliments."

"Is everything okay?" Victoria asked.

"It's just," Karina said. "You're as pretty as he said you were."

"As who said I was?" Victoria asked, befuddled.

Roars and screams and screeches drew her attention back to the battlefield. The monsters were leaving. Dragons, cavastil birds, and gargoyles all gathered overhead at different ends of the field. Like flocks of migratory birds that eat people, they flew away.

"What a mess," Angst said from behind her. "About what I expected. I wouldn't know what to do if it was easy."

"Angst," Victoria squealed, wrapping her arms around him. "You did it? You won?"

"I did," he said, sounding a little sad.

Angst pulled away, and she took several steps back in surprise. He'd entered the Vivek in black armor and came out wearing armor that was brushed silver. There were more wrinkles around his eyes, and his hair seemed a lighter gray and thinner. A peppered beard covered his chin and mouth. He smiled at her but looked more tired than ever.

"I don't understand," she said, looking him up and down. "Is it...you?"

"I missed you so very much," he said, his eyes glassy.

"You missed me?" Victoria asked. "You just left. What's going on? Why do you look older?"

"Later," he said with a wink.

Angst drew both swords and took a deep, reluctant breath.

"Jaden," he called out, throwing a foci to the young man.

"About time," Jaden said, catching the sword by the hilt. He raised it high as red lightning showered his body.

"Kala," Angst shouted, tossing his other foci to the teenager.

"Yes," she said, catching it. The blue lightning that surrounded her sword flashed in her eyes.

"Kala?" Nikkola asked.

"Wait until you see this," Kala said. She knelt beside the black lab pup, petting him several times. Pointing to the nearest attackers, she said, "Scar, fetch!"

The puppy rushed forward, growing with each step until it became a steel-coated monster with six glowing red eyes and three tails. She leaped on the dog's shoulders as he reared up, letting loose an earth-shaking bark.

"How can you stop a war without your swords?" Victoria asked.

"I won't be needing them anymore," he said. "I won the prize."

"What does that mean, exactly?" she said, her heart racing.

"I'm not completely sure, yet," he said. "But I've learned a few new tricks along the way. I think you'll like this one."

* * * *

Silence fell on the battlefield. The abrupt quiet from Angst's mute bomb had an unnerving effect. It was a great spell, one of his favorites. Who wouldn't love a spell that made everyone shut up? Soldiers from every nation became disoriented as swords struck shields without sound and war cries went unheard. The fighting abruptly slowed and within minutes stopped entirely.

Pressing a finger against his throat, he cast a spell so all would hear him.

"Hello, Ehrde," Angst shouted, holding out both hands. "I'm interrupting this war to tell you that it's over."

He took a breath to let that sink in. The sheer quantity of people in all their shapes and sizes was almost overwhelming. From tiny Meldusians to enormous Nordruaut, they all turned to face him.

"We've all been tricked into something we didn't want to do," he said. "Every two thousand years the elements come alive and go to war. They create weapons like dragons and gargoyles. When those weapons don't work, they use us instead."

The crowd continued paying attention, which brought a sigh of relief. There'd been enough dying. With every moment they took to think about what they were doing, there was a greater chance they would want to stop fighting. At least, that was what he hoped.

"That's right, the elements, especially Magic, used us to fight their war. Along my travels, I met people from every nation, and none of them wanted this. You were told that if I won the prize, my wish would destroy Ehrde. You came here to stop me, to protect your people and our world. I commend you.

"Well, I beat the elements, and I won the prize. I'm sure you noticed, I did not destroy Ehrde," he said, waiting for polite laughter until he remembered taking away their sound. "I'm also not here to destroy you. That's what elements do. That's what they did to Rohjek. We need to work together so that never happens again. Tonight, we bury our dead. Tomorrow, we go home. In six months, you will send leaders to meet at the former capital of Rohjek. There, we will decide how to rebuild that nation and defend Ehrde. If you have any complaints, feel free to share with my friends."

On cue, a hundred naked Berfemmian landed around him, hard enough to shake the entire battlefield. Armies stepped back as tribesmen approached their mates and stood beside them. Nordruaut and Fulk'han laid down their weapons while Melkier and Unsel armies took a knee.

"This is our Ehrde, not theirs. This is your Ehrde, not mine," Angst said. "Now do what's right."

He released the spell, and a cheer erupted. His shoulders dropped, and he let out a deep sigh. Turning around, he took in his friends. Jaden embraced Victoria. Nikkola held Kala as if she'd never let her go. Rose and Dallow's embrace seemed more out of relief than passion. Tarness winked at him even as Maarja smothered the large man. Tiny Meldusians surrounded them like small children, hopping up and down while cheering. It was all good.

Heather, Thom, Eila, and Scar approached, and he drew them all into a hug, holding them close until his kids complained.

"Thank you," he said. "Let's go home."

54

Several months later

"You're here," Alloria said, leaping forward and wrapping her arms around him.

"Just like I promised," Angst said. "I'll visit you as often as I can."

"I hate this place. I'm so lonely," she said, shoving him away. "How could you leave me here by myself?"

"I've been told you have all sorts of company," he said. "And how could you hate paradise?"

Alloria's island was roughly the size of the training field. She had more than enough space to run, and dance, and relax. A sizable dome made of stone, similar to those in Rookshire, stood several hundred feet from the shoreline. He could barely make out Angoria in the distance. This was a lonely place, but it was far better than the dungeon under Unsel. Or death. He'd promised to keep her out of that dungeon, and this was the best solution. He'd also promised to always be there for her, so he visited every week or so.

"I guess I don't completely hate it," she said, grudgingly. "And I *do* get a lot of visitors. Berfemmian stop by almost every day. They teach me how to do sealtian, and I show them how I dance. They are so nice, and beautiful. They bring me food, and sometimes I even get a kiss."

"Good," he said. "You deserve to be kissed."

Her eyes brightened. "Is that an offer?"

"I'll kiss your cheek any time you want," he said with a knowing smile.

She pouted cutely and stomped her foot. "You're no fun."

"I can leave," he said, turning away.

"Please don't, baby," she said. "You know I was teasing."

"Tell me more about your days," Angst said.

"I also get to visit with merpeople. They're friendly but different. I've even gotten to see their children... So cute!"

"I bet," he said with a smile.

"Your family comes to visit sometimes," she said, coyly. "I see your kids. Kala and Scar come to see me, and so do the twins. Bella and Karina sometimes bring mead, and we drink late into the night."

"Oh?" he asked, in surprise.

"Please don't tell them to stop," she pleaded. "They're so much fun. I promise I won't hurt them."

"I believe you," Angst said.

"Am I really so dangerous that I need to be stuck on this island?" she asked.

"Are you?" he asked. "You've been making daggers out of stone again. I sense three in your home, and two buried by the shore."

"Oh, those," she said, sucking in her lips. "They're for protection."

"You're safe," he said. "And like last time, I've turned them into sand."

"Whatever," she said, rolling her eyes. "Did you bring me something?"

"Just food." He withdrew a parcel from his satchel. "And a new dress."

"Oh," she said, taking the dress and holding it up. "It looks pretty... Is it boring? Did your wife pick it out again?"

"This one is from me," he said.

"I'll go try it on," she said. "Want to come watch?"

"Yes," he said. "But I'll wait here."

"Chicken," she said, sticking out her tongue before running to her hovel with the dress.

It shouldn't have taken that long to put on, and he was tempted to check on Alloria but knew better. Seconds before he actually became worried, she came out in a short, fitted dress. It was hot pink, and low cut in the best way possible. She absolutely owned the dress and reveled in his attention.

"Stunning," he said.

"Thank you," she said, bowing just enough so he could see everything nice.

"Are you going to tear this one up like the others?" he asked.

"No, but I get bored waiting for you," she said, pouting cutely. "Do you want to see the new decorations in my home?"

"Maybe after lunch," he said.

She nodded as he spread out a blanket and their meal. They feasted on roast meat sandwiches, hearty cakes, and a little sweet wine. She hurriedly shared stories about playing fetch with Scar, drinking with Bella and Karina, kissing Berfemmian, and missing boys.

He tried explaining that, despite Rose's failure to heal her, Dallow was still working to find a solution. All his friends were convinced that, even though Magic had somehow broken the young woman, there was still hope. Collectively, they continued searching for ways to make her whole. In a way, he felt her lack of sanity was almost worse than death. Angst tried his best to share their efforts, as encouragingly as possible. She merely nodded, dismissively, as if he were talking nonsense.

"I should go," he finally said.

"Are you sure you don't want to see my house?" she asked, her tone full of sultry. "You won't want to leave."

"I already don't want to leave," he said, standing and brushing sand off his leggings. "But I've got something to do."

"Okay," she said, in a heartbreaking tone. Alloria stood, placed her hands on his chest and leaned against him. "Will I ever get off this island?"

"I promise to bring you to Unsel every holiday," he said. "As long as you behave yourself."

"Boring," she said, nuzzling a bit. "And sex? You said we could have sex." She gyrated against him pleasantly.

He pulled away, holding her shoulders. "I did not say that, young temptress," Angst said with a wink.

"You're missing out," she said, sincerely.

"I believe you," he said.

"I hate that you're such a good man," she said, pulling him into another hug.

"Me too," he said, kissing her forehead. He took a step back. "I'll see you next week?"

"I can't wait," she said.

Angst created a portal. He brushed her cheek with his fingers, nodded once, and returned to Unsel.

55

Angst stood at the entrance of the throne room he'd broken when being chased by Magic. It felt like so long ago. Victoria stood in the center, her arms crossed and shoulders tense. His natural inclination was to walk across the room and rub them until they relaxed. Heather might not have appreciated that but would understand. So, choosing to respect his wife, he didn't and instead looked at the problem.

The great war had taken up all of Unsel's resources and restoring this room had been slow going to nowhere. His princess, his best friend, should be crowned in this throne room, not some grand hallway that was makeshift.

"Hey," he finally said.

"Angst," Tori said in surprise, spinning about. She tugged on her ivory bodice and gave him a glowing smile.

"You look stressed," he said. "Like you're going to be crowned queen of Unsel or something."

"Ha," she said, taking a deep breath. "Something like that. It suddenly feels very real."

"I apologize," he said. "It should've happened sooner. I feel like I delayed it."

"It's not that," Tori said, looking around. "It's this. I'm a big baby to complain, but I'll be the first queen of Unsel not to be crowned here. My mom was, my grandmother was, but me…"

"May I?" Angst asked, making a broad motion toward the

room.

"Really?" Tori asked in wonder.

"Really," he said.

He could do anything now, practically anything, but would always understand earth far better than the rest. Angst drew in his will and raised his hands. A blue glow surrounded them, ripe with the power he wielded. He needed material to work with. Most of the rubble had been cleared, so he reached far into distant mountains until he found white marble. The room shuddered as he drew that marble to them. Victoria stepped forward and wrapped her arms around him for protection, just as she had when they met at the maiden's courtyard. Like clay, the white marble formed columns, repaired floors, and molded into the ceiling. After several minutes, he smiled and nodded respectfully.

"Thank you," she said stepping back.

He bowed his head once again. They looked into each other's eyes for barely a moment before Tori blushed and searched the room as if admiring his handiwork. He moved in close like she used to. They met eyes again, and hers became sad. She inched away.

"Yes," he said.

"I...I'm sorry, what?" she asked, her voice nervous.

"You were going to ask me something," he said. "Before Alloria stabbed you. You said, 'Angst, would you be my...'" He shuddered at the memory. It seemed like forever had passed, but it would always be one of those key moments in his life, never forgotten.

"I did," she said, swallowing hard. "I remember."

"The answer is yes."

"How can you say yes when you don't even know the question, silly?" she said, failing to sound playful. Her face was wrought with worry.

"Because that's how much you mean to me," Angst said. "I love you, Tori. I always have. I always will. No matter what you ask, the answer will always be yes. All you need to do is ask the question."

She waited, her throat constricting as she swallowed hard. "Are you really an element, Angst?" she asked, a slight quaver to her voice.

"That's not what you were going to ask me," he teased.

She looked ready to smack his arm but hesitated. Was she really that scared of him? "Are you?"

He winked but provided no further answer. "What were you going to ask me, my queen?"

"I was going to...I was going to ask you..." Her face went pale, and she rocked slightly as if ready to pass out. "I was going to ask you if you would be my—"

"Champion?" he asked with a knowing smile.

The relief in her eyes was immediate. That wasn't what she'd been going to ask in her chambers. When he'd walked through the crystal cave on his way to Nordruaut, Angst had seen the future—a future where they were married, and he was king of Unsel. A part of her had wanted that, and a small part of him had as well. But much had happened, their futures were now unwritten, and they both controlled their own destinies.

He was married, happily on the good days, and there weren't really many bad days, not anymore. She had someone waiting who she loved very much. Angst and Victoria were friends, the best of friends now and forever, and nothing would ever get in the way of that.

This may have seemed a cruel way to clear the air, but it also ended any open questions forever.

"Yes," she said with a sigh. "Yes, please. I can't think of anyone else who could protect me better than you."

"Welllll," he drawled, placing his hands behind his back. He began to pace. "That sounds like a demanding job."

"It will be very rewarding." She gave him a full-lipped smile. "Both financially, and you get to see my pretty face every day."

"Bonuses are nice," he said, turning to wink at her. "Of course, I'm married with kids. I may need time away to tend my flock."

"I'm sure the crown can accommodate your schedule," she said. "All things considered."

"And, of course, other responsibilities may come up," he said. "In two thousand years or so."

"Oh." Her voice was worried again, and he realized that it was too much.

"Will travel be required for this job?" he asked. "I hear my queen likes to adventure."

"I'm sorry to say that travel will be a necessity," she said, hopeful once again. "Adventures are a requirement of the position."

"And what about Rookshire?" he asked.

She looked at the ground hesitantly, took a deep breath, and said, "Whatever you want."

"It's what they need," he said firmly. Angst turned on a heel and bowed deeply. "Then I accept, Your Majesty."

She clapped and giggled again, every bit the young teen he'd always loved. A queen who could keep her sense of humor, who could appreciate his, but would give up everything for a better kingdom, would indeed be a great queen. He stood at attention, with his chest sticking out barely farther than his sucked-in stomach, and hands behind his back.

"Angst, is this the right path?" she asked. "I can see so many futures, but I can't read you or your mind. Our future, our fate..."

"Is now ours to choose. That's everything I fought for," he said taking her hands in his. "And I couldn't be more grateful, or more honored, to be your best friend, now and always."

Their embrace was far more than a hug and far less than love lost. After a long time that would've left others feeling awkward, Angst pulled back.

"You will be an amazing queen," he said, proudly. "Let's see you crowned."

* * * *

Victoria bowed her head low as Wilfred gently laid the crown of Unsel onto it. The throne room was so still, Angst feared he'd broken time once again. Everyone from sirs to miladys looked on in wonder. Zyn'ight, wielders, and citizens all admired with wide eyes and hopeful smiles. This was as much a closure to the insanity, war, and strife the kingdom had faced as it was an open door to their unknown future. This wasn't just the crowning of his dear friend, their queen. This was hope, and it was about fel-king time.

She stood upright and nodded once at Wilfred, whose eyes were glassy with tears. Angst shed none, feeling nothing but pride for Tori, and everything he'd fought through to make this happen. The queen turned and looked over the room, making the briefest eye contact with him. His glance at Heather was met with the softest wife-look he'd ever enjoyed. Victoria's eyes met Jaden's as the young man approached to stand by her side.

Jaden turned around, held her hand, and raised it high. "Our queen!"

The room erupted like a crowd at a jousting tourney. Whistles and hoots and clapping echoed through the hall like nothing Angst had ever heard. His heart swelled with pride, and his anxiety wanted nothing more than to leave. He squeezed Heather's hand once, nodded, and pushed his way through the masses. Heather, Thom, and Eila followed him as he rushed to exit through the wide center aisle, and just beyond the soldiers at the back of the throne room.

"Mister Angst," Victoria called out.

He froze in place as though a spell had been cast. The crowd quieted immediately, and Heather held his hand tight.

"If we run, we can still make it," she whispered.

"Mo-om," Eila said.

"I said," Victoria's voice echoed throughout the throne room, "Mister Angst!"

Angst spun on a heel and took a step back, rearing at her steely gaze. "My queen," he said with a bow of his head.

"I have summoned you," she said stiffly. "You will approach."

He couldn't believe this. What now? She barely sounded like his Tori; she sounded more like her mother. He sighed and forced his legs forward. The sneak-out-through-the-crowd with his family had seemed much faster than the long walk back, wading through the heavy gazes of a hundred watchful eyes. He stopped before her parapet, looking up at his dear friend and seeing his new queen. There wasn't a thimbleful of emotion on her face, and despite their closeness, he could sense nothing. She merely stared at him.

"Am I not your queen?" she asked, looking from him to the ground.

"You are my queen, and my friend," he said, kneeling.

"Mister Angst," she said, her tone as cold as a Nordruaut winter. "Is it not true that you have destroyed all mage cities beyond restoration? Did you not destroy half the capitol of Melkier, driving them to declare war on Unsel? Were your actions not instrumental in the Fulk'han going to war with Unsel? Are you not responsible for the battle at Prendere? Is it true that you almost destroyed Ehrde?"

"It is true, Your Majesty," he said, his heart racing. "All of it."

"Is it also true that you freed two mage cities of their curses? Did you not end a terrible evil at the mage city Gyldorane? And were you responsible for killing all the living elements, ending the war, and bringing peace to our world?"

"Yes," he said in a small voice.

"The queen's sword," she commanded.

The crowd's muttering was ended by her fierce gaze.

"My first act as Queen of Unsel is this," she said. "Your heroic deeds and great sacrifice will not go unrecognized."

The reflection of gold caught his eye as the queen's longsword rested on his left shoulder.

"I dub thee Sir Angst of Rookshire," she said. "Knight of Unsel."

The sword rested on his right shoulder.

"Zyn'ight of Unsel," she continued.

The sword fell on his left shoulder.

"Champion of the Queen," she said with finality, gently resting the sword on his head.

And everything he'd ever wanted caught in his throat. He could only nod and fight tears.

"Rise, Sir Angst," she said. "And stand by my right side."

He stood shakily and stared into her green eyes. They were full of hope, and love. For a brief moment, he couldn't have cared less about those attending and just wanted to embrace her.

"Hugs later," she said in his mind, casually holding up a hand.

"Lots of them," he thought, moving to stand beside her.

The crowd erupted in cheers once again. He ignored them all, his eyes falling on Heather and his children. The pride in their faces was better than the surprise knighting. Mostly.

56

Epilogue One

It was more than a dream. It always had been. In the past, his nighttime visits to Prendere seemed out of his control. That was no longer the case. Now, the great golden field surrounded by snow-capped mountains felt as much like his home as the rest of Ehrde.

Almost every face staring down at Angst from on high appeared either curious, or perturbed, or furious. The five elements were larger than ever, their forms towering over the mountains they stood behind. Earth, the giant stone maiden, seemed surprised at what she'd helped create. Air hovered in its tornadic form, and Angst took his stormy demeanor to mean the element was as pleased as the others. Water's arms were crossed, and she leaned over like an angry mother, glaring at him with hollow eyes. Fire was fury, as always, and Angst was surprised that the element hadn't shot globs of flame toward him, yet. Magic was practically unrecognizable, a human-like form composed of darkness—not unlike the beam Angst had chased from Fulk'han to Unsel so long ago.

He stood there, naked before all the elements, in the middle of the field with cool grass beneath his feet. It was nice. The mountain-fresh air was warm against his bare skin. Despite the pending doom of five elements towering over him, Angst was surprisingly at peace. It was a welcome change from how he usually experienced these dreams. With the gentlest effort of will, he covered himself in armor—silver, not black—and stared up at the giants.

"Yes?" he asked calmly. "Did you need something?"

"Do you know what you have done?" Water asked.

"I'm pretty sure I won," Angst said, sticking his chest out and placing his fists on his hips.

Tantrum would be the best way to describe the next few minutes. The elements stomped and fretted and roared, or more accurately stormed, and rumbled, and blew. It went on for too long, and he sat down, leaning back against his arms to watch. This was, after all, a dream—and how often do you get to see the extremes of so much nature all at the same time?

"You never answered my question," he finally said. "Do you need something? I'm tired. I've earned the rest. Do you have something to share, or some advice to give?"

"Angst," Earth said, her tone grating like the crunch of boulders rolling down a hillside. "Since the beginning of time there have only been five elements, and now…"

"Do you even know what to do?" Air said, actually sounding concerned.

"Yes," Angst said. "I'll watch over everyone. I'll be a hero like I've always wanted."

"You aren't an element. You are tiny! You are nothing!" Fire roared. "We'll do everything we can to make your reign miserable. We'll destroy everything you care for and everyone you love and…and…"

"No," he said, his voice booming.

They stopped. To his surprise, they stood still, looking at him like upset children—made of fire and storm and everything frightening.

He sighed and shook his head. "This was my win," he said. "If I sense the slightest backlash, there will be consequences."

"What will you do now?" Water asked, practically sneering.

"Cover Ehrde in flesh?"

"Gross," he said, wincing at the image. "Don't you see? Your war has always been about domination when it should've been about balance. You're all equally important. We need air to breathe, fire for warmth, water to drink, earth to stand on, and magic to bind it all together."

"But we don't need you," Air said.

"Yes," Angst said. "You really do, or what's the point? Without life, Ehrde will die, and you all become nothing."

They looked at each other, and Angst expected to hear some sort of unknown 'twin language' between them.

"You'll see that life is part of this," he said, trying to sound hopeful. "Sharing isn't so bad. The six of us will work together, in harmony. In two thousand years, maybe you'll come back and not want to go to war."

"And if we come back ready to fight?" Fire asked.

Angst imagined himself in his dusky zyn'ight armor, and it appeared. With a deep breath, he willed himself to grow, and he did. He grew, and grew, and grew until he filled the field. He grew until he towered over them, and then he grew a little more. It was so ridiculous, he would've laughed if he wasn't so upset. A small part of him wondered if this was what it was like to be tall.

"I'll be waiting," Angst said, his voice booming. "Just ask Magic."

The elements turned to face Magic, who looked at the ground like a guilty child. They stood there, disgruntled, as if waiting for something. They shuffled their feet, stared at each other, and waited.

"You're still here?" he asked. "It's over. Go home. Go!"

Angst turned his back on them and left.

57

Epilogue Two

The Wizard's Revenge had never smelled so good. While the new location in Rookshire was only nine months old, Angst could already smell the familiar tinge of burnt grease. It was as if every piece of bacon had been cooked to a sharp crisp just for him. The stone floor was tacky from old booze, and the smell of stale alcohol wafted through the thick summer air. Someone's spell had generated a warm breeze from window to window across the bar. It was just enough to clear out the stench of sweaty drunks, both young and old. Honestly, it smelled pretty awful, much like the old Wizard's Revenge, but the nostalgia was delicious.

The room was huge, filled with patrons and noise. The old Wizard's Revenge at the capital would grow and shrink thanks to Graloon's magic. This new bar was created by Jaden to be spacious enough without the need for magic. And while Graloon grumbled about having more space to clean, the old barkeep didn't have to struggle with his spell to host large crowds or larger guests.

Maarja and Faeoris were already deep into their kegs. An impressive collection of emptied mugs on their table made Angst wonder if they'd challenged each other to drink, or merely planned to challenge Graloon's stores of liquor. Fortunately, the backslapping hadn't gotten so rough that Angst felt the need to intervene. Three tiny Meldusians stood before them, toasting with their thimble-sized goblets.

"I told you not to let Kala use those wings," Nikkola said, propped up by a less-drunk General Mirim.

"I can't imagine where she got them," Faeoris lied, hiding behind her mug.

Maarja laughed and they both drank. Despite the Berfemmian's prowess on the battlefield, it was impossible for her to out-drink Maarja. Marisha, the petite Berfemmian who sat beside Faeoris, sipped at her own drink and watched warily, as if ready to catch her drunk friend and fly her home at any moment. Exactly what he would expect from her *essent*.

Tarness sat between Maarja and Dallow, either fighting through a haze of alcohol or struggling to stay awake through Dallow's long-winded exposition of something or other. Tarness rubbed his mechanical arm awkwardly until Maarja took it, kissed it, and said in a low voice, "Stop."

"Just missing our son, Jarle," he said.

"He's in good hands with Gose," she said, "and we deserve the break. Now drink."

Angst tensed as his favorite barmaid approached Rose and bosomtastically leaned over the table. Rose whispered something in her ear that made her giggle before scurrying off. He was glad to see Rose smiling. She hadn't said much to him beyond rolling her eyes after Karina had made his lap her seat.

The twin was lost in a giggly conversation with her sister, Bella, who must've been drunk because her hand rested on his arm. He leaned around Karina awkwardly and took a long draw of sweet wine, careful not to disrupt his perch. It wasn't easy to reach his mug, and it also wasn't torture.

"...and then, after Dallow and I get back from visiting all the mage city ruins, I'm going to go on a bunch of naked adventures with the twins," Kala said. The young woman stood before him with hands on hips, leaning a little too close.

"What?" Angst asked, jerking his head up in surprise.

Bella and Karina laughed, the twin on his lap wiggling pleasantly.

"I knew if I said naked, I'd finally get your attention, old man," she said.

"Sorry, Kala," he said. "I've got a lot on my mind."

"A lot of booze on your mind and women on your lap," she said, winking at the twins. "I originally said that after gathering all the books we can from the old mage cities, we're going to open a school for wielders."

"It's about time!" he said too loudly, unable to hold back his excitement. "I'm sure our queen would be glad to help you recruit—"

"I've already spoken to Tori about it," she said hurriedly. "She thinks it's a good idea to welcome casters, uh, wielders from all of Ehrde."

"Tori, huh?" he asked in surprise. Wasn't he the only one who was supposed to use that nickname? "Well, she would know, and...oh boy, hold that thought."

Heather stormed into the bar looking slightly perturbed, Scar following closely, his puppy head skinny with guilt. She stomped past several pending hugs and waved Karina off his lap. The young woman squeezed between him and Bella.

"I thought you were supposed to watch him," Heather said to Kala. "Especially with those two."

"I can't tell them what to do," she said, jerking her head toward the twins. "You're the only one they listen to. You and maybe Faeoris."

Heather peered at the twins. They smiled innocently at her, hardening his wife's stony gaze.

"You didn't stomp in here just to yell at mah girls," Angst said, the alcohol-imbued words coming out too slowly.

"Your girls," Heather said, rolling her eyes.

The twins giggled, and Angst failed to hold back his grin.

"Do you know what Thom and Eila did?" she asked, not waiting for a reply. "It seems they took Scar and stole a piece of the

Ivan tree from the Fulk'han...again!"

"Are they okay?" Angst asked.

"Yes," she said snappily. "But you need to talk to them!"

"Were the Fulk'han upset?" he asked.

"Of course they were upset," Heather said, her cheeks red. Everyone around them seemed agitated as her emotions became theirs. "But the Fulk'han won't touch them because they're afraid of you."

"Good," Angst said dismissively, taking another sip of sweet wine.

"You're not going to talk to them, are you?" she asked.

Angst glanced at his empty lap, encouraging her to take a seat.

"It's all warmed up for you," Karina said, practically singing the words.

"Mine," Heather said, peering at the girls as she plopped down on Angst's lap.

Graloon approached with a flask and handed it to Heather with a slight bow.

"At least someone is a gentleman," she said. "Thank you."

"Angst, I wanted to thank—" Graloon bit off his words. He looked up and paled, his eyes wide. "I didn't know...you should have told me. I would have cleaned..."

Victoria and Jaden walked into the Wizard's Revenge, appearing quite regal. Despite being weeks away from marriage, they were already the perfect royal couple, and everyone wobbled to their feet as they entered. Jaden wore a deep crimson tunic and tan leggings, Dulgirgraut hovering ominously over his back. Tori had fashioned a pink satin corset dress that was incredibly flattering in his favorite way.

Angst patted his wife on the leg, and she sighed as they rose. He knelt, lowering his head, and everyone in the bar followed his lead. Tori and Jaden approached to stand before him.

"My queen," he said.

"I don't want my friends to kneel," she said. "Please rise, my champion."

He did, and before she could say anything else, wrapped his arms around her in a hug and didn't let go until he was done. Tori was blushing when he pulled away, and Jaden stared at the ground, his face set in a grimace. Angst didn't care.

"You came," he said.

"I wouldn't miss your party for anything." She accepted a goblet from Graloon, turned to face everyone, and raised it in a toast. "I would like everyone to know that the law was signed this morning, and Rookshire is officially a mage city. Autonomous to the crown."

There was a gentle round of clapping. When it slowed, Tori nodded to Jaden.

"More important than that," Jaden said, "the queen has decreed that magic is now legal in Unsel. No more restrictions."

Cheers, and tears, and back patting, and hugs overtook the room. Heather embraced Angst and held tight. When she was done, he sought Tori's eyes and nodded once in gratitude.

"A toast," Angst said, raising a glass. "To the queen and future king of Unsel!"

Everyone nodded respectfully and sipped from their cups.

"This wouldn't be possible without the sacrifice of so many," he said, unable to hold back the catch in his throat. "Queen Isabelle and Captain Tyrell. My friends Moyra and Marissa. Leaders like Rook and Janda. Sean and Simon. Jintorich and Aerella..."

Heather gripped his arm. Faeoris shoved past the twins to hold the other. He nodded to them both before continuing, barely choking out the words, "To Hector."

The room became bleary through his tears, and Angst lowered his head while lifting his mug. There were hugs and pats of encouragement, but all of them were a haze through the loss he felt. Maybe the sacrifice was worth it. Maybe his friends had died for a good reason. That didn't make it stop hurting, and honestly, they deserved his tears.

"Hey, Angst," Graloon asked, "how did you get to be so stinking old?"

It was the laugh everyone needed, and Angst wiped tears from his cheeks.

"Don't you know?" he asked. "Age is all in your head. It doesn't matter if you're tall or short, young or old, fat or thin, all that matters is who you choose to be. I'll always be Angst."

They all clapped, and he nodded respectfully.

"But you went into that beam of light alone," General Mirim said. "I've been told that everyone who came out, including your kids, are older too. How is that even possible? Do people get older just by being near you?"

He'd hoped the laughter and noise from the crowd would wash away the questions, but a quiet overtook the room. He waited, wishing for that one joke that would distract everyone, but it didn't come. Finally, his eyes met Tori's.

"I want to know, Angst," she said. "You don't have to tell your queen, but will you tell your friend?"

"You won't believe me," he said, wanting nothing more than to end this conversation. The entire adventure was so fresh that he was still exhausted from the memory. Tori continued to look at him with those eyes that he couldn't say no to. He sighed deeply. "My dog saved everyone by sending them two thousand years into the future. Every flash of light that appeared when someone was about to die was Scar trying to save those I love." He took a deep breath. "I went into that beam of light to fight Magic for the wish and didn't realize I was actually fighting my future self. Young Angst lost, and I threw him into that future so he could find everyone, including himself."

Silence filled the room until Graloon burst out in nervous laughter. Others followed, but the laughter didn't last long. When the room became quiet once more, all eyes were on him.

"Really?" Victoria asked. "How did you find everyone? How did you get back?"

"Really," Angst said with a smirk. He took a long draw of sweet wine, lowered his glass, and looked her in the eye. "But that's another story entirely," he said with a wink.

About the Author

David J. Pedersen is a native of Racine, WI who resides in his home town Kansas City, MO. He received a Bachelor of Arts degree in Philosophy from the University of Wisconsin - Madison. He has worked in sales, management, retail, video and film production, and IT. David has run 2 marathons, climbed several 14,000 foot mountains and marched in Thee University of Wisconsin Marching Band. He is a geek and a fanboy that enjoys carousing, picking on his wife and kids, playing video games, and slowly muddling through his next novel.

To learn more about David and his writing please visit his blog:
www.gotangst.com

www.ingramcontent.com/pod-product-compliance
Lightning Source LLC
Chambersburg PA
CBHW070202120726
47909CB00001B/211